CARTOON NETWORK

ADVENTURE TIME

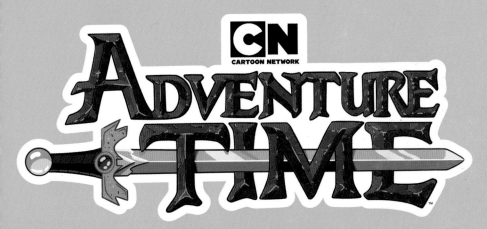

JAKE

kaboom!

Designer **Chelsea Roberts**
Assistant Editor **Michael Moccio**
Editor **Matthew Levine**

With Special Thanks to Marisa Marionakis, Janet No, Becky M. Yang, Conrad Montgomery, Kelly Crews, Scott Malchus, Adam Muto and the wonderful folks at Cartoon Network.

Ross Richie CEO & Founder
Joy Huffman CFO
Matt Gagnon Editor-in-Chief
Filip Sablik President, Publishing & Marketing
Stephen Christy President, Development
Lance Kreiter Vice President, Licensing & Merchandising
Phil Barbaro Vice President, Finance & Human Resources
Arune Singh Vice President, Marketing
Bryce Carlson Vice President, Editorial & Creative Strategy
Scott Newman Manager, Production Design
Kate Henning Manager, Operations
Spencer Simpson Manager, Sales
Sierra Hahn Executive Editor
Jeanine Schaefer Executive Editor
Dafna Pleban Senior Editor
Shannon Watters Senior Editor
Eric Harburn Senior Editor
Chris Rosa Editor
Matthew Levine Editor
Sophie Philips-Roberts Associate Editor
Gavin Gronenthal Assistant Editor

Michael Moccio Assistant Editor
Gwen Waller Assistant Editor
Amanda LaFranco Executive Assistant
Jillian Crab Design Coordinator
Michelle Ankley Design Coordinator
Kara Leopard Production Designer
Marie Krupina Production Designer
Grace Park Production Designer
Chelsea Roberts Production Design Assistant
Samantha Knapp Production Design Assistant
José Meza Live Events Lead
Stephanie Hocutt Digital Marketing Lead
Esther Kim Marketing Coordinator
Cat O'Grady Digital Marketing Coordinator
Holly Aitchison Digital Sales Coordinator
Morgan Perry Retail Sales Coordinator
Megan Christopher Operations Coordinator
Rodrigo Hernandez Mailroom Assistant
Zipporah Smith Operations Assistant
Breanna Sarpy Executive Assistant

ADVENTURE TIME: JAKE, May 2019. Published by KaBOOM!, a division of Boom Entertainment, Inc. ADVENTURE TIME, CARTOON NETWORK, the logos, and all related characters and elements are trademarks of and © Cartoon Network. A WarnerMedia Company. All rights reserved. (S19) Originally published in single magazine form as ADVENTURE TIME No. 9, 13, 36-39, 51-53, ADVENTURE TIME COMICS No. 2, 4, 13, 20, ADVENTURE TIME: MARCELINE AND THE SCREAM QUEENS No. 5, ADVENTURE TIME 2013 ANNUAL No. 1. © Cartoon Network. A WarnerMedia Company. All Rights Reserved. (S12, S13, S15, S16, S17, S18) KaBOOM!™ and the KaBOOM! logo are trademarks of Boom Entertainment, Inc., registered in various countries and categories. All characters, events, and institutions depicted herein are fictional. Any similarity between any of the names, characters, persons, events, and/or institutions in this publication to actual names, characters, and persons, whether living or dead, events, and/or institutions is unintended and purely coincidental. KaBOOM! does not read or accept unsolicited submissions of ideas, stories, or artwork.

BOOM! Studios, 5670 Wilshire Boulevard, Suite 400, Los Angeles, CA 90036-5679. Printed in China. First Printing.

ISBN: 978-1-68415-350-3, eISBN: 978-1-64144-333-3

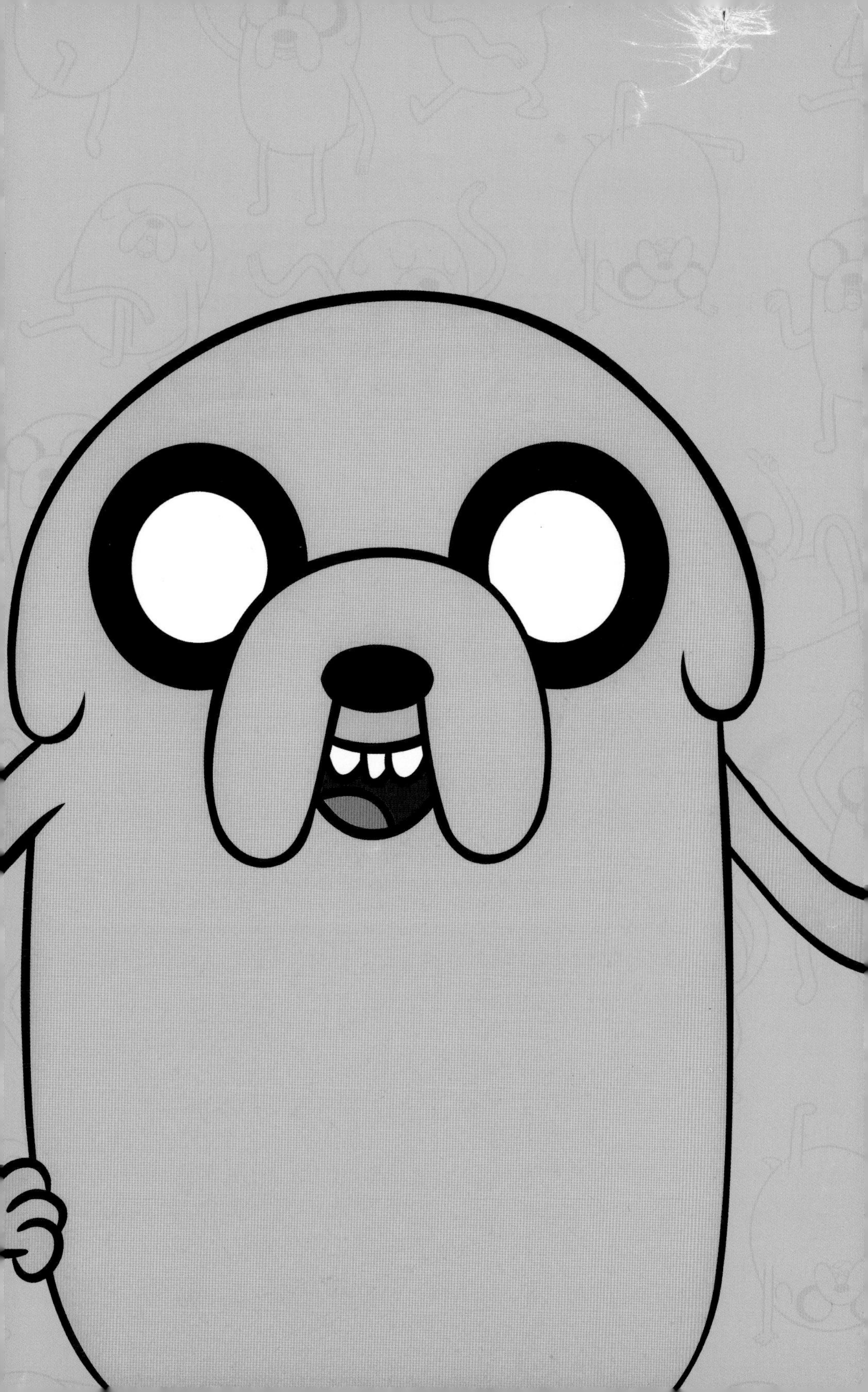

Created by **Pendleton Ward**

"Fishsling"
Written and Illustrated by **Shane & Chris Houghton**
Colors by **Josh Ulrich**

"Communication Issue"
Written and Illustrated by **Polly Guo**

**"The Devilish Devourer of
Delicious Delicacies"**
Written and Illustrated by **Josh Lesnick**

"Forgotten Feasts"
Written by **Christopher Hastings**
Illustrated by **Zachary Sterling**
Colors by **Maarta Laiho**
Letters by **Steve Wands**

"The Summiteers"
Written and Illustrated by Derek Fridolfs
Colors by Whitney Cogar
Letters by Mad Rupert

"Dirty Dungeon"
Written and Illustrated by Box Brown

"To the North"
Written by Nicole Andelfinger
Illustrated by Anissa Espinosa

"Stolen Youth"
Written by Christopher Hastings
Illustrated by Ian McGinty
Colors by Maarta Laiho
Letters by Steve Wands

"Body by Jake"
Written by Max Davison
Illustrated by Luca Claretti
Colors by Eleonora Bruni
Letters by Taylor Esposito

"Chock Full O' Stuff"
Written and Illustrated by David DeGrand

"Epic Yard Sale"
Written by James Asmus
Illustrated by Cristina Rose Chua
Letters by Mike Fiorentino

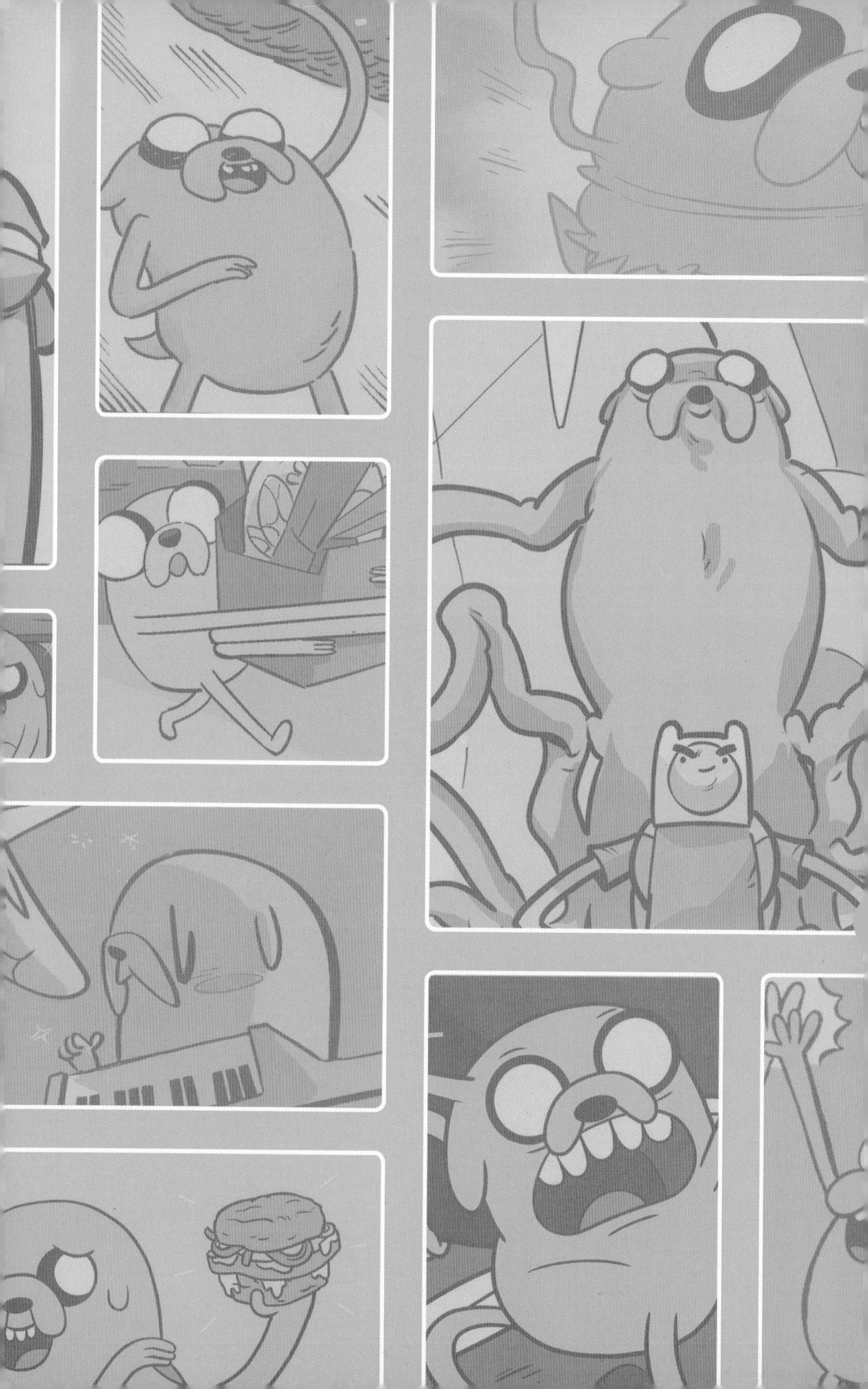

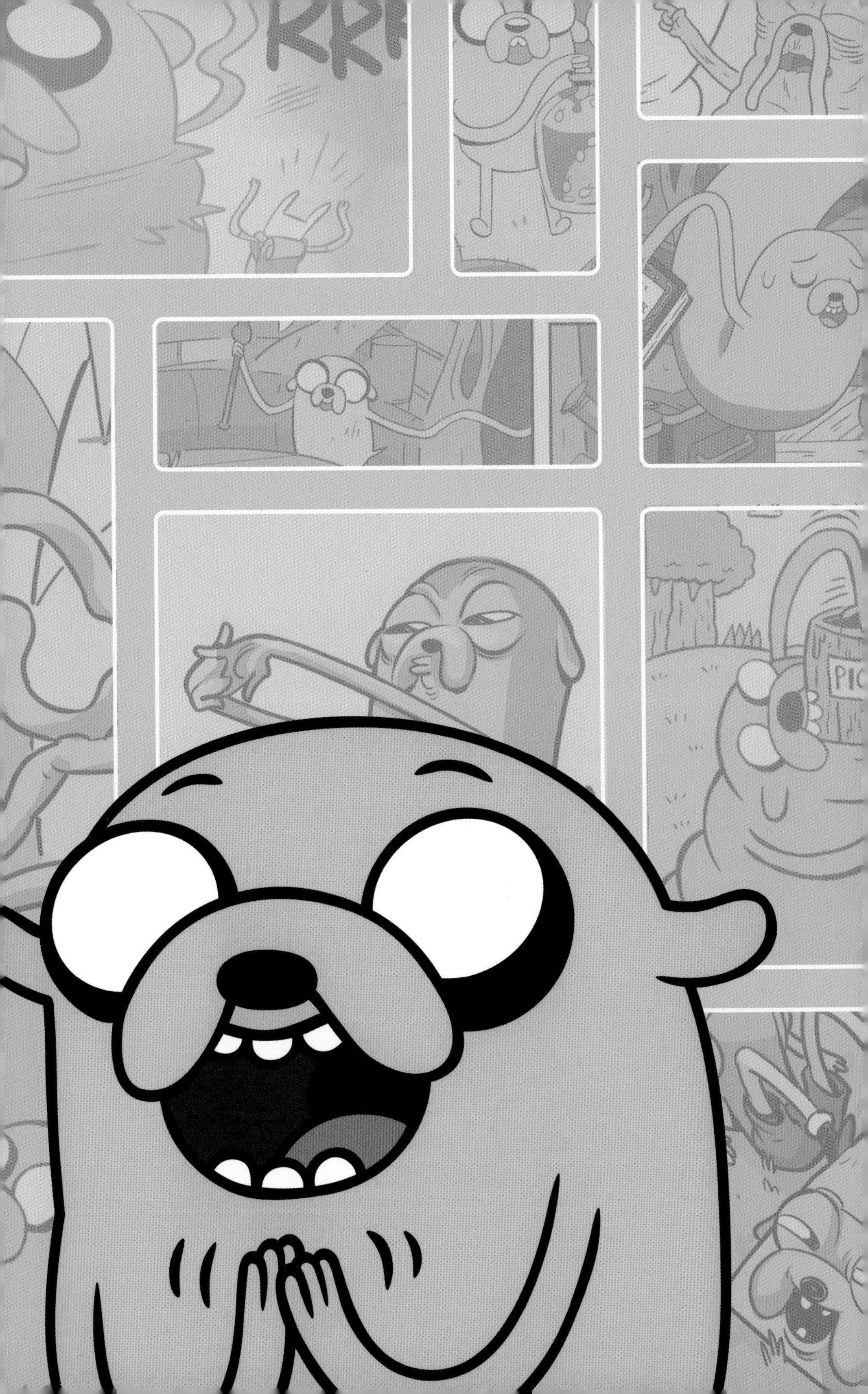

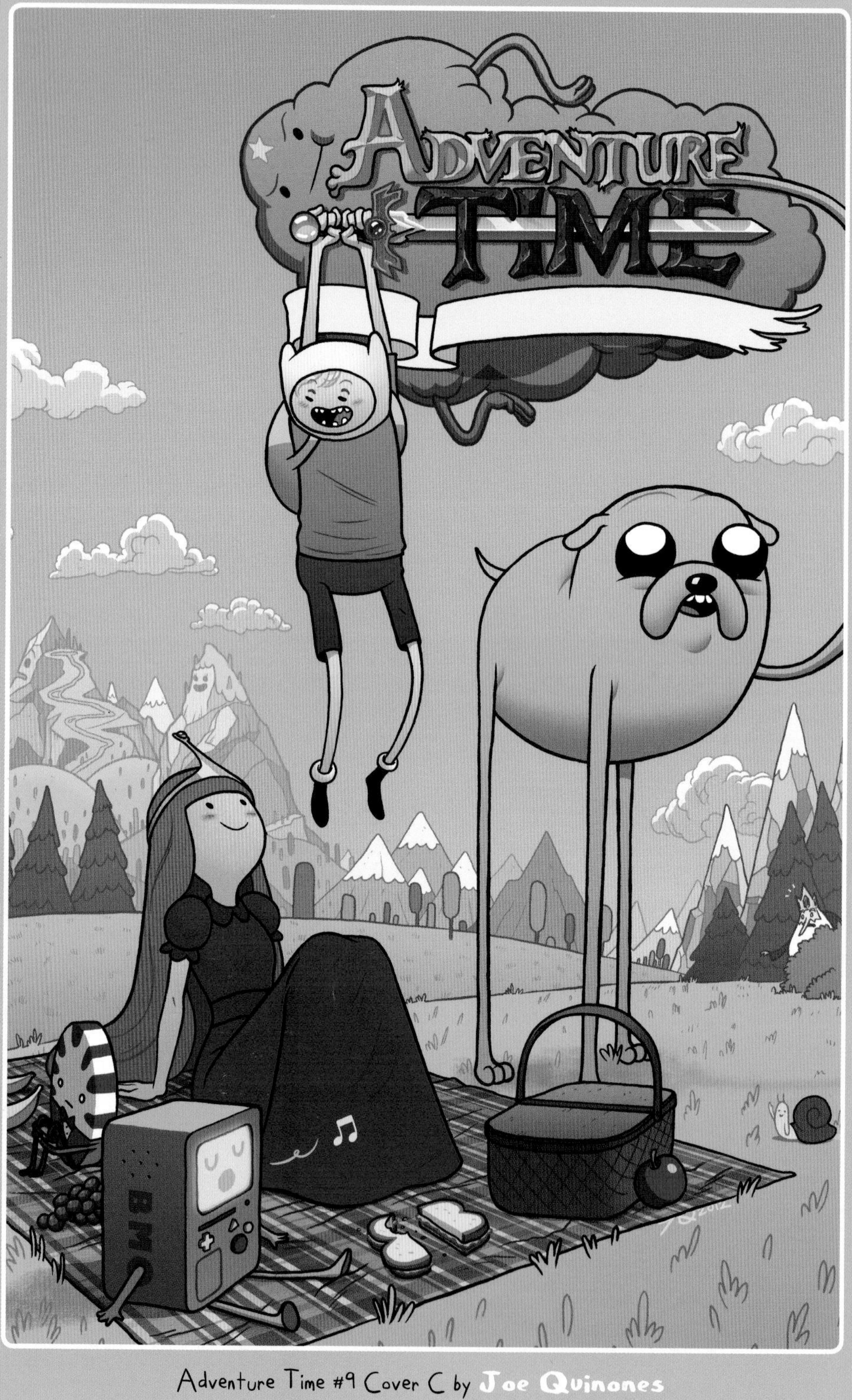
ADVENTURE
TIME
BMO

Adventure Time #9 Cover C by **Joe Quinones**

"Fishsling"

Written and Illustrated by **Shane & Chris Houghton**

Letters by **Josh Ulrich**

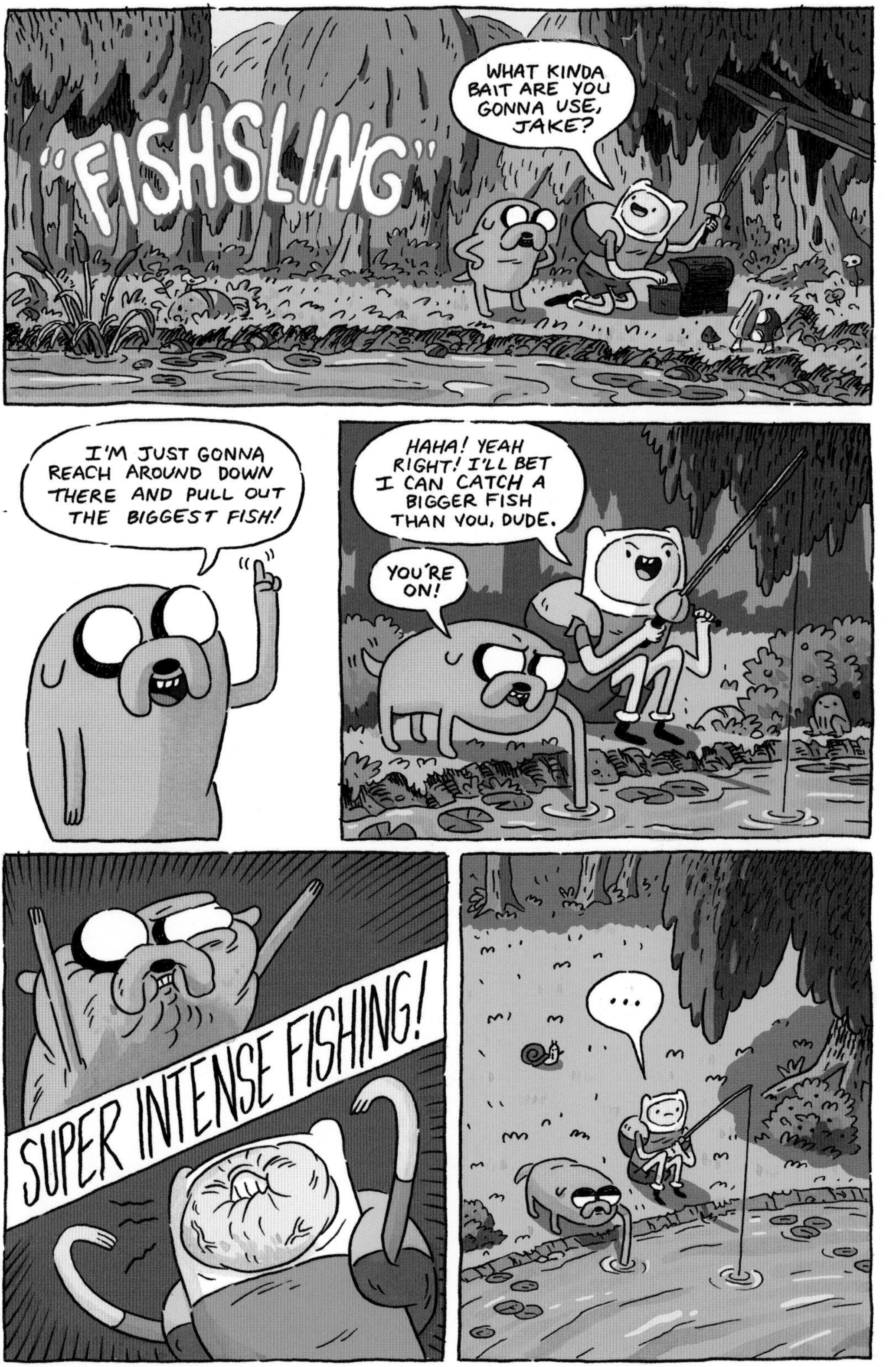
"FISHSLING"
WHAT KINDA BAIT ARE YOU GONNA USE, JAKE?
I'M JUST GONNA REACH AROUND DOWN THERE AND PULL OUT THE BIGGEST FISH!
HAHA! YEAH RIGHT! I'LL BET I CAN CATCH A BIGGER FISH THAN YOU, DUDE.
YOU'RE ON!
SUPER INTENSE FISHING!
...

WRITTEN BY: SHANE HOUGHTON DRAWN BY: CHRIS HOUGHTON COLORED BY: JOSH ULRICH

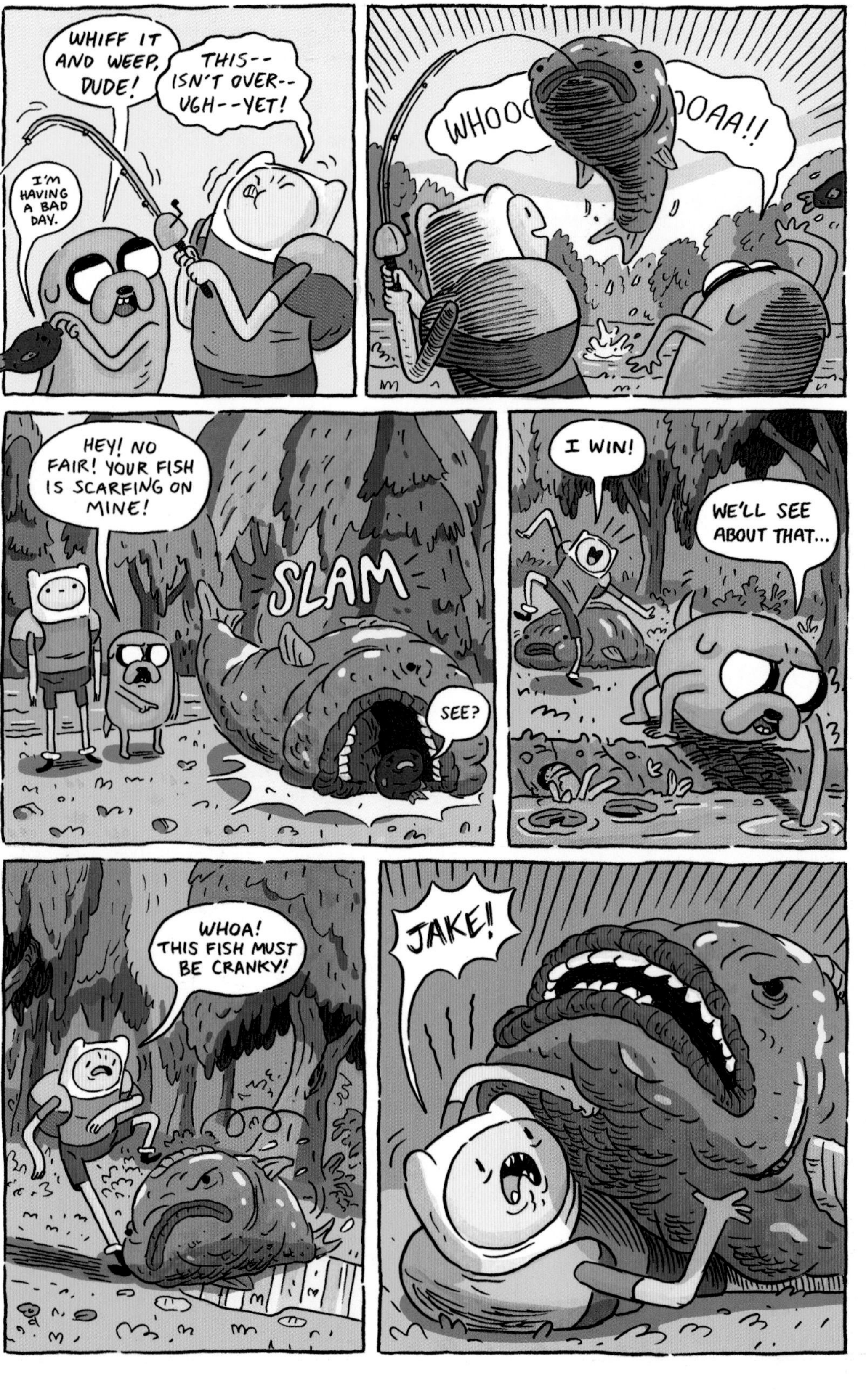
WHIFF IT AND WEEP, DUDE!
THIS-- ISN'T OVER-- UGH--YET!
I'M HAVING A BAD DAY.
WHOOOOOAA!!
HEY! NO FAIR! YOUR FISH IS SCARFING ON MINE!
SLAM
SEE?
I WIN!
WE'LL SEE ABOUT THAT...
WHOA! THIS FISH MUST BE CRANKY!
JAKE!

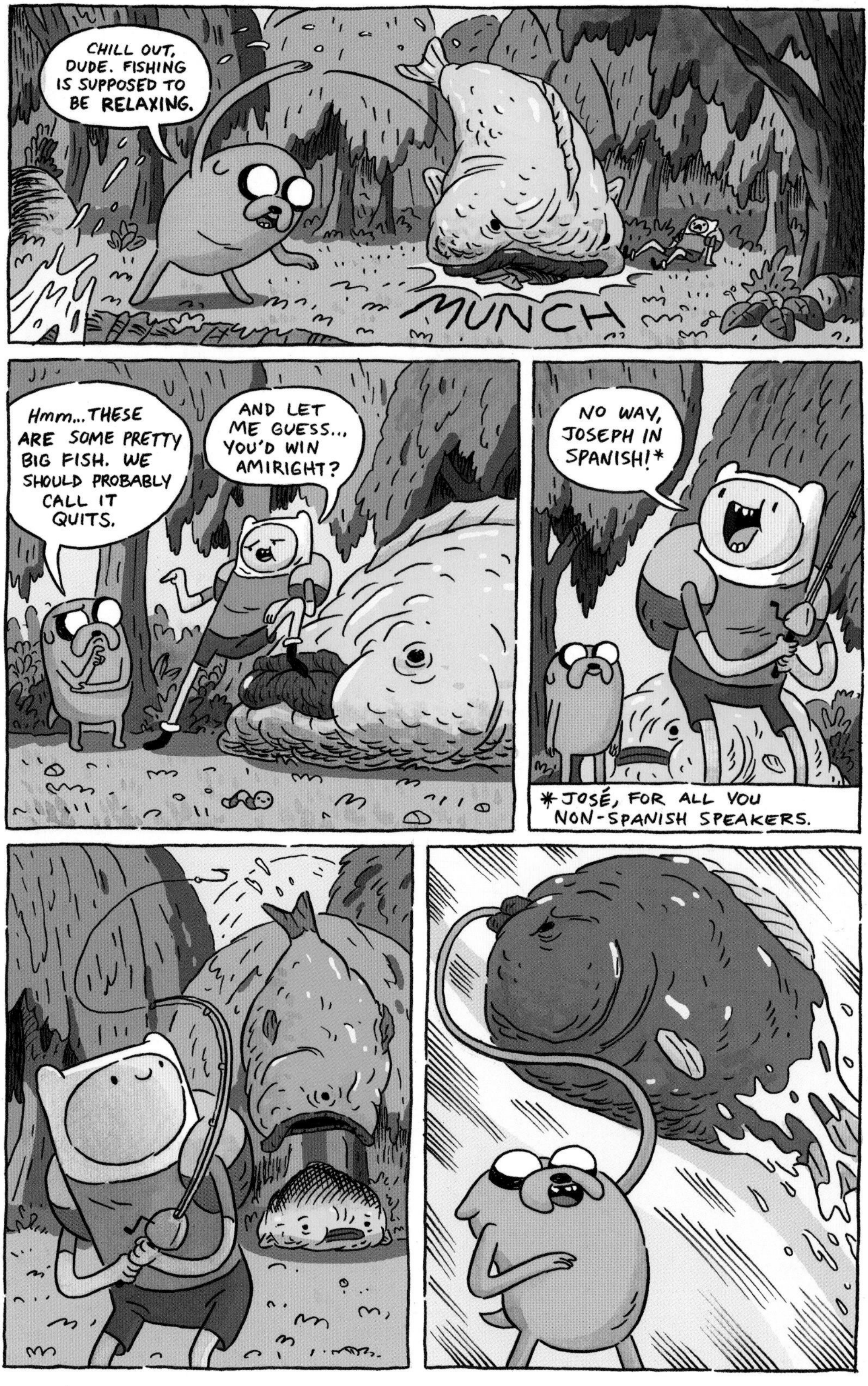
CHILL OUT, DUDE. FISHING IS SUPPOSED TO BE RELAXING.
MUNCH
Hmm... THESE ARE SOME PRETTY BIG FISH. WE SHOULD PROBABLY CALL IT QUITS.
AND LET ME GUESS... YOU'D WIN AMIRIGHT?
NO WAY, JOSEPH IN SPANISH!*
*JOSÉ, FOR ALL YOU NON-SPANISH SPEAKERS.

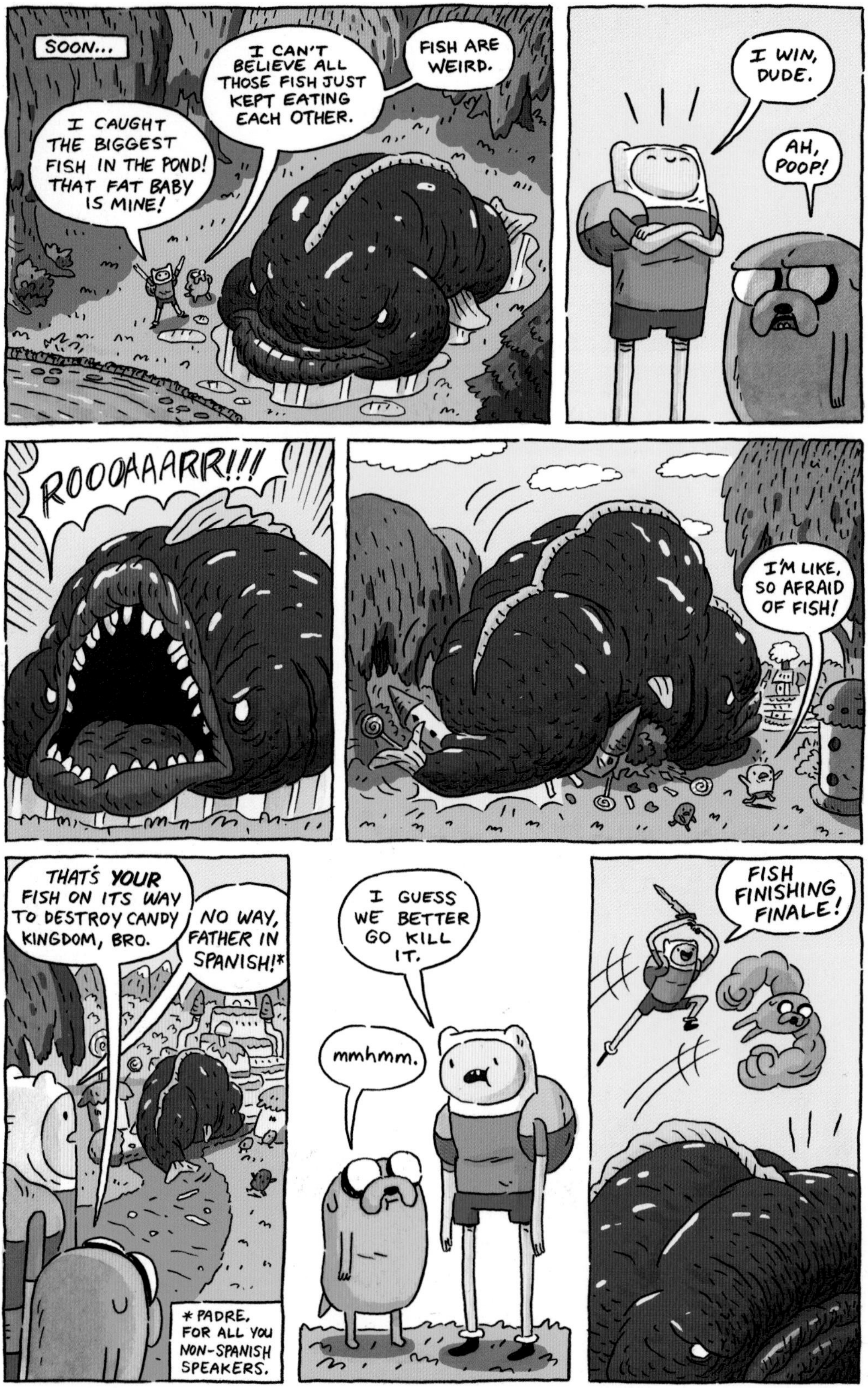
SOON...
I CAUGHT THE BIGGEST FISH IN THE POND! THAT FAT BABY IS MINE!
I CAN'T BELIEVE ALL THOSE FISH JUST KEPT EATING EACH OTHER.
FISH ARE WEIRD.
I WIN, DUDE.
AH, POOP!
ROOOAAARR!!!
I'M LIKE, SO AFRAID OF FISH!
THAT'S YOUR FISH ON ITS WAY TO DESTROY CANDY KINGDOM, BRO.
NO WAY, FATHER IN SPANISH!*
*PADRE, FOR ALL YOU NON-SPANISH SPEAKERS.
I GUESS WE BETTER GO KILL IT.
mmhmm.
FISH FINISHING FINALE!

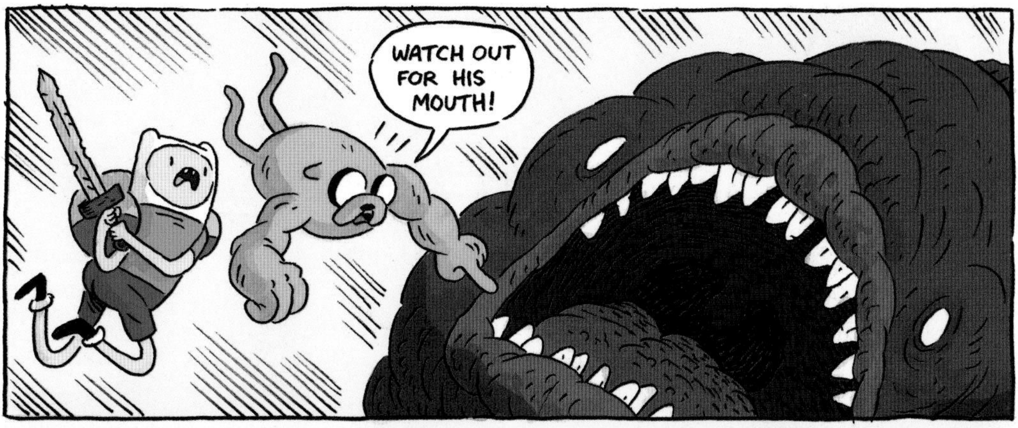
WATCH OUT FOR HIS MOUTH!

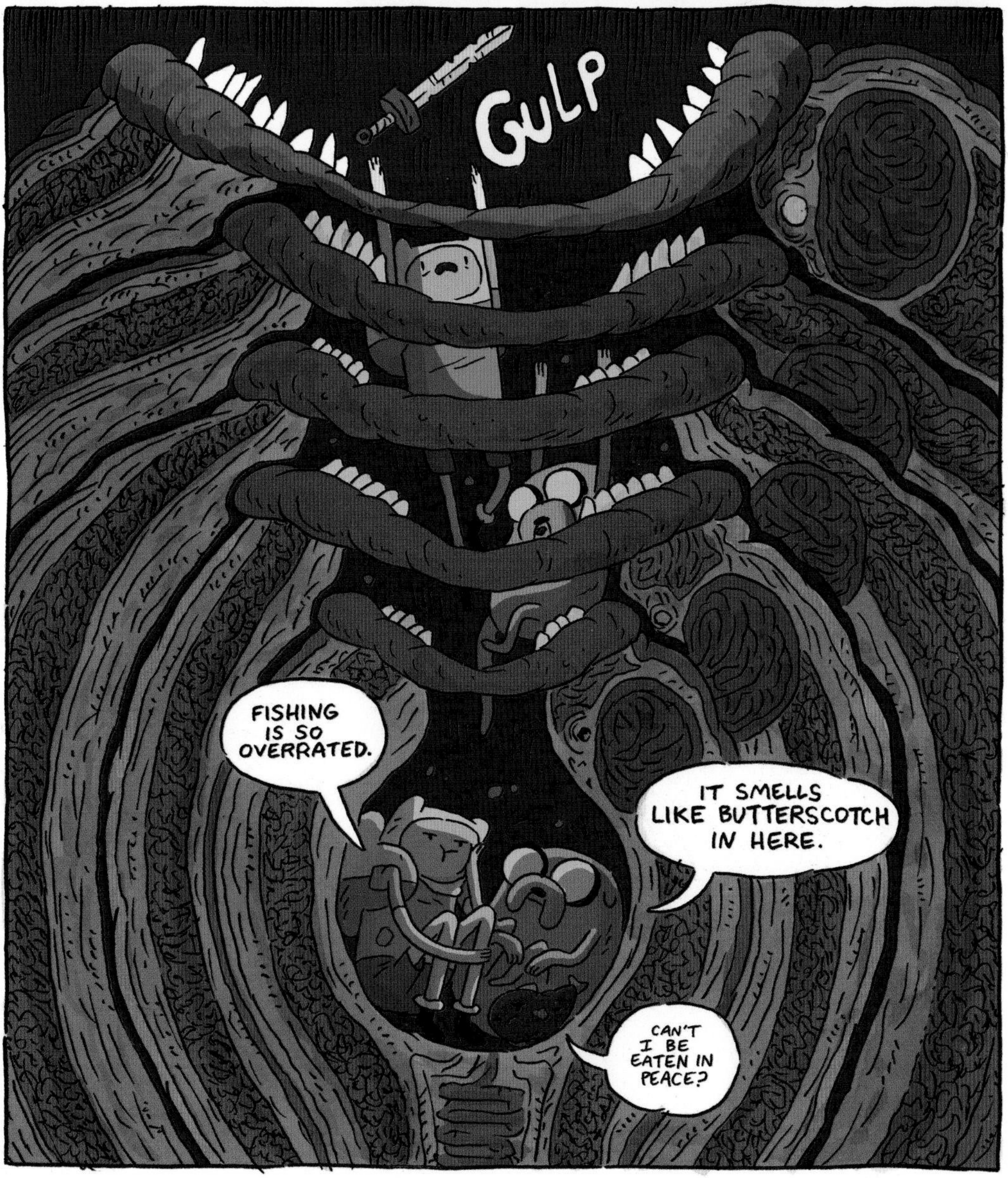
GULP
FISHING IS SO OVERRATED.
IT SMELLS LIKE BUTTERSCOTCH IN HERE.
CAN'T I BE EATEN IN PEACE?

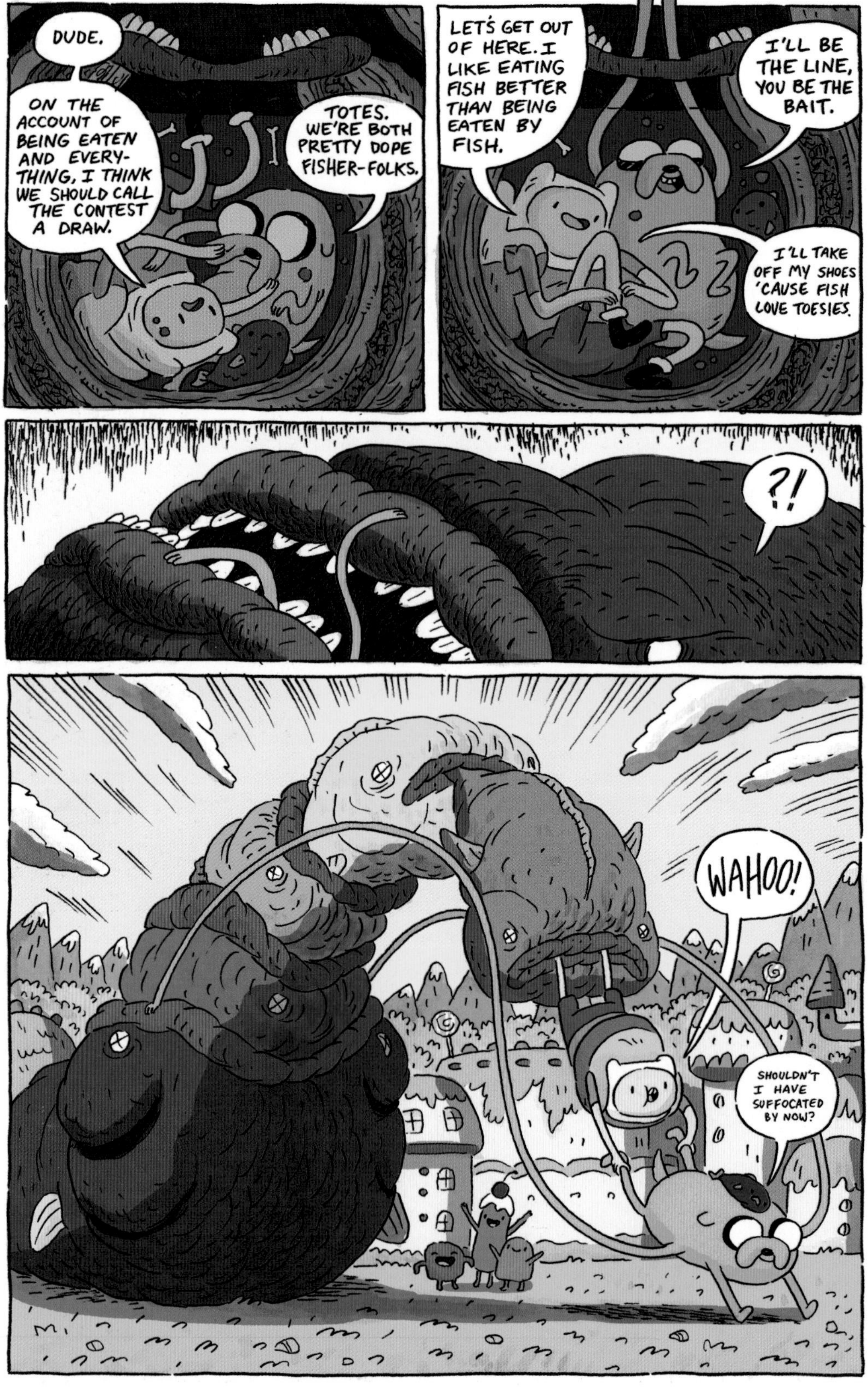
DUDE.
ON THE ACCOUNT OF BEING EATEN AND EVERYTHING, I THINK WE SHOULD CALL THE CONTEST A DRAW.
TOTES. WE'RE BOTH PRETTY DOPE FISHER-FOLKS.
LET'S GET OUT OF HERE. I LIKE EATING FISH BETTER THAN BEING EATEN BY FISH.
I'LL BE THE LINE, YOU BE THE BAIT.
I'LL TAKE OFF MY SHOES 'CAUSE FISH LOVE TOESIES.
?!
WAHOO!
SHOULDN'T I HAVE SUFFOCATED BY NOW?

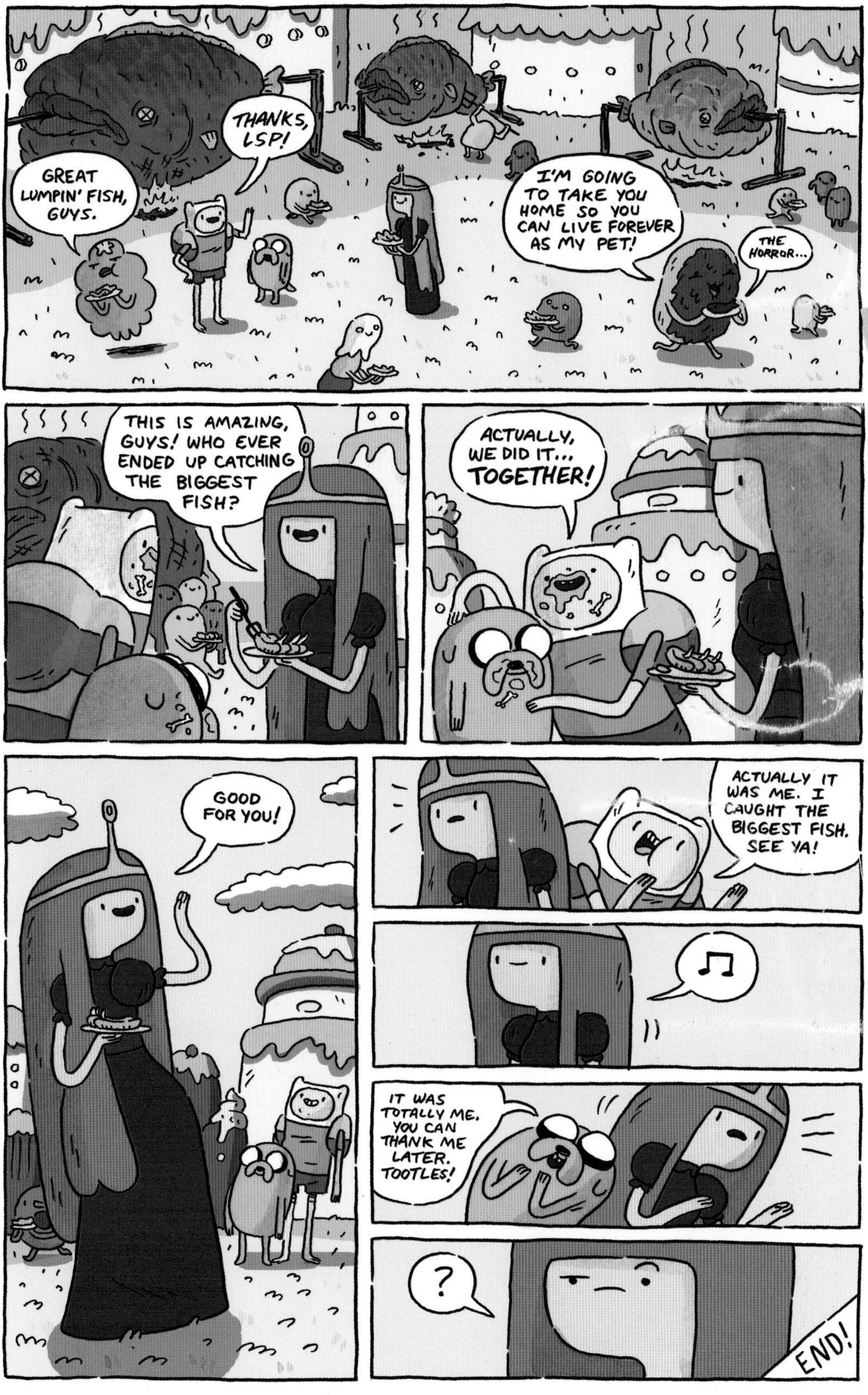
GREAT LUMPIN' FISH, GUYS.
THANKS, LSP!
I'M GOING TO TAKE YOU HOME SO YOU CAN LIVE FOREVER AS MY PET!
THE HORROR...
THIS IS AMAZING, GUYS! WHO EVER ENDED UP CATCHING THE BIGGEST FISH?
ACTUALLY, WE DID IT... TOGETHER!
GOOD FOR YOU!
ACTUALLY IT WAS ME. I CAUGHT THE BIGGEST FISH. SEE YA!
IT WAS TOTALLY ME. YOU CAN THANK ME LATER. TOOTLES!
?
END!

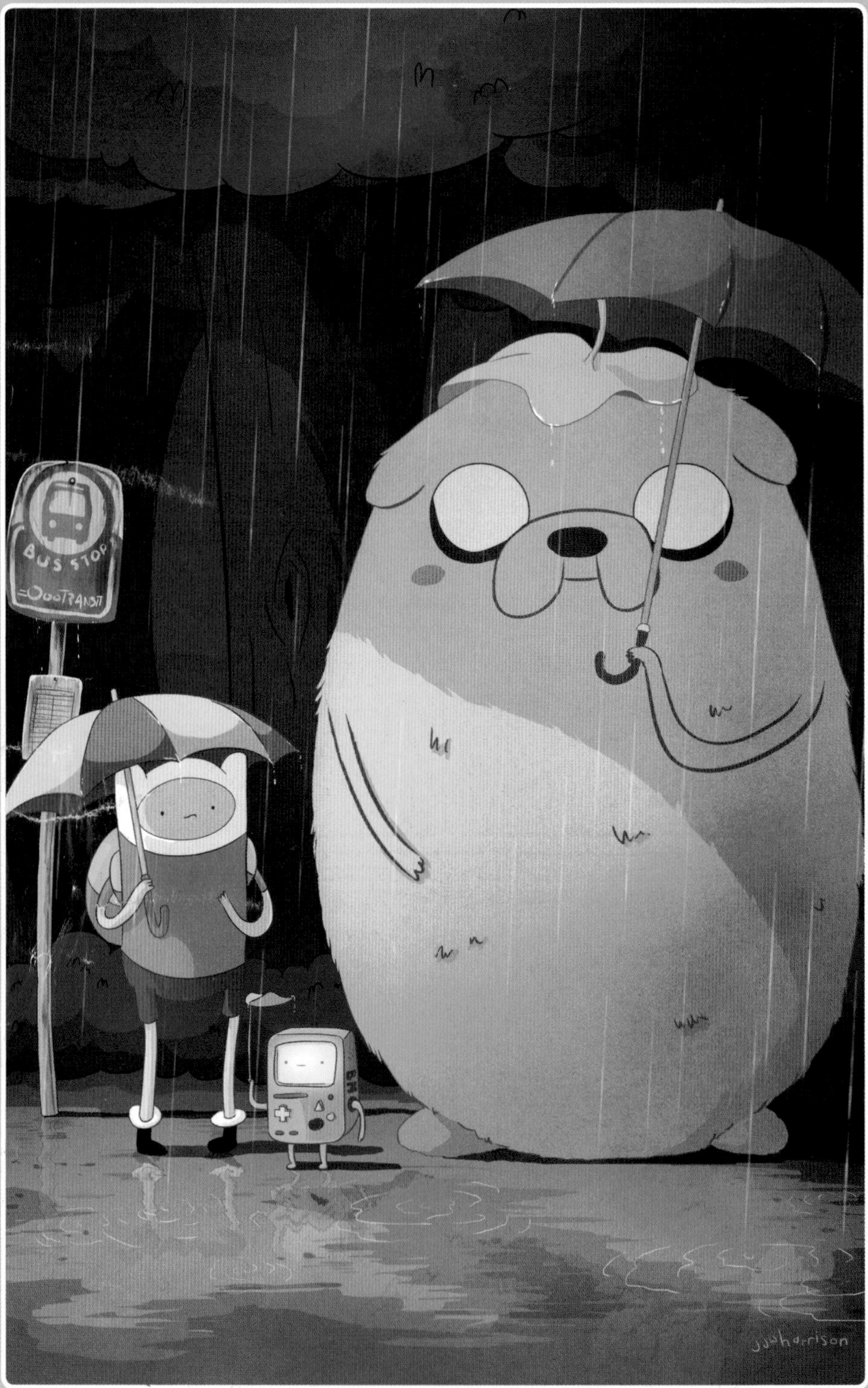
BUS STOP
=OOOTRANSIT
jjharrison

Adventure Time Comics #10 Dynamic Forces Exclusive Cover by **JJ Harrison**

"Communication Issues"

Written and Illustrated by **Polly Guo**

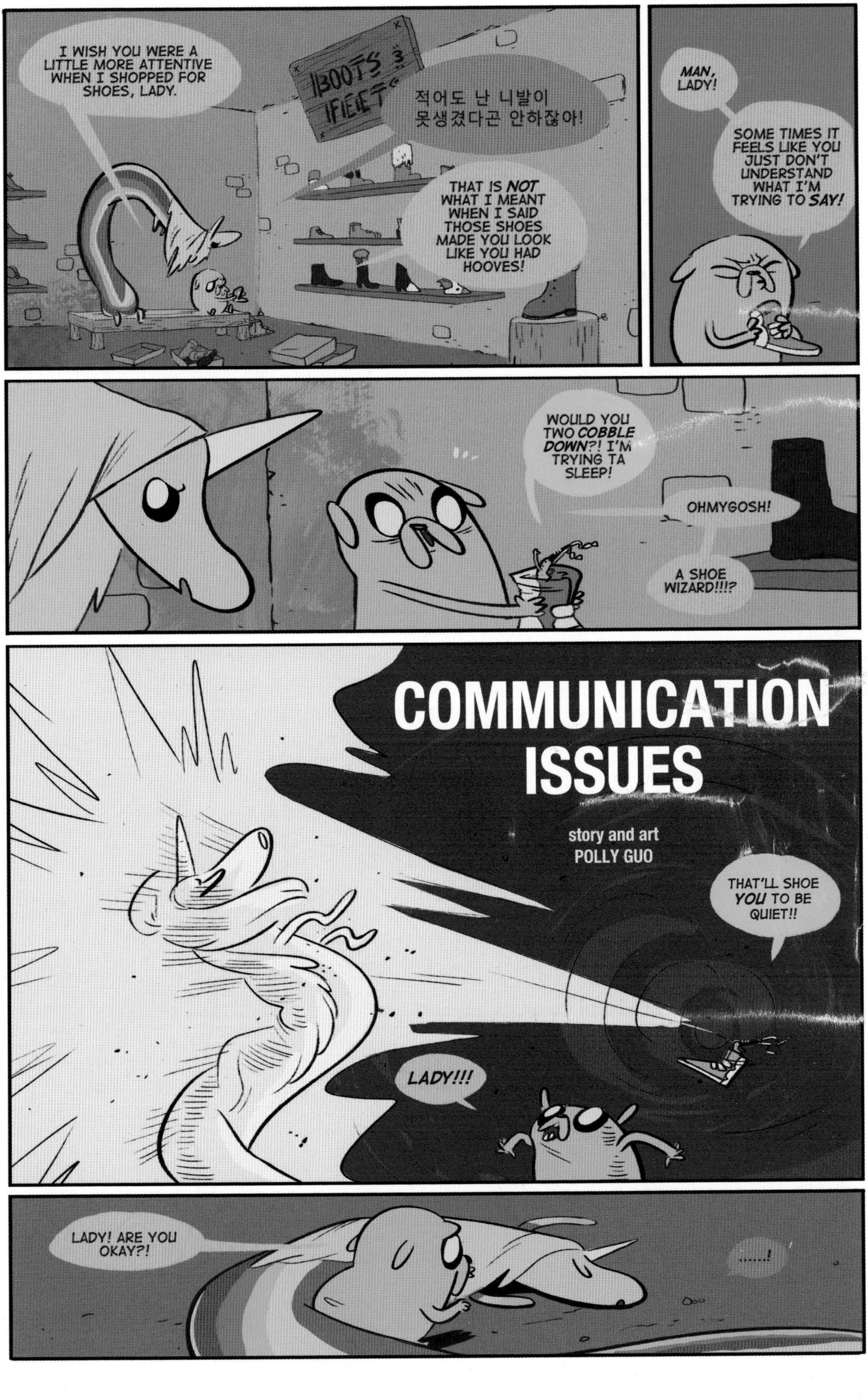
I WISH YOU WERE A LITTLE MORE ATTENTIVE WHEN I SHOPPED FOR SHOES, LADY.
적어도 난 니발이 못생겼다곤 안하잖아!
THAT IS NOT WHAT I MEANT WHEN I SAID THOSE SHOES MADE YOU LOOK LIKE YOU HAD HOOVES!
MAN, LADY!
SOME TIMES IT FEELS LIKE YOU JUST DON'T UNDERSTAND WHAT I'M TRYING TO SAY!
WOULD YOU TWO COBBLE DOWN?! I'M TRYING TA SLEEP!
OHMYGOSH!
A SHOE WIZARD!!!?
COMMUNICATION ISSUES
story and art
POLLY GUO
THAT'LL SHOE YOU TO BE QUIET!!
LADY!!!
LADY! ARE YOU OKAY?!
......!

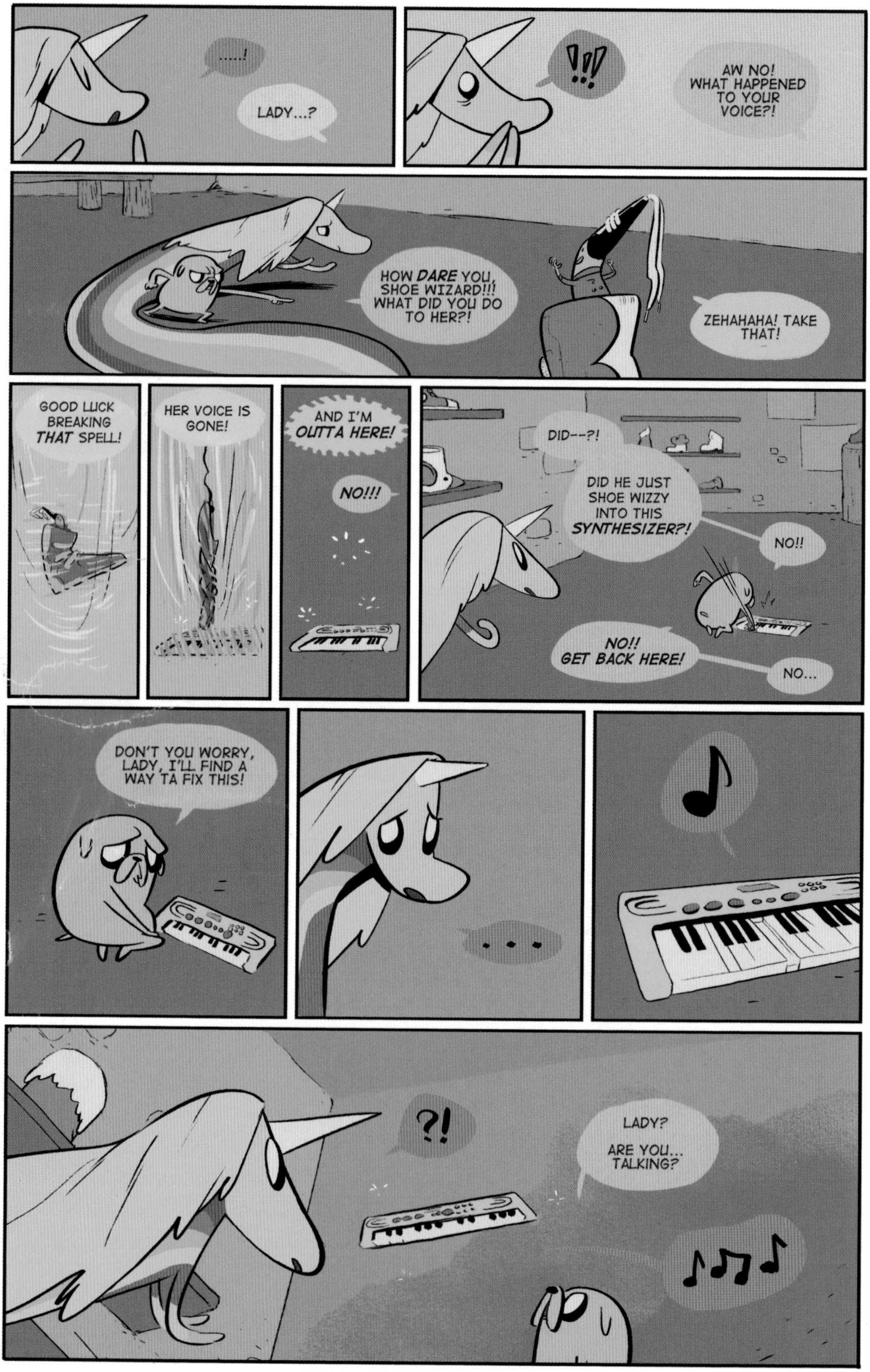
.....!
LADY...?
!?!/
AW NO! WHAT HAPPENED TO YOUR VOICE?!
HOW DARE YOU, SHOE WIZARD!!! WHAT DID YOU DO TO HER?!
ZEHAHAHA! TAKE THAT!
GOOD LUCK BREAKING THAT SPELL!
HER VOICE IS GONE!
AND I'M OUTTA HERE!
NO!!!
DID--?!
DID HE JUST SHOE WIZZY INTO THIS SYNTHESIZER?!
NO!!
NO!! GET BACK HERE!
NO...
DON'T YOU WORRY, LADY, I'LL FIND A WAY TA FIX THIS!
...
♪
?!
LADY?
ARE YOU... TALKING?
♪♫♪

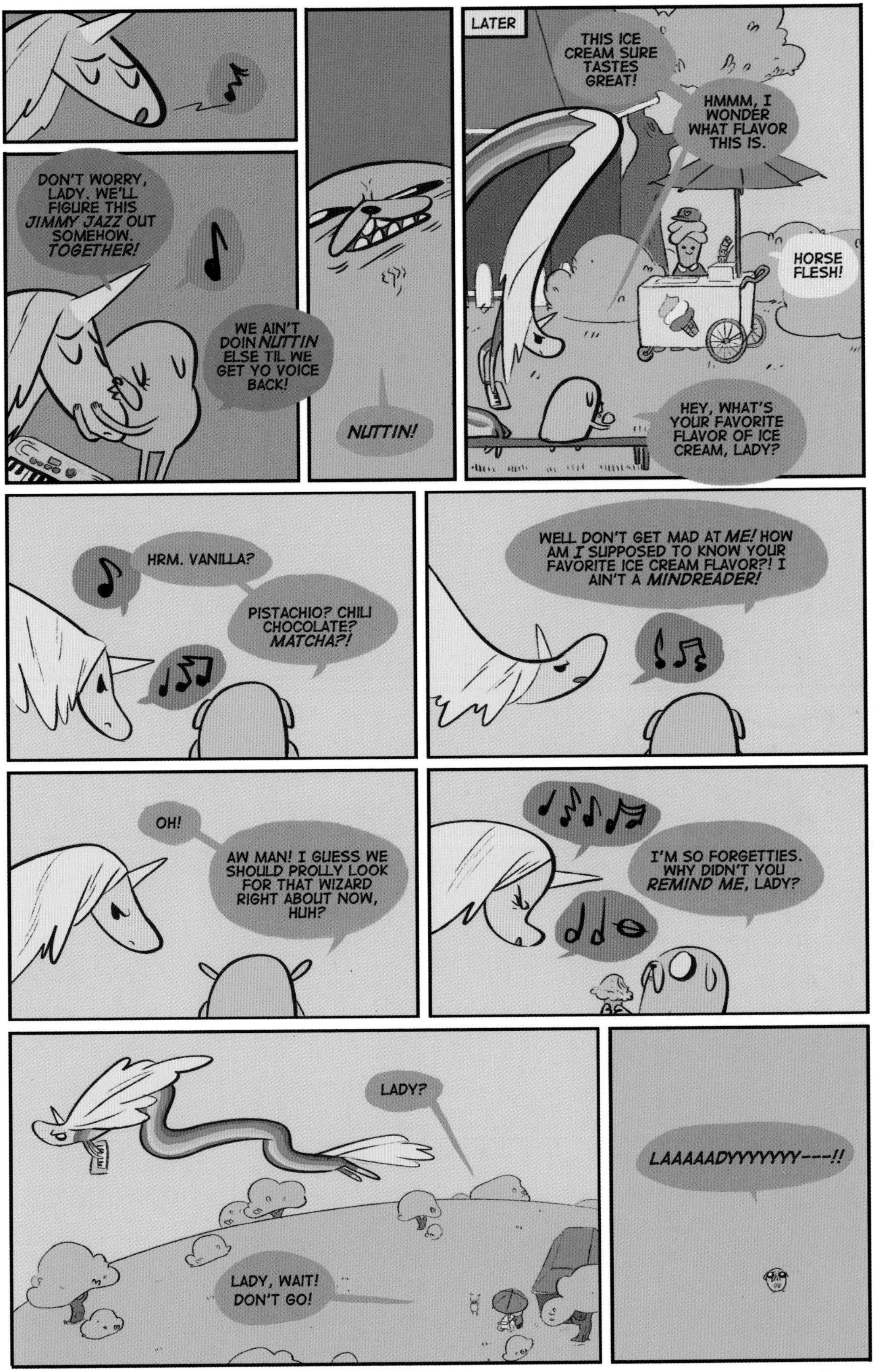

DON'T WORRY, LADY. WE'LL FIGURE THIS *JIMMY JAZZ* OUT SOMEHOW. *TOGETHER!*
WE AIN'T DOIN *NUTTIN* ELSE TIL WE GET YO VOICE BACK!
NUTTIN!
LATER
THIS ICE CREAM SURE TASTES GREAT!
HMMM, I WONDER WHAT FLAVOR THIS IS.
HORSE FLESH!
HEY, WHAT'S YOUR FAVORITE FLAVOR OF ICE CREAM, LADY?
HRM. VANILLA?
PISTACHIO? CHILI CHOCOLATE? *MATCHA?!*
WELL DON'T GET MAD AT *ME!* HOW AM *I* SUPPOSED TO KNOW YOUR FAVORITE ICE CREAM FLAVOR?! I AIN'T A *MINDREADER!*
OH!
AW MAN! I GUESS WE SHOULD PROLLY LOOK FOR THAT WIZARD RIGHT ABOUT NOW, HUH?
I'M SO FORGETTIES. WHY DIDN'T YOU *REMIND ME*, LADY?
LADY?
LADY, WAIT! DON'T GO!
LAAAAADYYYYYYY---!!

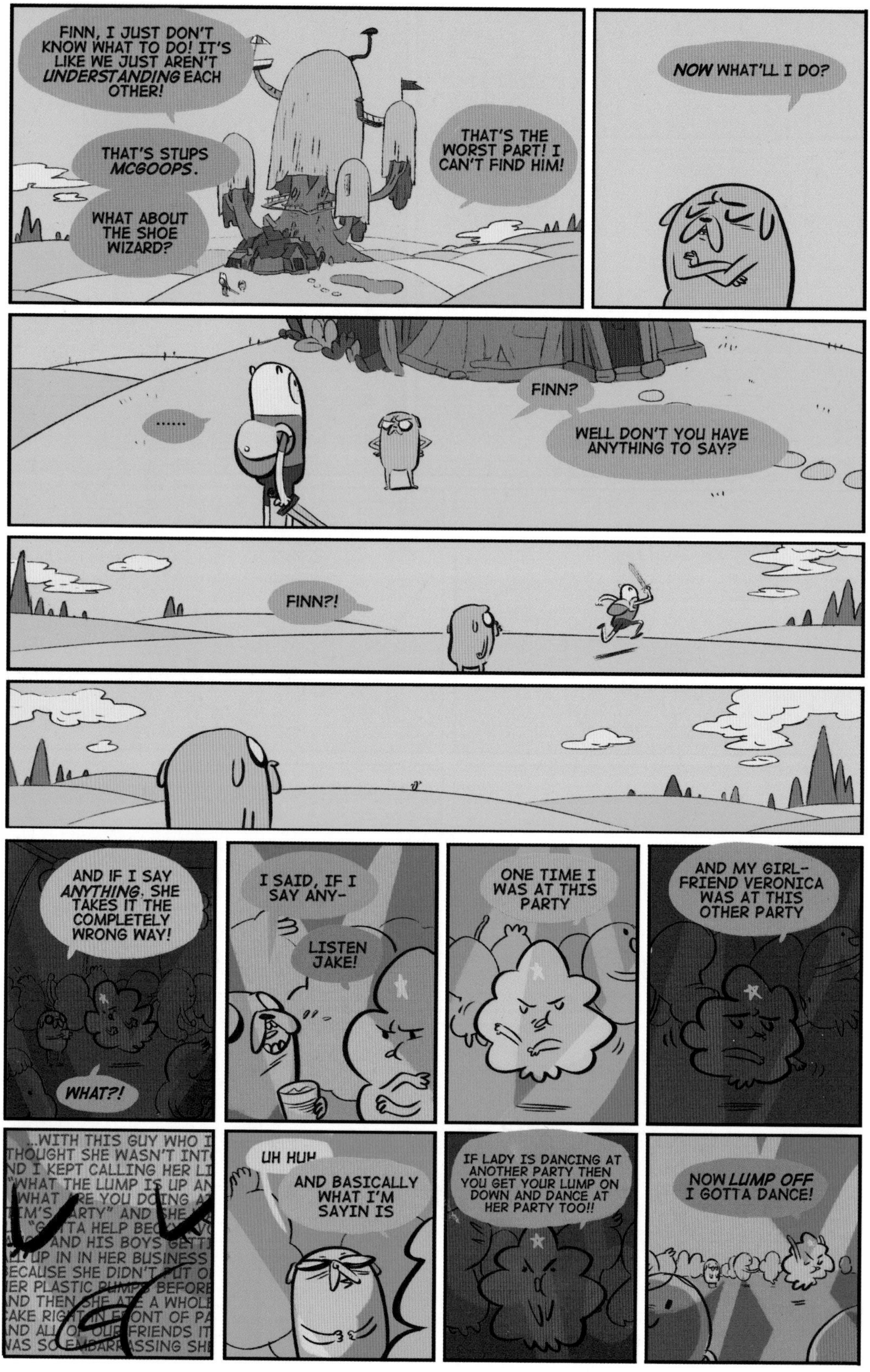
FINN, I JUST DON'T KNOW WHAT TO DO! IT'S LIKE WE JUST AREN'T UNDERSTANDING EACH OTHER!
THAT'S STUPS MCGOOPS.
WHAT ABOUT THE SHOE WIZARD?
THAT'S THE WORST PART! I CAN'T FIND HIM!
NOW WHAT'LL I DO?
......
FINN?
WELL DON'T YOU HAVE ANYTHING TO SAY?
FINN?!
AND IF I SAY ANYTHING, SHE TAKES IT THE COMPLETELY WRONG WAY!
WHAT?!
I SAID, IF I SAY ANY-
LISTEN JAKE!
ONE TIME I WAS AT THIS PARTY
AND MY GIRL-FRIEND VERONICA WAS AT THIS OTHER PARTY
...WITH THIS GUY WHO I
UP IN IN HER BUSINESS
BECAUSE SHE DIDN'T
ER PLASTIC
AND THEN
AKE RIGHT
ND ALL
UH HUH
AND BASICALLY WHAT I'M SAYIN IS
IF LADY IS DANCING AT ANOTHER PARTY THEN YOU GET YOUR LUMP ON DOWN AND DANCE AT HER PARTY TOO!!
NOW LUMP OFF I GOTTA DANCE!

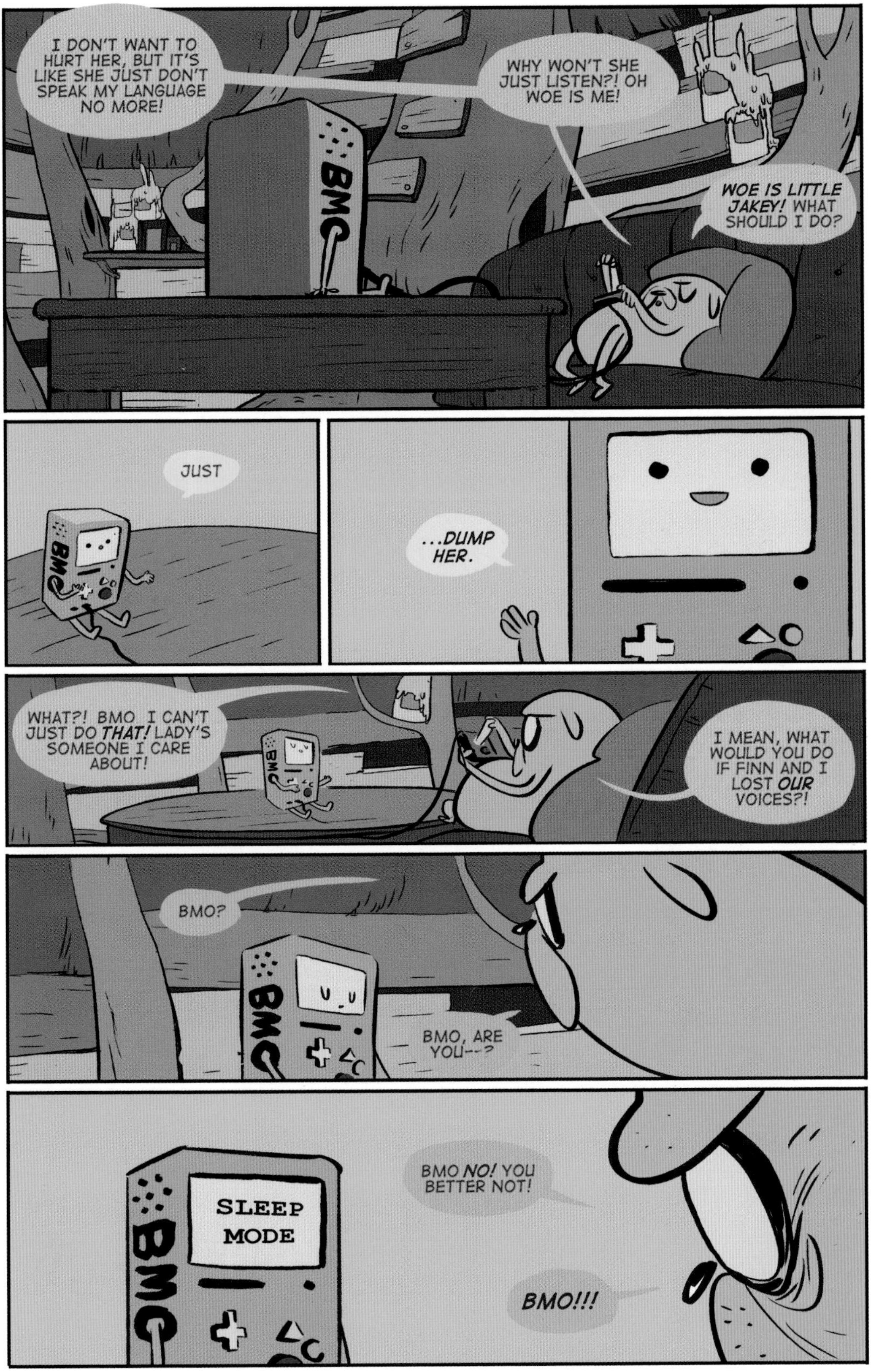

I DON'T WANT TO HURT HER, BUT IT'S LIKE SHE JUST DON'T SPEAK MY LANGUAGE NO MORE!
WHY WON'T SHE JUST LISTEN?! OH WOE IS ME!
WOE IS LITTLE JAKEY! WHAT SHOULD I DO?
BMO
JUST
...DUMP HER.
WHAT?! BMO I CAN'T JUST DO THAT! LADY'S SOMEONE I CARE ABOUT!
I MEAN, WHAT WOULD YOU DO IF FINN AND I LOST OUR VOICES?!
BMO?
BMO, ARE YOU--?
SLEEP MODE
BMO NO! YOU BETTER NOT!
BMO!!!

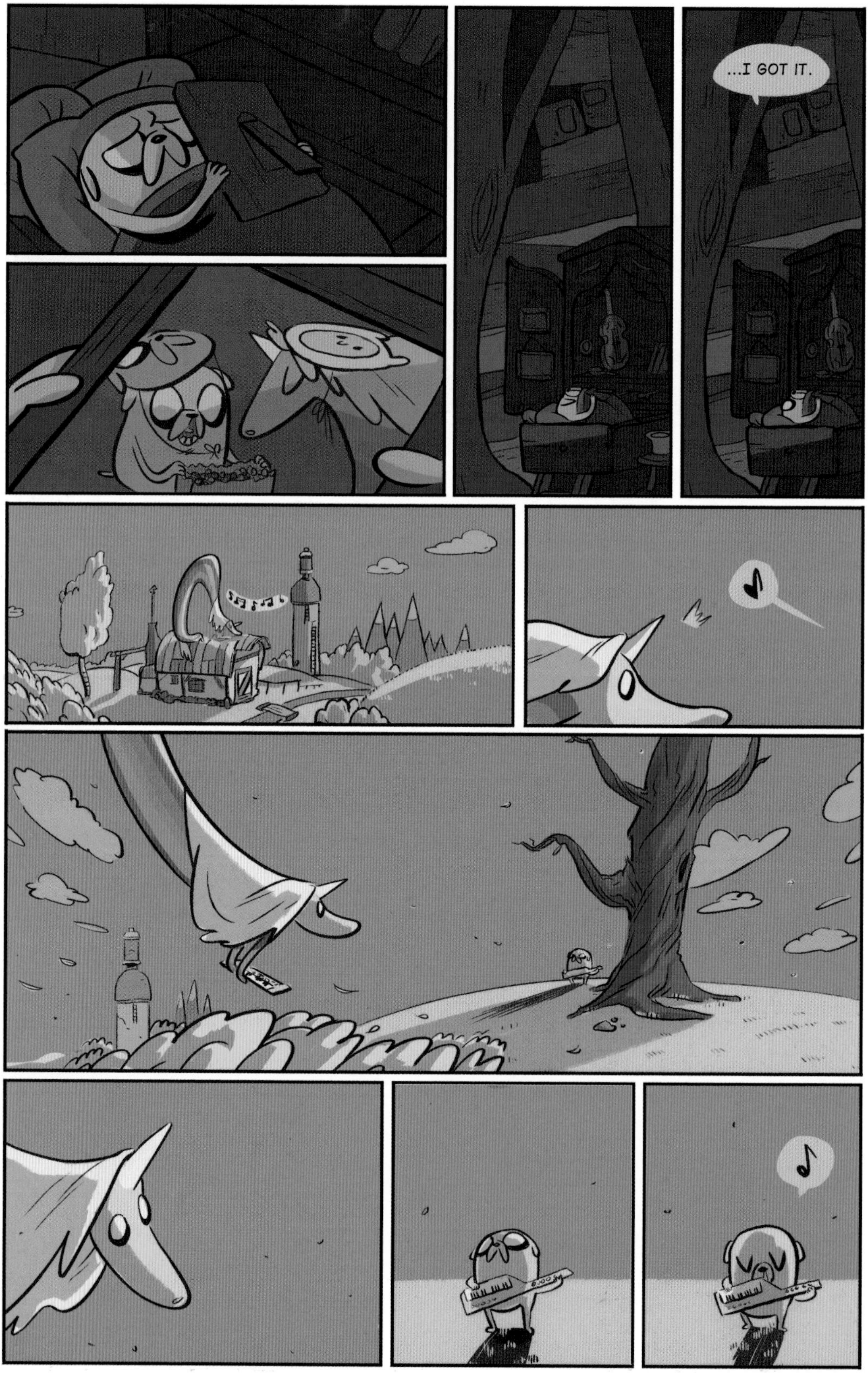
...I GOT IT.

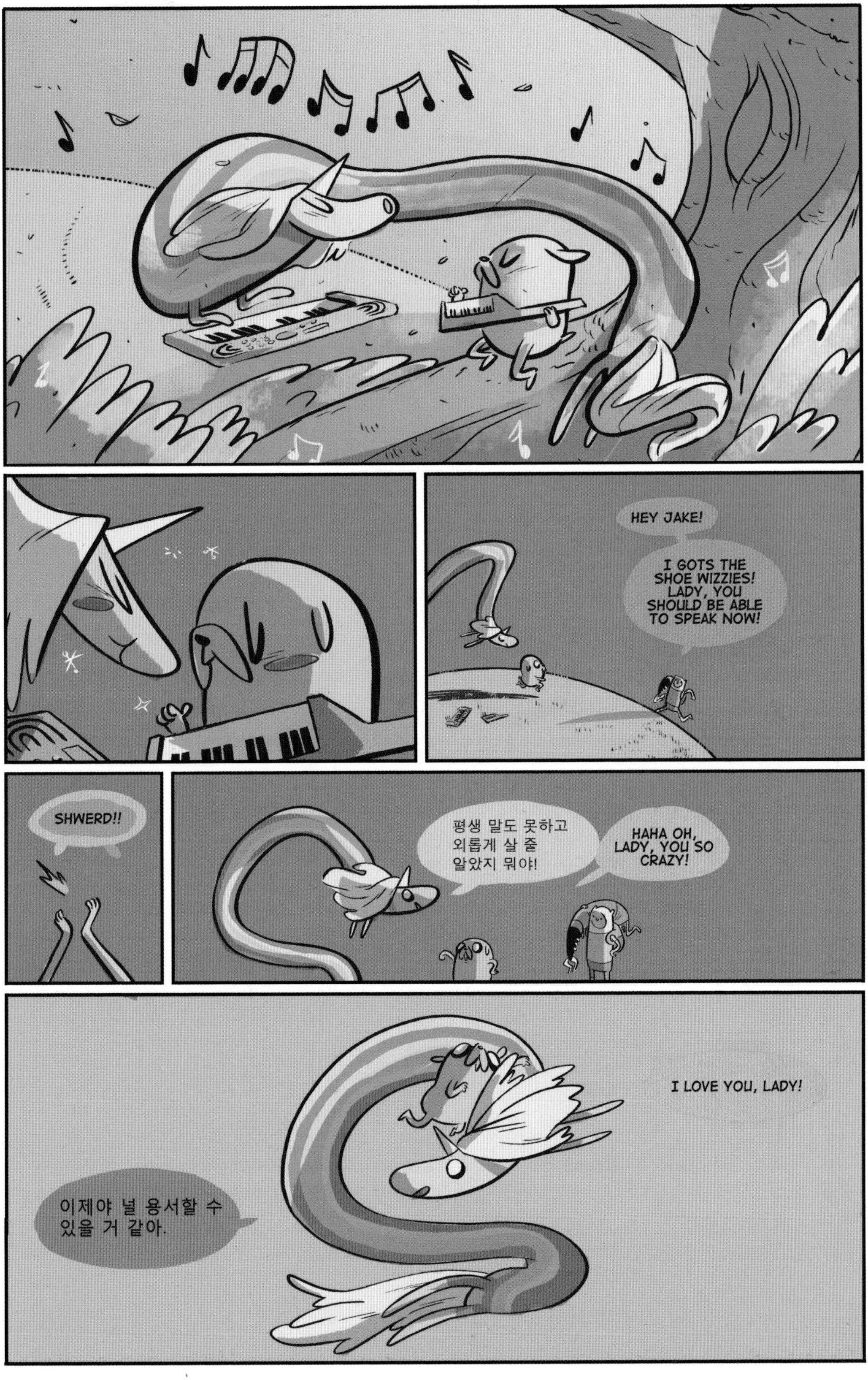
HEY JAKE!
I GOTS THE SHOE WIZZIES! LADY, YOU SHOULD BE ABLE TO SPEAK NOW!
SHWERD!!
평생 말도 못하고 외롭게 살 줄 알았지 뭐야!
HAHA OH, LADY, YOU SO CRAZY!
I LOVE YOU, LADY!
이제야 널 용서할 수 있을 거 같아.

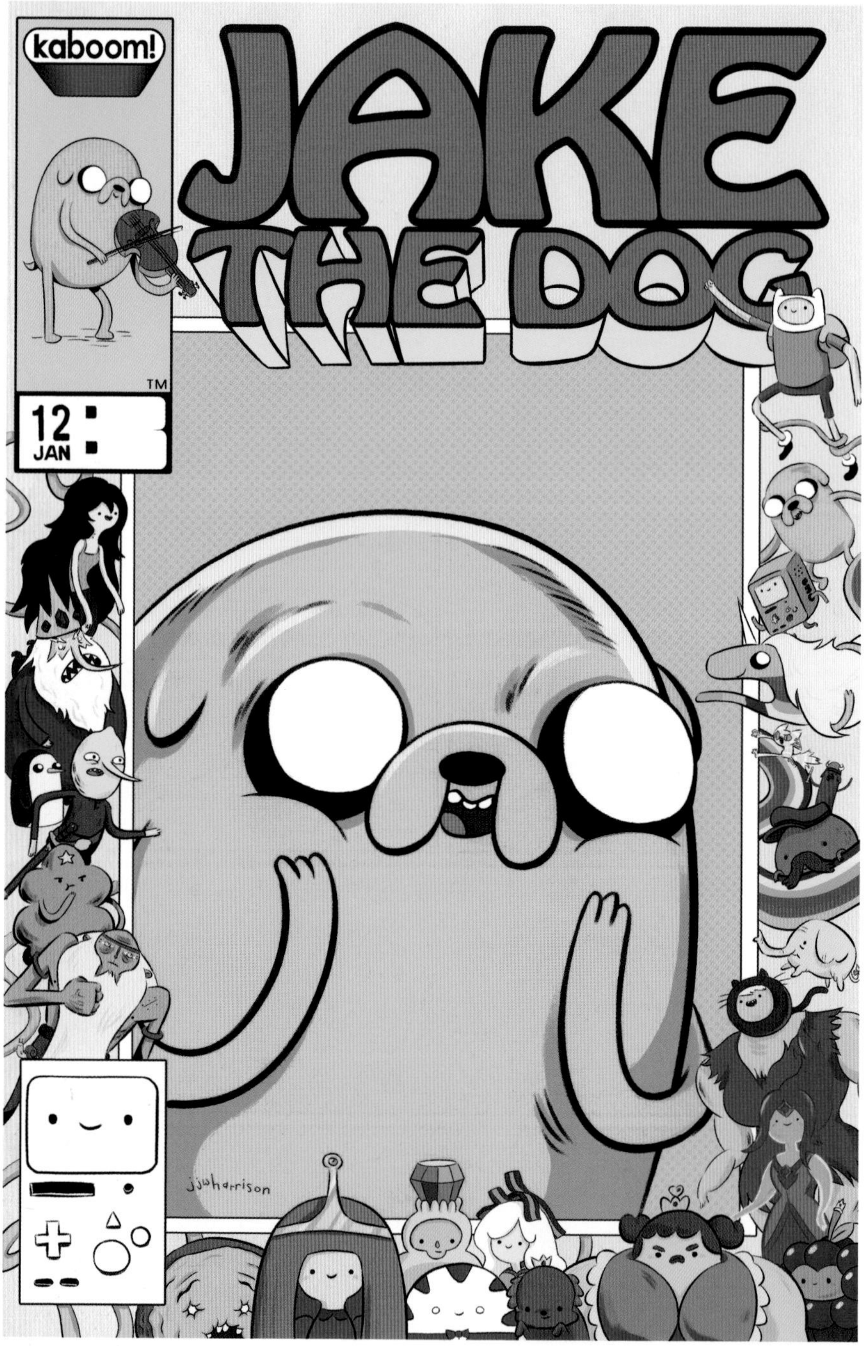
kaboom!
JAKE THE DOG
TM
12
JAN
jjwharrison

Adventure Time #12 Brett's Comics Pile Exclusive Cover by **JJ Harrison**

"The Devilish Devourer of Delicious Delicacies"

Written and Illustrated by **Josh Lesnick**

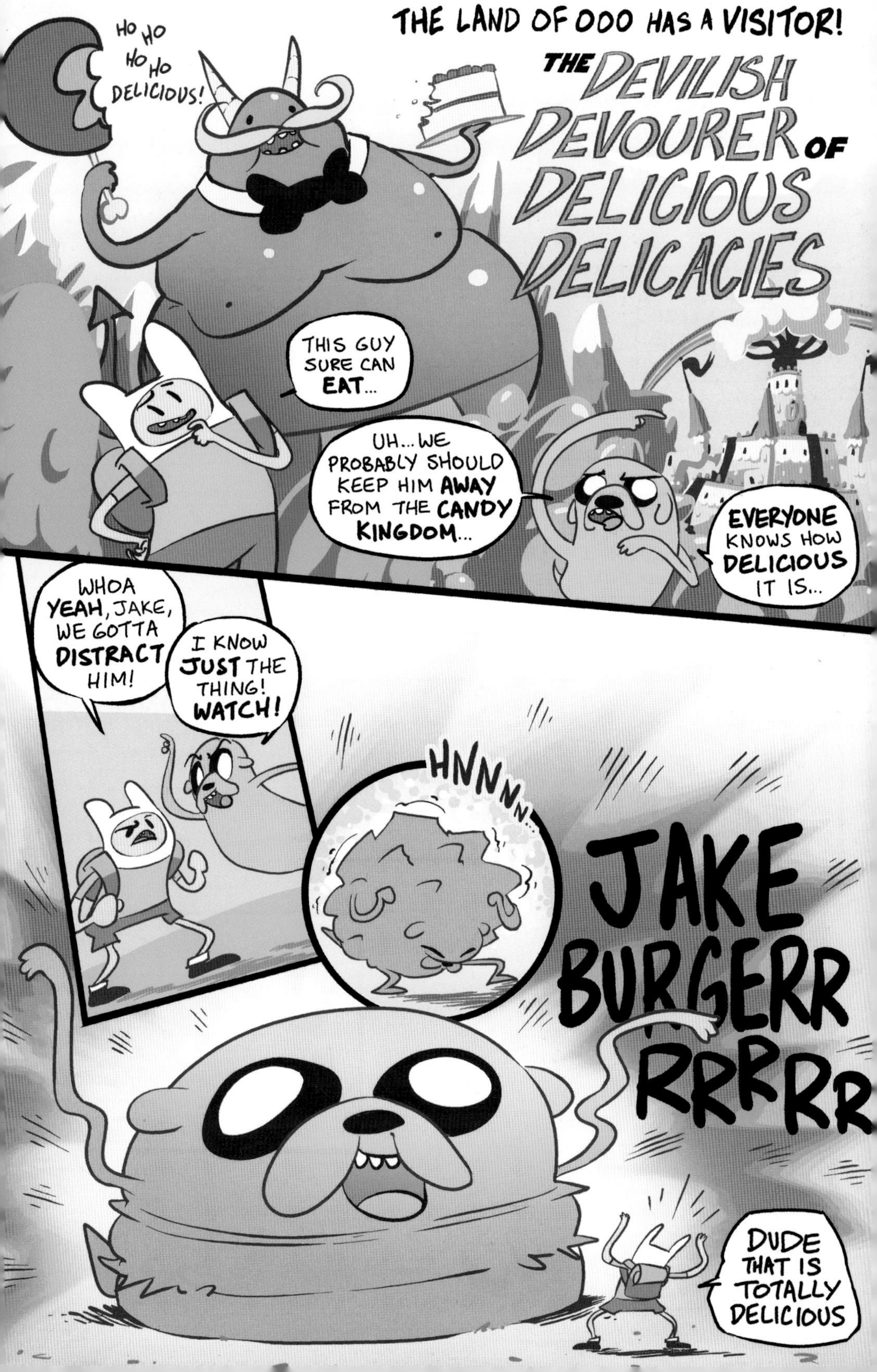

THE LAND OF OOO HAS A VISITOR!
THE DEVILISH DEVOURER OF DELICIOUS DELICACIES
HO HO HO HO DELICIOUS!
THIS GUY SURE CAN EAT...
UH... WE PROBABLY SHOULD KEEP HIM AWAY FROM THE CANDY KINGDOM...
EVERYONE KNOWS HOW DELICIOUS IT IS...
WHOA YEAH, JAKE, WE GOTTA DISTRACT HIM!
I KNOW JUST THE THING! WATCH!
HNNNN...
JAKE BURGERRRRRRR
DUDE THAT IS TOTALLY DELICIOUS

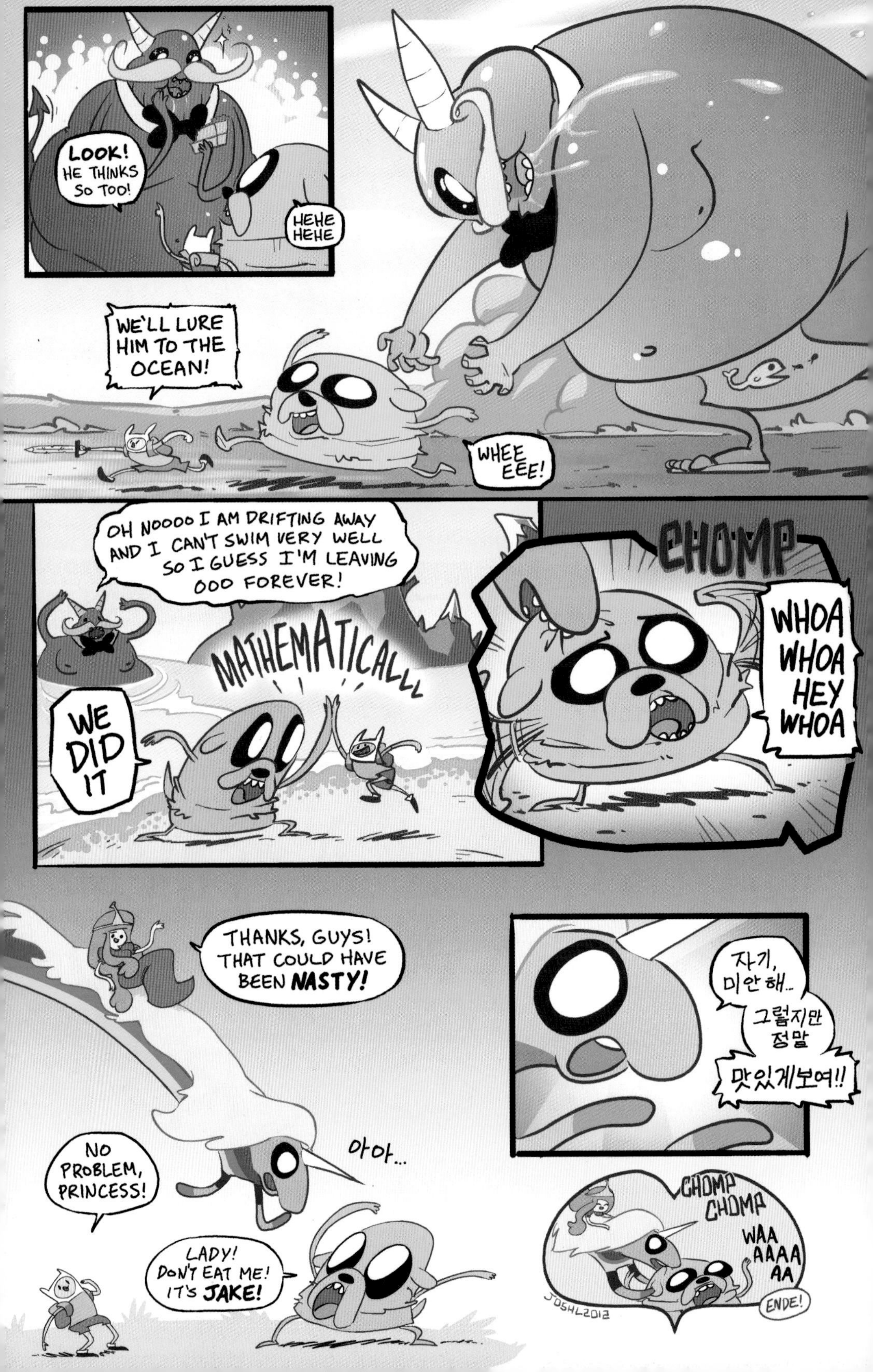

LOOK! HE THINKS SO TOO!
HEHE HEHE
WE'LL LURE HIM TO THE OCEAN!
WHEE EEE!
OH NOOOO I AM DRIFTING AWAY AND I CAN'T SWIM VERY WELL SO I GUESS I'M LEAVING OOO FOREVER!
MATHEMATICALLL
WE DID IT
CHOMP
WHOA WHOA HEY WHOA
THANKS, GUYS! THAT COULD HAVE BEEN NASTY!
NO PROBLEM, PRINCESS!
아아...
LADY! DON'T EAT ME! IT'S JAKE!
자기, 미안해..
그렇지만 정말
맛있게보여!!
CHOMP CHOMP
WAA AAAA AA
JOSHL2012
ENDE!

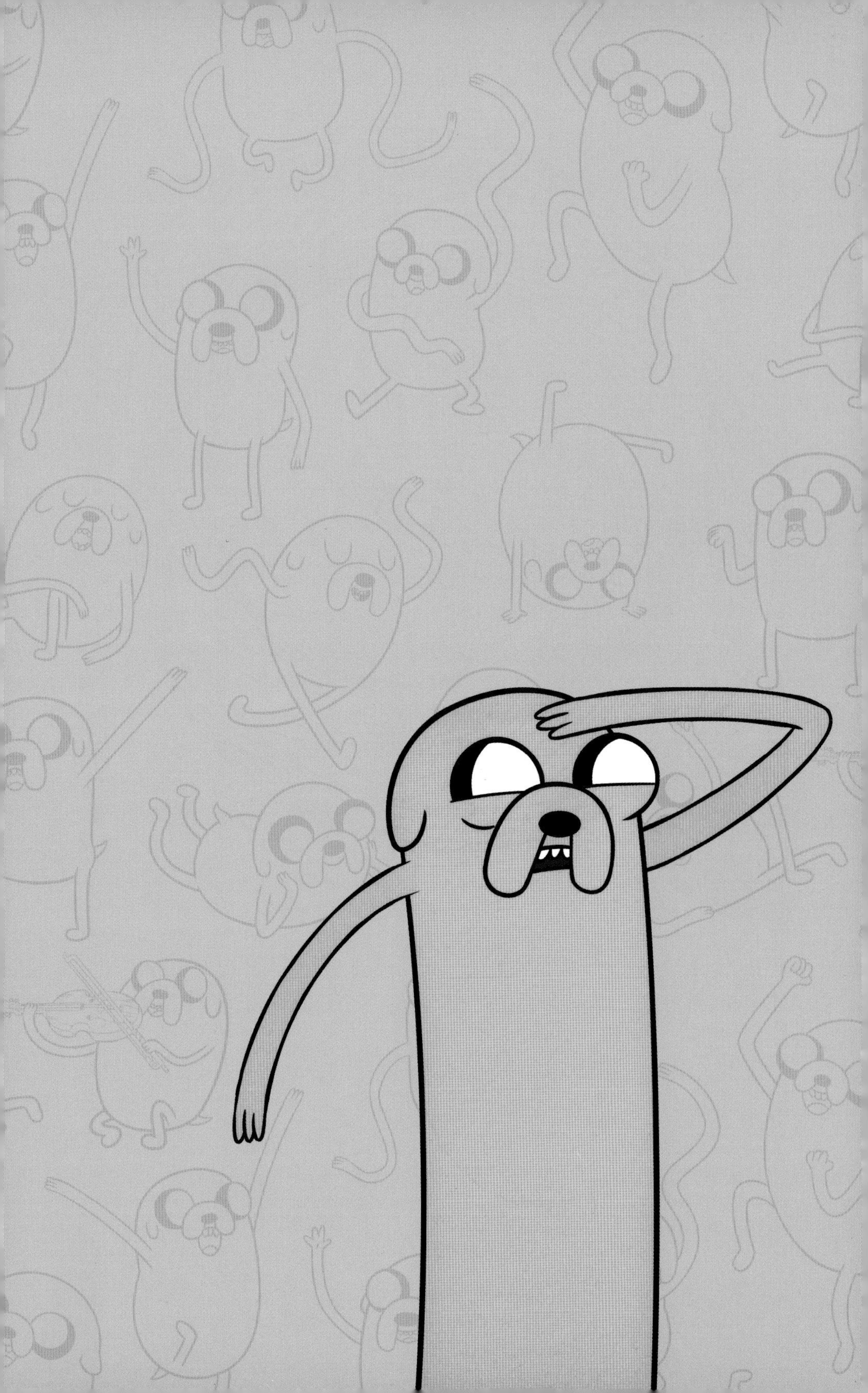

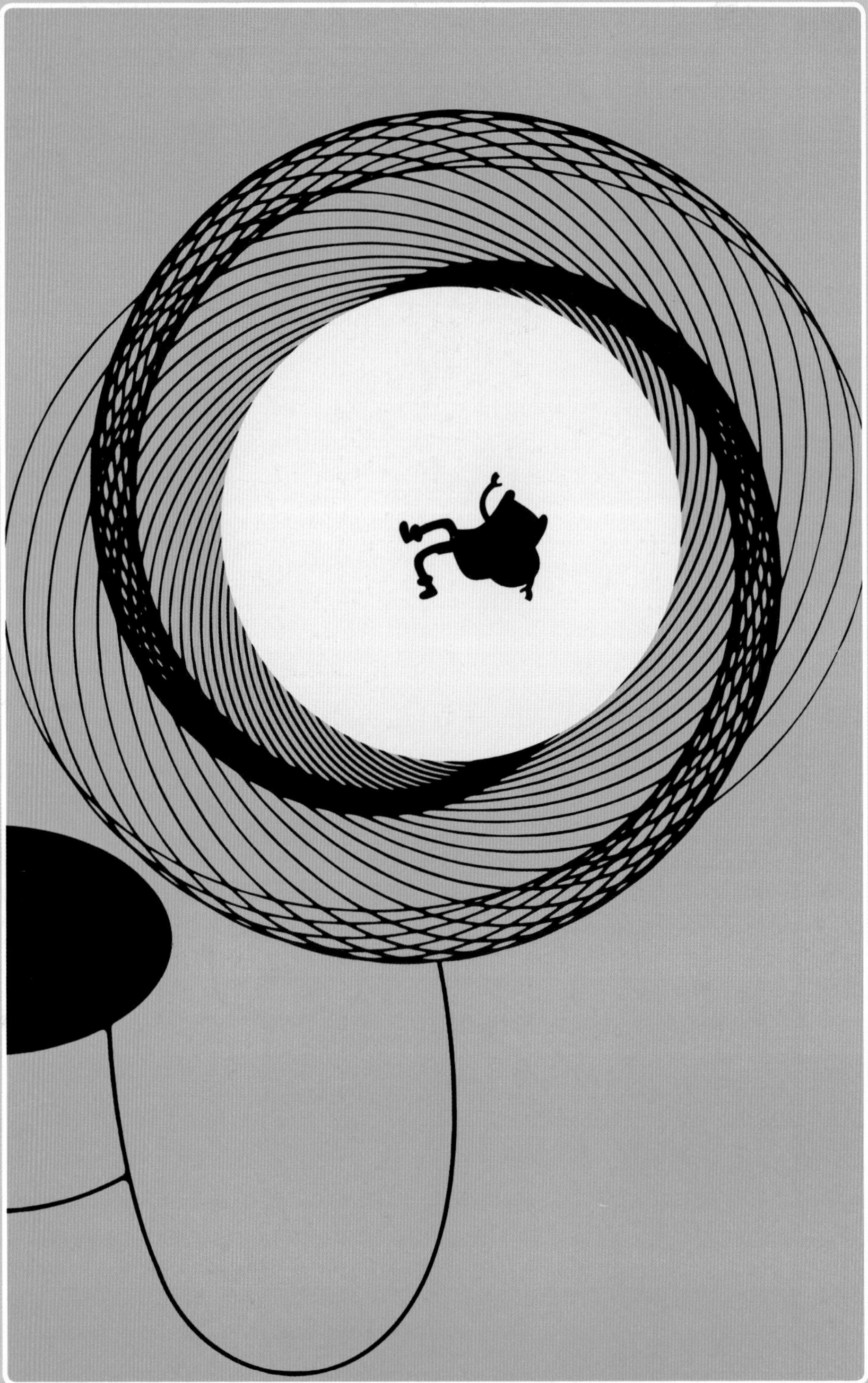

Adventure Time #36 Second Print Cover by **Jay Shaw**

"Forgotten Feasts"

Written by **Christopher Hastings** Illustrated by **Zachary Sterling**

Colors by **Maarta Laiho** Letters by **Steve Wands**

It went in that portal. Are we ADVENTURERS not SURELY TASKED to BOLDY FOLLOW?
I don't know man. MYSTERIOUS PORTALS give me the spookie-ookies.
Even if you ARE talkin' all knightly.
Afraid of portals? What are you, Jake the CLOG?
'Cause like, you're CLOGGING my good times?
I'm Jake the DOG. The MAGIC DOG. Bark bark bark!
Ha ha, I know, buddy. Jay kay. You're not a good times clog.
Bark bark bark!
Ha ha
Okay. Okay. Gotta get you back. Are you...
...Finn the HU--
--MAN?
Or Fin the huuuuuu....
Reach for it, dude. I believe in you.
...uuuuge WUSS?
Nice.
I'm Finn the human, baby! Let's DO THIS.
YEAH!
Wait did you trick me into motivating BOTH of us to jump in?
I did!
Oh dang. Oh dang oh dang oh dang.
Where ARE we?

Are YOU afraid of portals? It's okay if you are! What if one went into space? It's a reasonable fear.

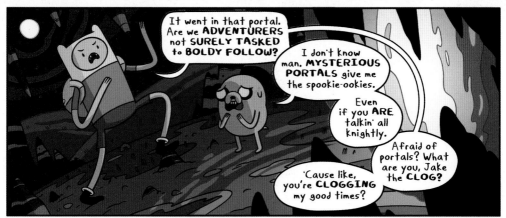

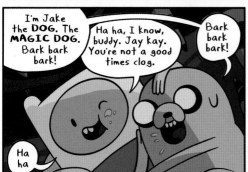

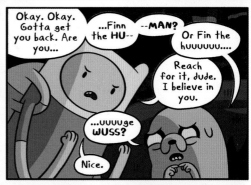

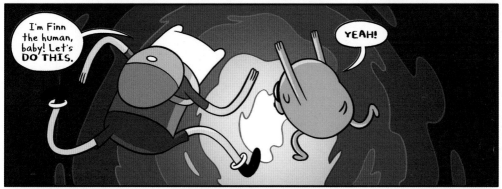

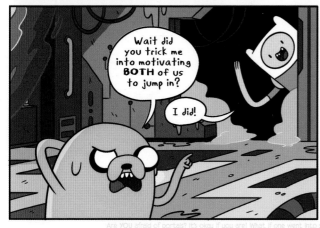

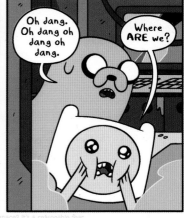

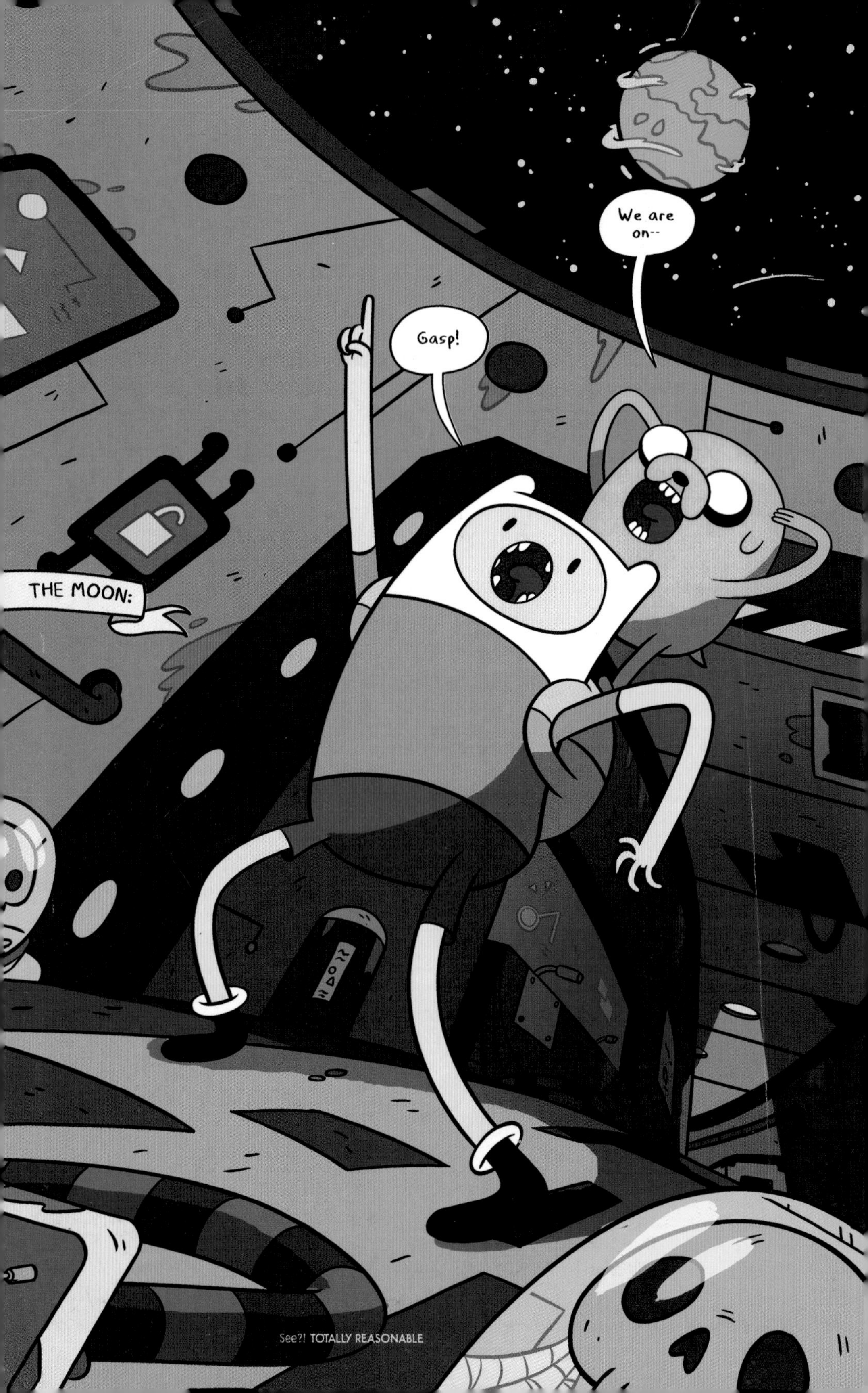
THE MOON:
Gasp!
We are on--
See?! TOTALLY REASONABLE

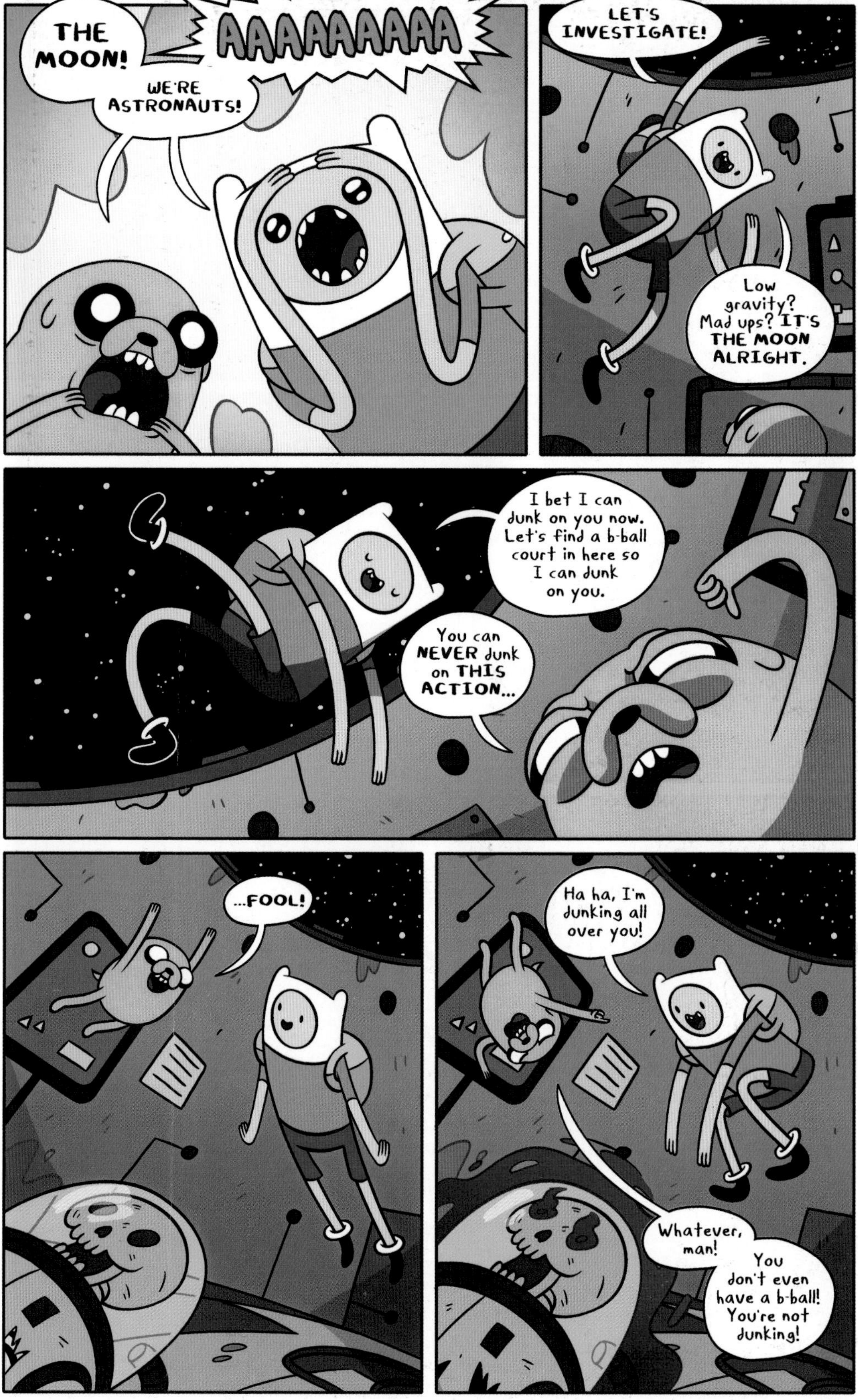
THE MOON!
AAAAAAAAA
WE'RE ASTRONAUTS!
LET'S INVESTIGATE!
Low gravity? Mad ups? IT'S THE MOON ALRIGHT.
I bet I can dunk on you now. Let's find a b-ball court in here so I can dunk on you.
You can NEVER dunk on THIS ACTION...
...FOOL!
Ha ha, I'm dunking all over you!
Whatever, man!
You don't even have a b-ball! You're not dunking!

It's very difficult to play basketball with a dog with legs that can stretch to infinity. That dog's gonna win, friend. He's got infinity legs.

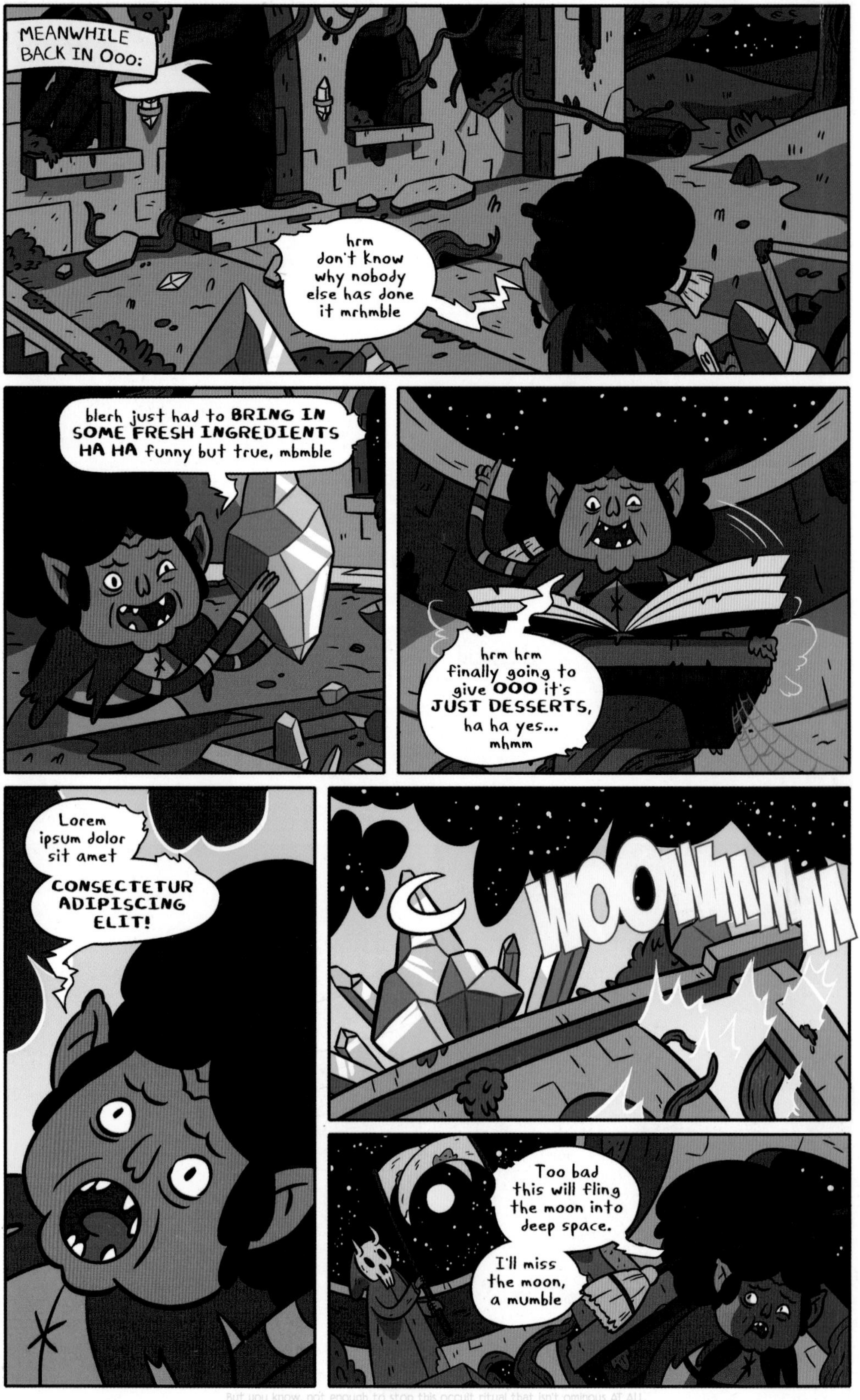
MEANWHILE BACK IN Ooo:
hrm don't know why nobody else has done it mrhmble
blerh just had to BRING IN SOME FRESH INGREDIENTS HA HA funny but true, mbmble
hrm hrm finally going to give OOO it's JUST DESSERTS, ha ha yes... mhmm
Lorem ipsum dolor sit amet
CONSECTETUR ADIPISCING ELIT!
WOOWMMM
Too bad this will fling the moon into deep space.
I'll miss the moon, a mumble

But you know, not enough to stop this occult ritual that isn't ominous AT ALL.

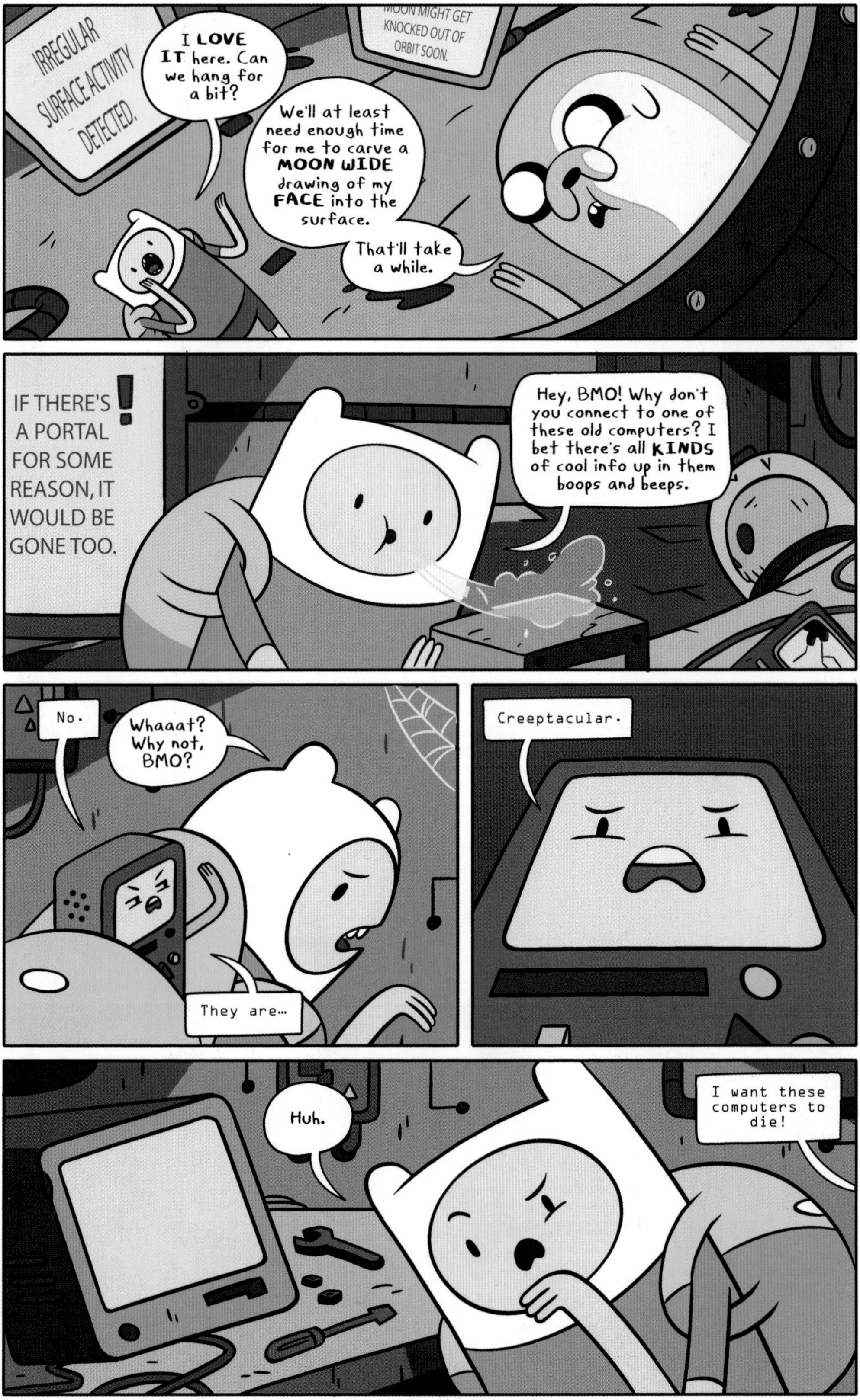
IRREGULAR SURFACE ACTIVITY DETECTED.
MOON MIGHT GET KNOCKED OUT OF ORBIT SOON.
I LOVE IT here. Can we hang for a bit?
We'll at least need enough time for me to carve a MOON WIDE drawing of my FACE into the surface.
That'll take a while.
IF THERE'S A PORTAL FOR SOME REASON, IT WOULD BE GONE TOO.
Hey, BMO! Why don't you connect to one of these old computers? I bet there's all KINDS of cool info up in them boops and beeps.
No.
Whaaat? Why not, BMO?
They are...
Creeptacular.
Huh.
I want these computers to die!

Let's all refer to our desktop hard drives as "boops and beeps" from now on, kay? Cool.

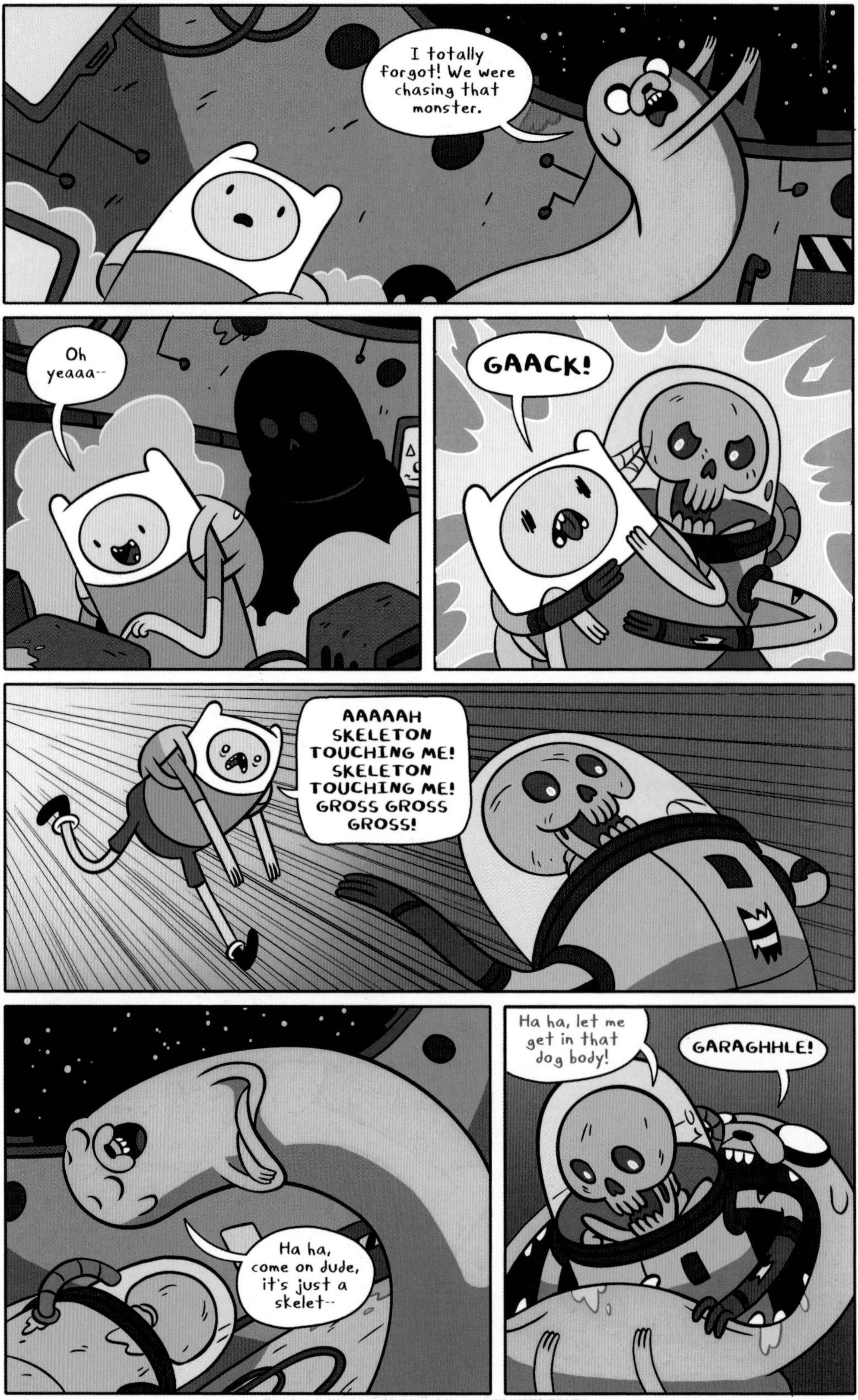
I totally forgot! We were chasing that monster.
Oh yeaaa--
GAACK!
AAAAAH SKELETON TOUCHING ME! SKELETON TOUCHING ME! GROSS GROSS GROSS!
Ha ha, come on dude, it's just a skelet--
Ha ha, let me get in that dog body!
GARAGHHLE!

There's a skeleton touching you right now! IT'S INSIDE OF YOU.

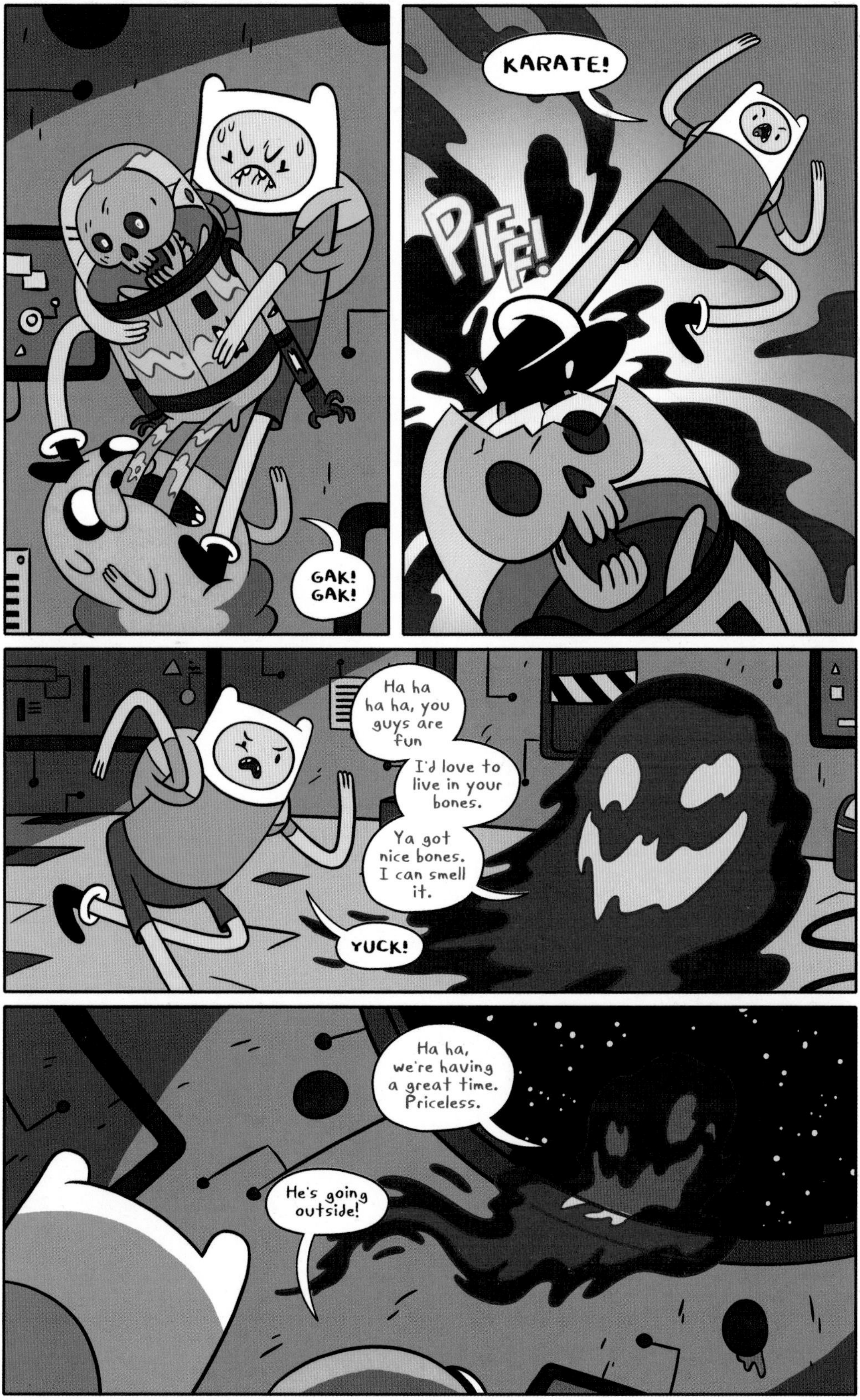
GAK! GAK!
KARATE!
PIFF!
Ha ha ha ha, you guys are fun
I'd love to live in your bones.
Ya got nice bones. I can smell it.
YUCK!
Ha ha, we're having a great time. Priceless.
He's going outside!

Who smells BONES anyway? Weirdo.

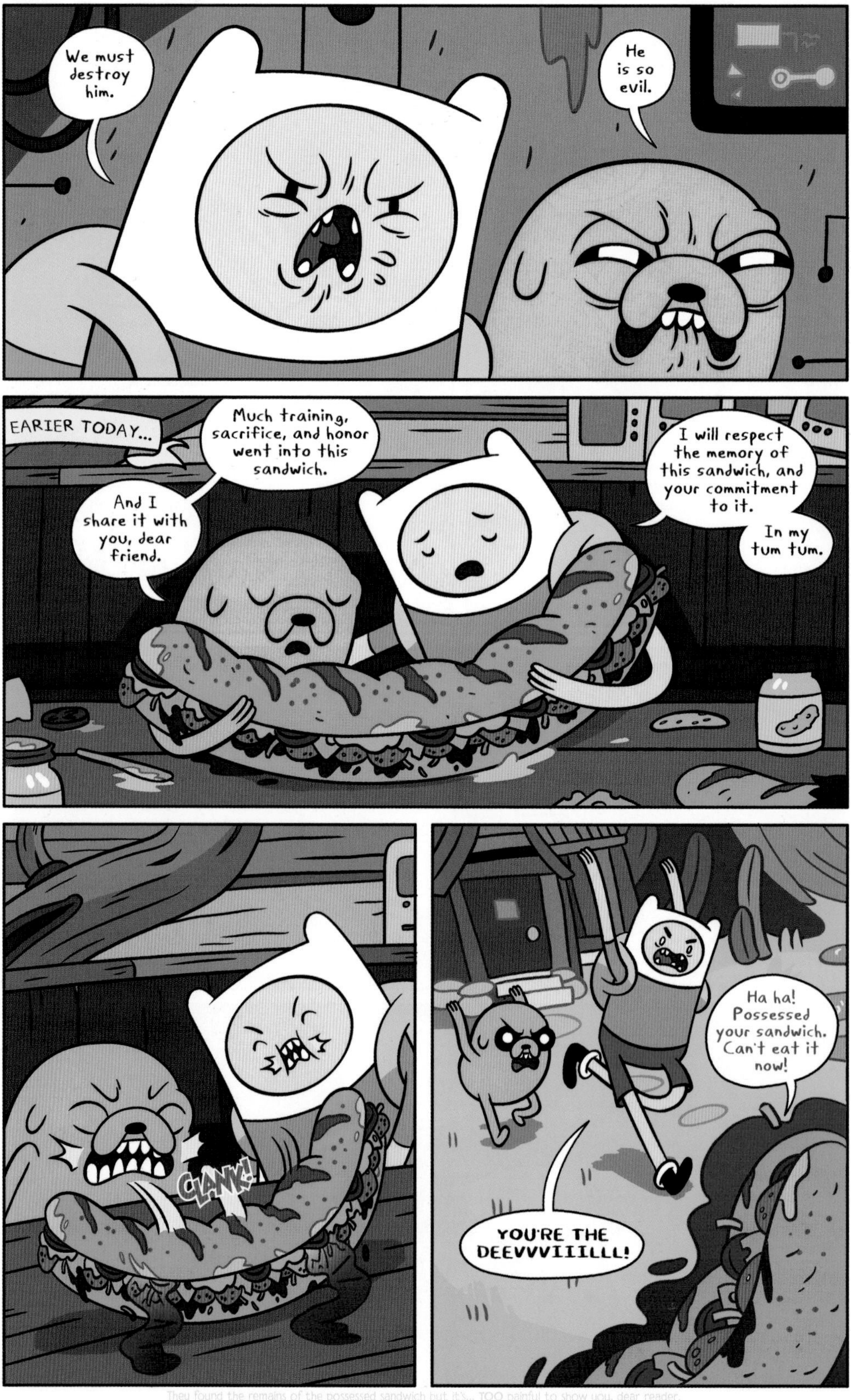
We must destroy him.
He is so evil.
EARIER TODAY...
Much training, sacrifice, and honor went into this sandwich.
And I share it with you, dear friend.
I will respect the memory of this sandwich, and your commitment to it.
In my tum tum.
CLANK!
Ha ha! Possessed your sandwich. Can't eat it now!
YOU'RE THE DEEVVVIIILLL!

They found the remains of the possessed sandwich but it's... TOO painful to show you, dear reader.

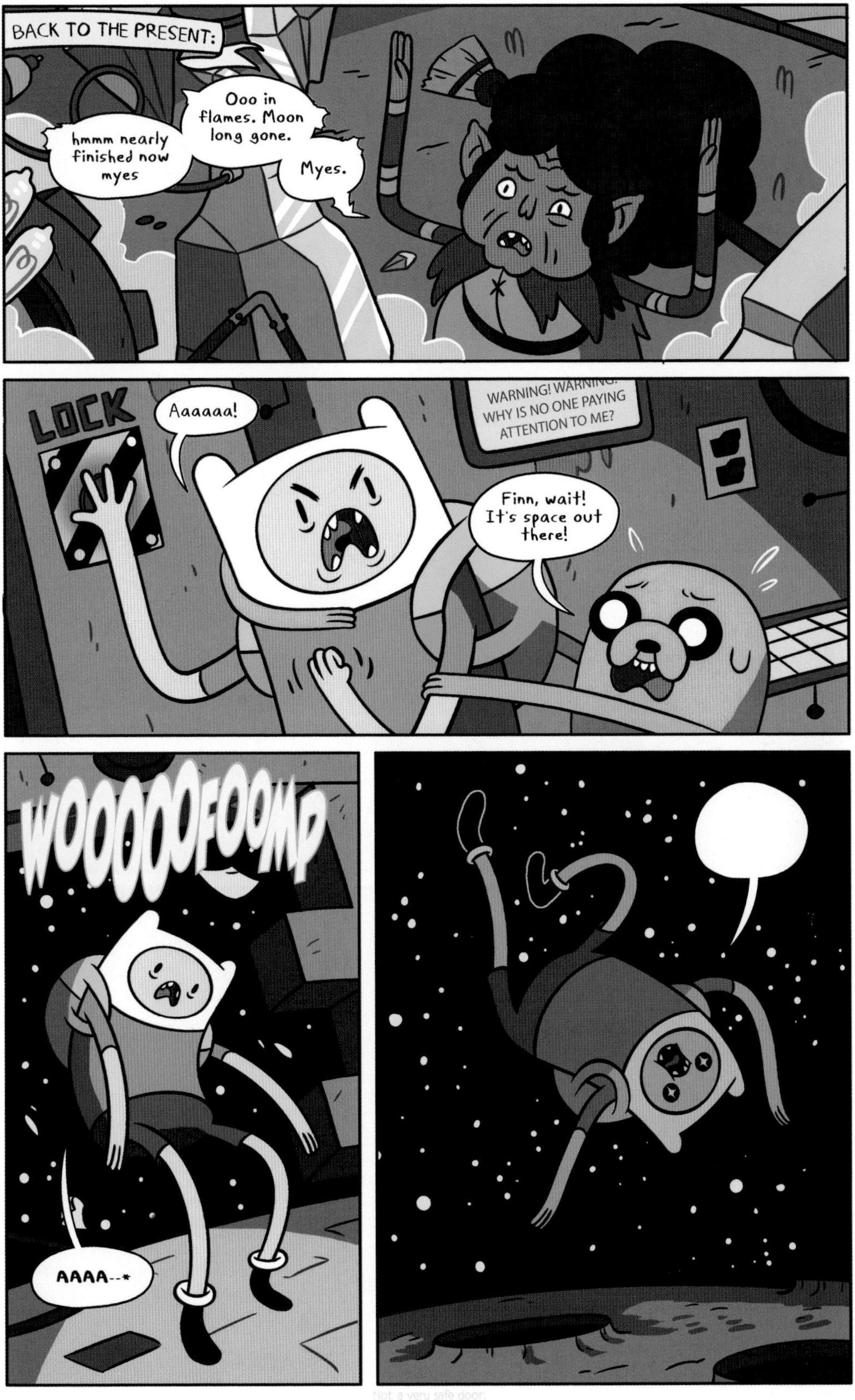
BACK TO THE PRESENT:
hmmm nearly finished now myes
Ooo in flames. Moon long gone.
Myes.
LOCK
Aaaaaa!
WARNING! WARNING! WHY IS NO ONE PAYING ATTENTION TO ME?
Finn, wait! It's space out there!
WOOOOFOOMP
AAAA--*

*Not a very safe door.

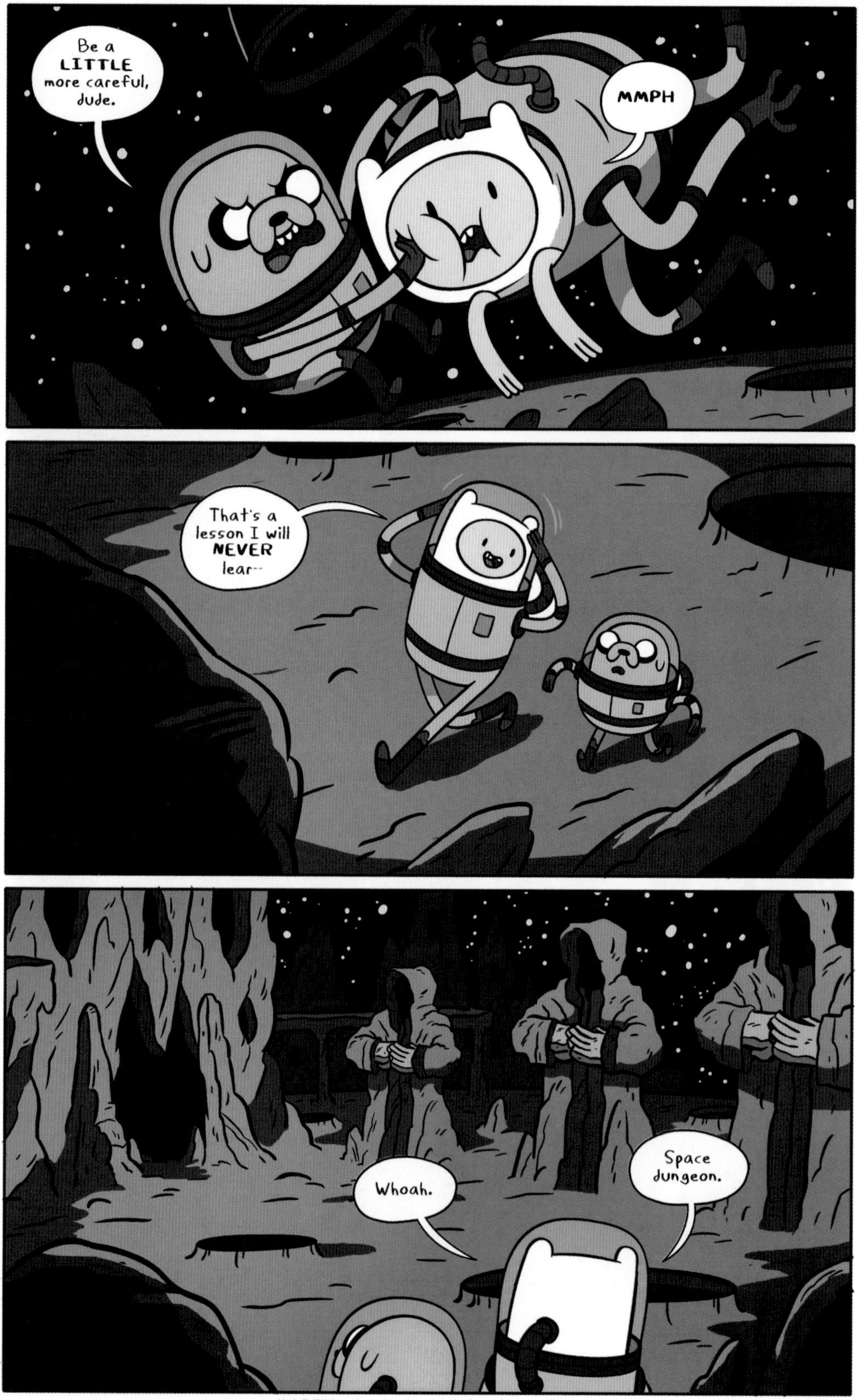
Be a LITTLE more careful, dude.
MMPH
That's a lesson I will NEVER lear--
Whoah.
Space dungeon.

Not EVERY ancient structure has to be a dungeon, Finn.

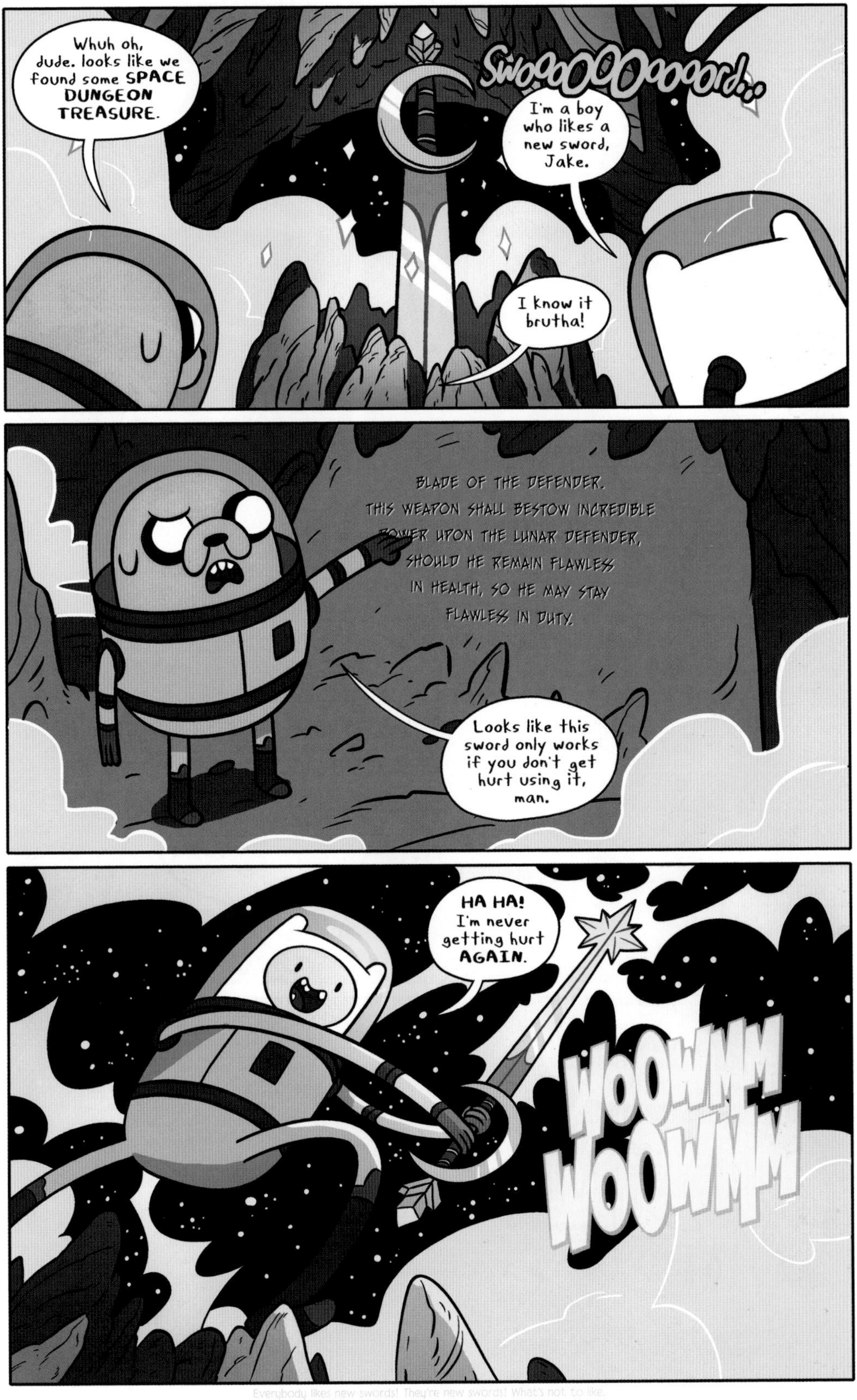
Whuh oh, dude. looks like we found some SPACE DUNGEON TREASURE.
SWOOOOOOOOOOORD..
I'm a boy who likes a new sword, Jake.
I know it brutha!
BLADE OF THE DEFENDER. THIS WEAPON SHALL BESTOW INCREDIBLE POWER UPON THE LUNAR DEFENDER, SHOULD HE REMAIN FLAWLESS IN HEALTH, SO HE MAY STAY FLAWLESS IN DUTY.
Looks like this sword only works if you don't get hurt using it, man.
HA HA! I'm never getting hurt AGAIN.
WOOWMM WOOWMM

Everybody likes new swords! They're new swords! What's not to like.

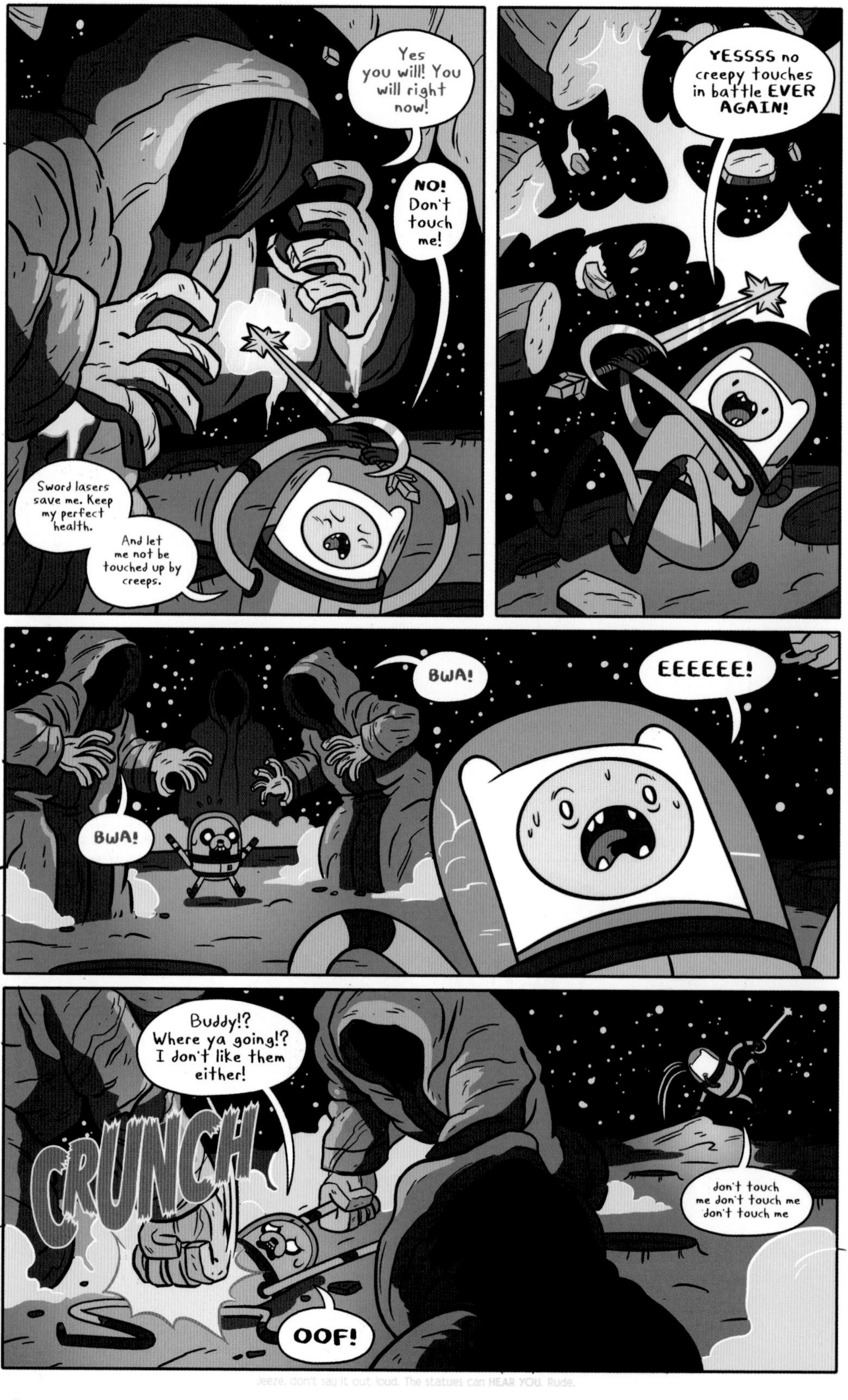
Yes you will! You will right now!
NO! Don't touch me!
Sword lasers save me. Keep my perfect health.
And let me not be touched up by creeps.
YESSSS no creepy touches in battle EVER AGAIN!
BWA!
EEEEEE!
BWA!
Buddy!? Where ya going!? I don't like them either!
CRUNCH
don't touch me don't touch me don't touch me
OOF!

Jeeze, don't say it out loud. The statues can HEAR YOU. Rude.

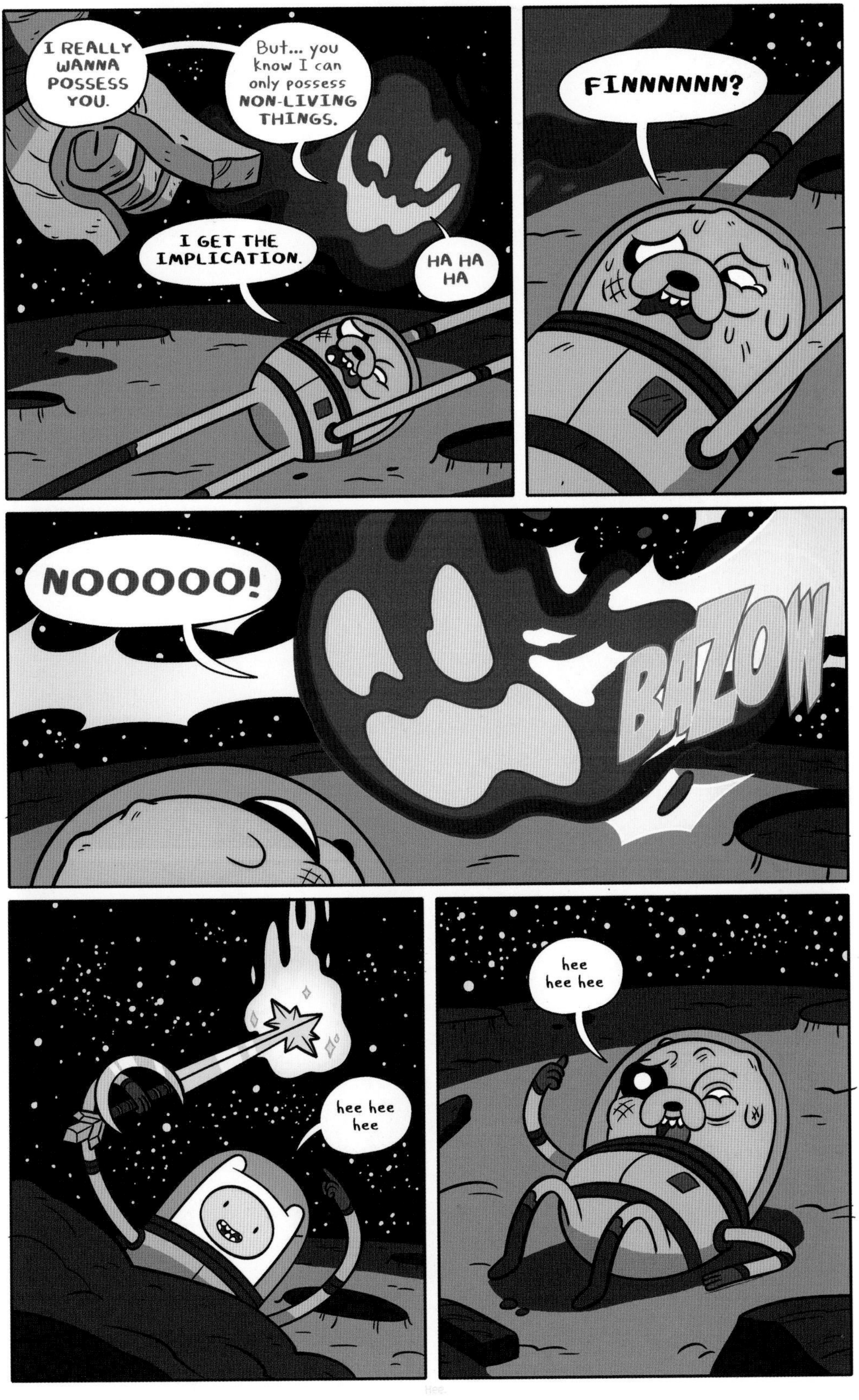
I REALLY WANNA POSSESS YOU.
But... you know I can only possess NON-LIVING THINGS.
I GET THE IMPLICATION.
HA HA HA
FINNNNNN?
NOOOOO!
BAZOW
hee hee hee
hee hee hee

Hee.

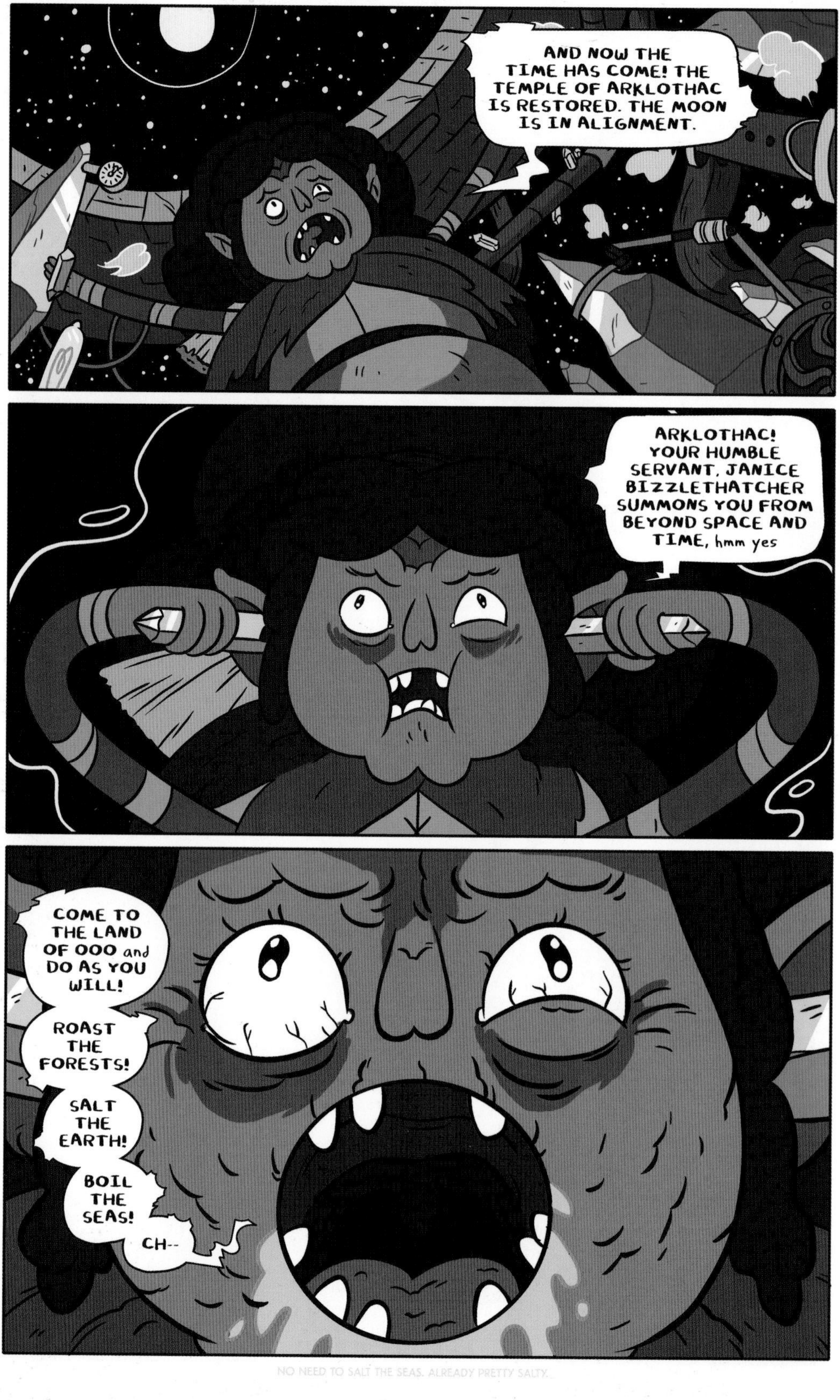
AND NOW THE TIME HAS COME! THE TEMPLE OF ARKLOTHAC IS RESTORED. THE MOON IS IN ALIGNMENT.
ARKLOTHAC! YOUR HUMBLE SERVANT, JANICE BIZZLETHATCHER SUMMONS YOU FROM BEYOND SPACE AND TIME, hmm yes
COME TO THE LAND OF OOO and DO AS YOU WILL!
ROAST THE FORESTS!
SALT THE EARTH!
BOIL THE SEAS!
CH--

NO NEED TO SALT THE SEAS. ALREADY PRETTY SALTY.

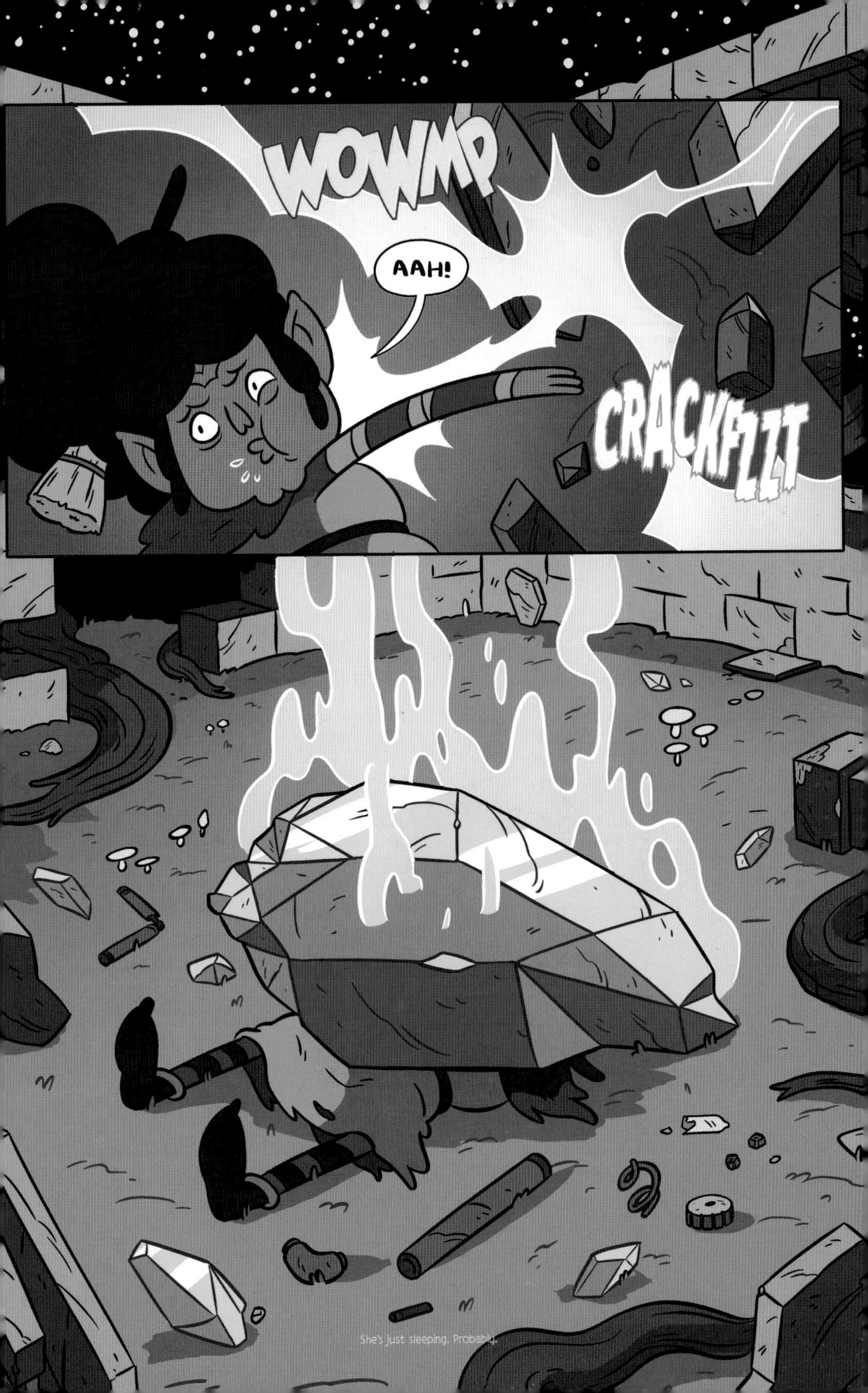
WOWMP
AAH!
CRACKFZZT
She's just sleeping. Probably.

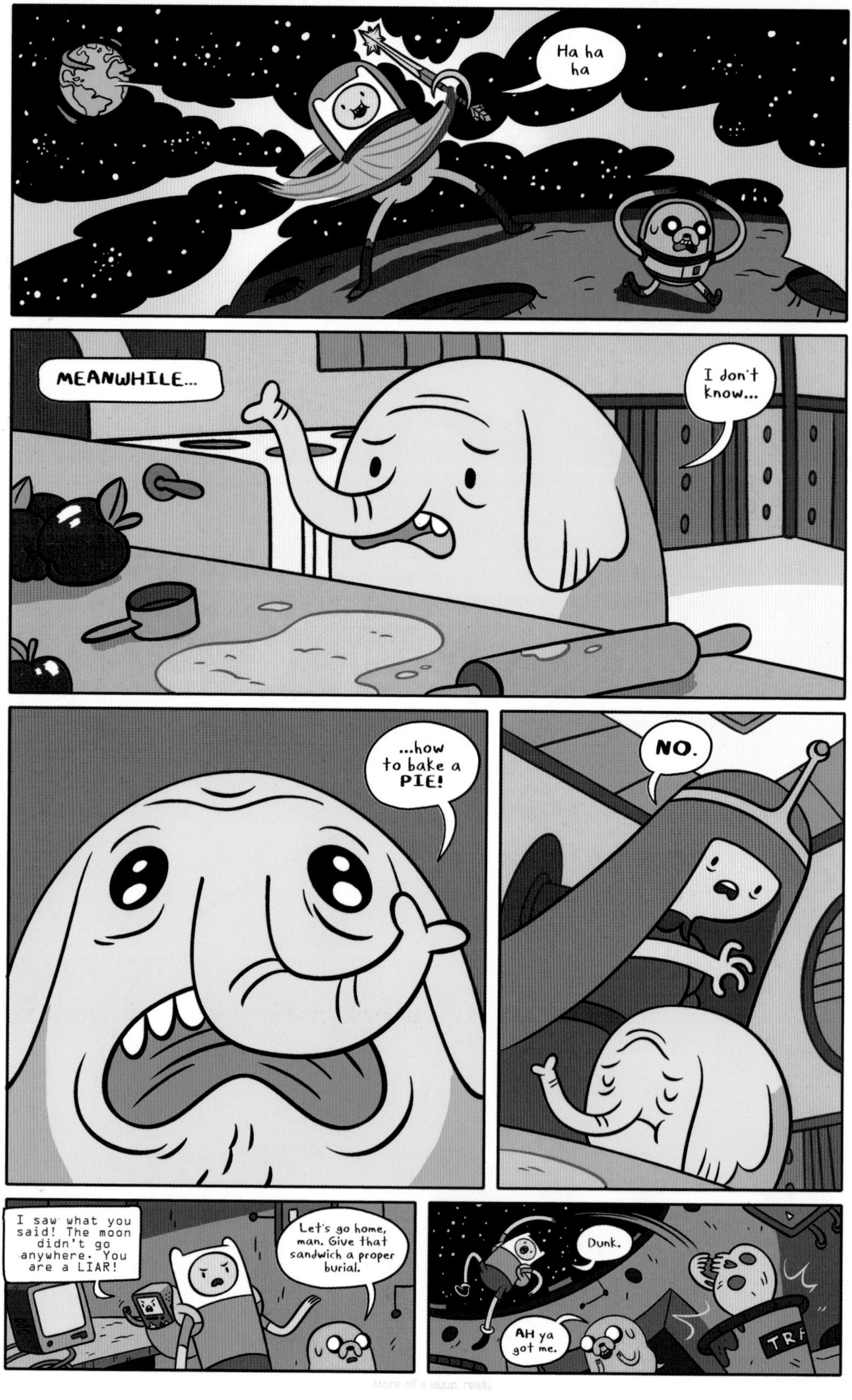
Ha ha ha
MEANWHILE...
I don't know...
...how to bake a PIE!
NO.
I saw what you said! The moon didn't go anywhere. You are a LIAR!
Let's go home, man. Give that sandwich a proper burial.
Dunk.
AH ya got me.

More of a layup, really.

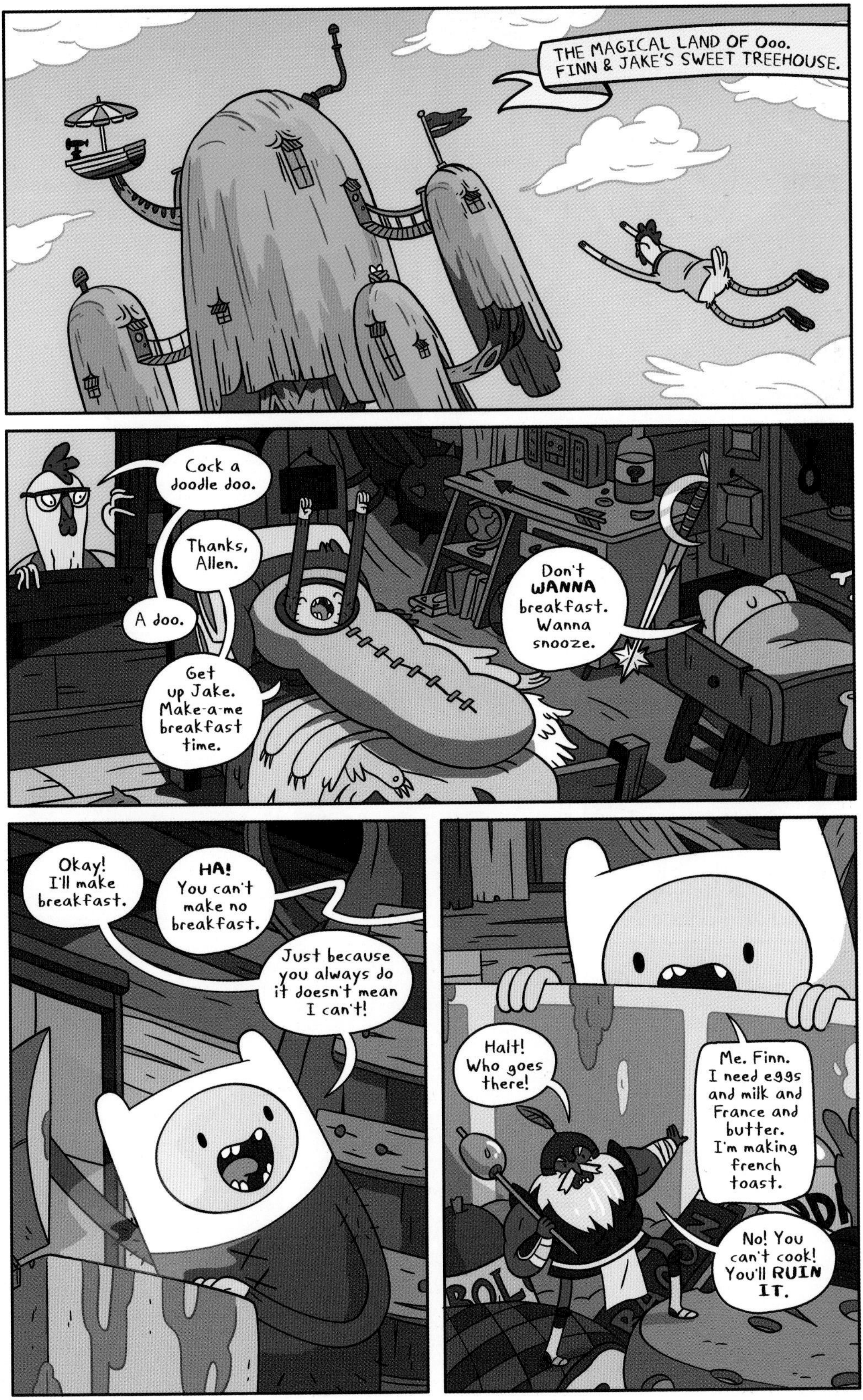
THE MAGICAL LAND OF Ooo.
FINN & JAKE'S SWEET TREEHOUSE.
Cock a doodle doo.
Thanks, Allen.
A doo.
Get up Jake. Make-a-me breakfast time.
Don't **WANNA** breakfast. Wanna snooze.
Okay! I'll make breakfast.
HA! You can't make no breakfast.
Just because you always do it doesn't mean I can't!
Halt! Who goes there!
Me. Finn. I need eggs and milk and France and butter. I'm making french toast.
No! You can't cook! You'll **RUIN IT.**

France is refrigerated, but the toast is in the cupboard.

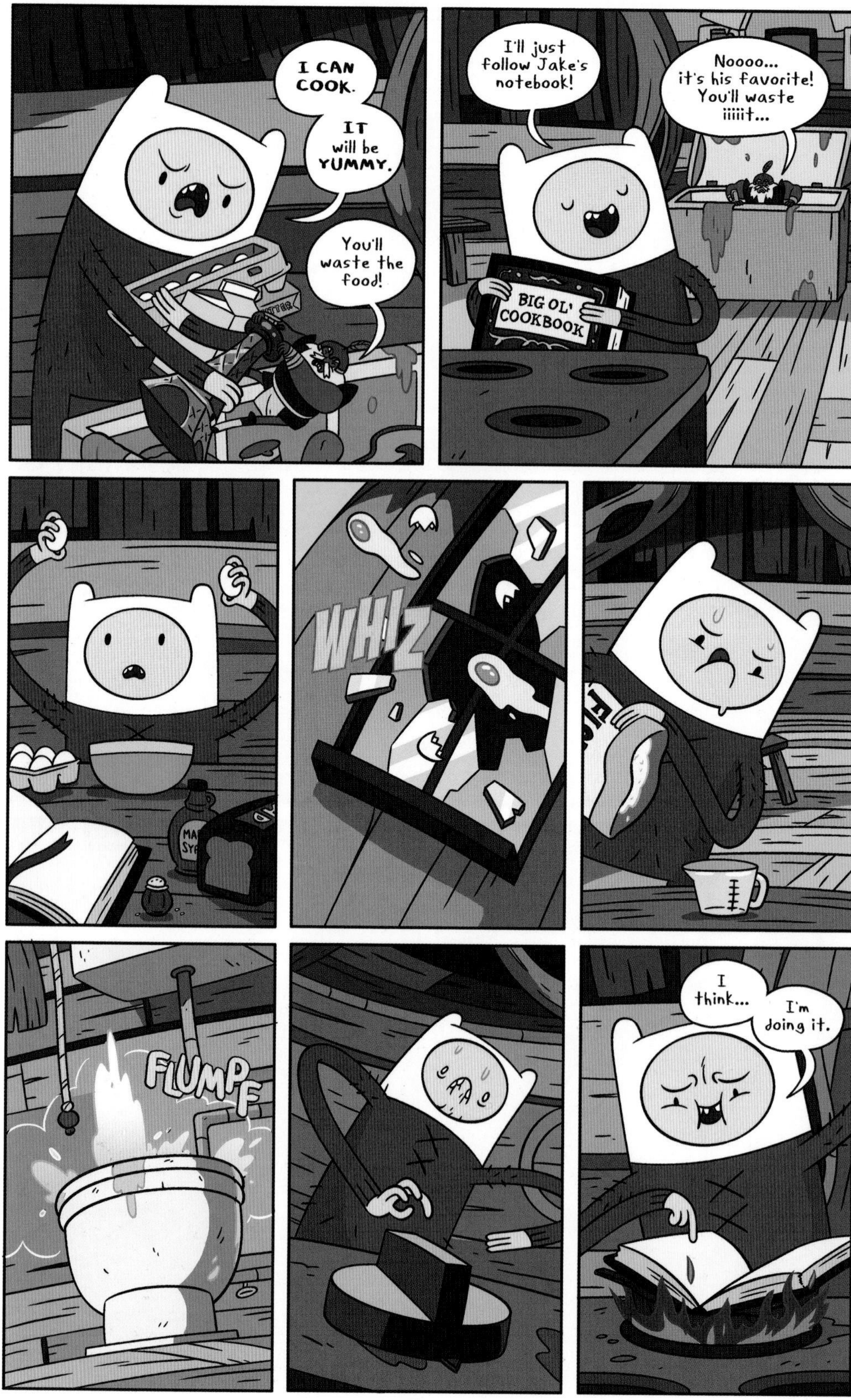
I CAN COOK.
IT will be YUMMY.
You'll waste the food!
I'll just follow Jake's notebook!
Noooo... it's his favorite! You'll waste iiiiit...
BIG OL' COOKBOOK
WHIZ
FLUMPF
I think...
I'm doing it.

Nope.

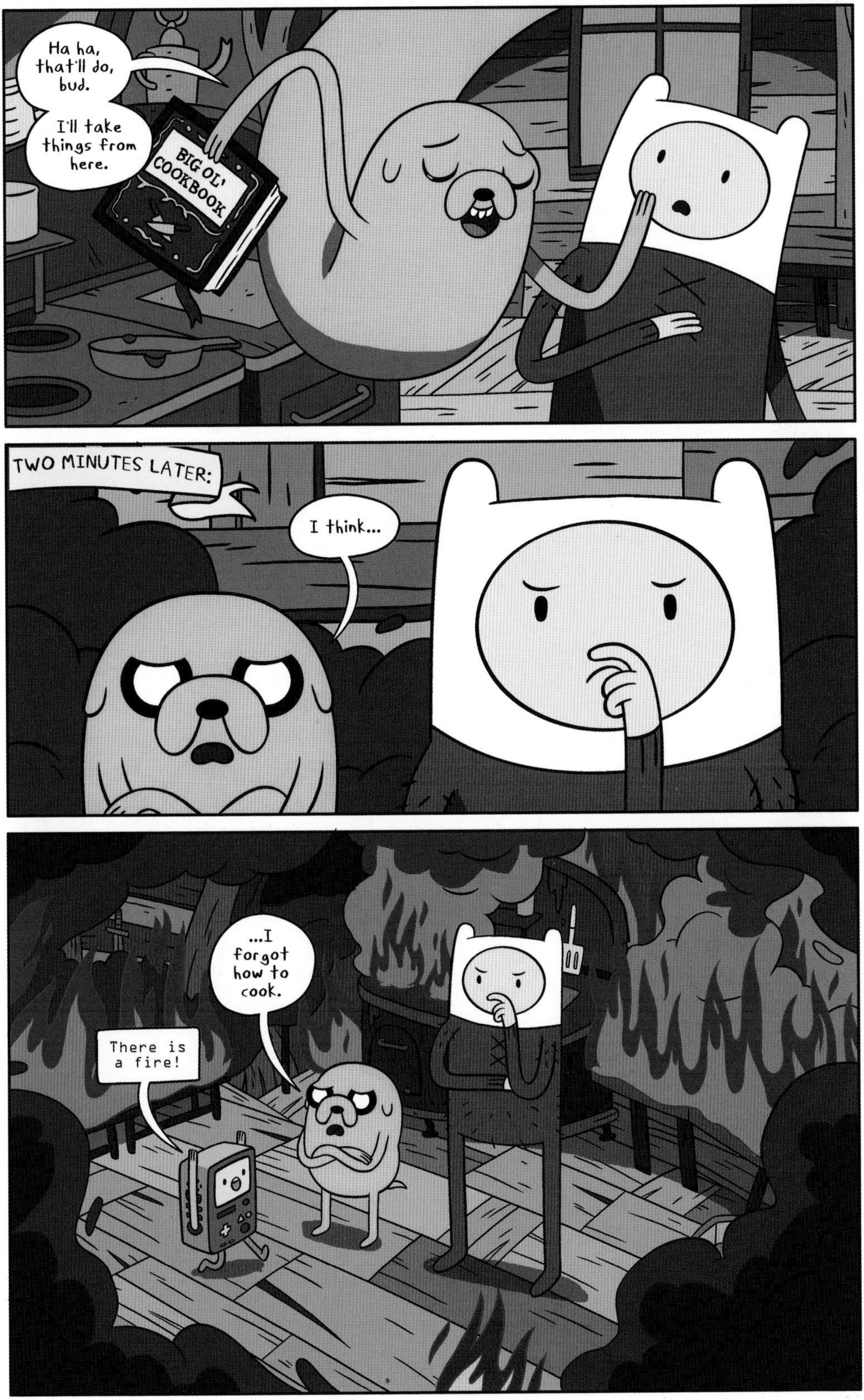
Ha ha, that'll do, bud.
I'll take things from here.
BIG OL' COOKBOOK
TWO MINUTES LATER:
I think...
...I forgot how to cook.
There is a fire!

And this is a comic book! Sorry, we're all just saying things that are true?

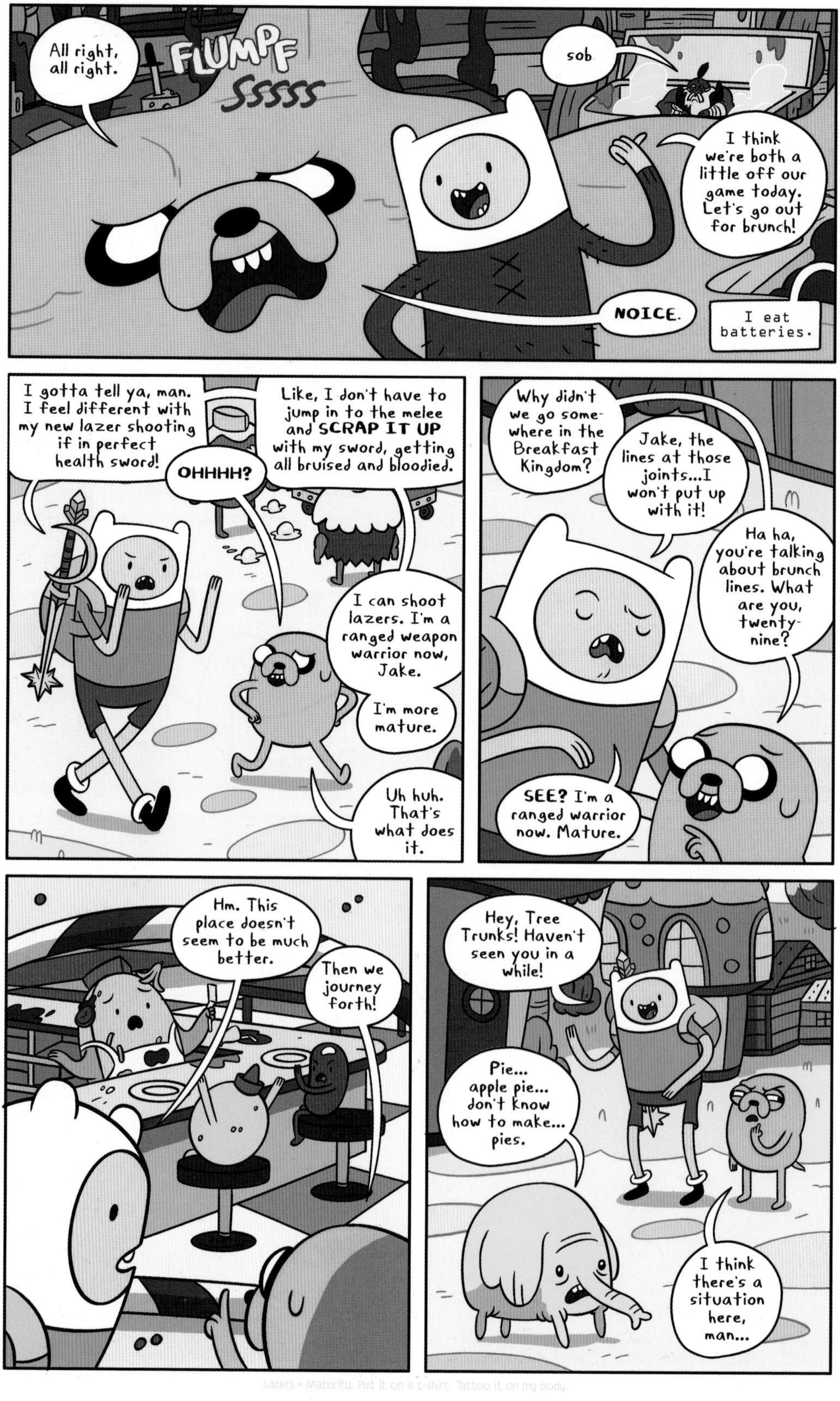

All right, all right.
FLUMPF
SSSSS
sob
I think we're both a little off our game today. Let's go out for brunch!
NOICE.
I eat batteries.
I gotta tell ya, man. I feel different with my new lazer shooting if in perfect health sword!
Like, I don't have to jump in to the melee and **SCRAP IT UP** with my sword, getting all bruised and bloodied.
OHHHH?
I can shoot lazers. I'm a ranged weapon warrior now, Jake.
I'm more mature.
Uh huh. That's what does it.
Why didn't we go somewhere in the Breakfast Kingdom?
Jake, the lines at those joints...I won't put up with it!
Ha ha, you're talking about brunch lines. What are you, twenty-nine?
SEE? I'm a ranged warrior now. Mature.
Hm. This place doesn't seem to be much better.
Then we journey forth!
Hey, Tree Trunks! Haven't seen you in a while!
Pie... apple pie... don't know how to make... pies.
I think there's a situation here, man...

Lazers = Maturity. Put it on a t-shirt. Tattoo it on my body.

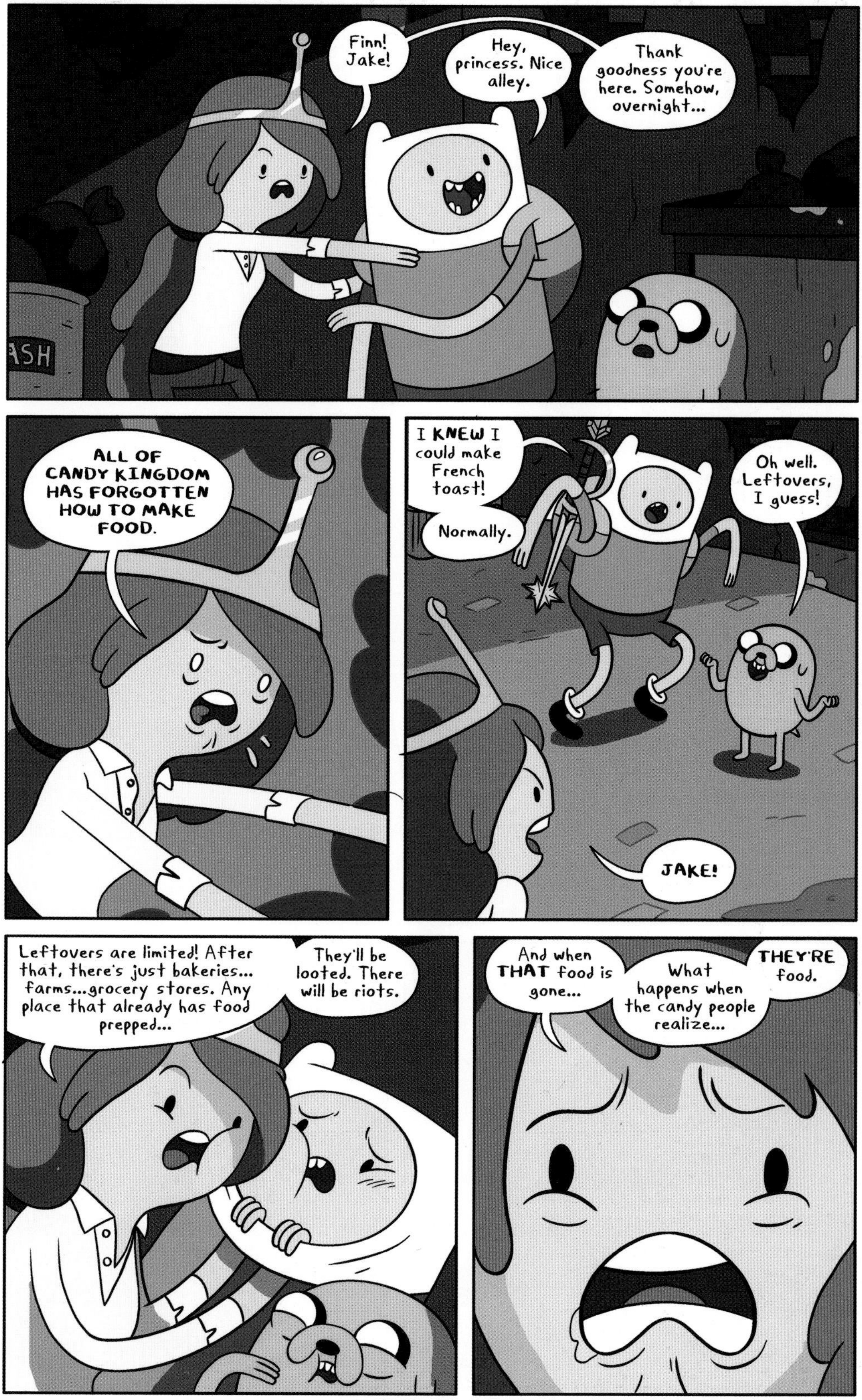
Finn! Jake!
Hey, princess. Nice alley.
Thank goodness you're here. Somehow, overnight...
ALL OF CANDY KINGDOM HAS FORGOTTEN HOW TO MAKE FOOD.
I **KNEW** I could make French toast!
Normally.
Oh well. Leftovers, I guess!
JAKE!
Leftovers are limited! After that, there's just bakeries... farms...grocery stores. Any place that already has food prepped...
They'll be looted. There will be riots.
And when **THAT** food is gone...
What happens when the candy people realize...
THEY'RE food.

An existential crisis, probably.

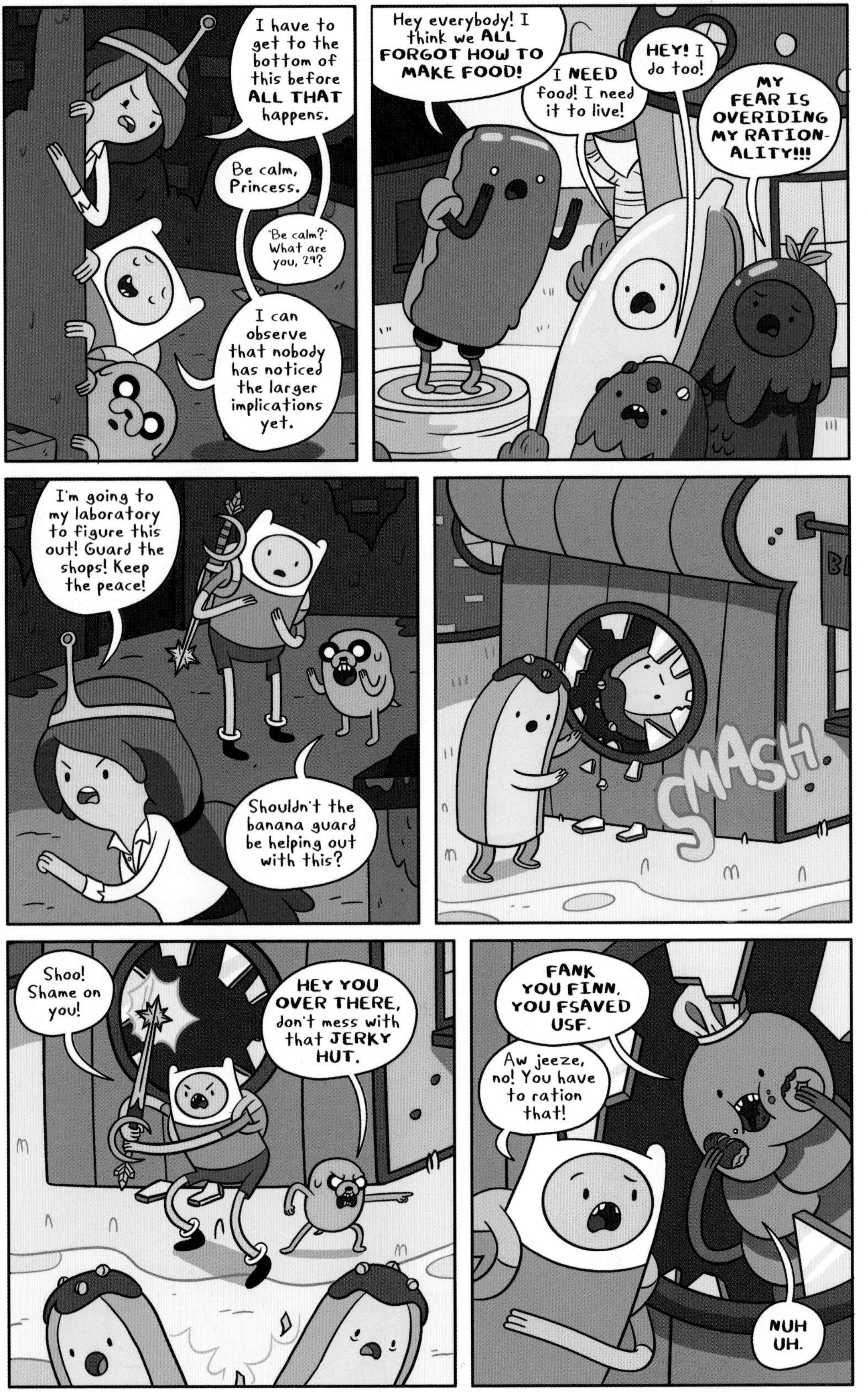
I have to get to the bottom of this before ALL THAT happens.
Be calm, Princess.
"Be calm?" What are you, 29?
I can observe that nobody has noticed the larger implications yet.
Hey everybody! I think we ALL FORGOT HOW TO MAKE FOOD!
I NEED food! I need it to live!
HEY! I do too!
MY FEAR IS OVERIDING MY RATION-ALITY!!!
I'm going to my laboratory to figure this out! Guard the shops! Keep the peace!
Shouldn't the banana guard be helping out with this?
SMASH!
Shoo! Shame on you!
HEY YOU OVER THERE, don't mess with that JERKY HUT.
FANK YOU FINN, YOU FSAVED USF.
Aw jeeze, no! You have to ration that!
NUH UH.

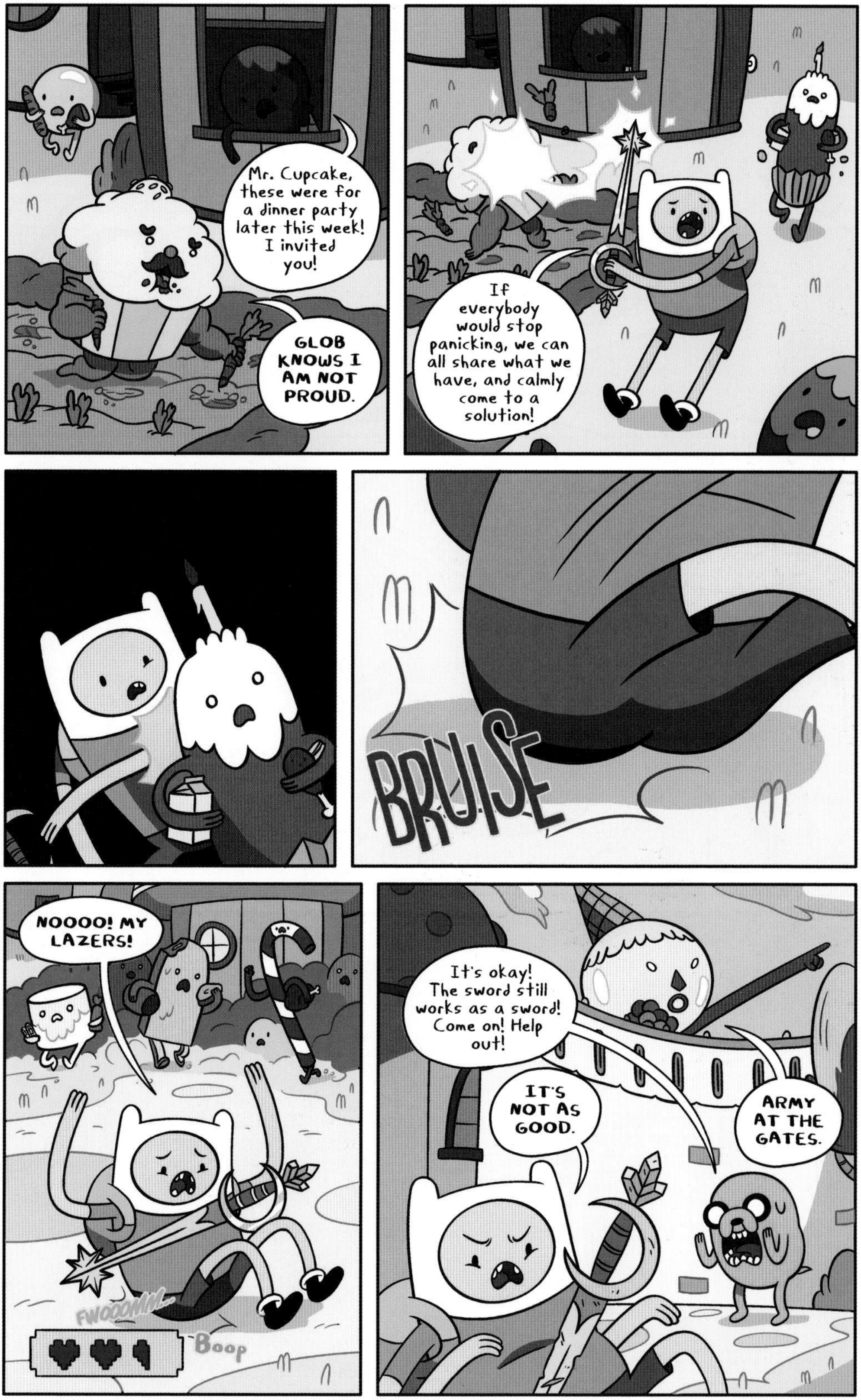
Mr. Cupcake, these were for a dinner party later this week! I invited you!
GLOB KNOWS I AM NOT PROUD.
If everybody would stop panicking, we can all share what we have, and calmly come to a solution!
BRUISE
NOOOO! MY LAZERS!
FWOOOMM...
Boop
It's okay! The sword still works as a sword! Come on! Help out!
IT'S NOT AS GOOD.
ARMY AT THE GATES.

The sword is clearly not as good, Jake.

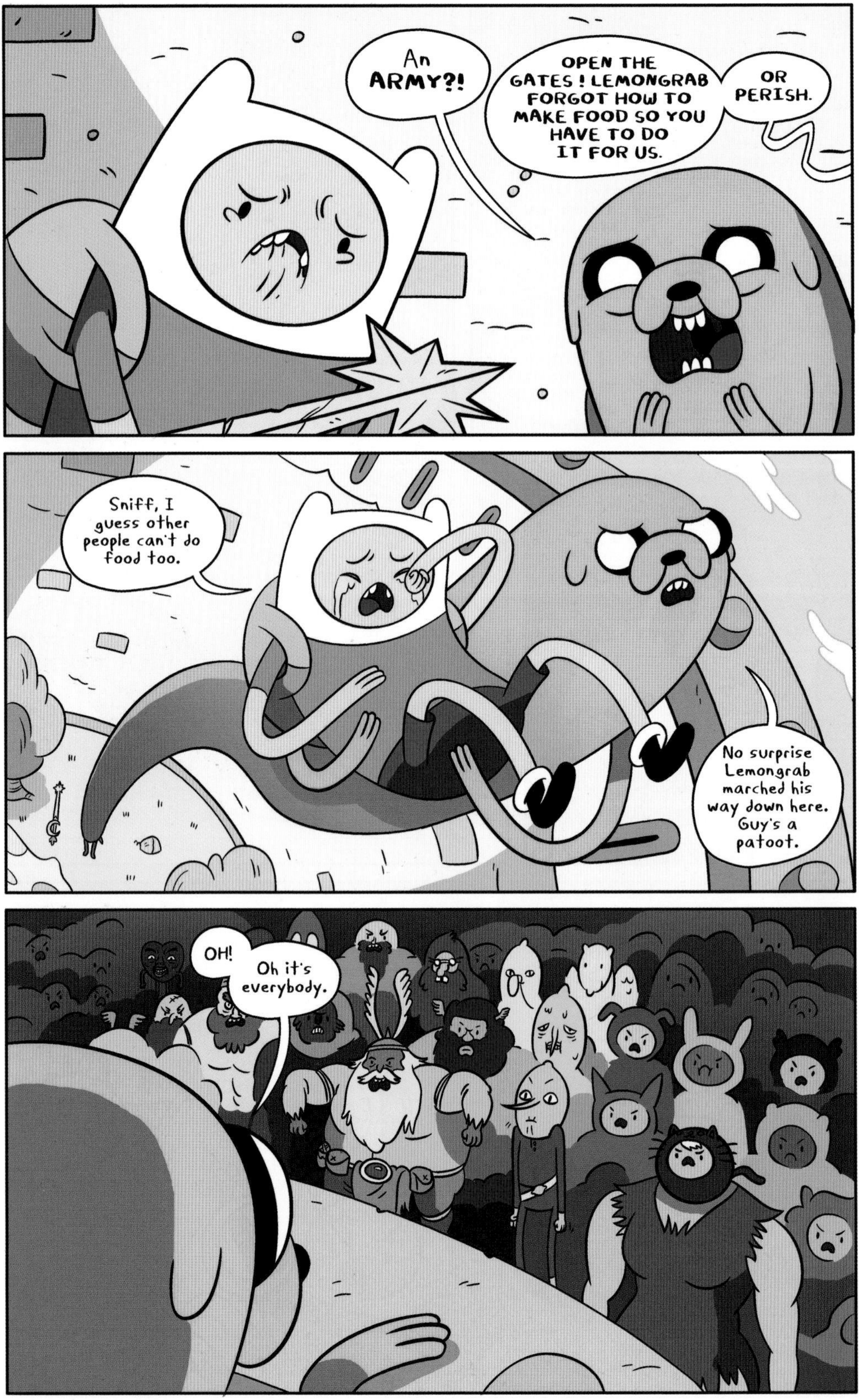
An ARMY?!
OPEN THE GATES! LEMONGRAB FORGOT HOW TO MAKE FOOD SO YOU HAVE TO DO IT FOR US.
OR PERISH.
Sniff, I guess other people can't do food too.
No surprise Lemongrab marched his way down here. Guy's a patoot.
OH!
Oh it's everybody.

Hi everybody.

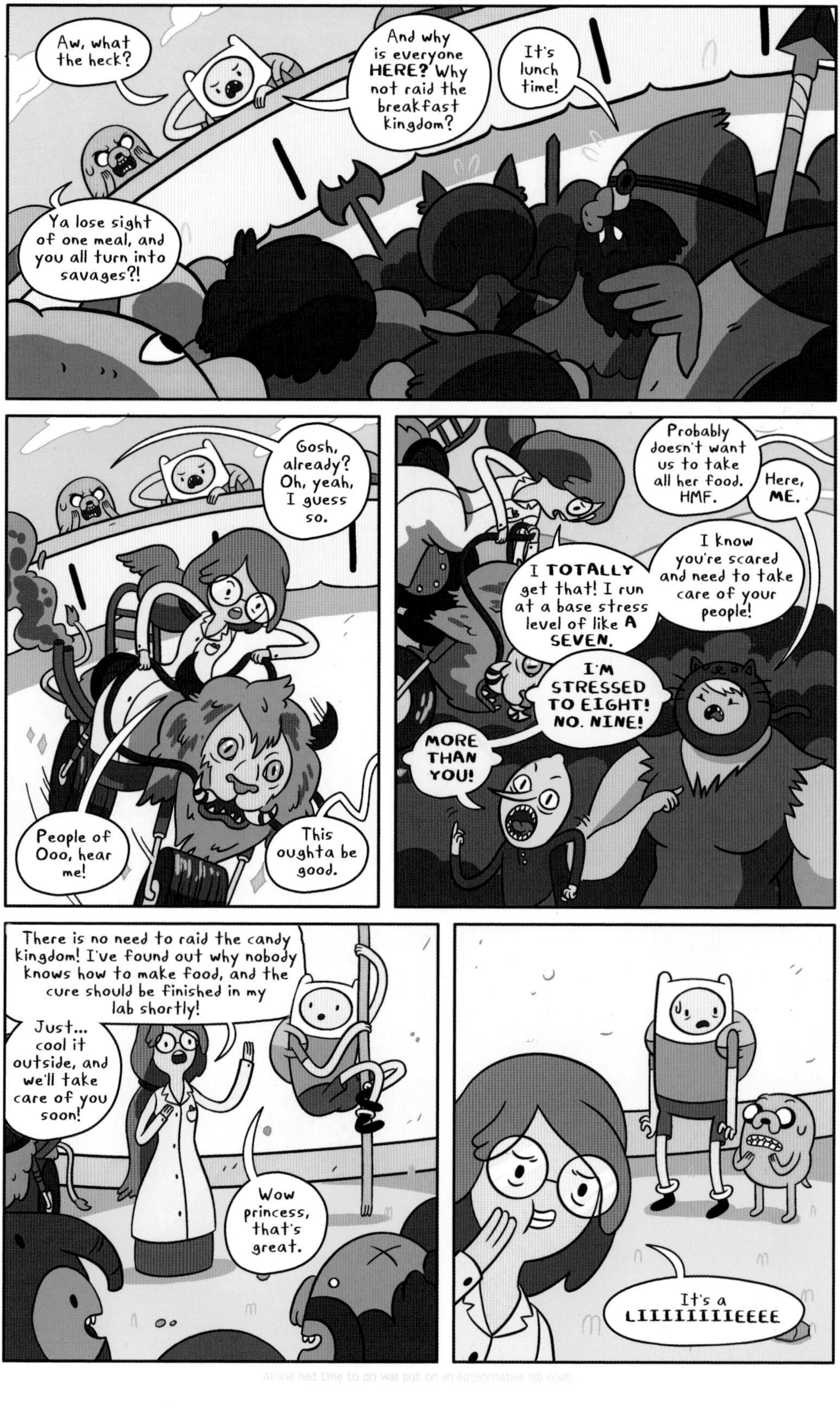
Aw, what the heck?
And why is everyone HERE? Why not raid the breakfast kingdom?
It's lunch time!
Ya lose sight of one meal, and you all turn into savages?!
Gosh, already? Oh, yeah, I guess so.
People of Ooo, hear me!
This oughta be good.
Probably doesn't want us to take all her food. HMF.
Here, ME.
I TOTALLY get that! I run at a base stress level of like A SEVEN.
I know you're scared and need to take care of your people!
I'M STRESSED TO EIGHT! NO. NINE!
MORE THAN YOU!
There is no need to raid the candy kingdom! I've found out why nobody knows how to make food, and the cure should be finished in my lab shortly!
Just... cool it outside, and we'll take care of you soon!
Wow princess, that's great.
It's a LIIIIIIIIEEEE

All she had time to do was put on an authoritative lab coat.

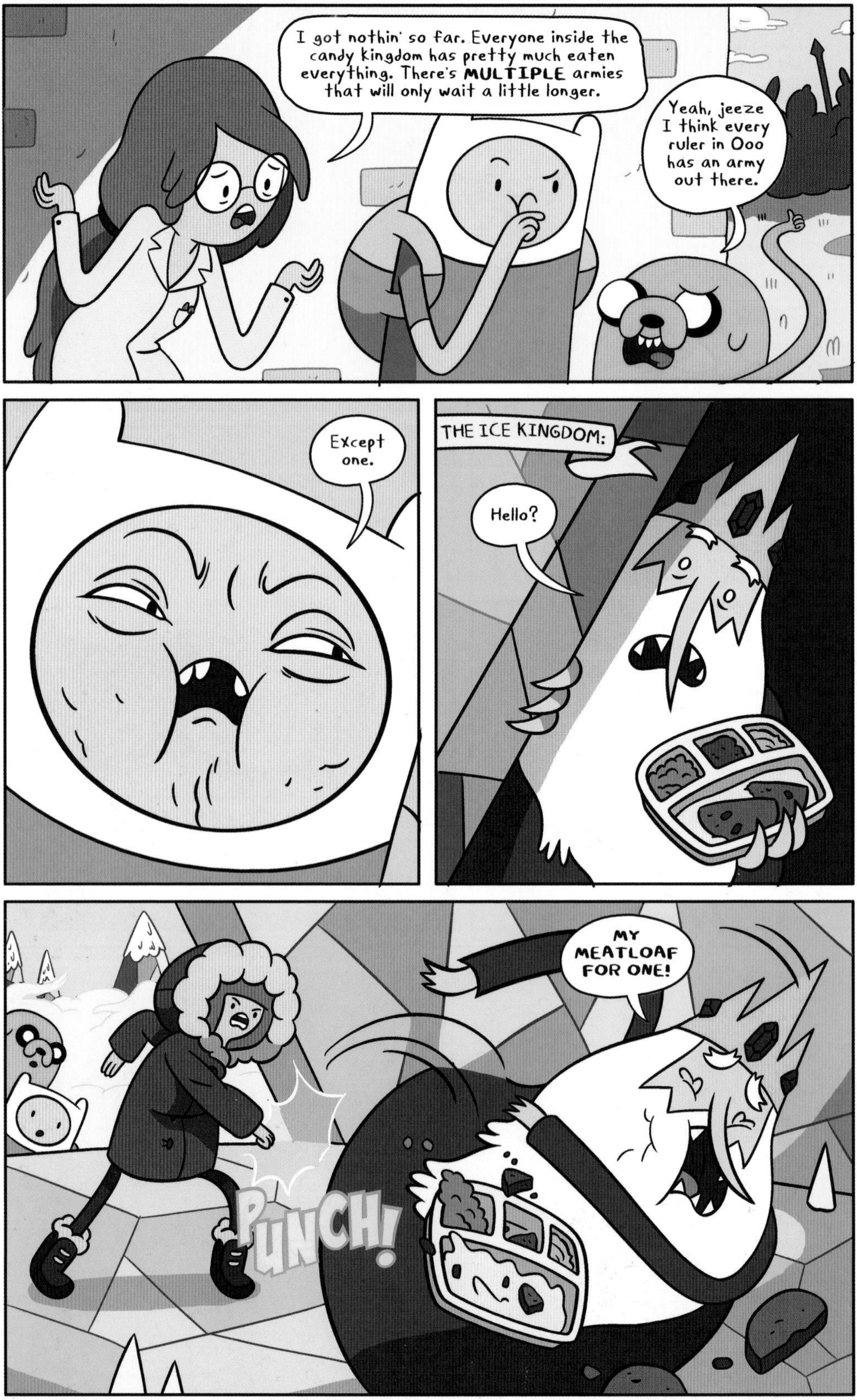

I got nothin' so far. Everyone inside the candy kingdom has pretty much eaten everything. There's MULTIPLE armies that will only wait a little longer.
Yeah, jeeze I think every ruler in Ooo has an army out there.
Except one.
THE ICE KINGDOM:
Hello?
MY MEATLOAF FOR ONE!
PUNCH!

It totally says on the box it's for two, you GLUTTON.

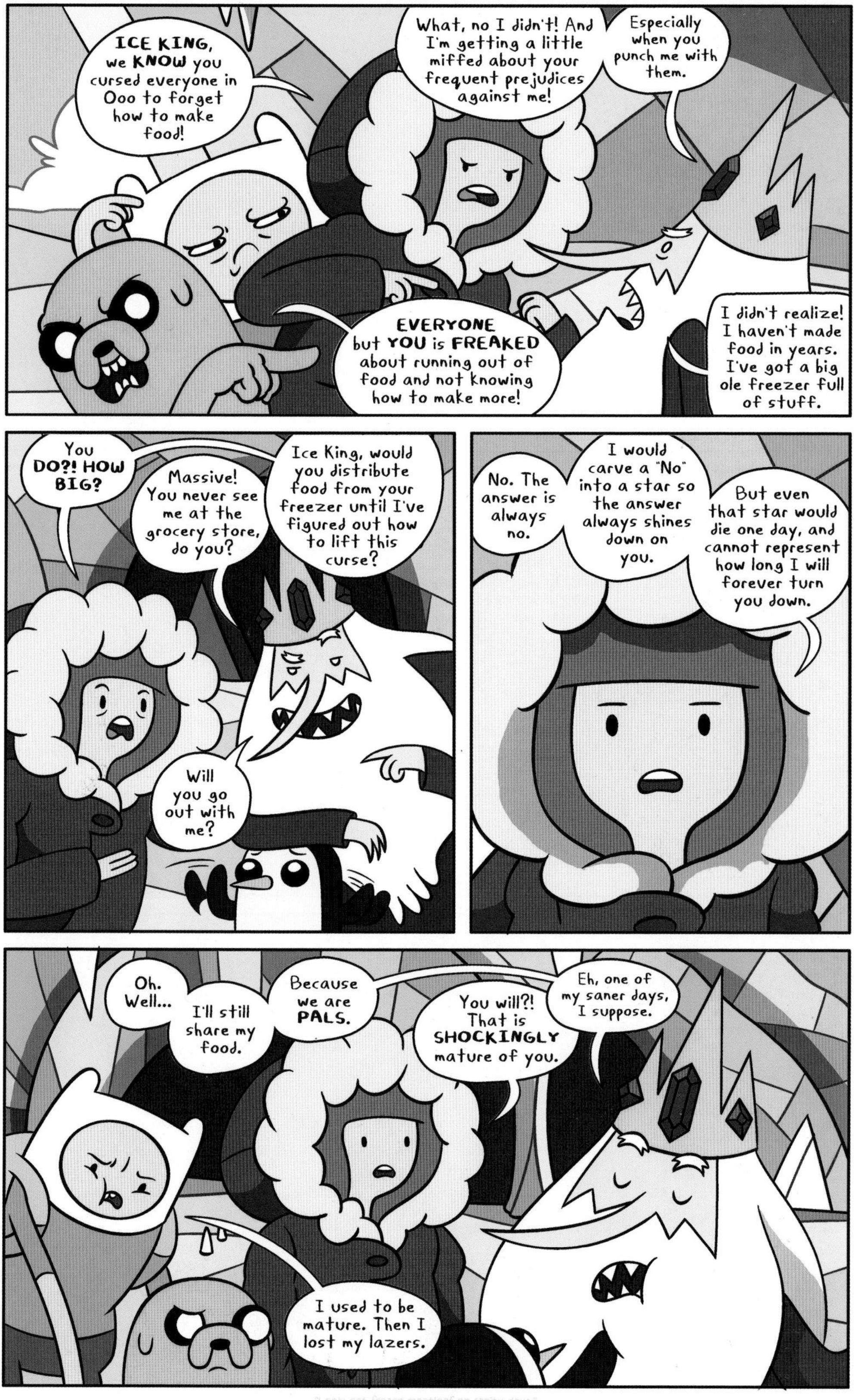
ICE KING, we KNOW you cursed everyone in Ooo to forget how to make food!
What, no I didn't! And I'm getting a little miffed about your frequent prejudices against me!
Especially when you punch me with them.
EVERYONE but YOU is FREAKED about running out of food and not knowing how to make more!
I didn't realize! I haven't made food in years. I've got a big ole freezer full of stuff.
You DO?! HOW BIG?
Massive! You never see me at the grocery store, do you?
Ice King, would you distribute food from your freezer until I've figured out how to lift this curse?
Will you go out with me?
No. The answer is always no.
I would carve a "No" into a star so the answer always shines down on you.
But even that star would die one day, and cannot represent how long I will forever turn you down.
Oh. Well...
I'll still share my food.
Because we are PALS.
You will?! That is SHOCKINGLY mature of you.
Eh, one of my saner days, I suppose.
I used to be mature. Then I lost my lazers.

"I only eat frozen meatloaf on sanity days."

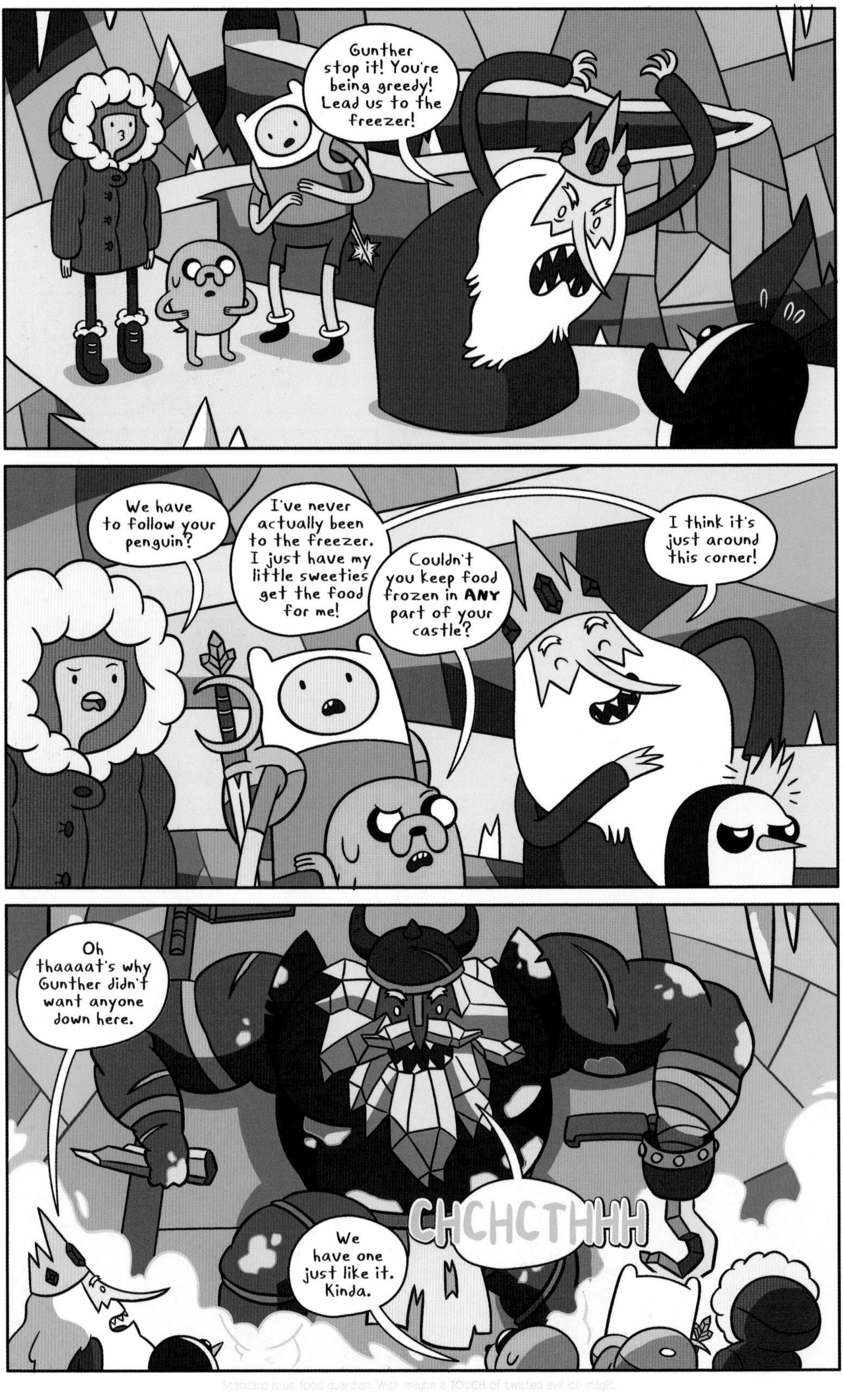
Gunther stop it! You're being greedy! Lead us to the freezer!
We have to follow your penguin?
I've never actually been to the freezer. I just have my little sweeties get the food for me!
Couldn't you keep food frozen in **ANY** part of your castle?
I think it's just around this corner!
Oh thaaaat's why Gunther didn't want anyone down here.
CHCHCTHHH
We have one just like it. Kinda.

Standard issue food guardian. With maybe a TOUCH of twisted evil ice magic.

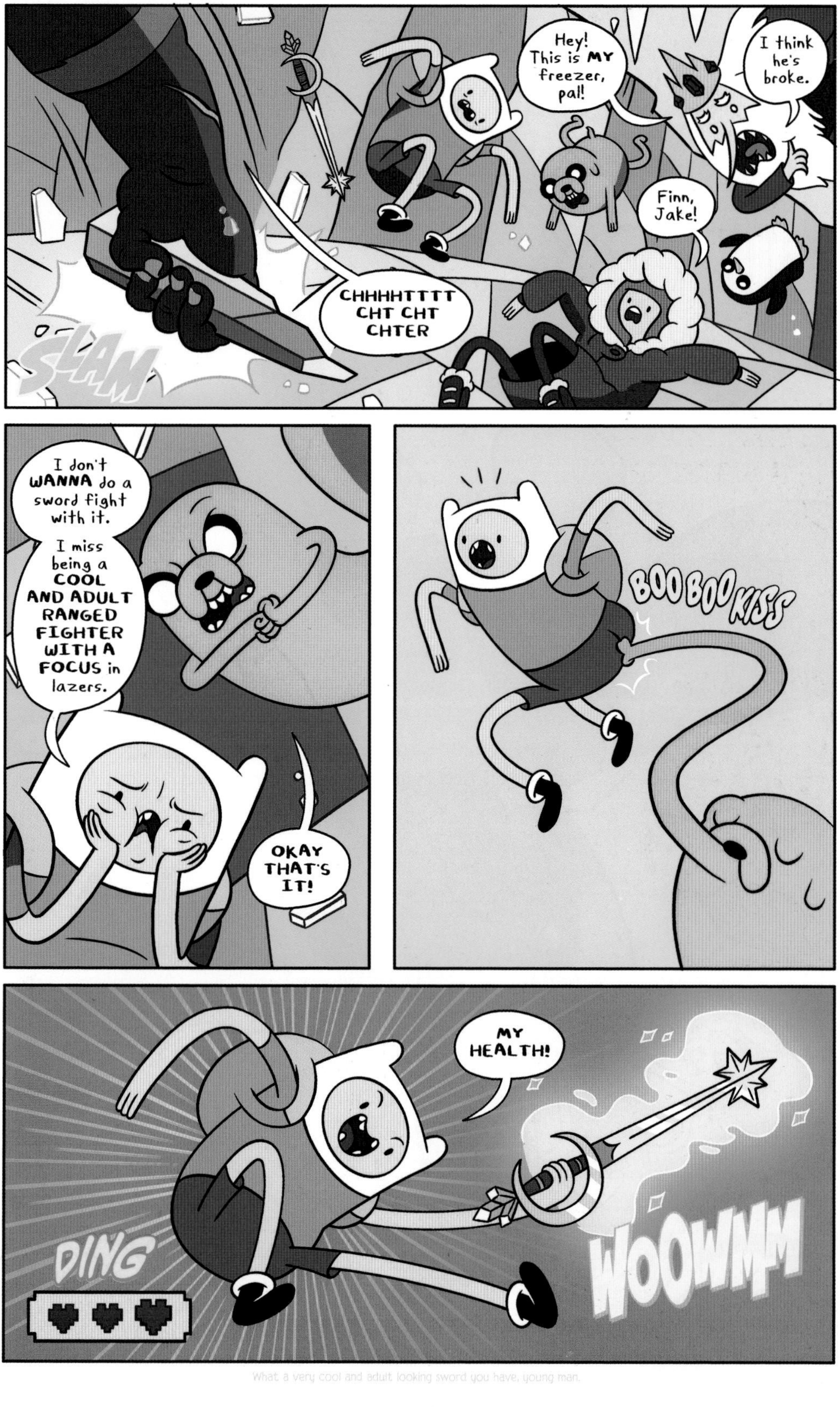
SLAM
CHHHHTTTT CHT CHT CHTER
Hey! This is MY freezer, pal!
I think he's broke.
Finn, Jake!
I don't WANNA do a sword fight with it.
I miss being a COOL AND ADULT RANGED FIGHTER WITH A FOCUS in lazers.
OKAY THAT'S IT!
BOO BOO KISS
MY HEALTH!
WOOWMM
DING

What a very cool and adult looking sword you have, young man.

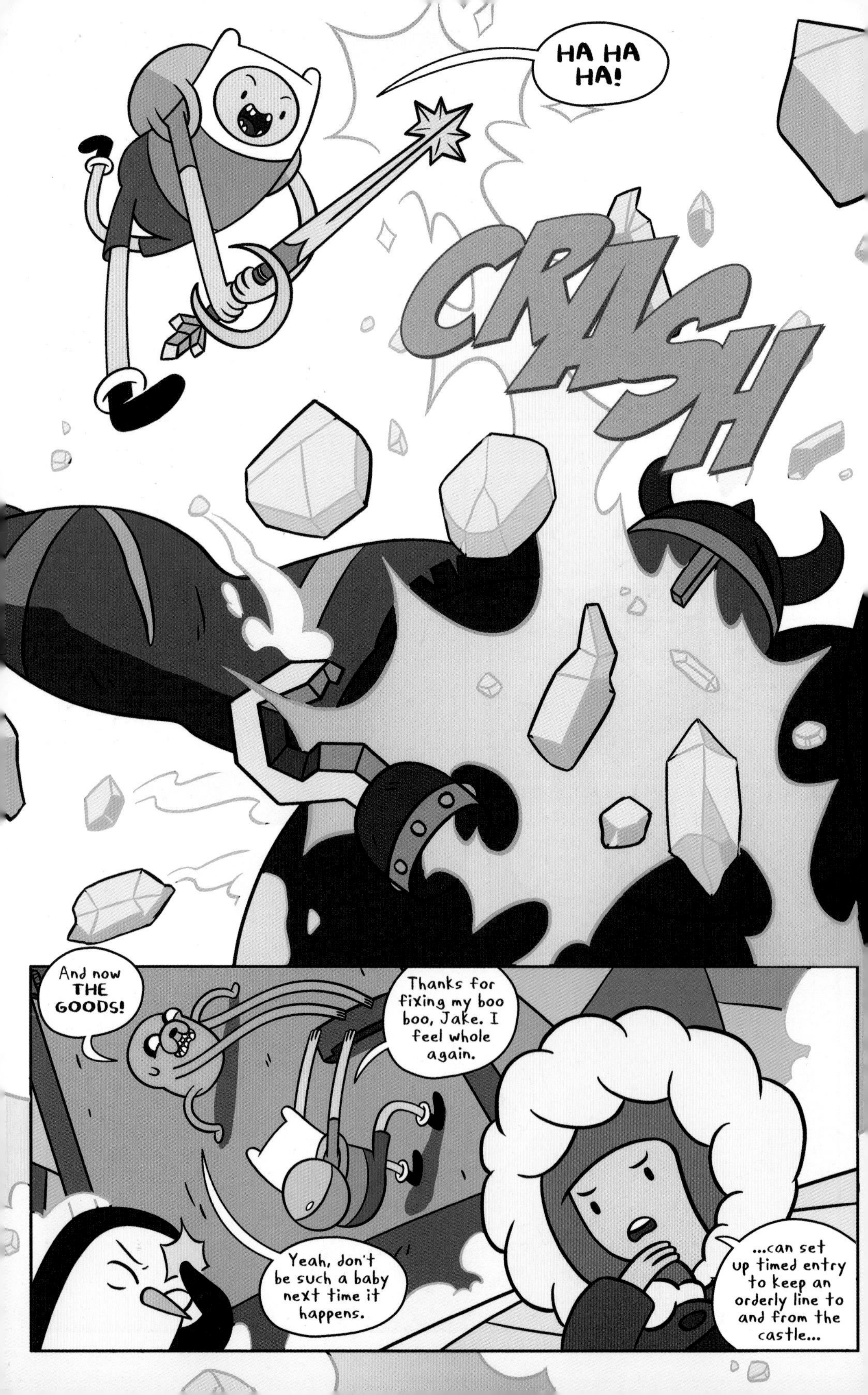
HA HA HA!
CRASH
And now THE GOODS!
Thanks for fixing my boo boo, Jake. I feel whole again.
Yeah, don't be such a baby next time it happens.
...can set up timed entry to keep an orderly line to and from the castle...

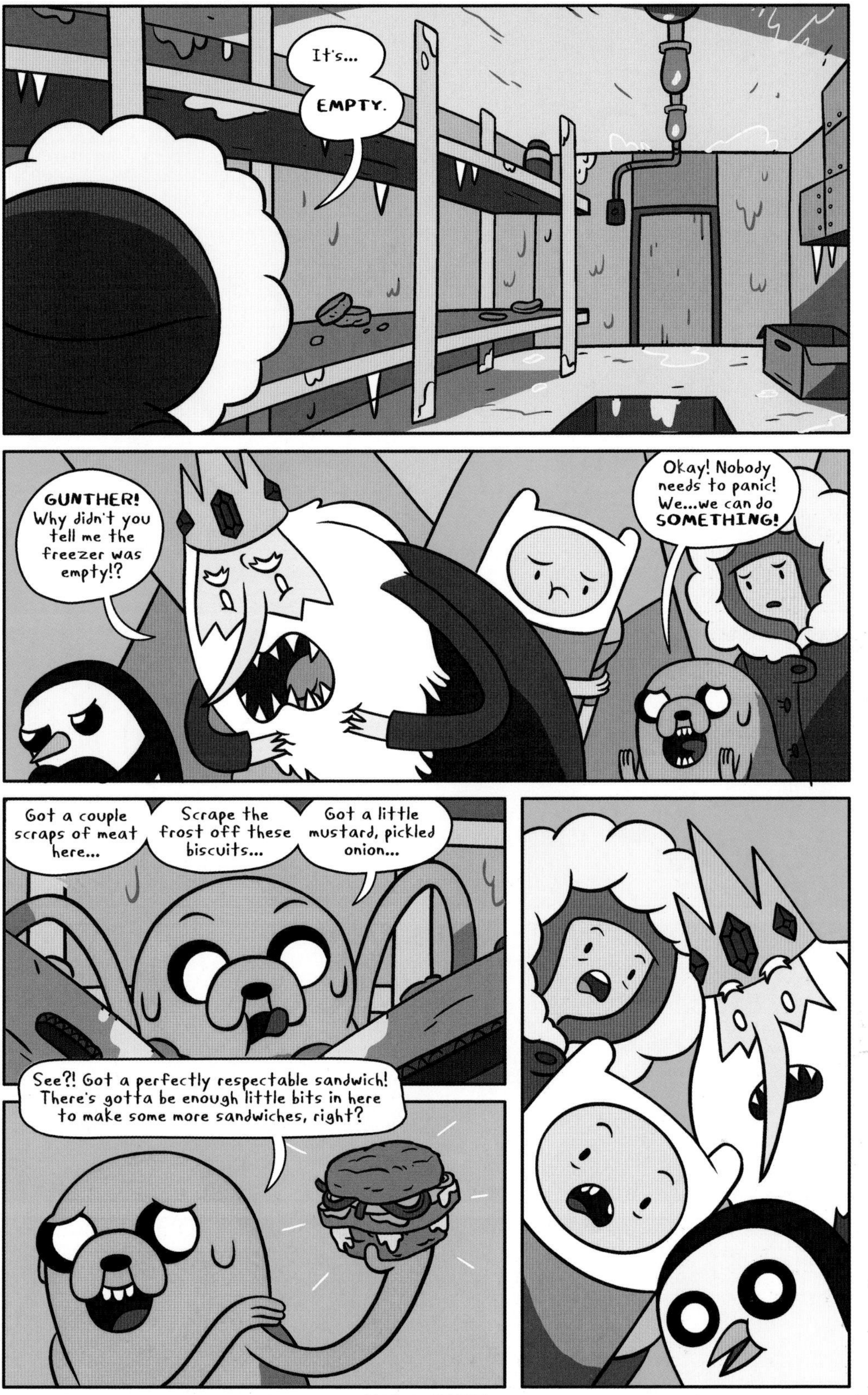

It's...
EMPTY.
GUNTHER! Why didn't you tell me the freezer was empty!?
Okay! Nobody needs to panic! We...we can do SOMETHING!
Got a couple scraps of meat here...
Scrape the frost off these biscuits...
Got a little mustard, pickled onion...
See?! Got a perfectly respectable sandwich! There's gotta be enough little bits in here to make some more sandwiches, right?

Who freezes MUSTARD?

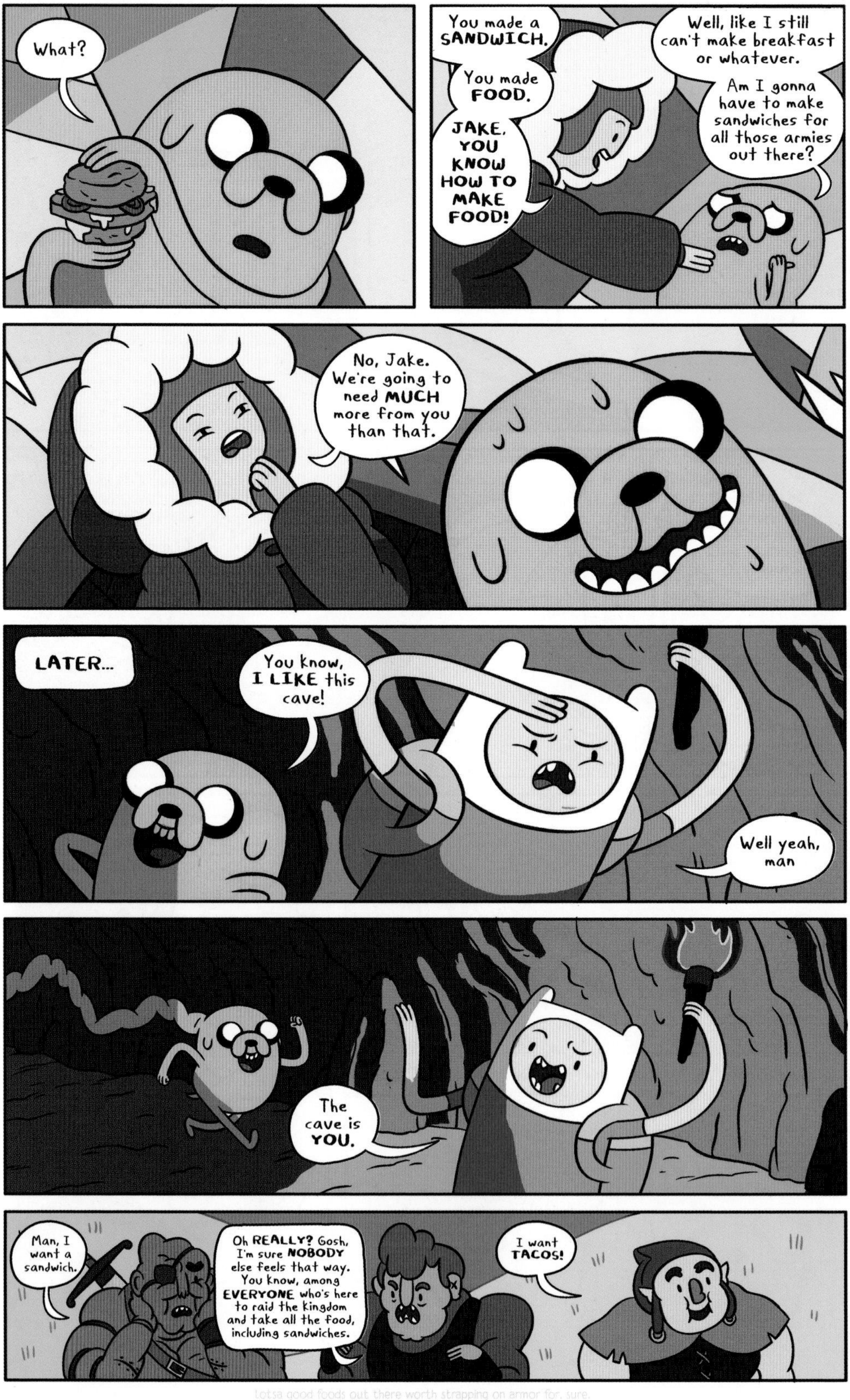
What?
You made a SANDWICH.
You made FOOD.
JAKE, YOU KNOW HOW TO MAKE FOOD!
Well, like I still can't make breakfast or whatever.
Am I gonna have to make sandwiches for all those armies out there?
No, Jake. We're going to need MUCH more from you than that.
LATER...
You know, I LIKE this cave!
Well yeah, man
The cave is YOU.
Man, I want a sandwich.
Oh REALLY? Gosh, I'm sure NOBODY else feels that way. You know, among EVERYONE who's here to raid the kingdom and take all the food, including sandwiches.
I want TACOS!

Lotsa good foods out there worth strapping on armor for, sure.

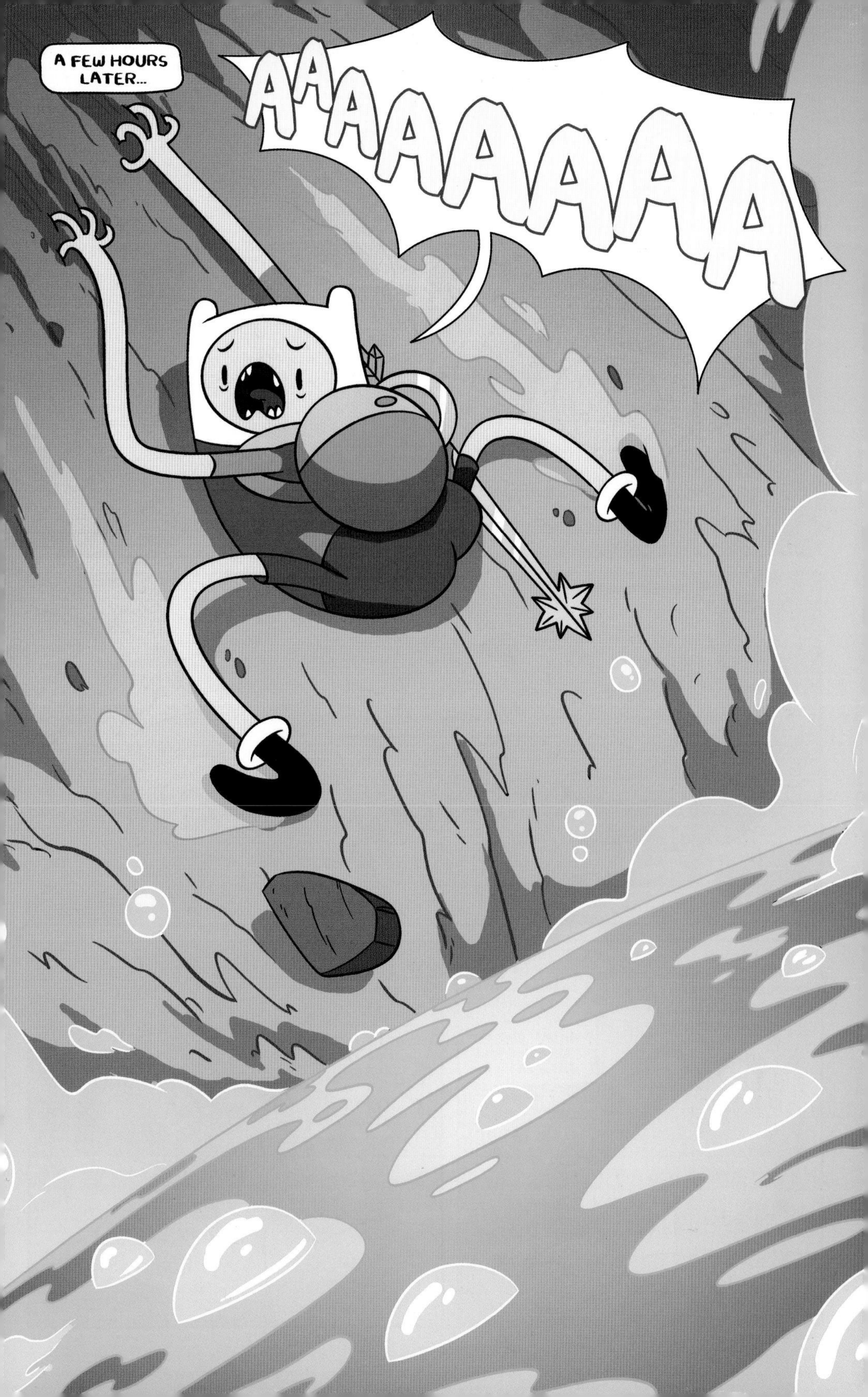
A FEW HOURS LATER...
AAAAAAAAAA

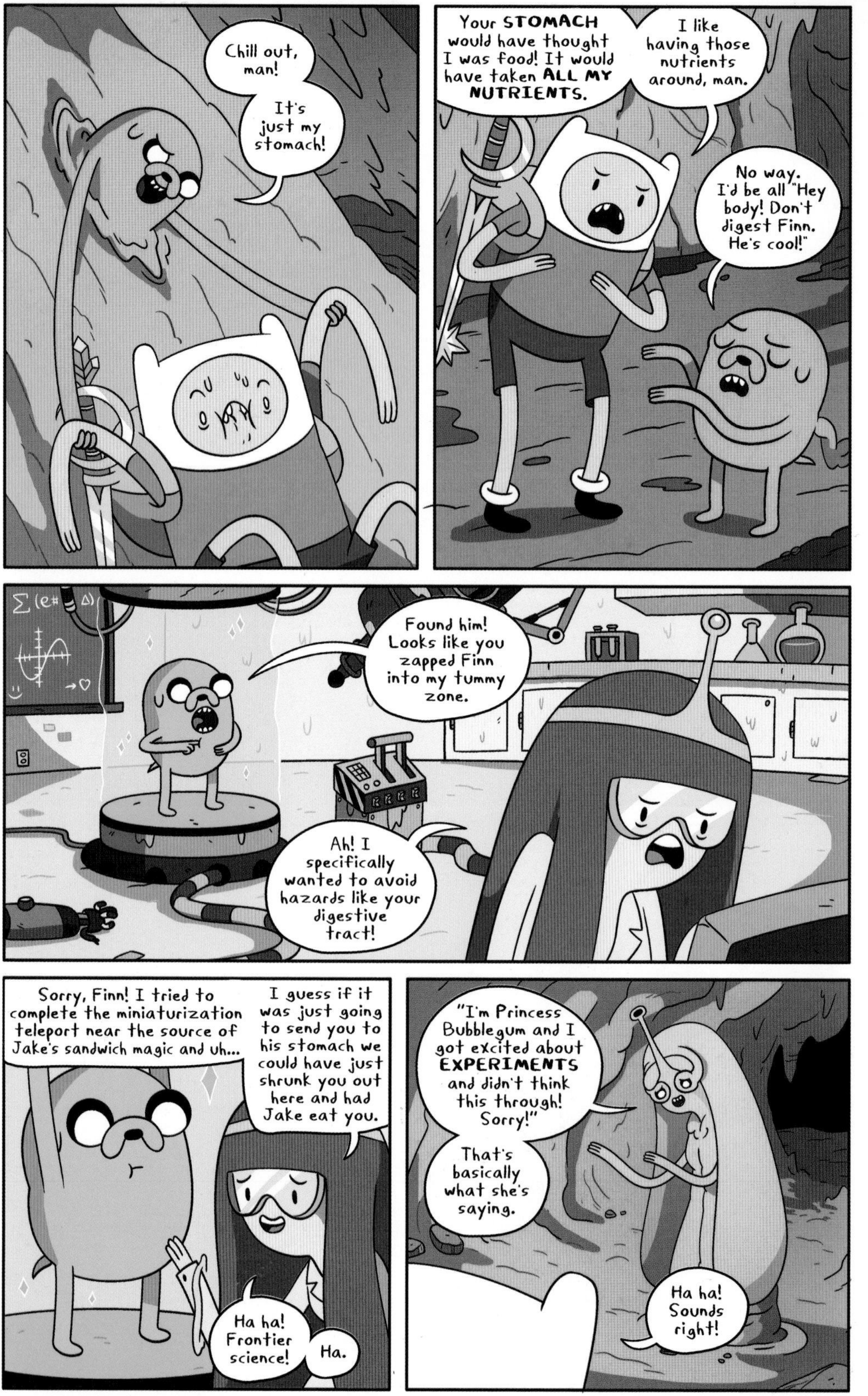
Chill out, man!
It's just my stomach!
Your STOMACH would have thought I was food! It would have taken ALL MY NUTRIENTS.
I like having those nutrients around, man.
No way. I'd be all "Hey body! Don't digest Finn. He's cool!"
Found him! Looks like you zapped Finn into my tummy zone.
Ah! I specifically wanted to avoid hazards like your digestive tract!
Sorry, Finn! I tried to complete the miniaturization teleport near the source of Jake's sandwich magic and uh...
I guess if it was just going to send you to his stomach we could have just shrunk you out here and had Jake eat you.
Ha ha! Frontier science!
Ha.
"I'm Princess Bubblegum and I got excited about EXPERIMENTS and didn't think this through! Sorry!"
That's basically what she's saying.
Ha ha! Sounds right!

Jake: Good on faces. Bad on words.

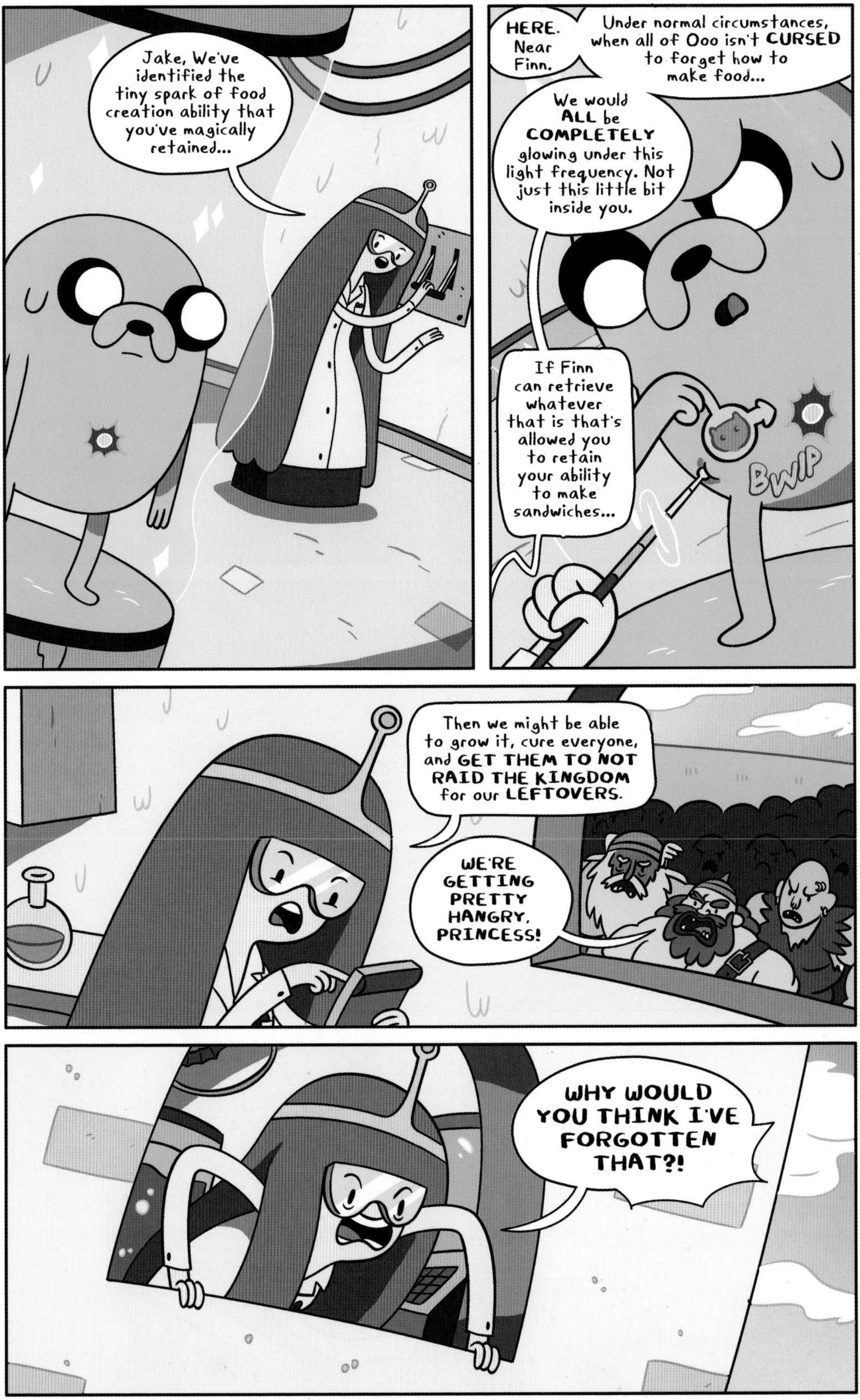

Jake, We've identified the tiny spark of food creation ability that you've magically retained...
HERE. Near Finn.
Under normal circumstances, when all of Ooo isn't CURSED to forget how to make food...
We would ALL be COMPLETELY glowing under this light frequency. Not just this little bit inside you.
If Finn can retrieve whatever that is that's allowed you to retain your ability to make sandwiches...
BWIP
Then we might be able to grow it, cure everyone, and GET THEM TO NOT RAID THE KINGDOM for our LEFTOVERS.
WE'RE GETTING PRETTY HANGRY, PRINCESS!
WHY WOULD YOU THINK I'VE FORGOTTEN THAT?!

"Hangry" is a mix of "Angry" and "Hungry" but deep down inside, you knew that.

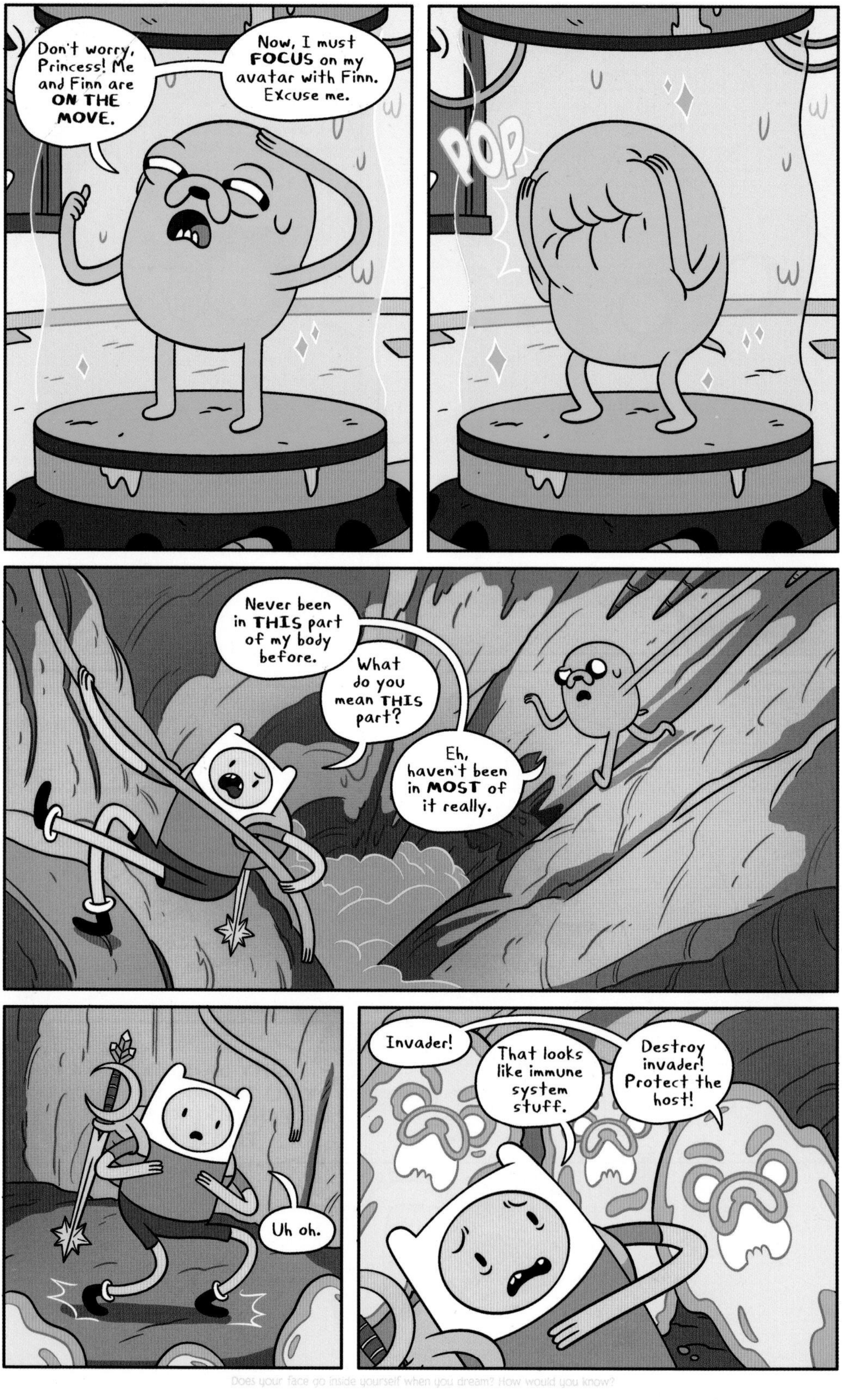
Don't worry, Princess! Me and Finn are **ON THE MOVE.**
Now, I must **FOCUS** on my avatar with Finn. Excuse me.
POP
Never been in **THIS** part of my body before.
What do you mean **THIS** part?
Eh, haven't been in **MOST** of it really.
Uh oh.
Invader!
That looks like immune system stuff.
Destroy invader! Protect the host!

Does your face go inside yourself when you dream? How would you know?

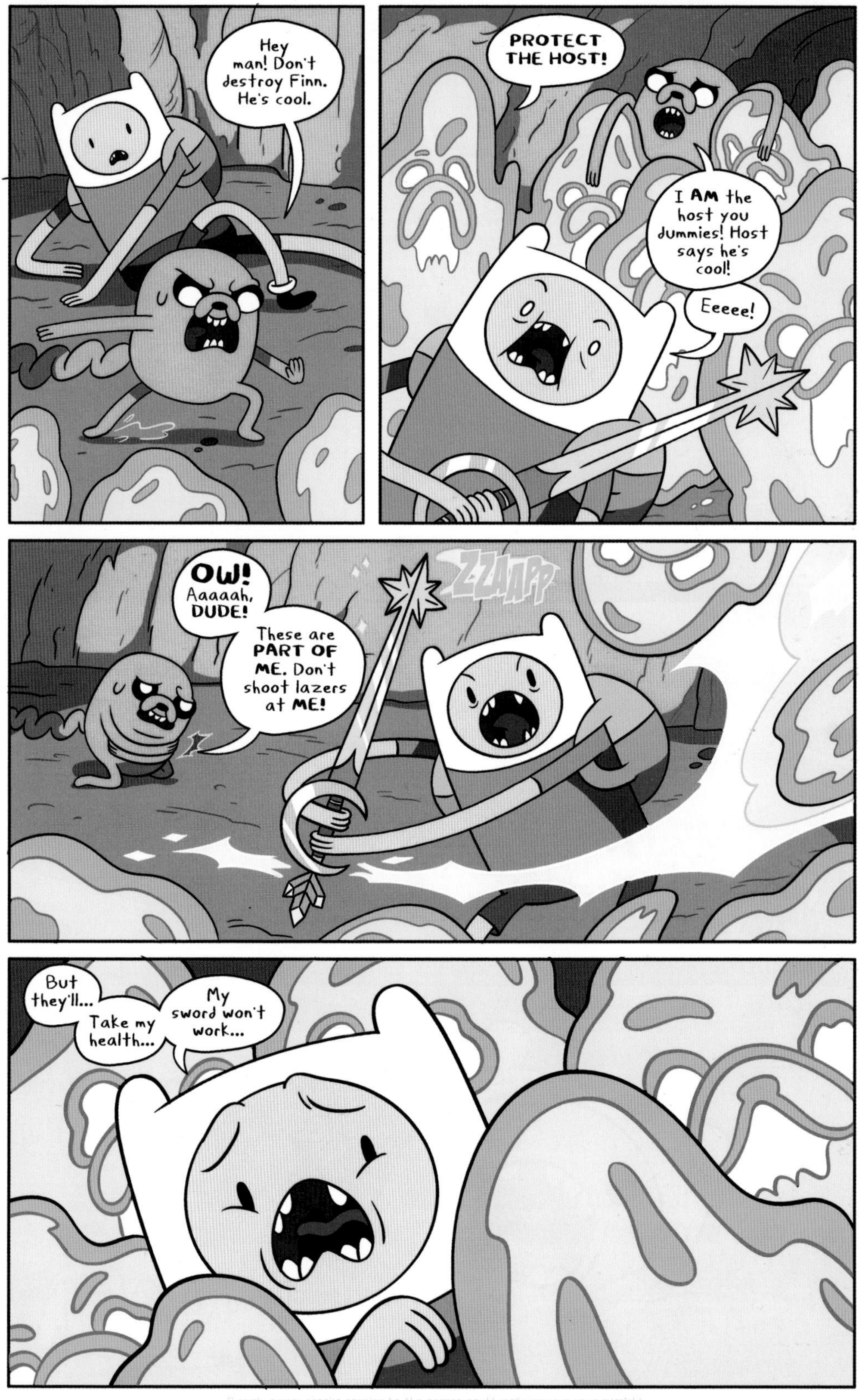
Hey man! Don't destroy Finn. He's cool.
PROTECT THE HOST!
I AM the host you dummies! Host says he's cool!
Eeeee!
ZZAAPP
OW! Aaaaah, DUDE!
These are PART OF ME. Don't shoot lazers at ME!
But they'll...
Take my health...
My sword won't work...

Though, a very precise zapping to the cornea could really improve your eyesight.

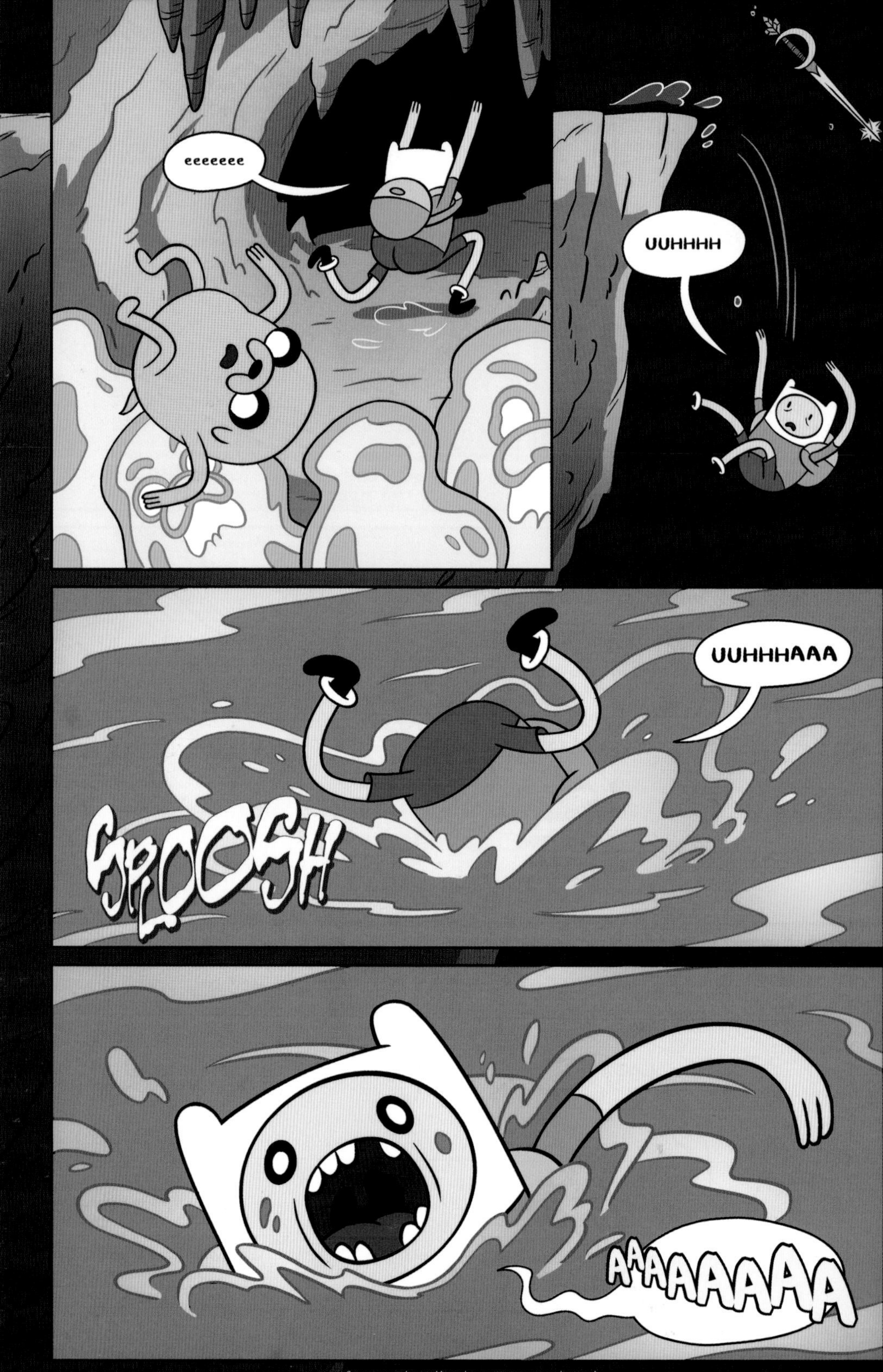
eeeeeee
UUHHHH
UUHHHAAA
SPLOOSH
AAAAAAAA

So many noise options to announce your horror!

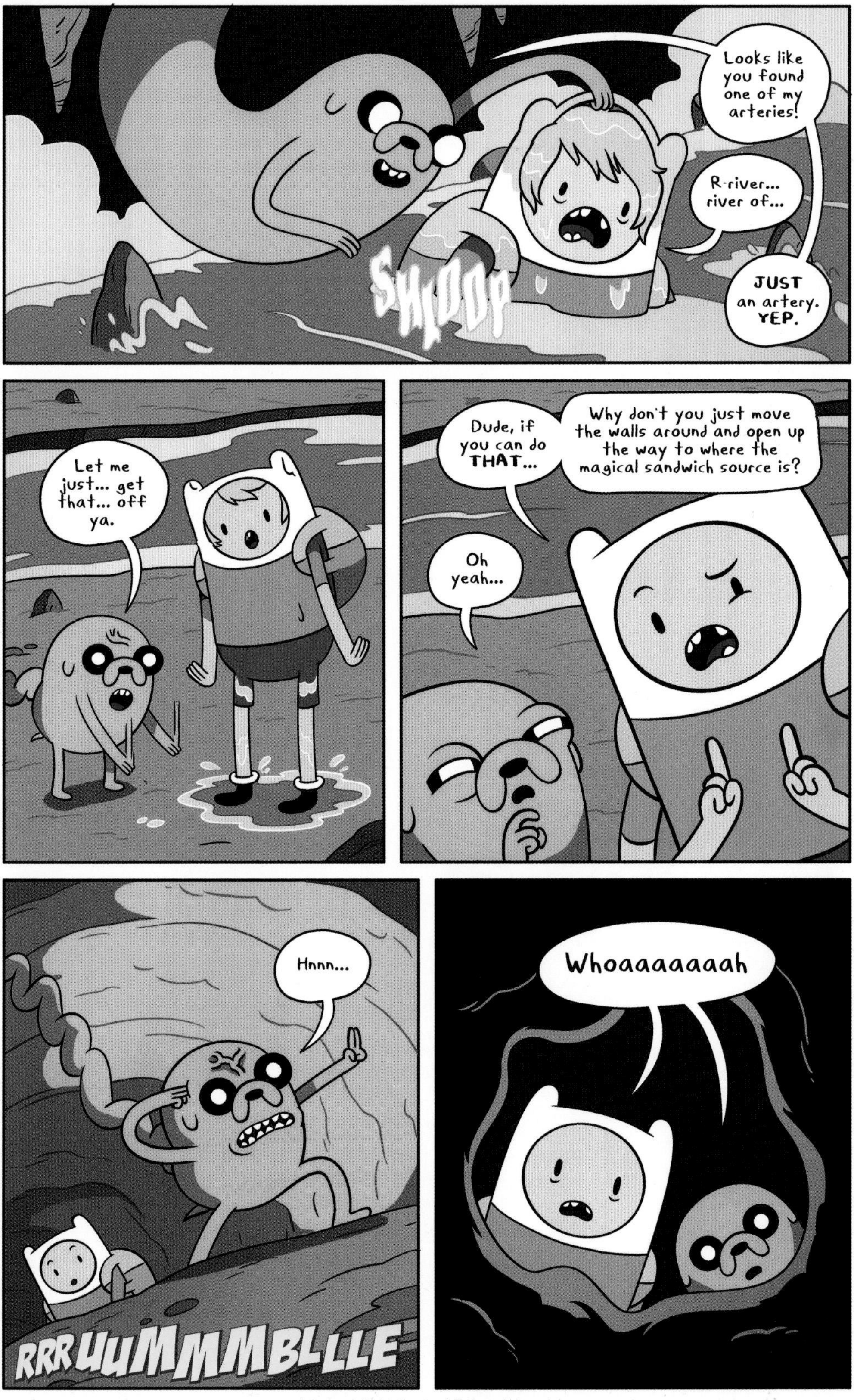
Looks like you found one of my arteries!
R-river... river of...
SHLOOP
JUST an artery. YEP.
Let me just... get that... off ya.
Dude, if you can do THAT...
Why don't you just move the walls around and open up the way to where the magical sandwich source is?
Oh yeah...
Hnnn...
RRRUUMMMMBLLLE
Whoaaaaaaah

Is it a part that isn't yellow? That would be weird.

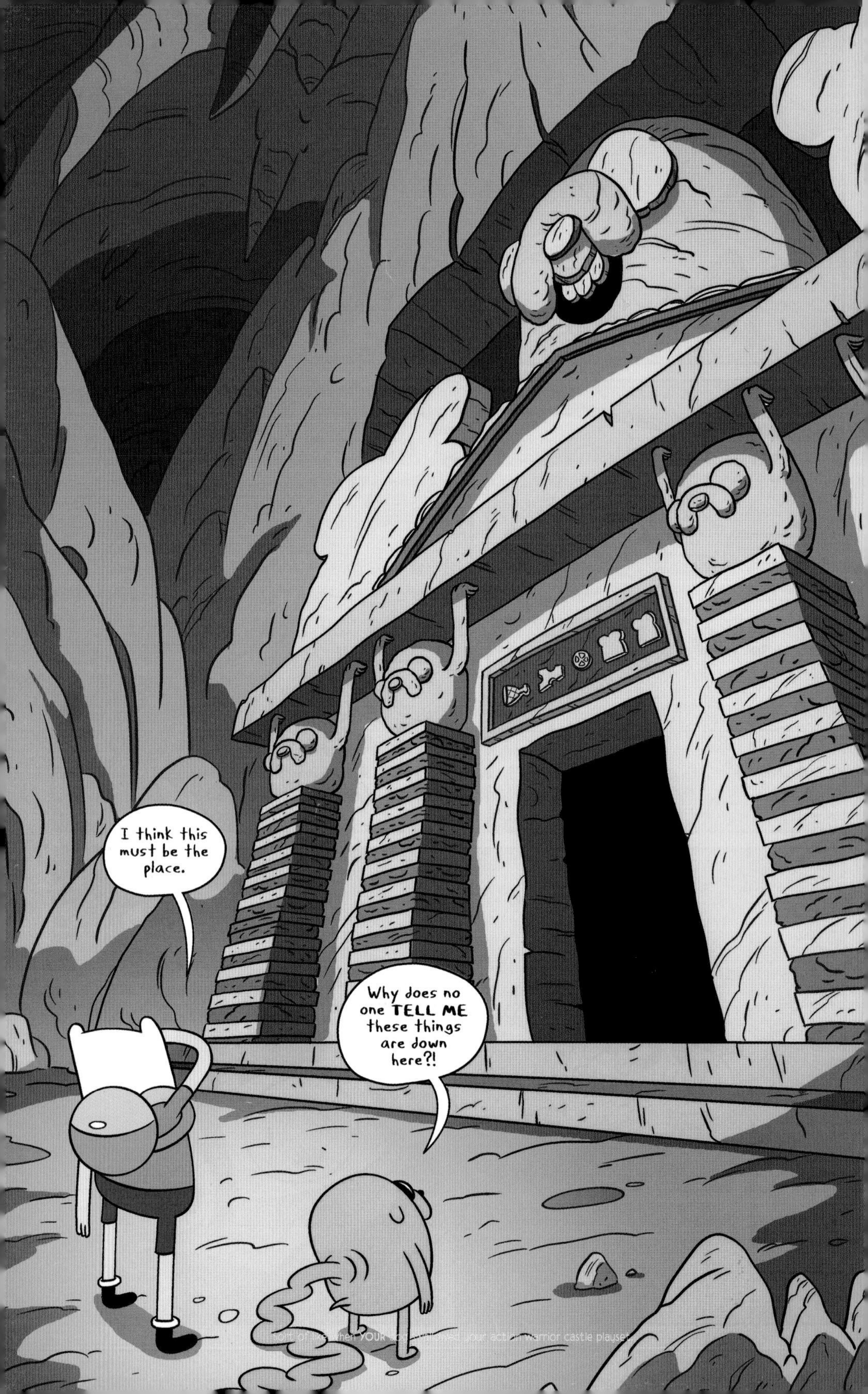
I think this must be the place.
Why does no one **TELL ME** these things are down here?!
Sort of like when YOUR dog swallowed your action warrior castle playset.

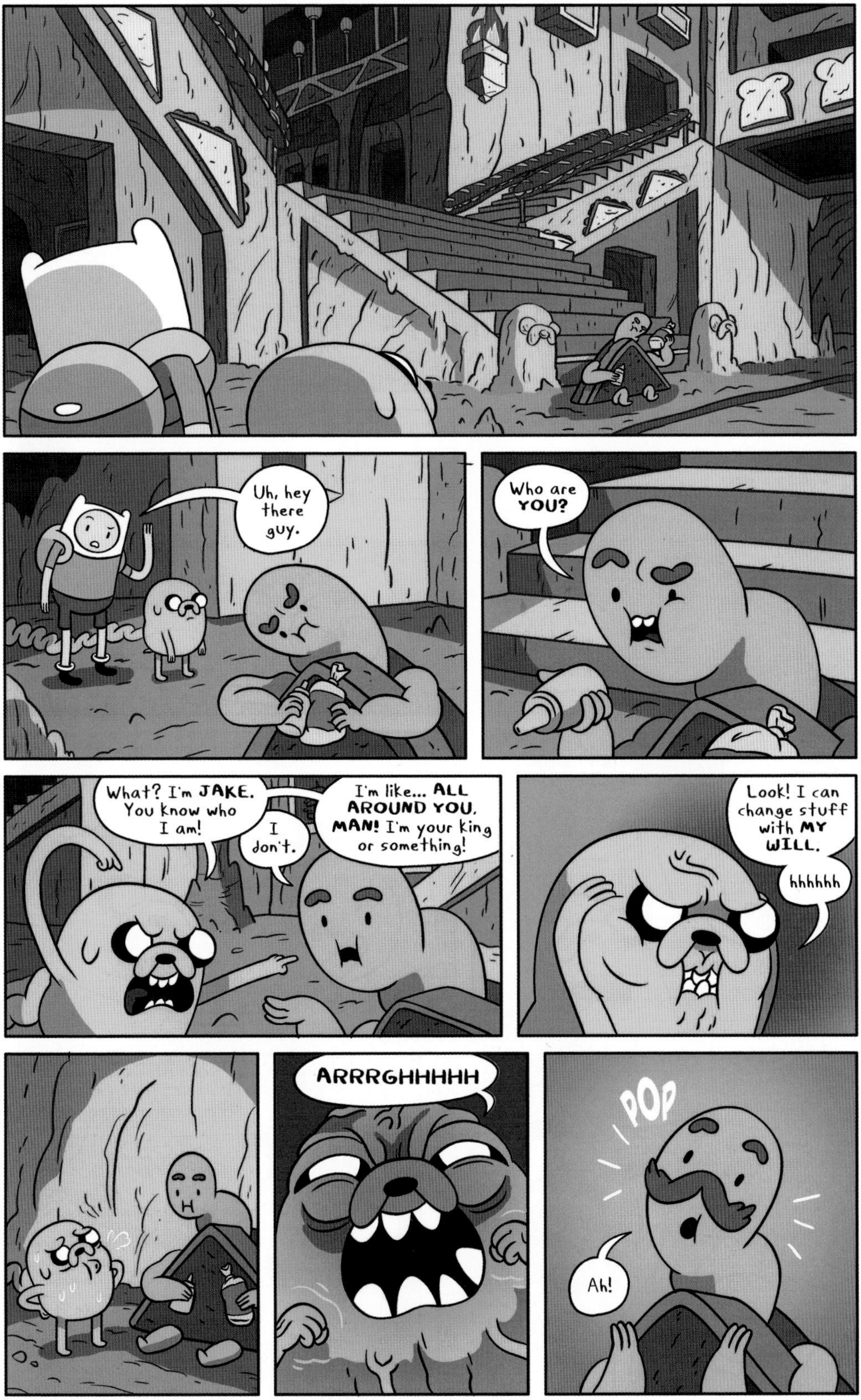

Uh, hey there guy.
Who are YOU?
What? I'm JAKE. You know who I am!
I don't.
I'm like... ALL AROUND YOU, MAN! I'm your king or something!
Look! I can change stuff with MY WILL.
hhhhhh
ARRRGHHHHH
POP
Ah!

Secretly though, Jake was trying to get like... a long braided beard on the guy. Don't tell.

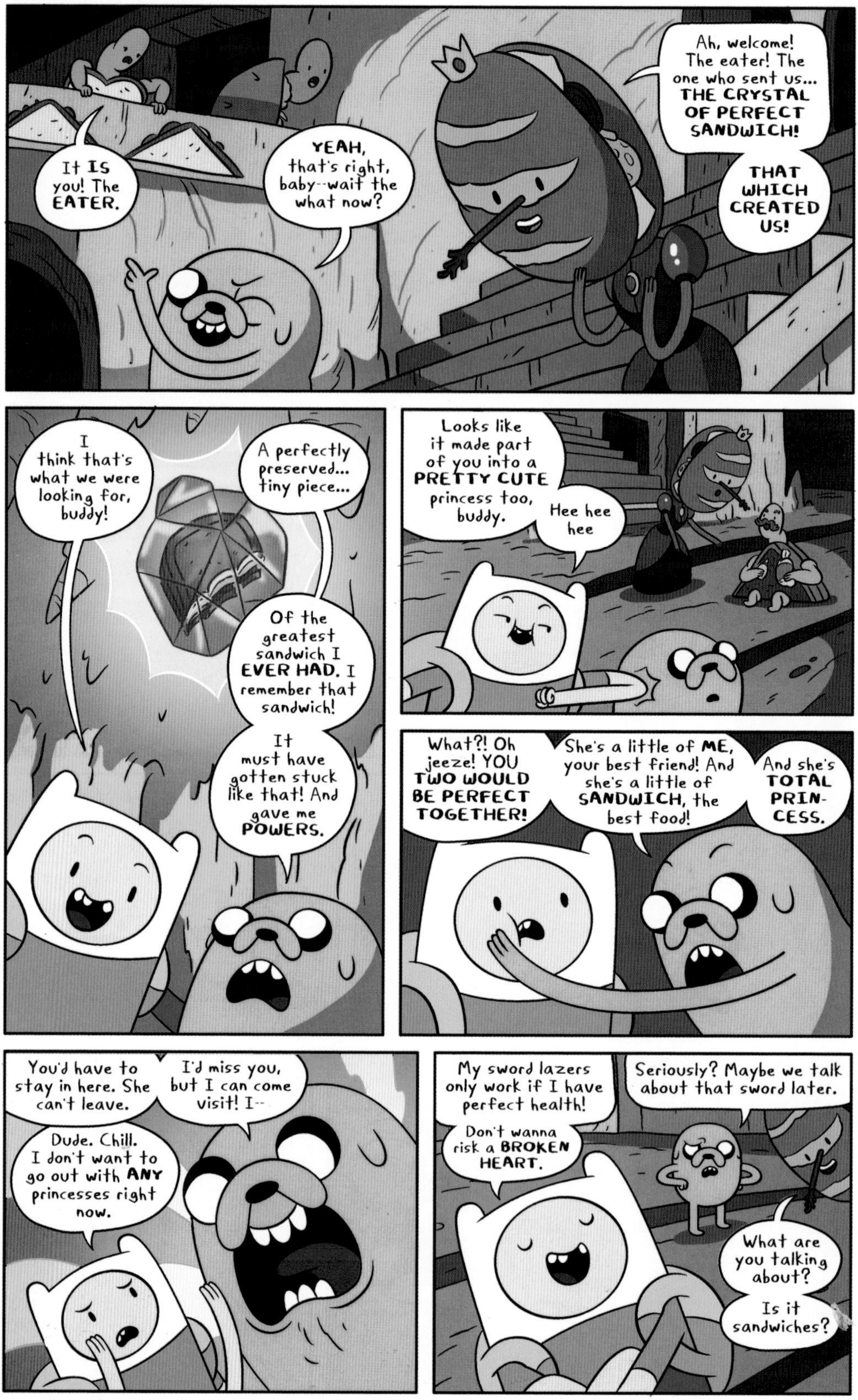

Ah, welcome! The eater! The one who sent us... THE CRYSTAL OF PERFECT SANDWICH!
THAT WHICH CREATED US!
It IS you! The EATER.
YEAH, that's right, baby--wait the what now?
I think that's what we were looking for, buddy!
A perfectly preserved... tiny piece...
Of the greatest sandwich I EVER HAD. I remember that sandwich!
It must have gotten stuck like that! And gave me POWERS.
Looks like it made part of you into a PRETTY CUTE princess too, buddy.
Hee hee hee
What?! Oh jeeze! YOU TWO WOULD BE PERFECT TOGETHER!
She's a little of ME, your best friend! And she's a little of SANDWICH, the best food!
And she's TOTAL PRIN-CESS.
You'd have to stay in here. She can't leave.
I'd miss you, but I can come visit! I--
Dude. Chill. I don't want to go out with ANY princesses right now.
My sword lazers only work if I have perfect health!
Don't wanna risk a BROKEN HEART.
Seriously? Maybe we talk about that sword later.
What are you talking about?
Is it sandwiches?

Well, whatever you were talking about, it was with your mouths, which is where sandwiches go, so I'll just assume it was about sandwiches.

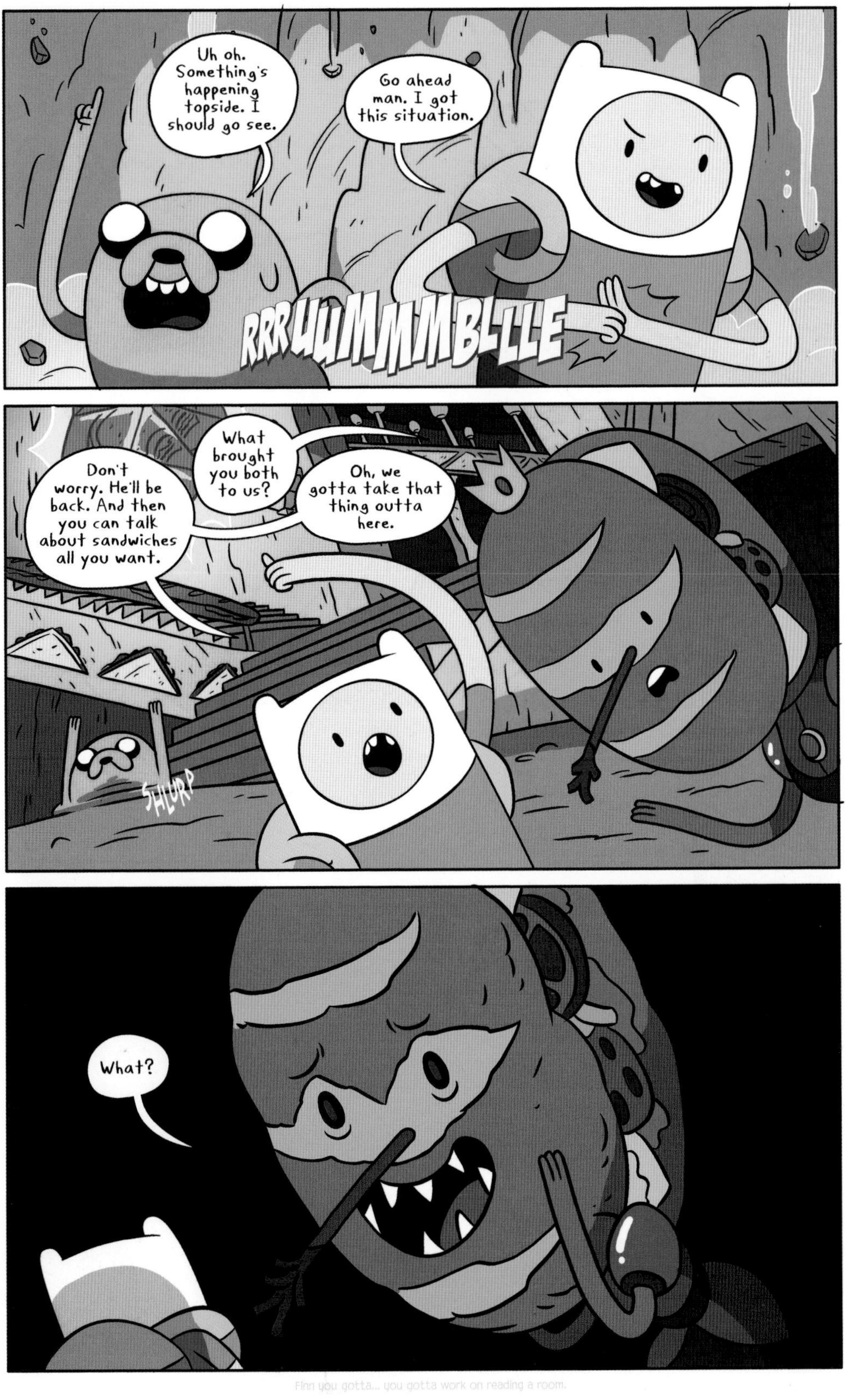
Uh oh. Something's happening topside. I should go see.
Go ahead man. I got this situation.
RRRUUMMMMBLLLE
Don't worry. He'll be back. And then you can talk about sandwiches all you want.
What brought you both to us?
Oh, we gotta take that thing outta here.
SHLURP
What?

Finn you gotta... you gotta work on reading a room.

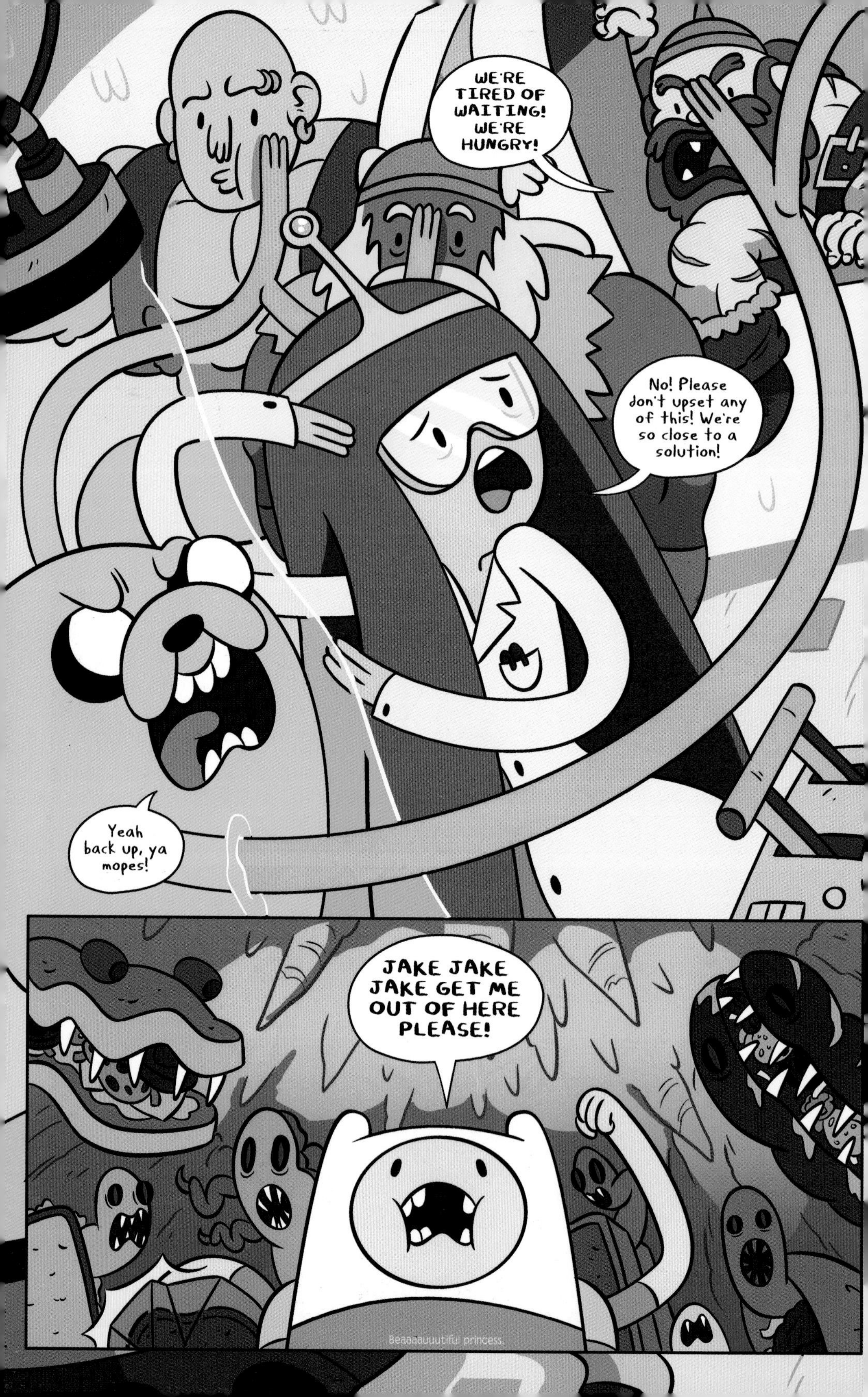
WE'RE TIRED OF WAITING! WE'RE HUNGRY!
No! Please don't upset any of this! We're so close to a solution!
Yeah back up, ya mopes!
JAKE JAKE JAKE GET ME OUT OF HERE PLEASE!
Beaaaauuutiful princess.

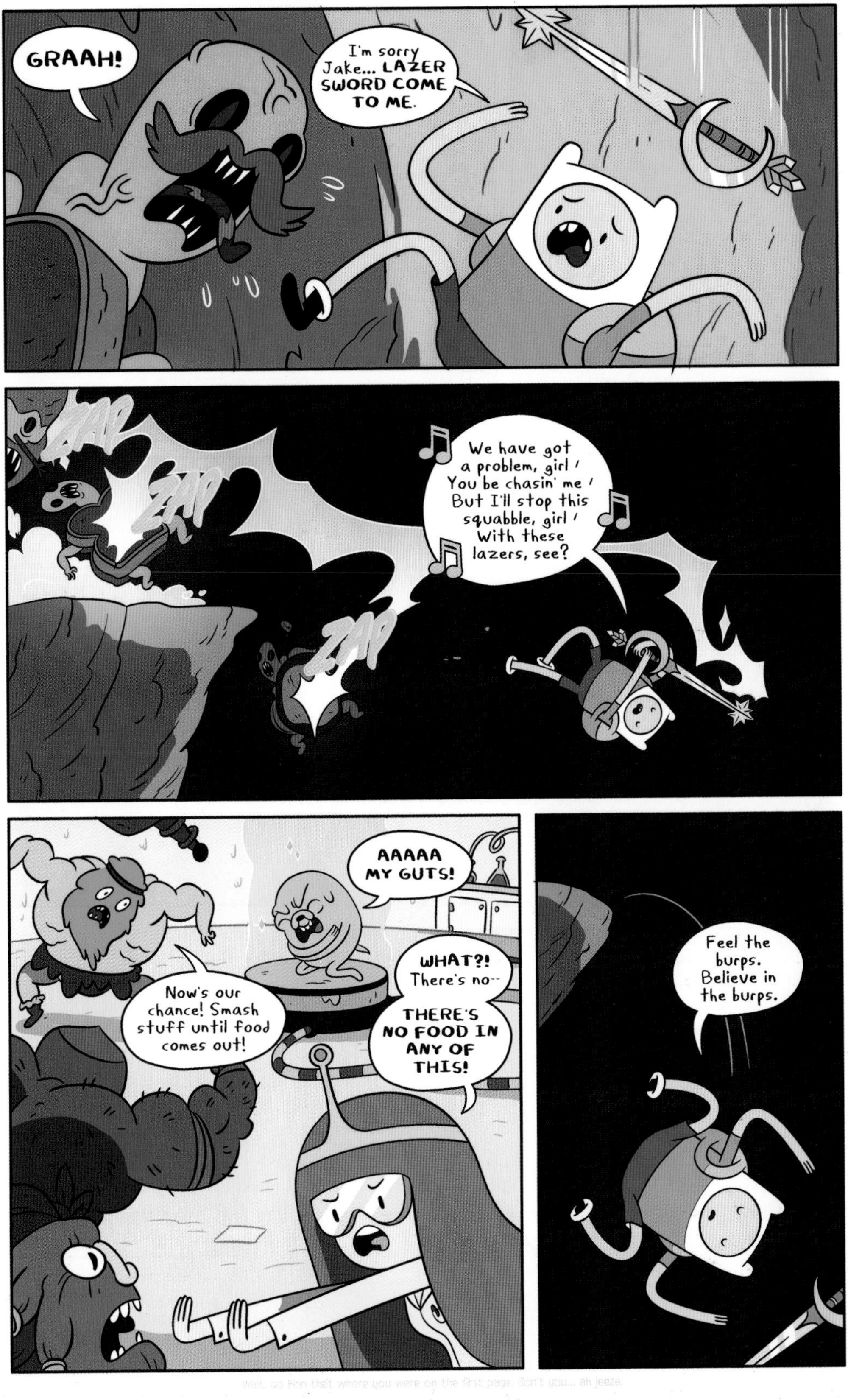
GRAAH!
I'm sorry Jake... LAZER SWORD COME TO ME.
ZAP
ZAP
We have got a problem, girl / You be chasin' me / But I'll stop this squabble, girl / With these lazers, see?
ZAP
AAAAA MY GUTS!
Now's our chance! Smash stuff until food comes out!
WHAT?! There's no--
THERE'S NO FOOD IN ANY OF THIS!
Feel the burps. Believe in the burps.

wait, so Finn that where you were on the first page, don't you... ah jeeze.

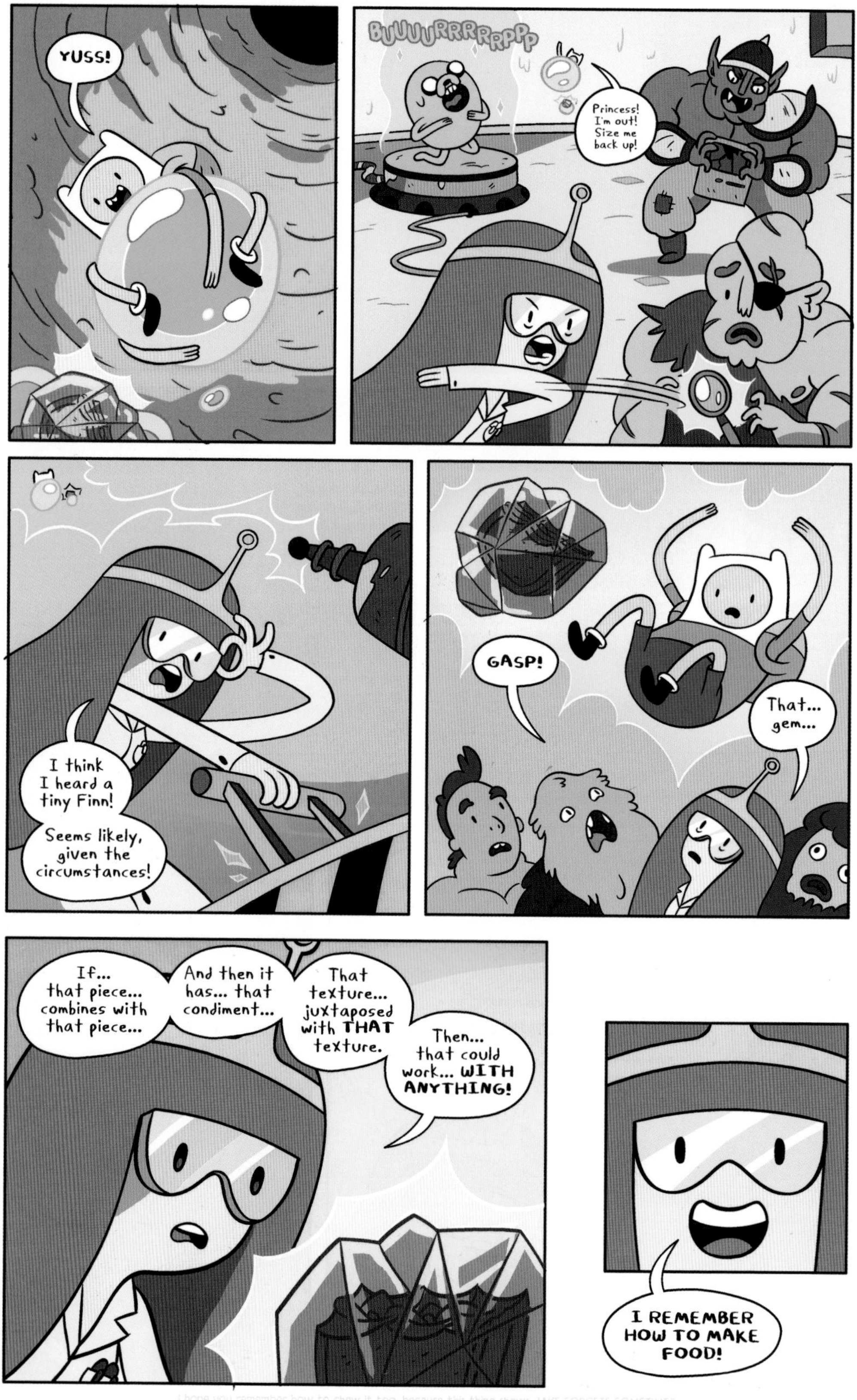
YUSS!
BUUUURRRRRPPP
Princess! I'm out! Size me back up!
I think I heard a tiny Finn!
Seems likely, given the circumstances!
GASP!
That... gem...
If... that piece... combines with that piece...
And then it has... that condiment...
That texture... juxtaposed with THAT texture.
Then... that could work... WITH ANYTHING!
I REMEMBER HOW TO MAKE FOOD!

I hope you remember how to chew it too. because this thing shows JAKE FORGETS SOMETIMES.

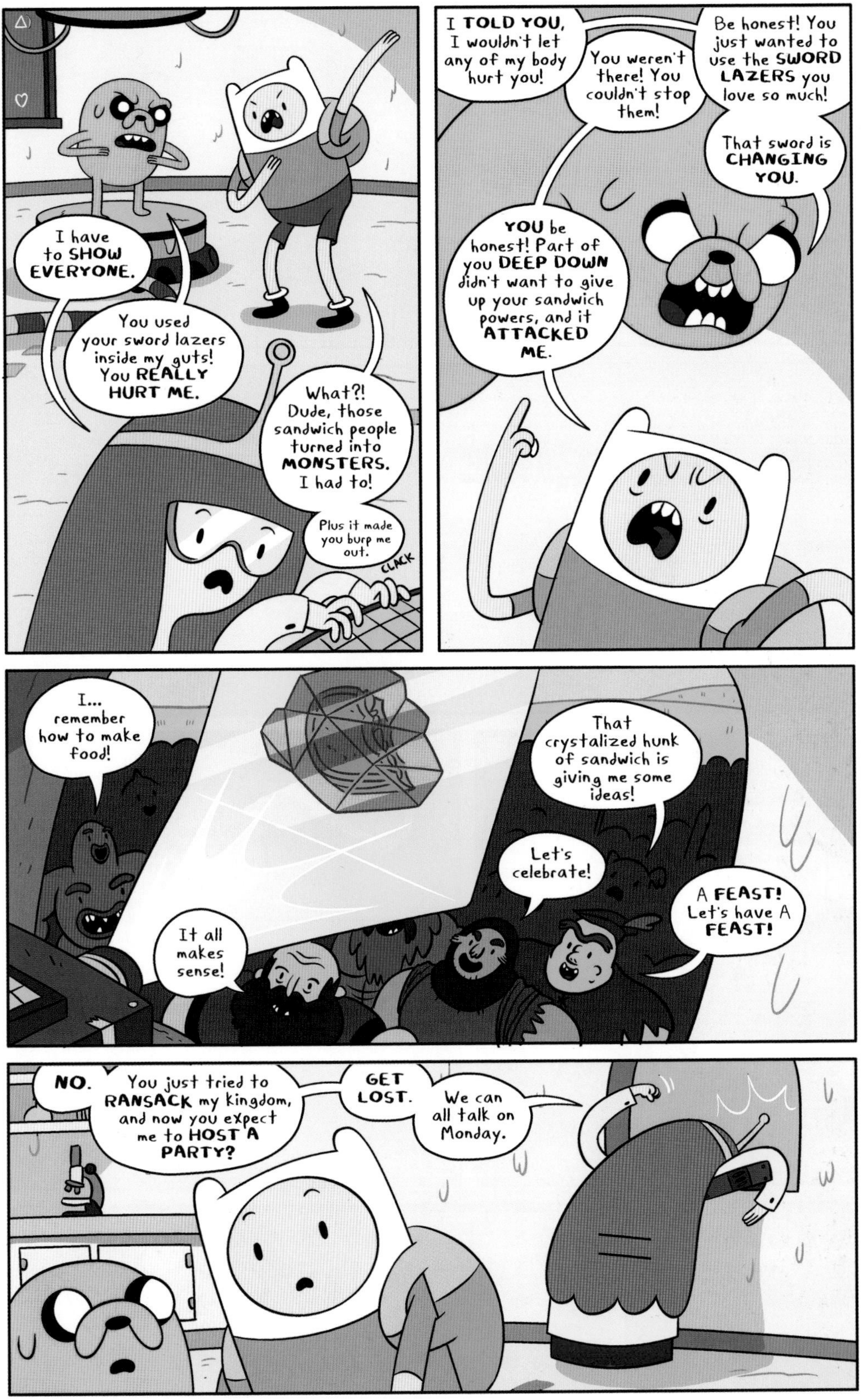
I have to SHOW EVERYONE.
You used your sword lazers inside my guts! You REALLY HURT ME.
What?! Dude, those sandwich people turned into MONSTERS. I had to!
Plus it made you burp me out.
CLACK
I TOLD YOU, I wouldn't let any of my body hurt you!
You weren't there! You couldn't stop them!
Be honest! You just wanted to use the SWORD LAZERS you love so much!
That sword is CHANGING YOU.
YOU be honest! Part of you DEEP DOWN didn't want to give up your sandwich powers, and it ATTACKED ME.
I... remember how to make food!
That crystalized hunk of sandwich is giving me some ideas!
Let's celebrate!
A FEAST! Let's have A FEAST!
It all makes sense!
NO.
You just tried to RANSACK my kingdom, and now you expect me to HOST A PARTY?
GET LOST.
We can all talk on Monday.

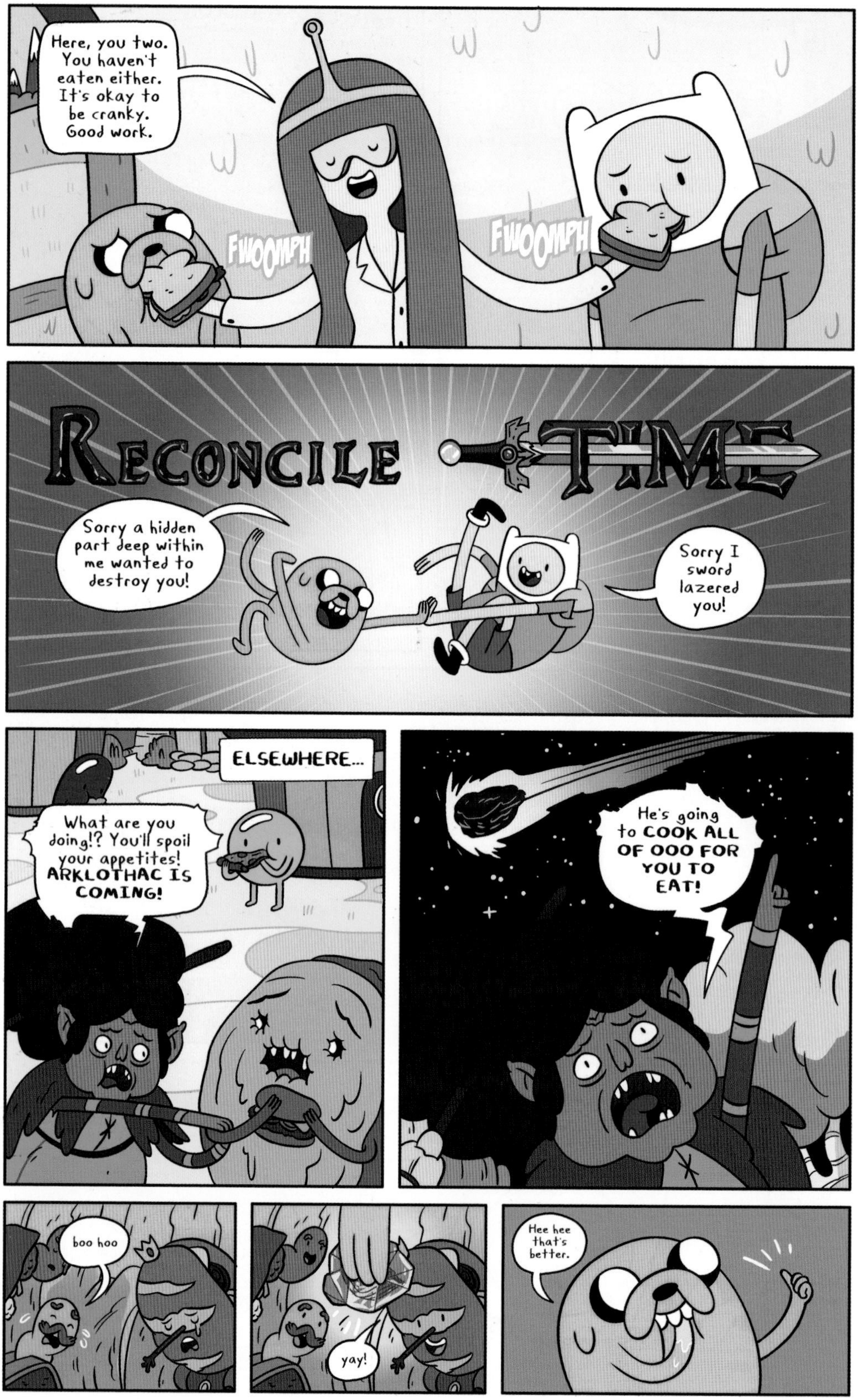
Here, you two. You haven't eaten either. It's okay to be cranky. Good work.
FWOOMPH
FWOOMPH
RECONCILE TIME
Sorry a hidden part deep within me wanted to destroy you!
Sorry I sword lazered you!
ELSEWHERE...
What are you doing!? You'll spoil your appetites! ARKLOTHAC IS COMING!
He's going to COOK ALL OF OOO FOR YOU TO EAT!
boo hoo
yay!
Hee hee that's better.

Don't shop for groceries hungry. Don't argue hungry. Don't rally your kingdom to go raid another kingdom hungry... There's a lesson here.

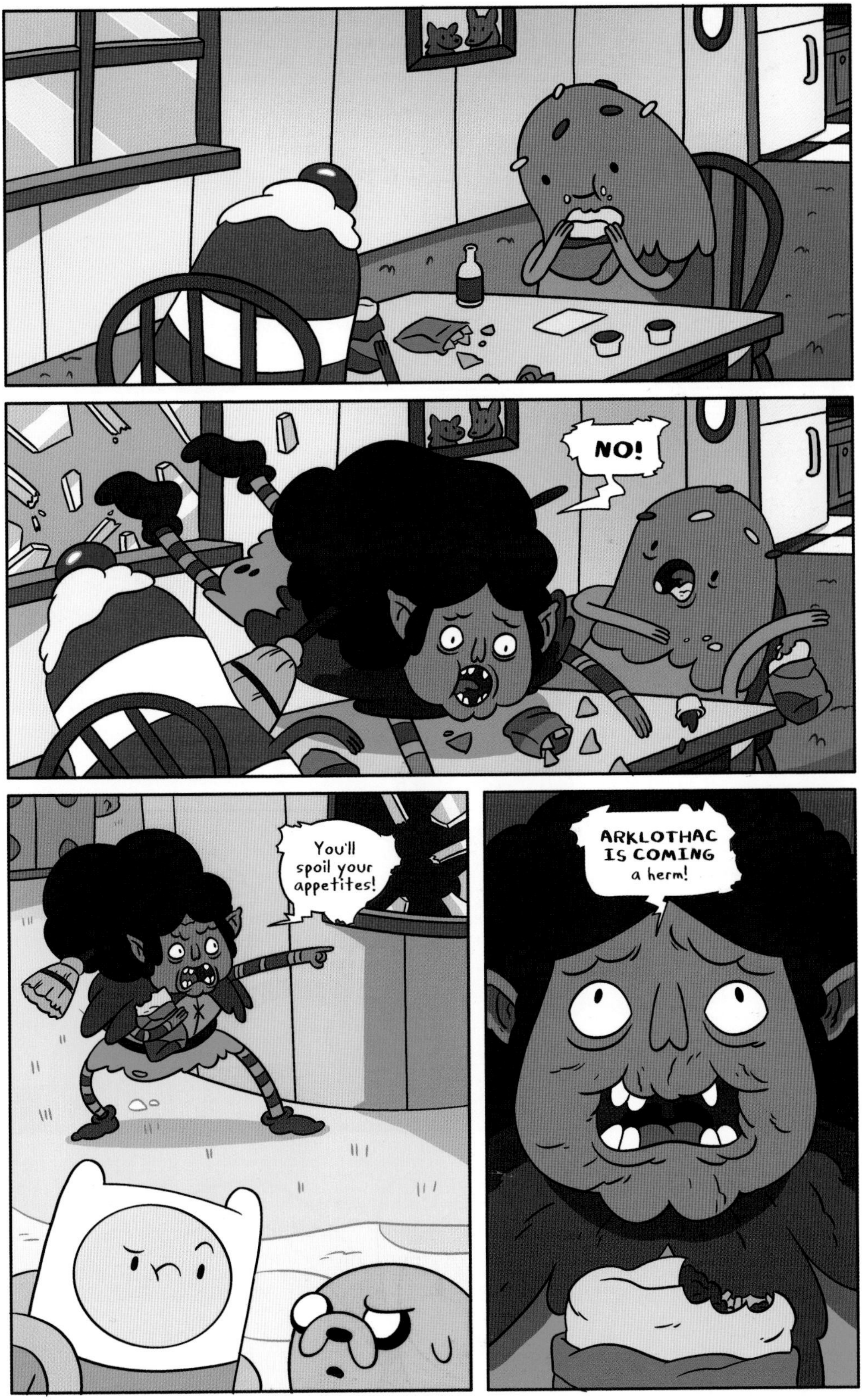
NO!
You'll spoil your appetites!
ARKLOTHAC IS COMING a herm!

A name I literally got from a "monster name generator".

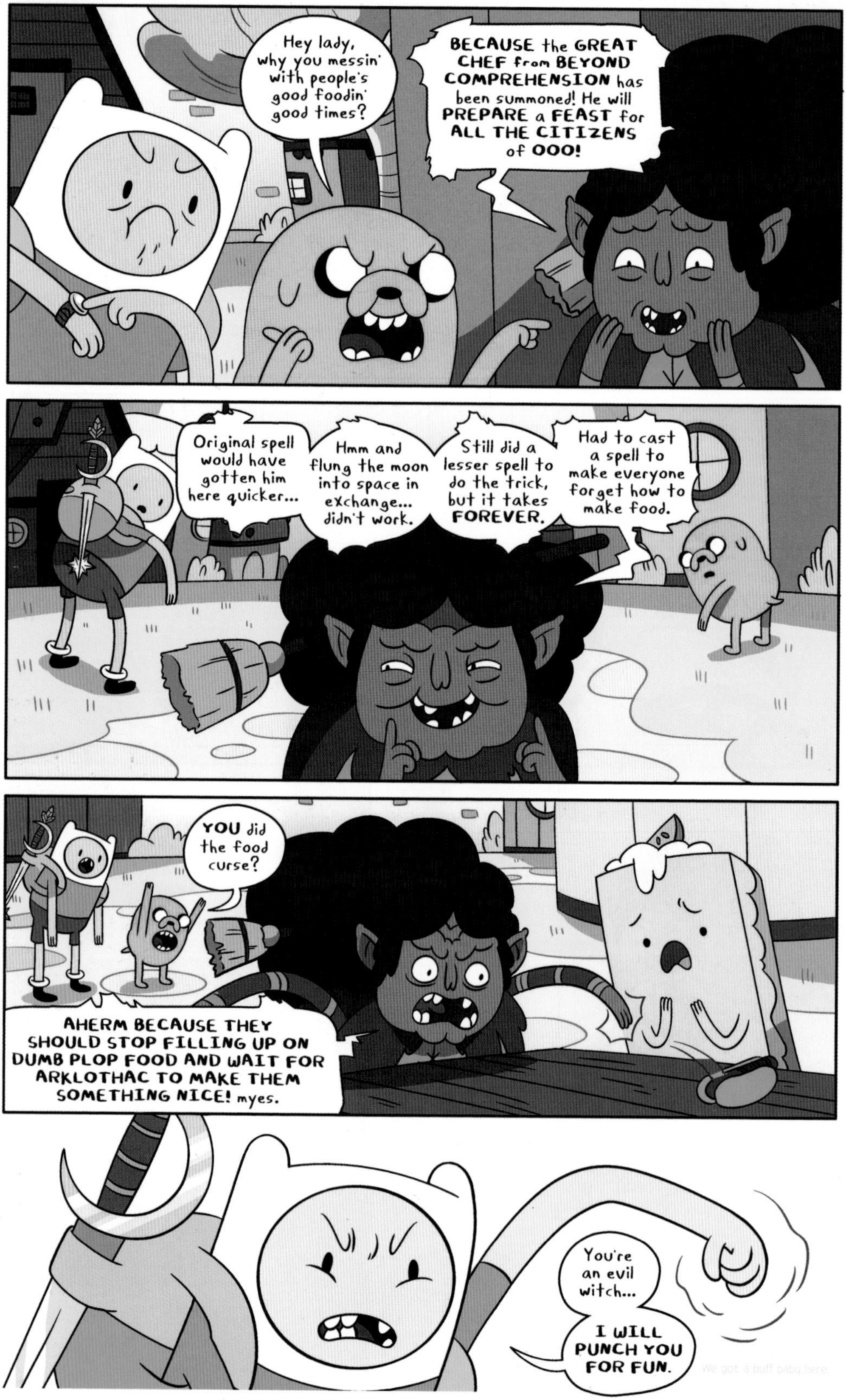

Hey lady, why you messin' with people's good foodin' good times?
BECAUSE the GREAT CHEF from BEYOND COMPREHENSION has been summoned! He will PREPARE a FEAST for ALL THE CITIZENS of OOO!
Original spell would have gotten him here quicker...
Hmm and flung the moon into space in exchange... didn't work.
Still did a lesser spell to do the trick, but it takes FOREVER.
Had to cast a spell to make everyone forget how to make food.
YOU did the food curse?
AHERM BECAUSE THEY SHOULD STOP FILLING UP ON DUMB PLOP FOOD AND WAIT FOR ARKLOTHAC TO MAKE THEM SOMETHING NICE! myes.
You're an evil witch...
I WILL PUNCH YOU FOR FUN.
We got a buff baby here.

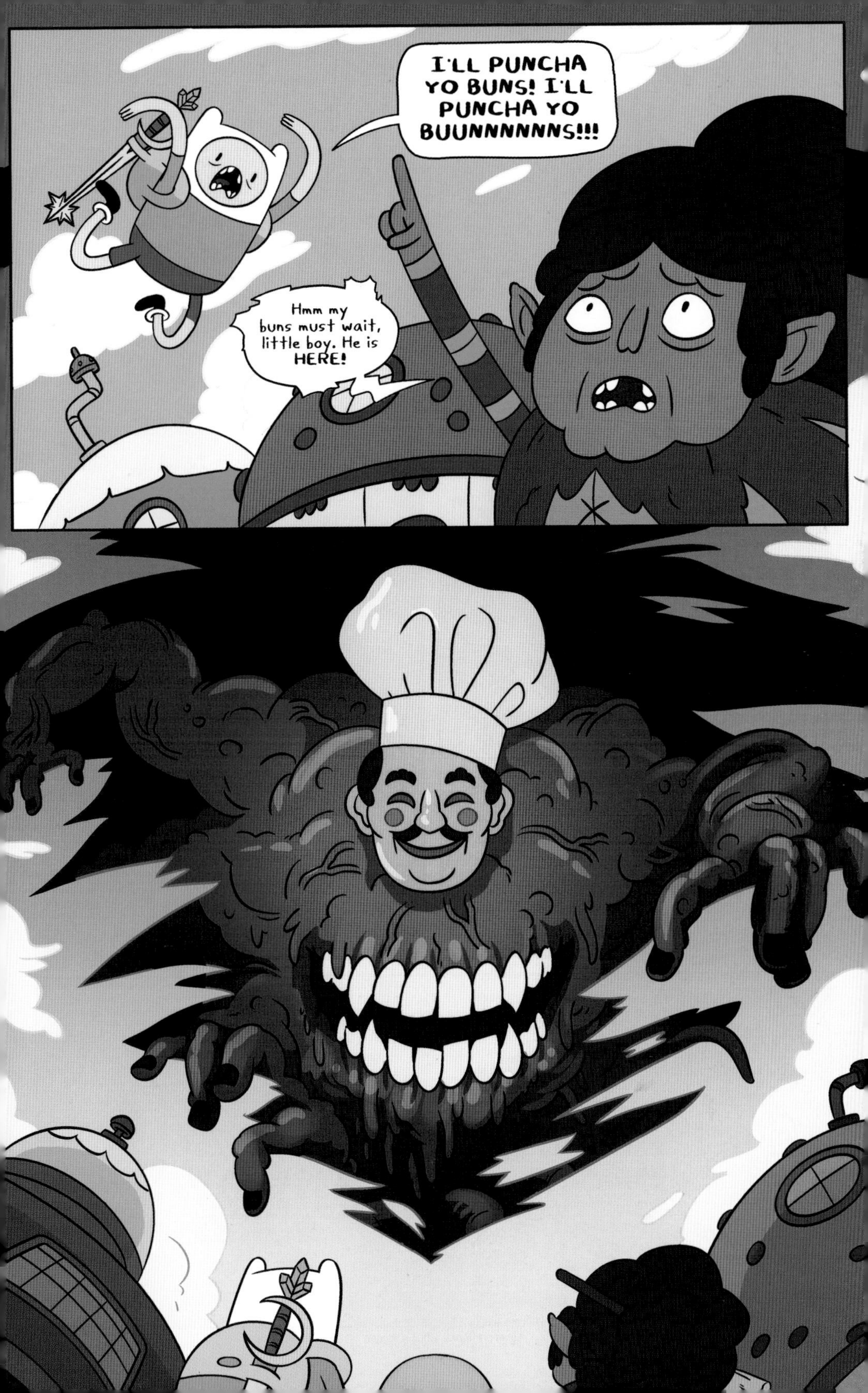
I'LL PUNCHA YO BUNS! I'LL PUNCHA YO BUUNNNNNNS!!!
Hmm my buns must wait, little boy. He is HERE!

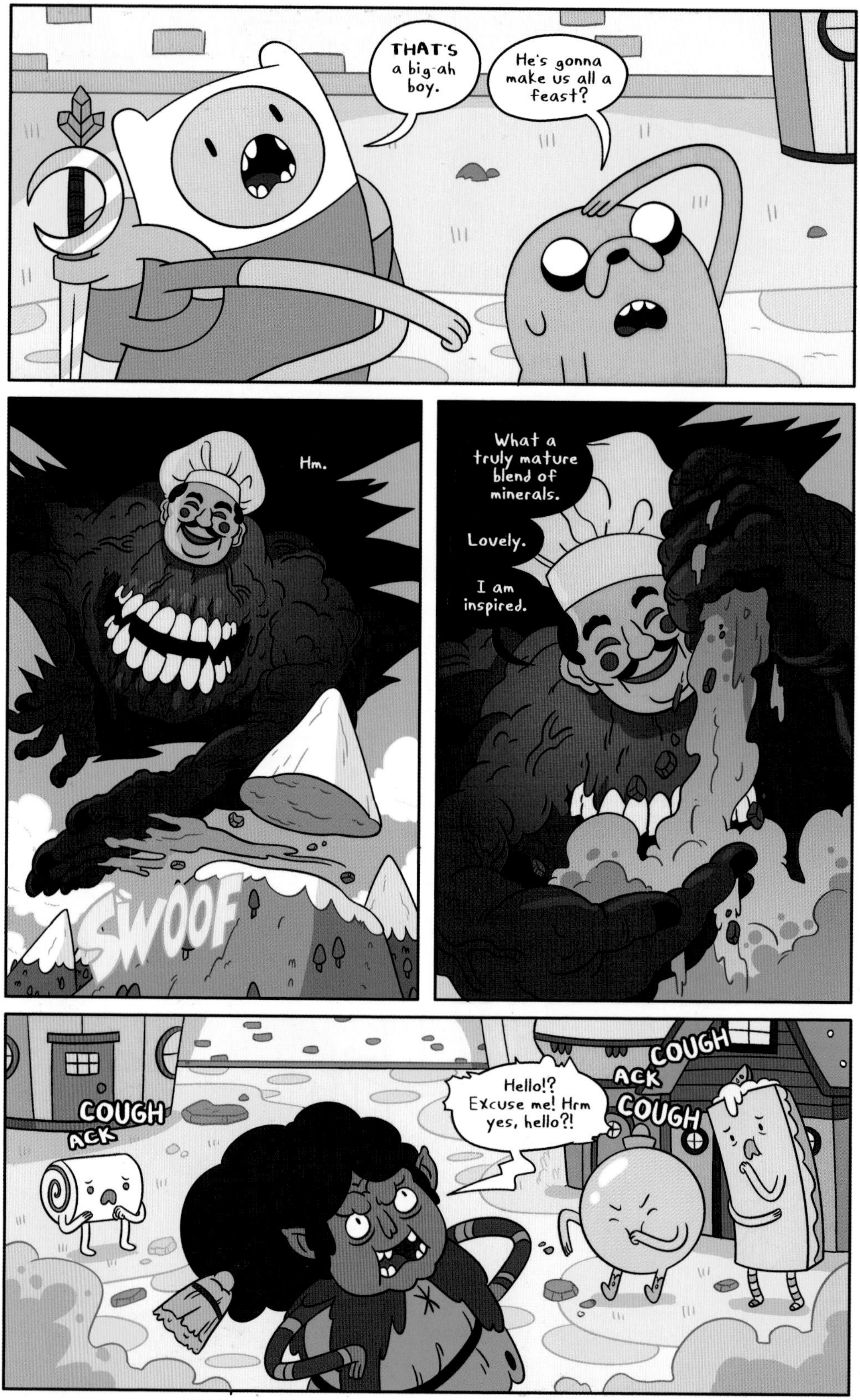
THAT'S a big-ah boy.
He's gonna make us all a feast?
Hm.
SWOOF
What a truly mature blend of minerals.
Lovely.
I am inspired.
COUGH
ACK
Hello!? Excuse me! Hrm yes, hello?!
COUGH
ACK
COUGH

Hello! Oh, you're not talking to me. You're talking to another character in the book. Carry on.

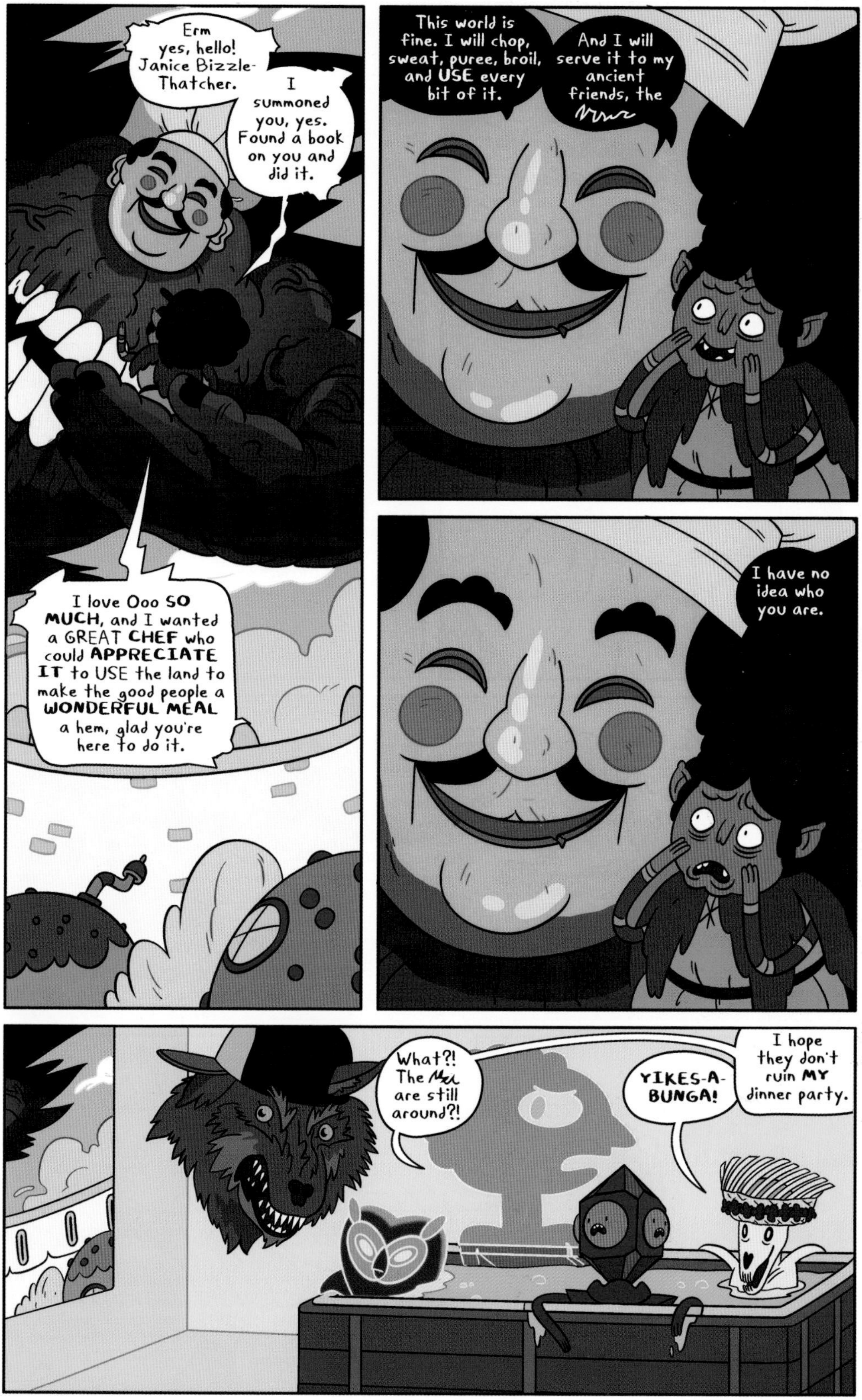
Erm yes, hello! Janice Bizzle-Thatcher.
I summoned you, yes. Found a book on you and did it.
I love Ooo **SO MUCH**, and I wanted a GREAT **CHEF** who could **APPRECIATE IT** to USE the land to make the good people a **WONDERFUL MEAL** a hem, glad you're here to do it.
This world is fine. I will chop, sweat, puree, broil, and **USE** every bit of it.
And I will serve it to my ancient friends, the
I have no idea who you are.
What?! The
are still around?!
YIKES-A-BUNGA!
I hope they don't ruin **MY** dinner party.

That's not a saying, Death.

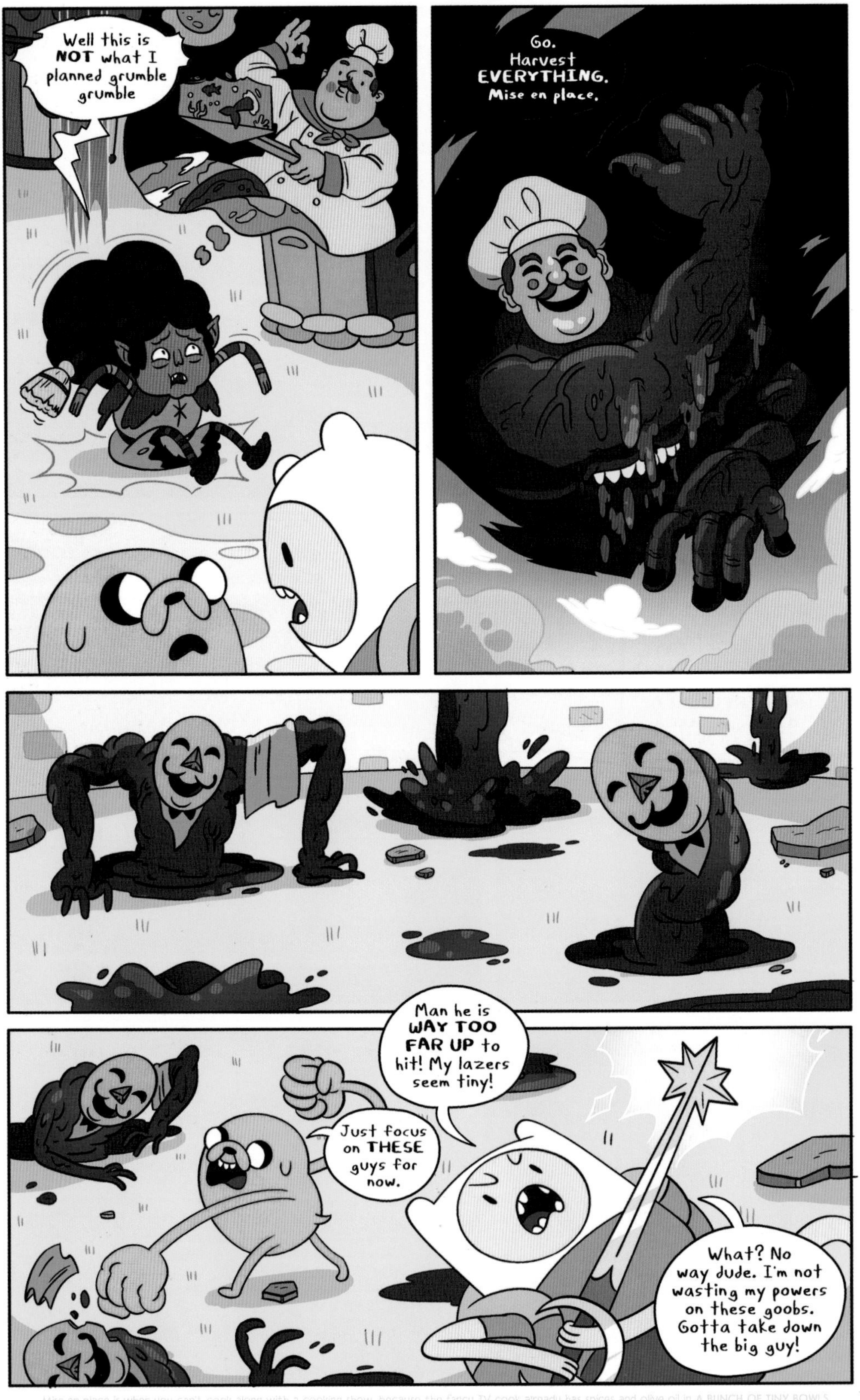
Well this is **NOT** what I planned grumble grumble
Go. Harvest **EVERYTHING.** Mise en place.
Man he is **WAY TOO FAR UP** to hit! My lazers seem tiny!
Just focus on **THESE** guys for now.
What? No way dude. I'm not wasting my powers on these goobs. Gotta take down the big guy!

Mise en place is when you can't cook along with a cooking show, because the fancy TV cook already has spices and olive oil in A BUNCH OF TINY BOWLS.

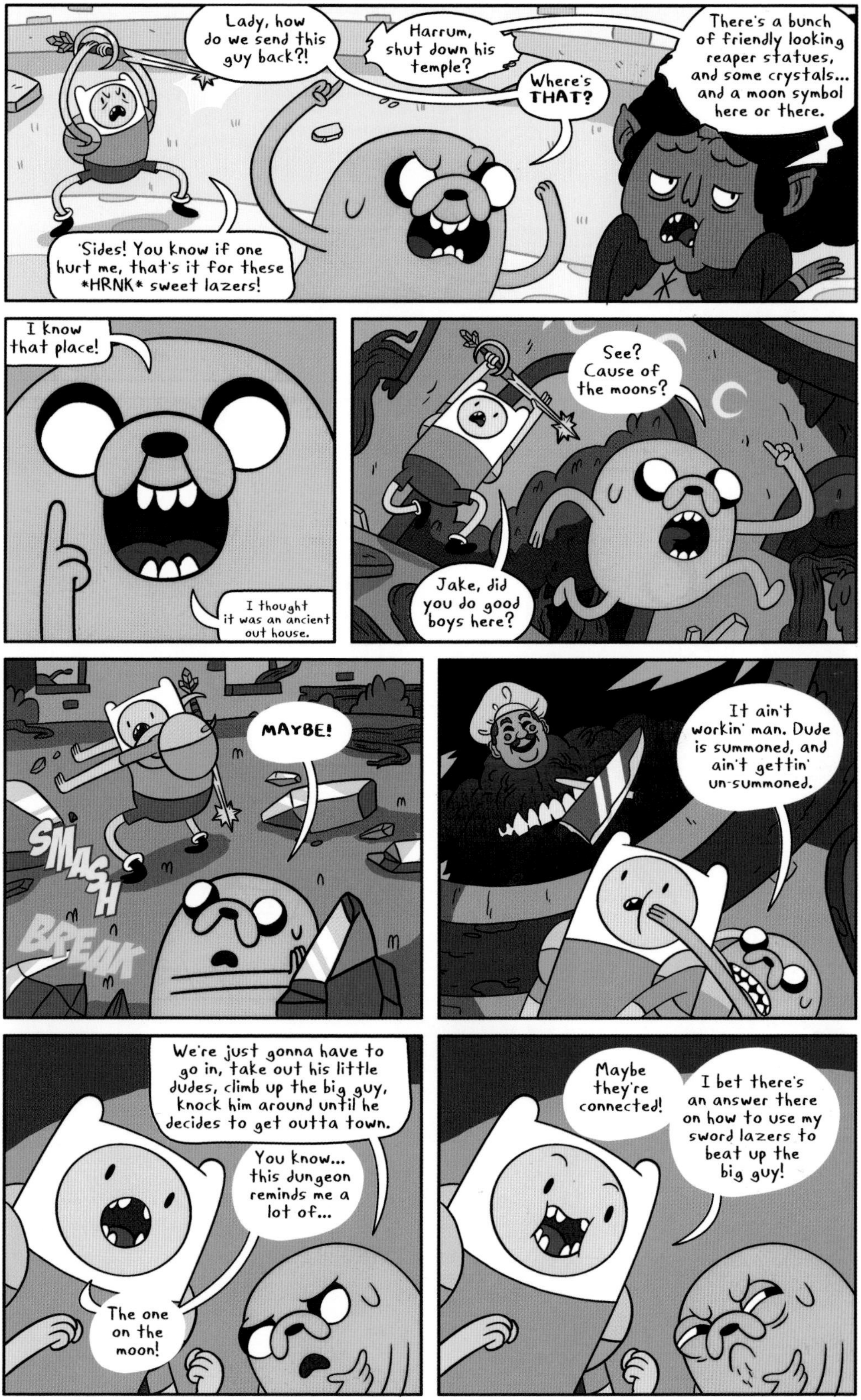

Lady, how do we send this guy back?!
Harrum, shut down his temple?
Where's THAT?
There's a bunch of friendly looking reaper statues, and some crystals... and a moon symbol here or there.
'Sides! You know if one hurt me, that's it for these *HRNK* sweet lazers!
I know that place!
I thought it was an ancient out house.
See? Cause of the moons?
Jake, did you do good boys here?
MAYBE!
SMASH
BREAK
It ain't workin' man. Dude is summoned, and ain't gettin' un-summoned.
We're just gonna have to go in, take out his little dudes, climb up the big guy, knock him around until he decides to get outta town.
You know... this dungeon reminds me a lot of...
The one on the moon!
Maybe they're connected!
I bet there's an answer there on how to use my sword lazers to beat up the big guy!

You kids are probably too young to remember little moons on outhouses. Not me! I've pottied like A COWBOY.

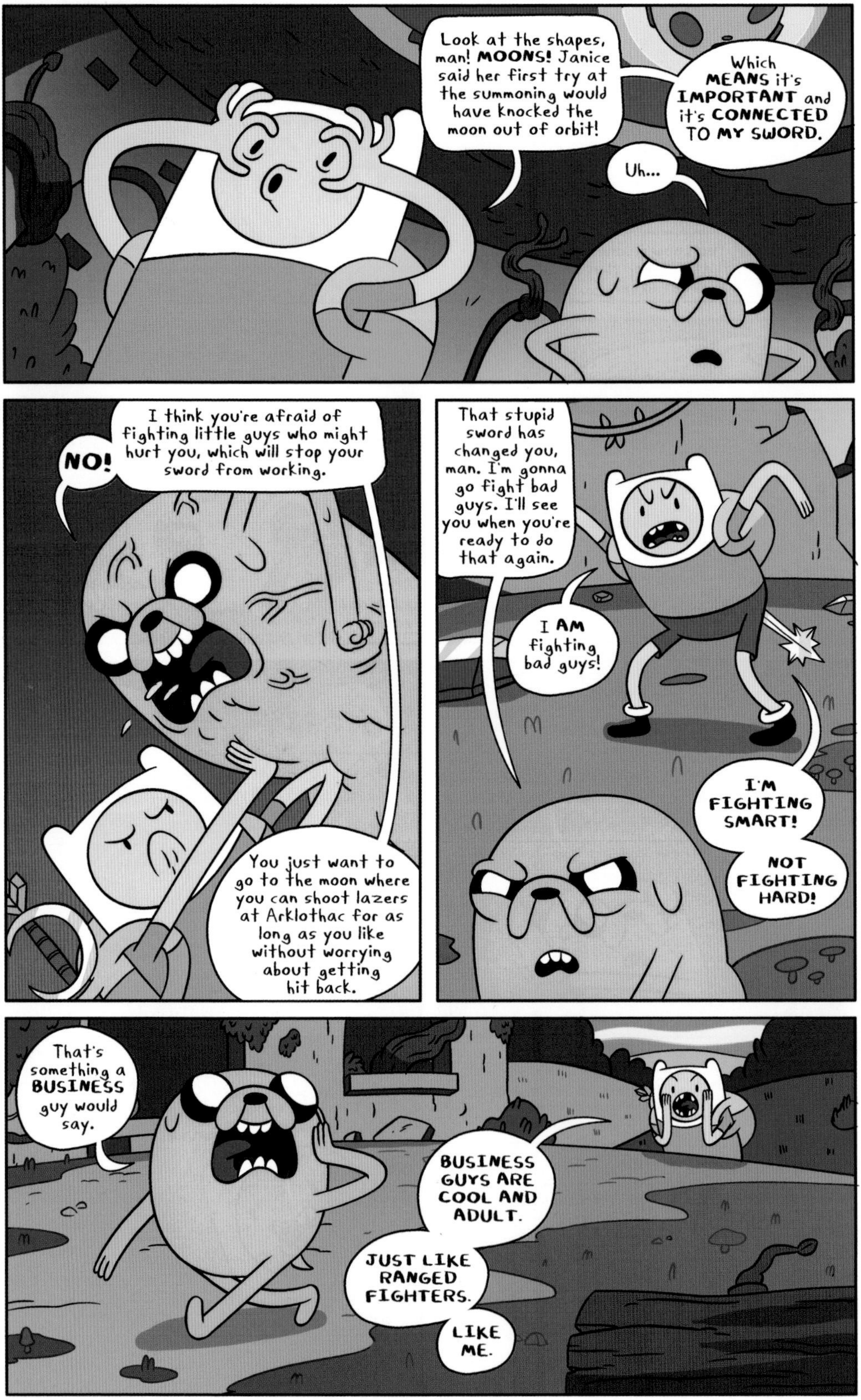
Look at the shapes, man! **MOONS!** Janice said her first try at the summoning would have knocked the moon out of orbit!
Which **MEANS** it's **IMPORTANT** and it's **CONNECTED TO MY SWORD.**
Uh...
I think you're afraid of fighting little guys who might hurt you, which will stop your sword from working.
NO!
You just want to go to the moon where you can shoot lazers at Arklothac for as long as you like without worrying about getting hit back.
That stupid sword has changed you, man. I'm gonna go fight bad guys. I'll see you when you're ready to do that again.
I **AM** fighting bad guys!
I'M FIGHTING SMART!
NOT FIGHTING HARD!
That's something a **BUSINESS** guy would say.
BUSINESS GUYS ARE COOL AND ADULT.
JUST LIKE RANGED FIGHTERS.
LIKE ME.

I'm just picturing an elf archer, kick-flipping on a calculator skateboard, saying "BUDGETS ARE DOPE"

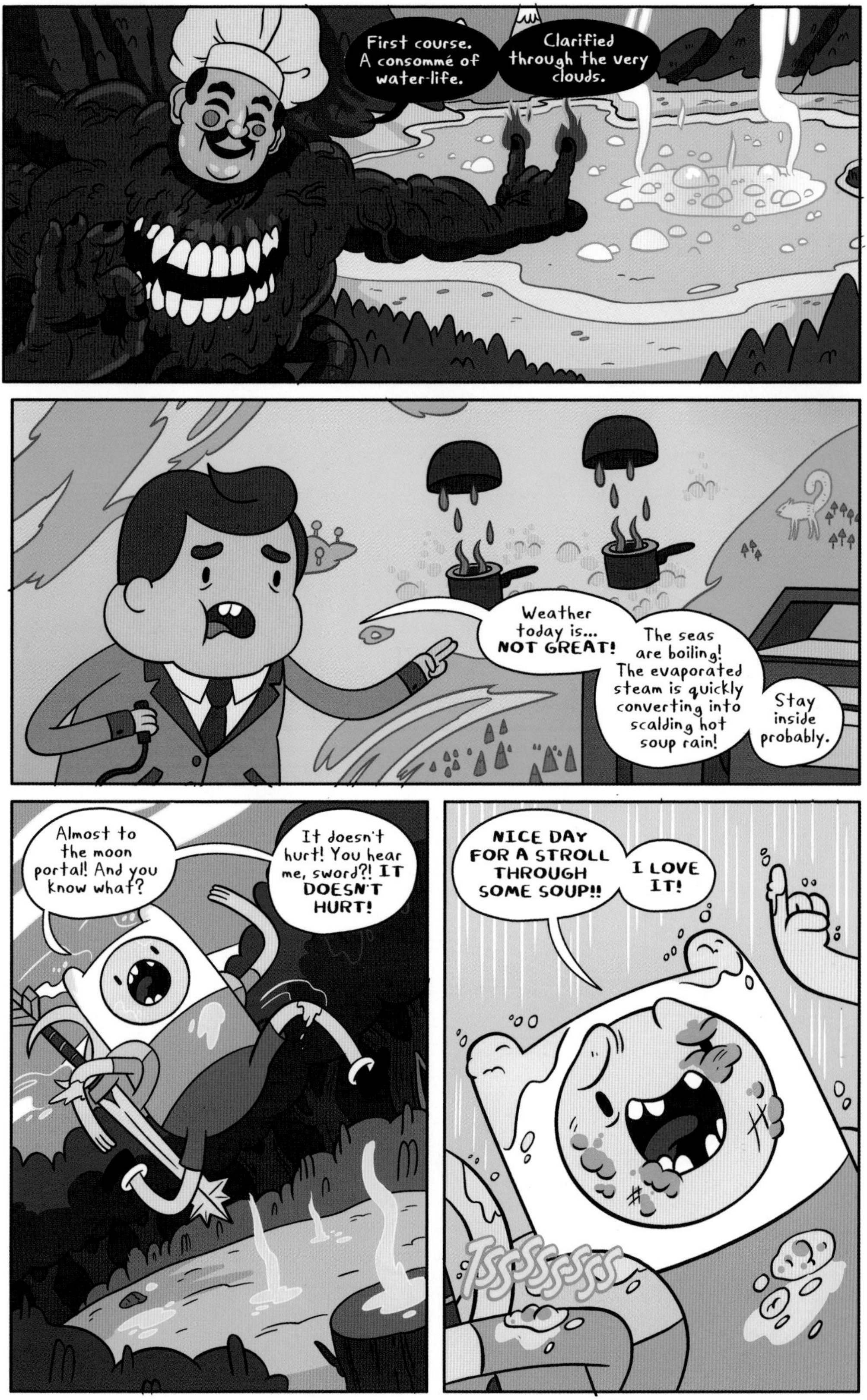
First course. A consommé of water-life.
Clarified through the very clouds.
Weather today is... **NOT GREAT!**
The seas are boiling! The evaporated steam is quickly converting into scalding hot soup rain!
Stay inside probably.
Almost to the moon portal! And you know what?
It doesn't hurt! You hear me, sword?! **IT DOESN'T HURT!**
NICE DAY FOR A STROLL THROUGH SOME SOUP!!
I LOVE IT!
TSSSSSSS

Writing this story arc has made me so flippin' hungry. Pie. Sandwiches. Now soup rain? I WANT ALL OF IT.

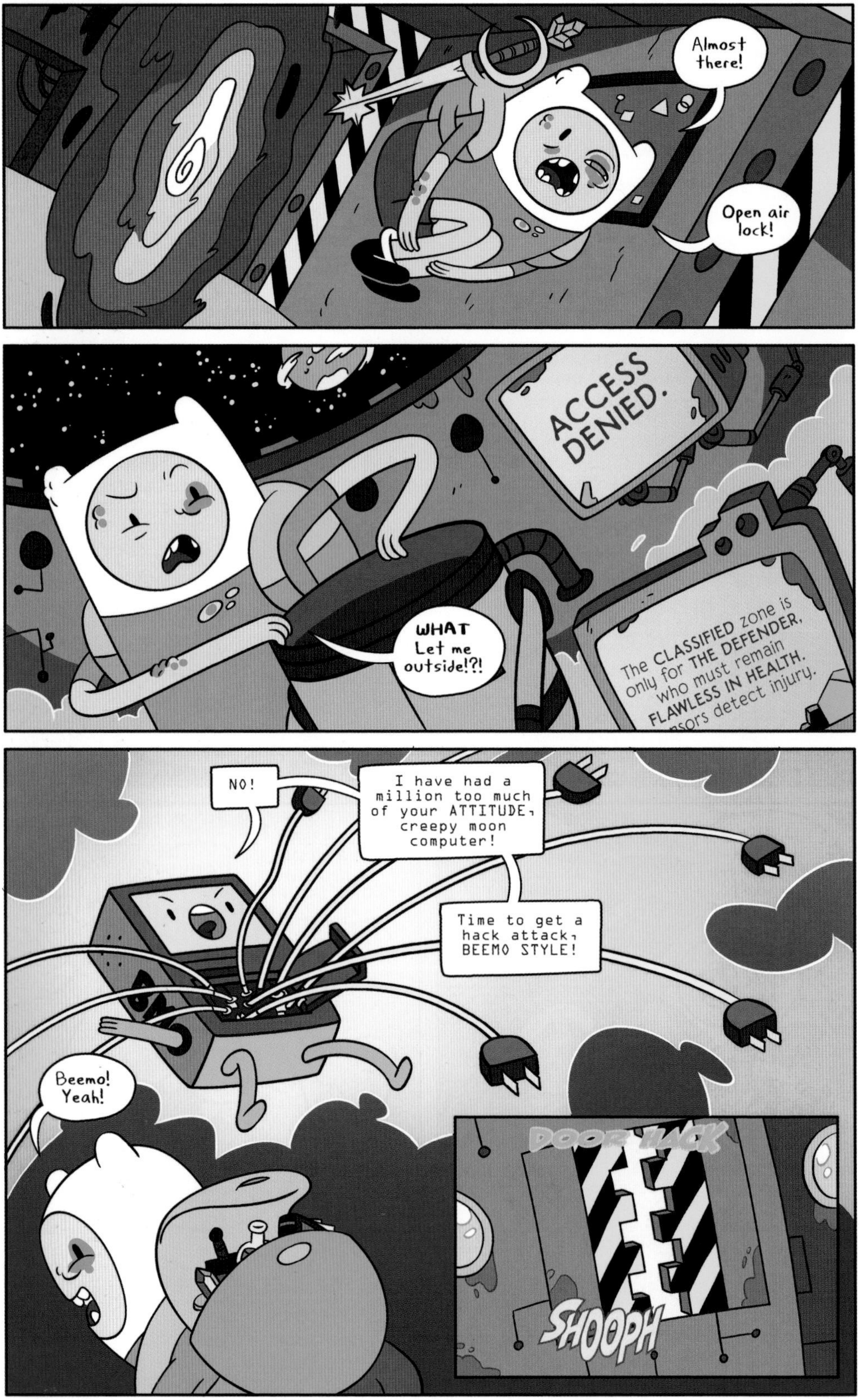
Almost there!
Open air lock!
ACCESS DENIED.
WHAT Let me outside!?!
The CLASSIFIED zone is only for THE DEFENDER, who must remain FLAWLESS IN HEALTH. nsors detect injury.
NO!
I have had a million too much of your ATTITUDE, creepy moon computer!
Time to get a hack attack, BEEMO STYLE!
Beemo! Yeah!
DOOR HACK
SHOOPH

Shove your old Nintendo into a garage door to play this scene at home!

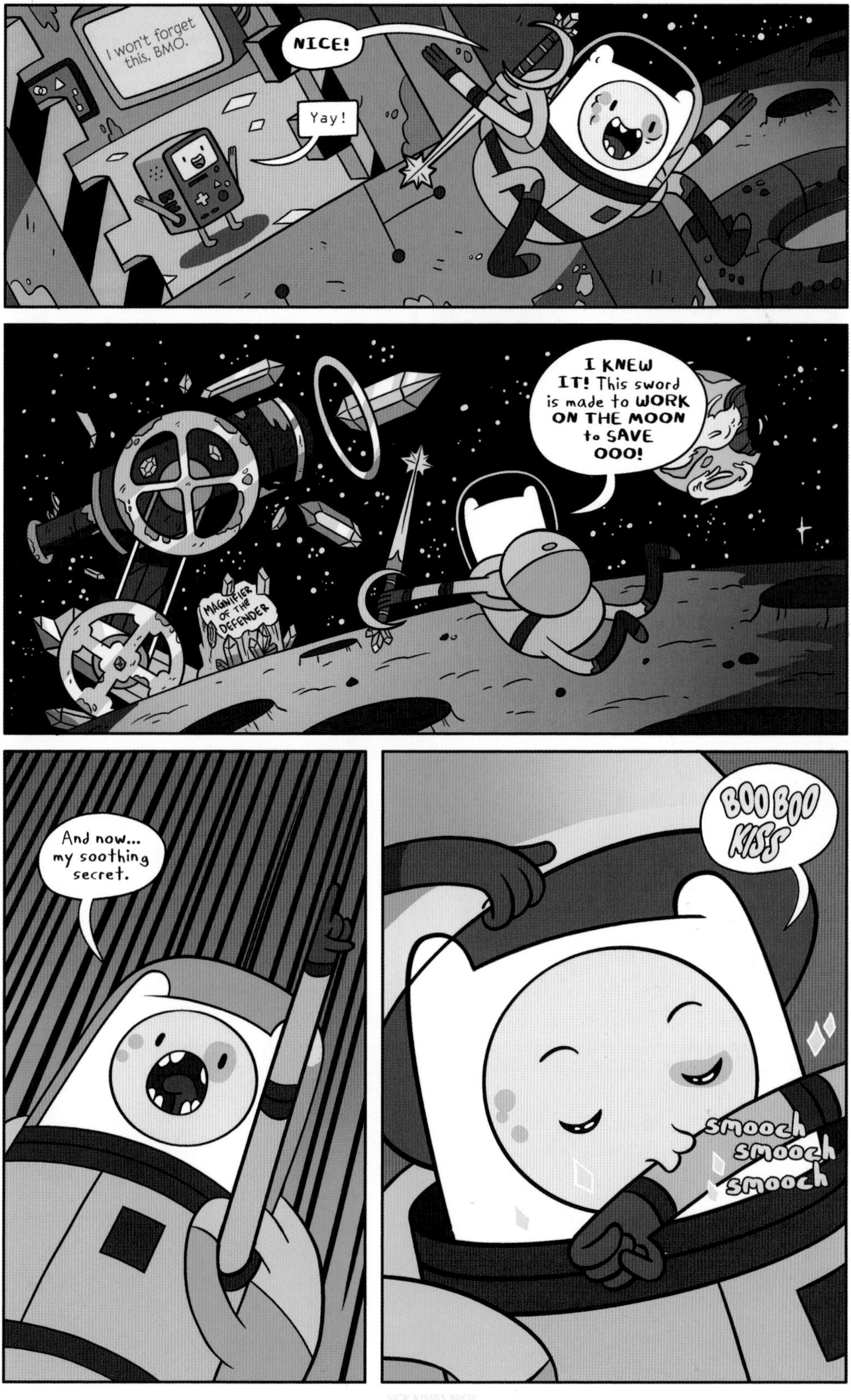
I won't forget this, BMO.
NICE!
Yay!
I KNEW IT! This sword is made to WORK ON THE MOON to SAVE OOO!
MAGNIFIER OF THE DEFENDER
And now... my soothing secret.
BOO BOO KISS
smooch smooch smooch

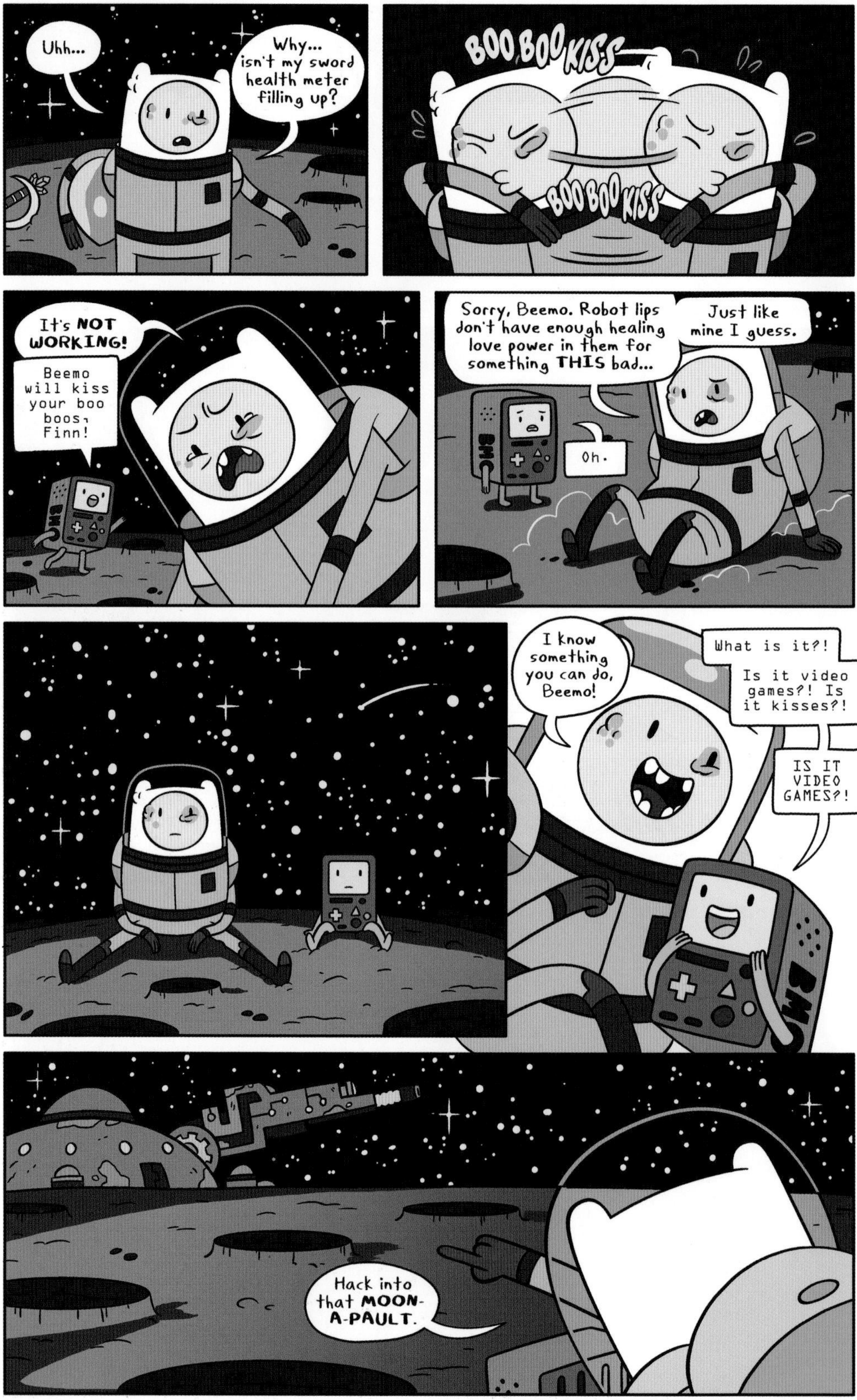
Uhh...
Why... isn't my sword health meter filling up?
BOO BOO KISS
BOO BOO KISS
It's NOT WORKING!
Beemo will kiss your boo boos, Finn!
Sorry, Beemo. Robot lips don't have enough healing love power in them for something THIS bad...
Oh.
Just like mine I guess.
I know something you can do, Beemo!
What is it?!
Is it video games?! Is it kisses?!
IS IT VIDEO GAMES?!
Hack into that MOON-A-PAULT.

It's... kind of video games.

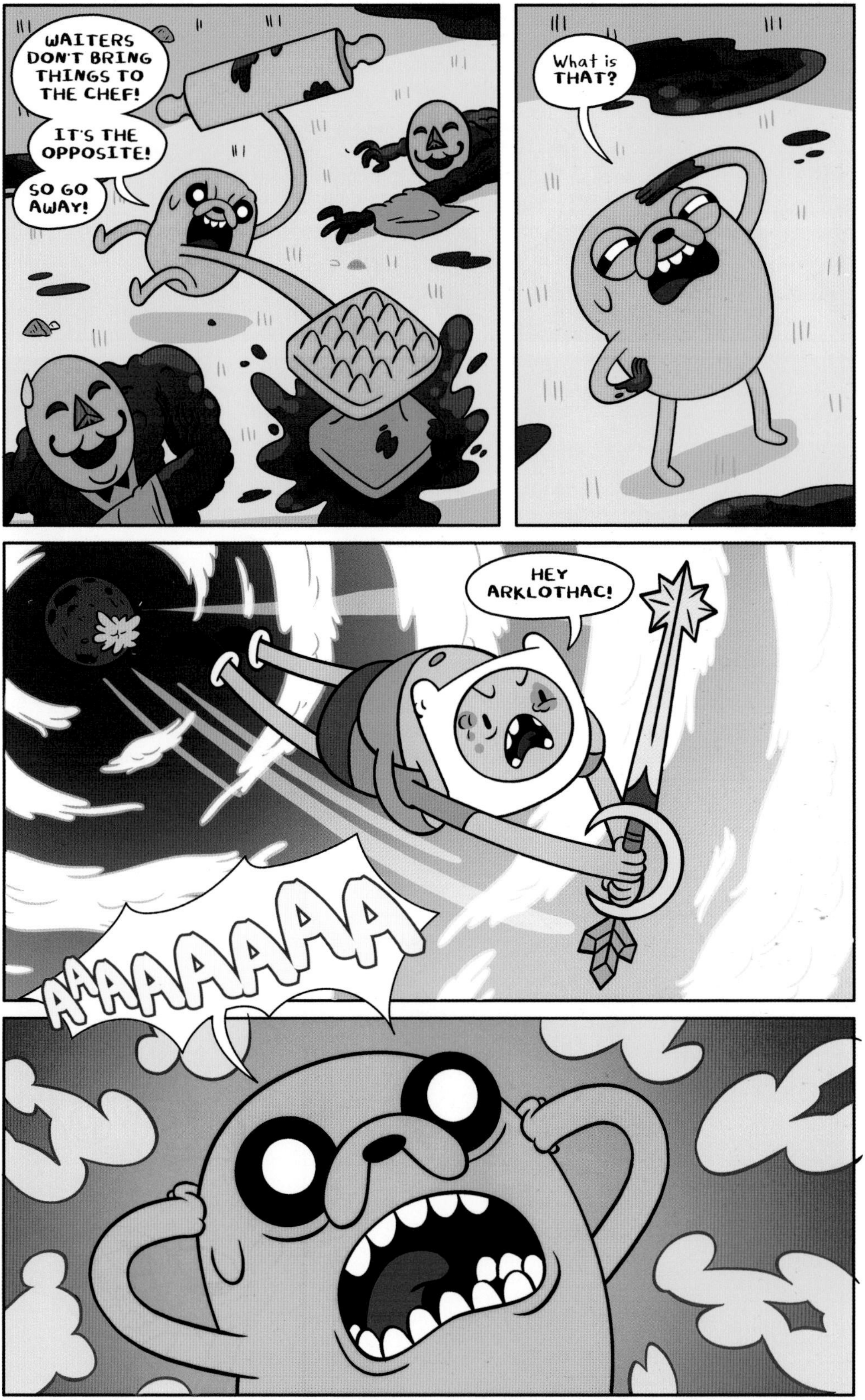
WAITERS DON'T BRING THINGS TO THE CHEF!
IT'S THE OPPOSITE!
SO GO AWAY!
What is THAT?
HEY ARKLOTHAC!
AAAAAAAA

Jake, you're making a lot of people sad that you're not fighting Arklothac at the same scale as him. BUT THOSE PEOPLE DON'T KNOW YOU ARE WORRIED ABOUT STEPPING ON PEOPLE AND THEIR HOUSES.

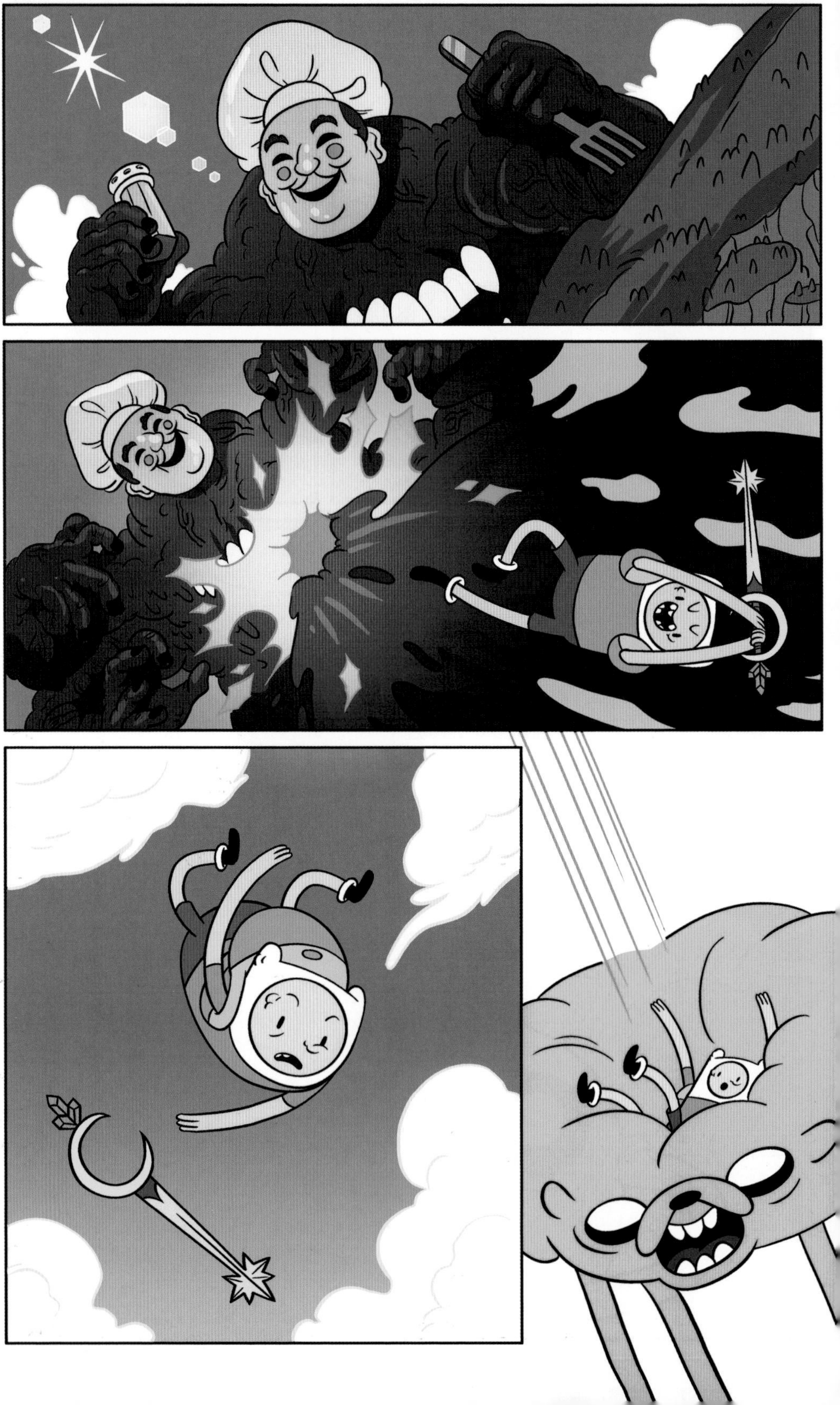

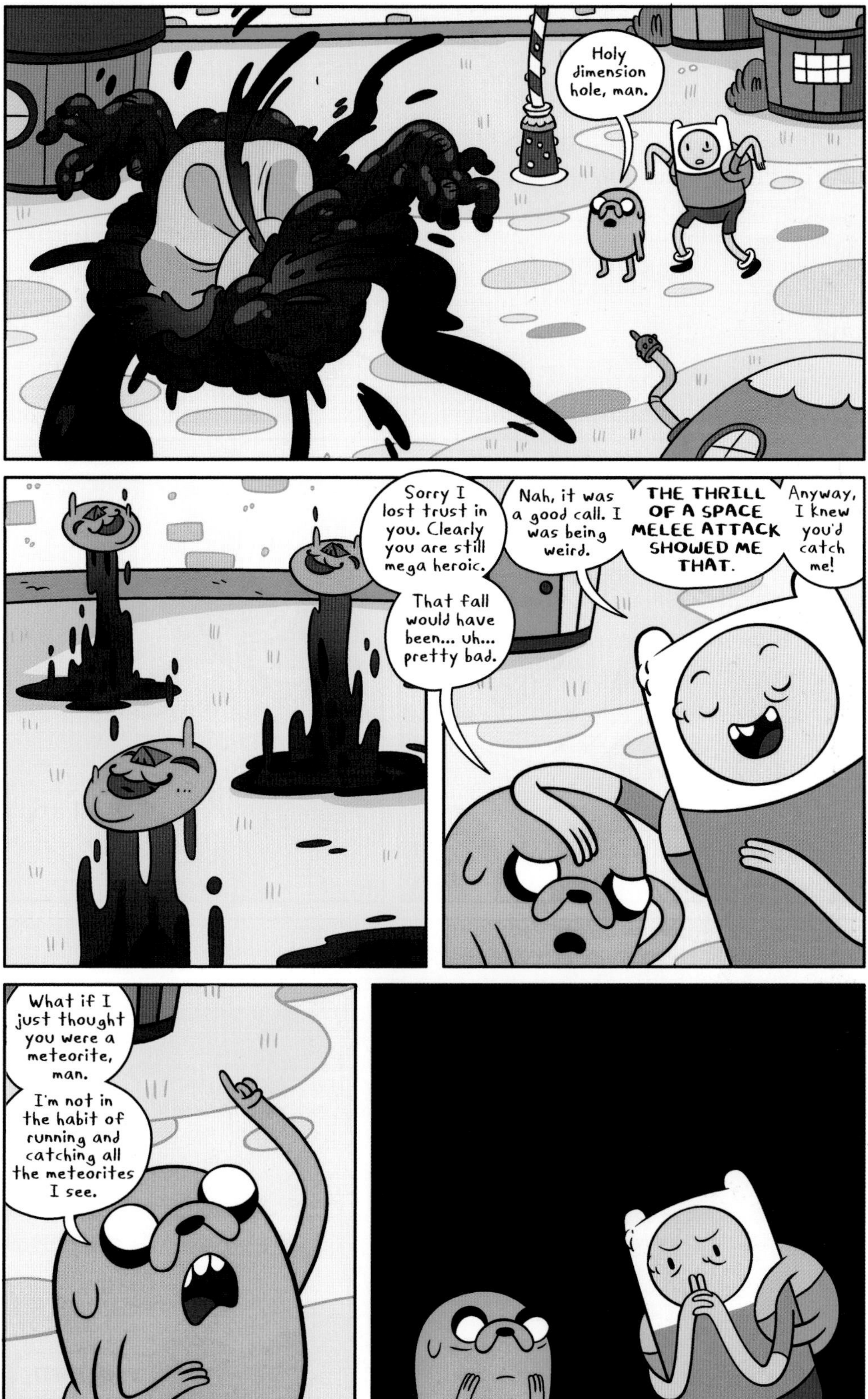
Holy dimension hole, man.
Sorry I lost trust in you. Clearly you are still mega heroic.
That fall would have been... uh... pretty bad.
Nah, it was a good call. I was being weird.
THE THRILL OF A SPACE MELEE ATTACK SHOWED ME THAT.
Anyway, I knew you'd catch me!
What if I just thought you were a meteorite, man.
I'm not in the habit of running and catching all the meteorites I see.

Yikes-a-bunga.

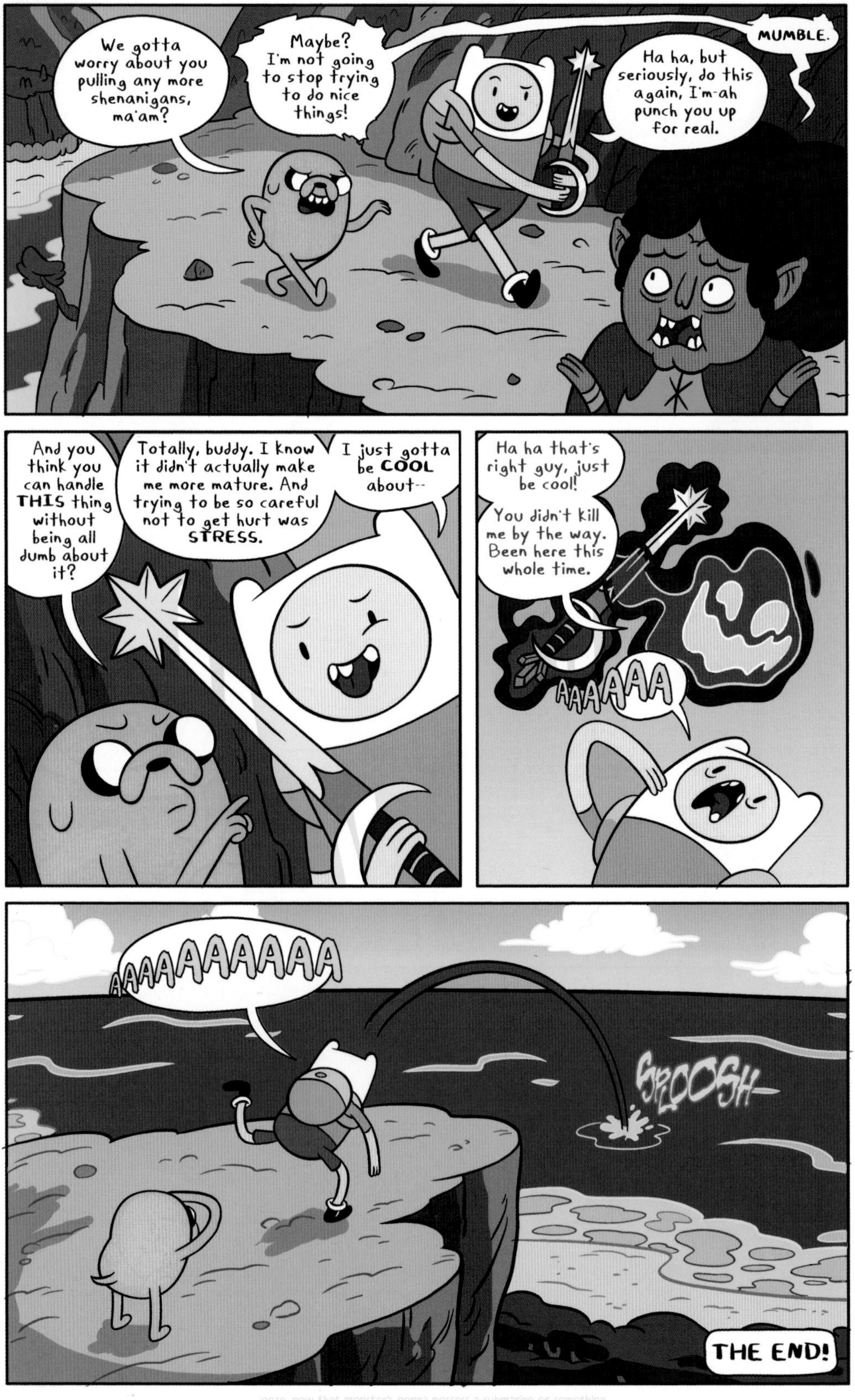
We gotta worry about you pulling any more shenanigans, ma'am?
Maybe? I'm not going to stop trying to do nice things!
MUMBLE.
Ha ha, but seriously, do this again, I'm-ah punch you up for real.
And you think you can handle THIS thing without being all dumb about it?
Totally, buddy. I know it didn't actually make me more mature. And trying to be so careful not to get hurt was STRESS.
I just gotta be COOL about--
Ha ha that's right guy, just be cool!
You didn't kill me by the way. Been here this whole time.
AAAAAAA
AAAAAAAAAAA
SPLOOSH--
THE END!

Jeeze, now that monster's gonna possess a submarine or something.

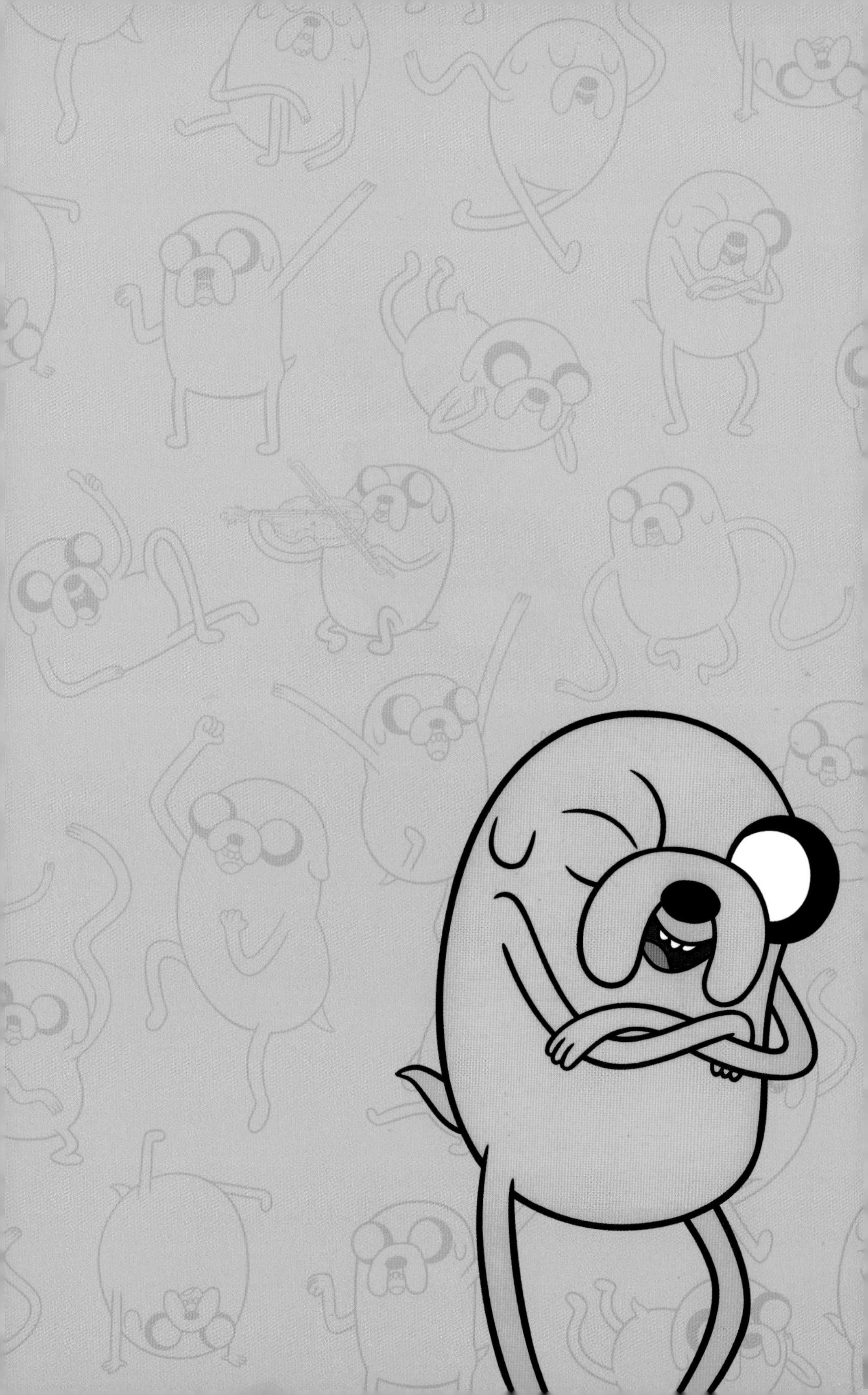

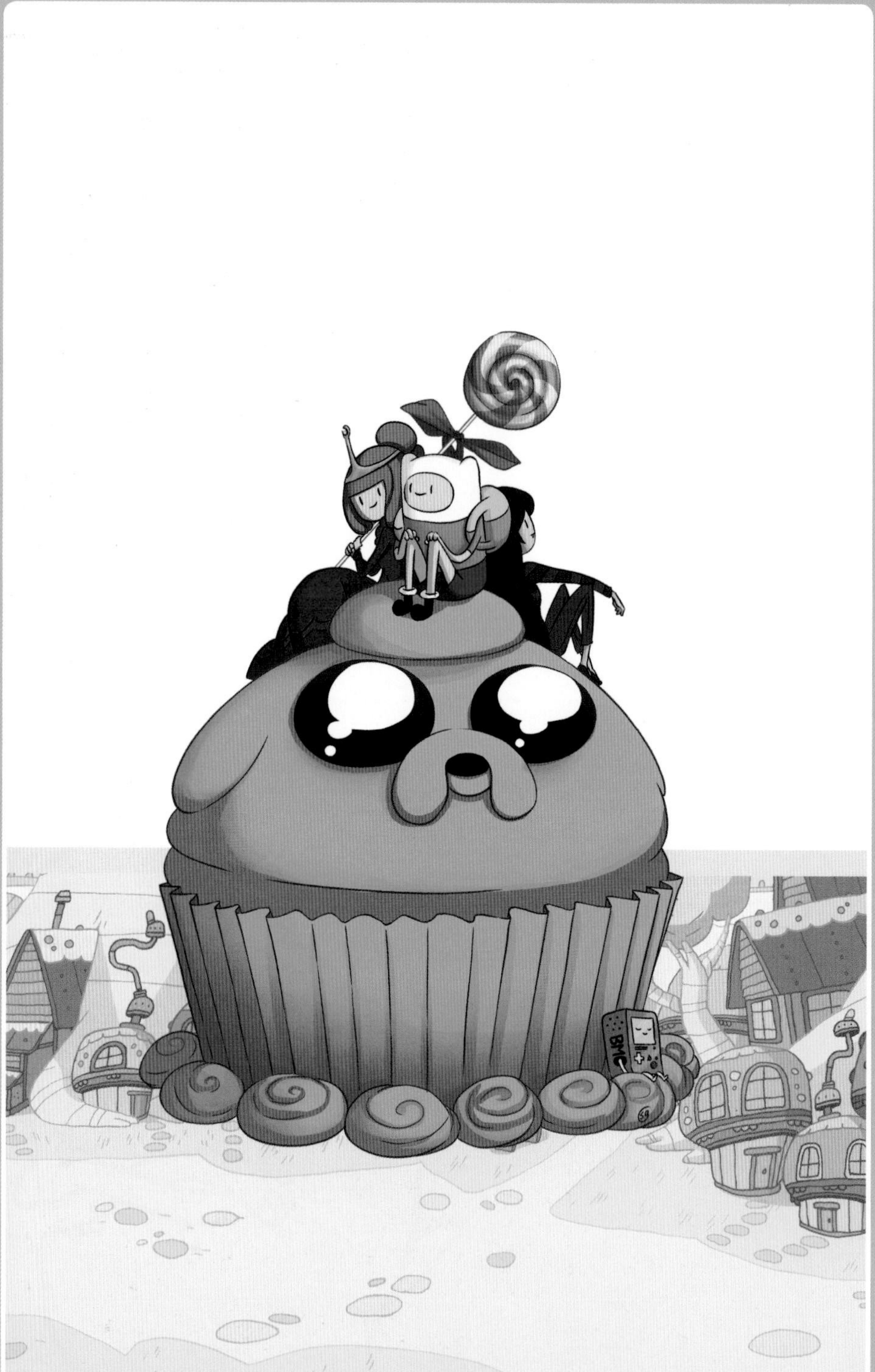
BMO

Adventure Time: Eye Candy Vol. 1 Cover by **Paul Pope**

"The Summiteers"

Written and Illustrated by **Derek Fridolfs**

Colors by **Whitney Cogar** Letters by **Mad Rupert**

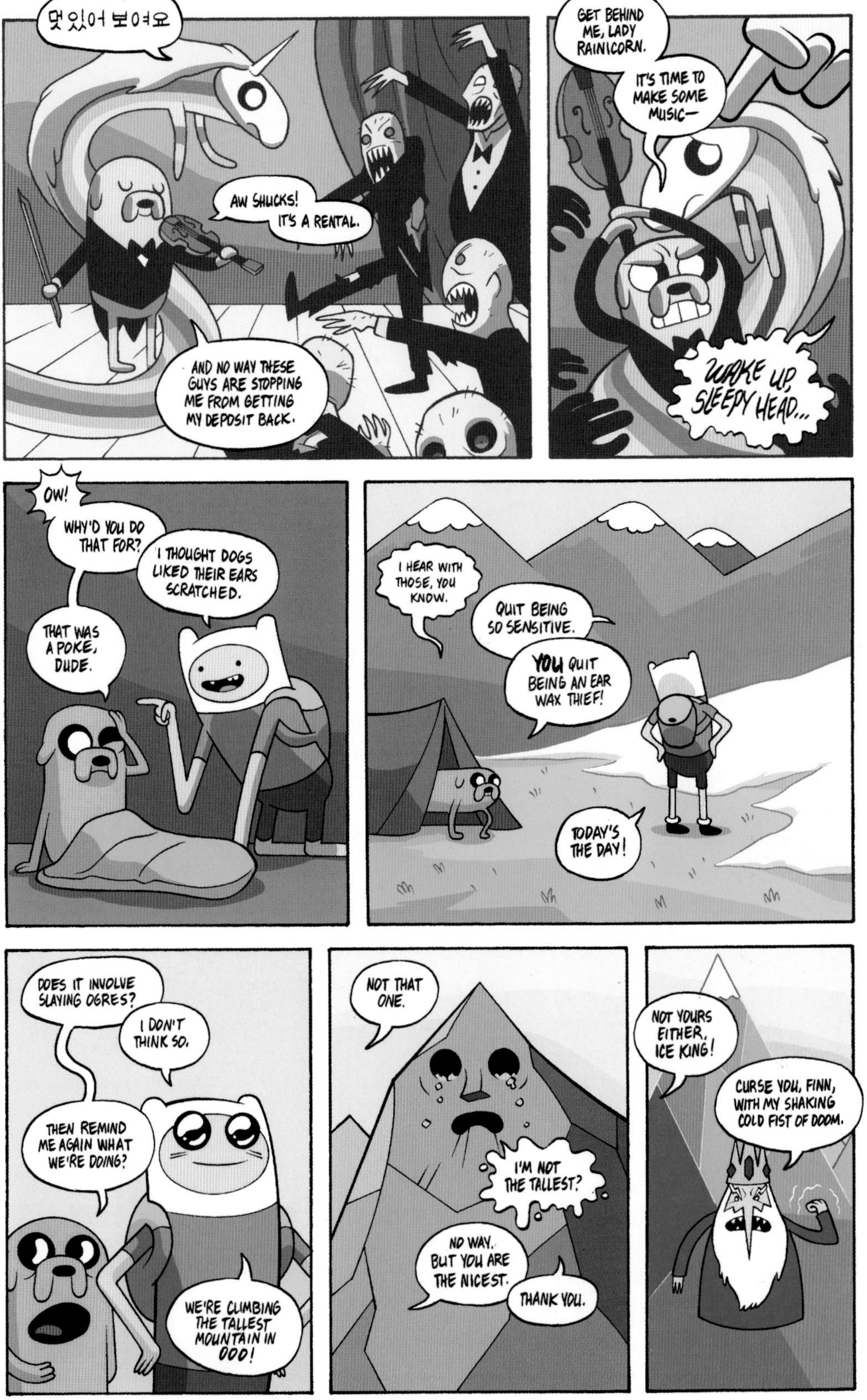

맛있어 보여요
AW SHUCKS! IT'S A RENTAL.
AND NO WAY THESE GUYS ARE STOPPING ME FROM GETTING MY DEPOSIT BACK.
GET BEHIND ME, LADY RAINICORN.
IT'S TIME TO MAKE SOME MUSIC—
WAKE UP, SLEEPY HEAD...
OW!
WHY'D YOU DO THAT FOR?
I THOUGHT DOGS LIKED THEIR EARS SCRATCHED.
THAT WAS A POKE, DUDE.
I HEAR WITH THOSE, YOU KNOW.
QUIT BEING SO SENSITIVE.
YOU QUIT BEING AN EAR WAX THIEF!
TODAY'S THE DAY!
DOES IT INVOLVE SLAYING OGRES?
I DON'T THINK SO.
THEN REMIND ME AGAIN WHAT WE'RE DOING?
WE'RE CLIMBING THE TALLEST MOUNTAIN IN OOO!
NOT THAT ONE.
I'M NOT THE TALLEST?
NO WAY. BUT YOU ARE THE NICEST.
THANK YOU.
NOT YOURS EITHER, ICE KING!
CURSE YOU, FINN, WITH MY SHAKING COLD FIST OF DOOM.

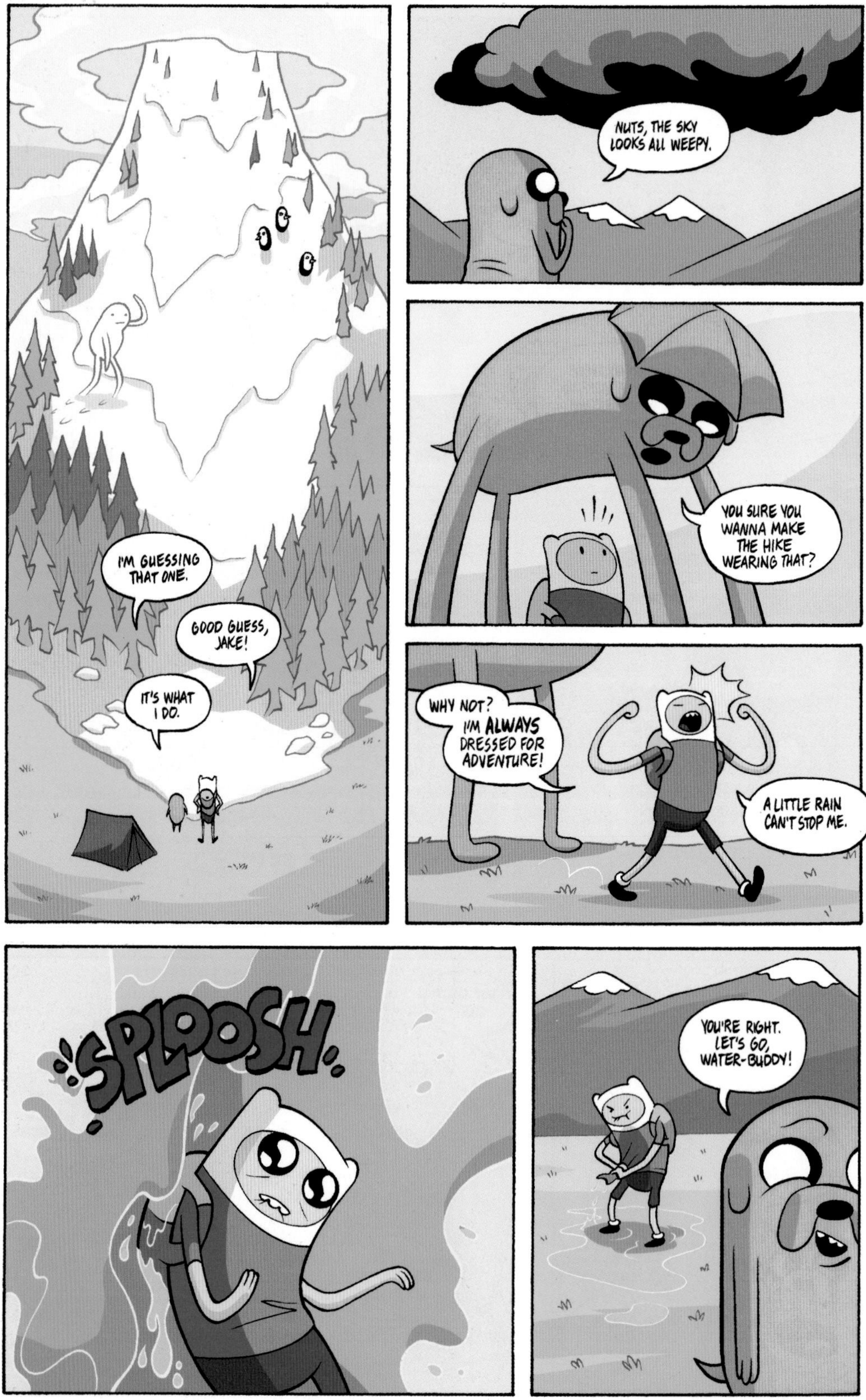
I'M GUESSING THAT ONE.
GOOD GUESS, JAKE!
IT'S WHAT I DO.
NUTS, THE SKY LOOKS ALL WEEPY.
YOU SURE YOU WANNA MAKE THE HIKE WEARING THAT?
WHY NOT? I'M ALWAYS DRESSED FOR ADVENTURE!
A LITTLE RAIN CAN'T STOP ME.
SPLOOSH
YOU'RE RIGHT. LET'S GO, WATER-BUDDY!

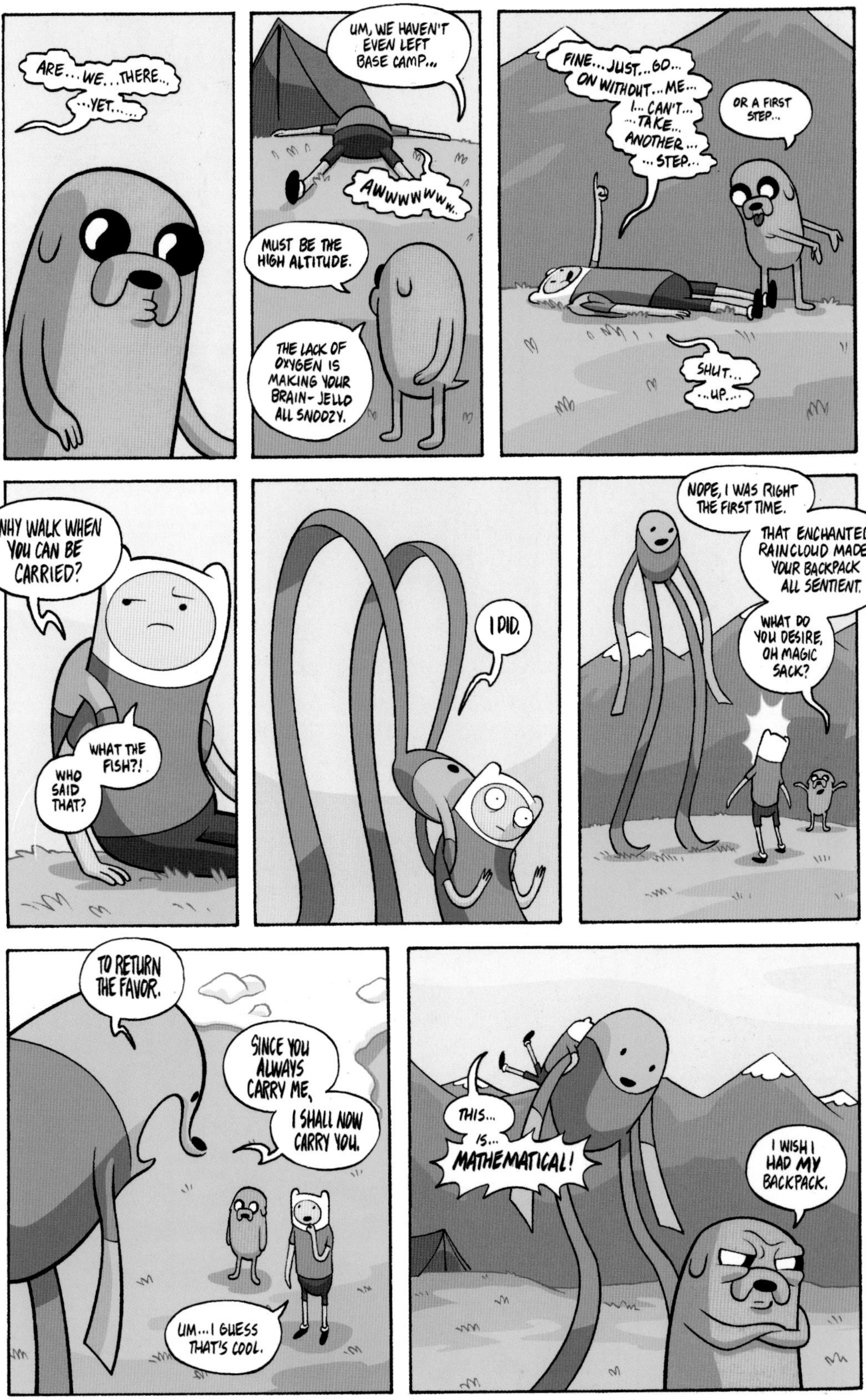

ARE... WE... THERE... ...YET.....
UM, WE HAVEN'T EVEN LEFT BASE CAMP...
AWWWWWWW...
MUST BE THE HIGH ALTITUDE.
THE LACK OF OXYGEN IS MAKING YOUR BRAIN-JELLO ALL SNOOZY.
FINE... JUST... GO... ON WITHOUT... ME... I... CAN'T... ...TAKE... ANOTHER... ...STEP...
OR A FIRST STEP...
SHUT... ...UP....
WHY WALK WHEN YOU CAN BE CARRIED?
WHO SAID THAT?
WHAT THE FISH?!
I DID.
NOPE, I WAS RIGHT THE FIRST TIME.
THAT ENCHANTED RAINCLOUD MADE YOUR BACKPACK ALL SENTIENT.
WHAT DO YOU DESIRE, OH MAGIC SACK?
TO RETURN THE FAVOR.
SINCE YOU ALWAYS CARRY ME,
I SHALL NOW CARRY YOU.
UM... I GUESS THAT'S COOL.
THIS... IS... MATHEMATICAL!
I WISH I HAD MY BACKPACK.

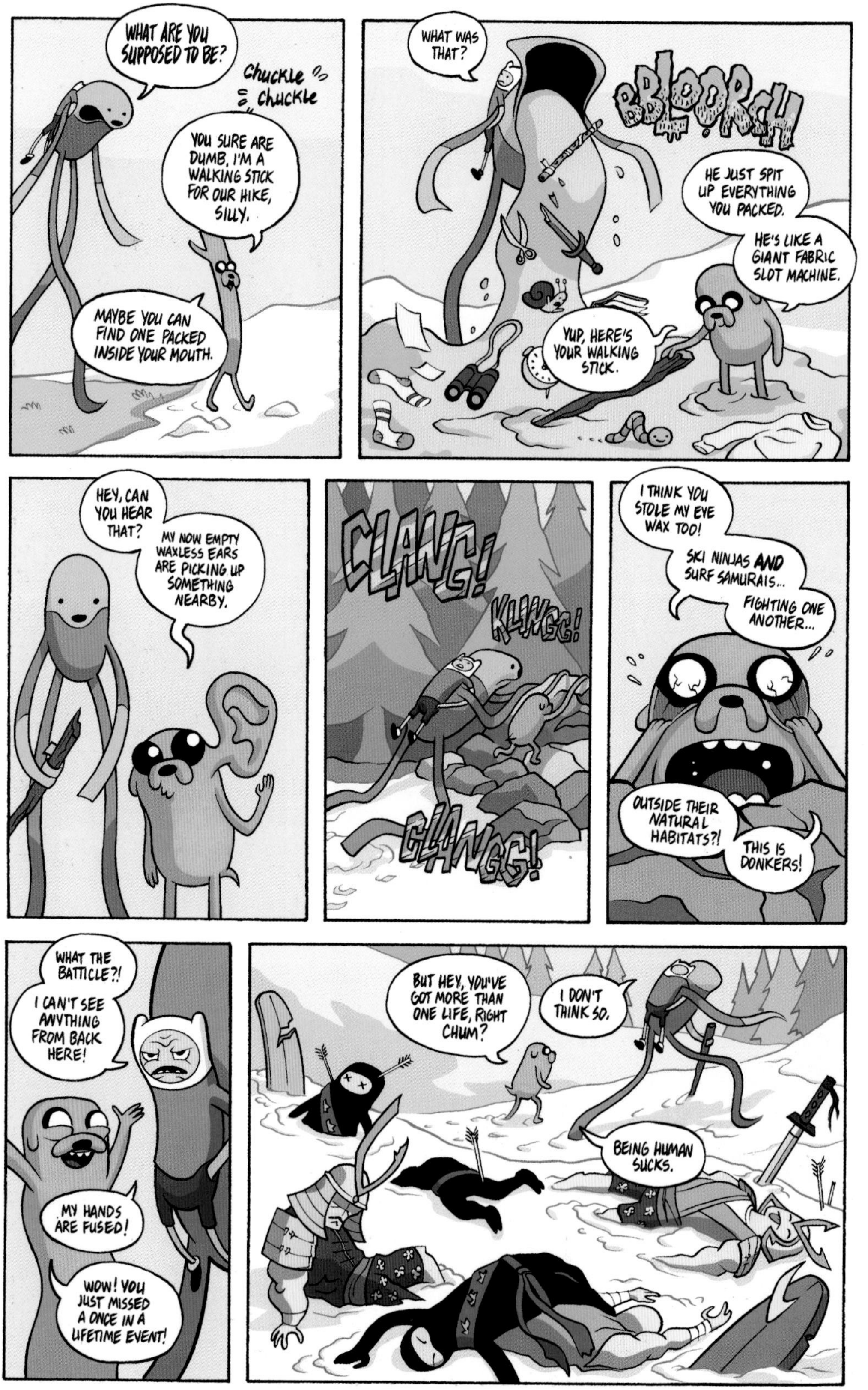
WHAT ARE YOU SUPPOSED TO BE?
chuckle chuckle
YOU SURE ARE DUMB, I'M A WALKING STICK FOR OUR HIKE, SILLY.
MAYBE YOU CAN FIND ONE PACKED INSIDE YOUR MOUTH.
WHAT WAS THAT?
BBLOORGH
HE JUST SPIT UP EVERYTHING YOU PACKED.
HE'S LIKE A GIANT FABRIC SLOT MACHINE.
YUP, HERE'S YOUR WALKING STICK.
HEY, CAN YOU HEAR THAT?
MY NOW EMPTY WAXLESS EARS ARE PICKING UP SOMETHING NEARBY.
CLANG!
KLINGG!
CLANGG!
I THINK YOU STOLE MY EYE WAX TOO!
SKI NINJAS **AND** SURF SAMURAIS...
FIGHTING ONE ANOTHER...
OUTSIDE THEIR NATURAL HABITATS?!
THIS IS DONKERS!
WHAT THE BATTICLE?!
I CAN'T SEE ANYTHING FROM BACK HERE!
MY HANDS ARE FUSED!
WOW! YOU JUST MISSED A ONCE IN A LIFETIME EVENT!
BUT HEY, YOU'VE GOT MORE THAN ONE LIFE, RIGHT CHUM?
I DON'T THINK SO.
BEING HUMAN SUCKS.

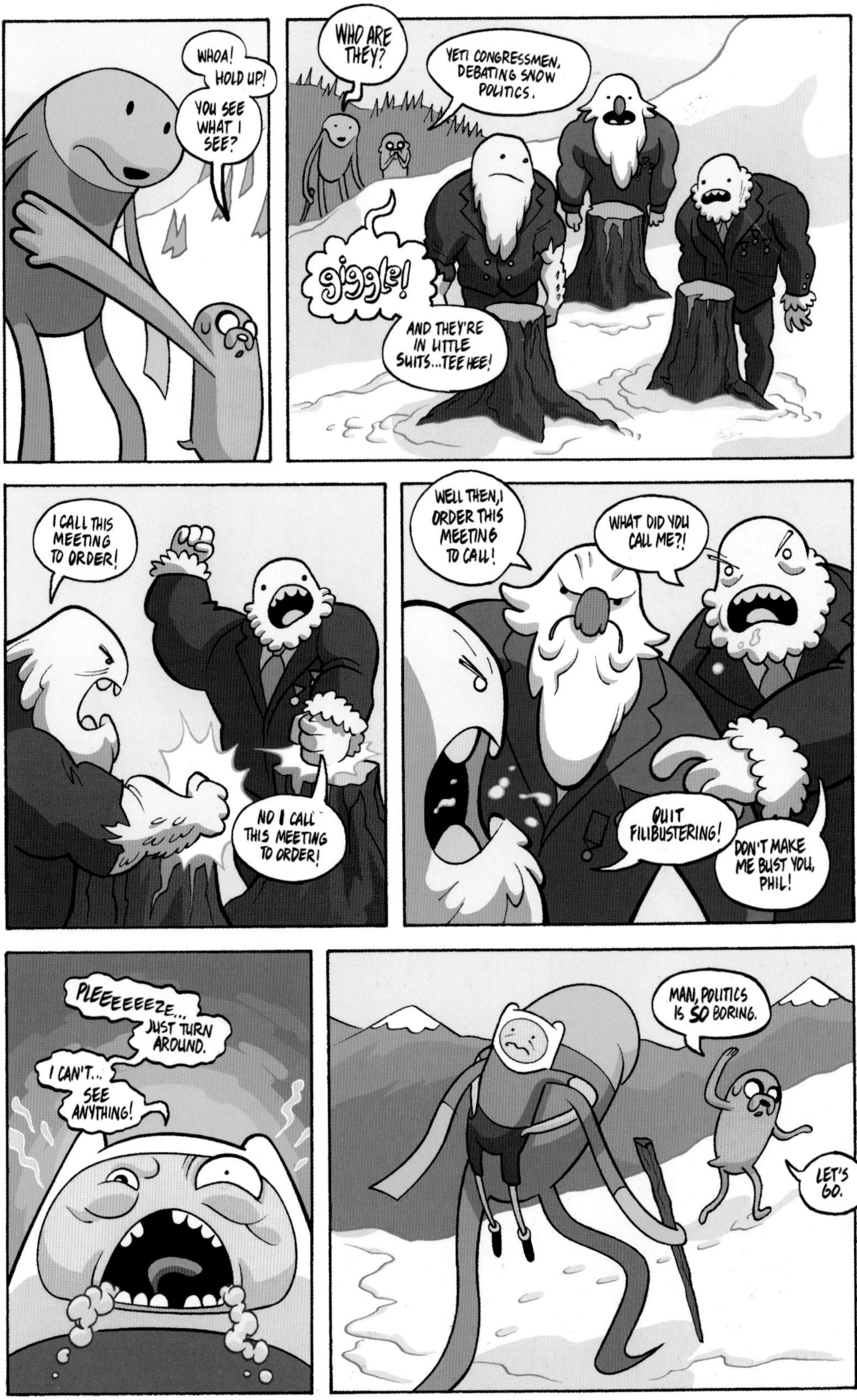
WHOA! HOLD UP!
YOU SEE WHAT I SEE?
WHO ARE THEY?
YETI CONGRESSMEN, DEBATING SNOW POLITICS.
giggle!
AND THEY'RE IN LITTLE SUITS...TEE HEE!
I CALL THIS MEETING TO ORDER!
NO I CALL THIS MEETING TO ORDER!
WELL THEN, I ORDER THIS MEETING TO CALL!
WHAT DID YOU CALL ME?!
QUIT FILIBUSTERING!
DON'T MAKE ME BUST YOU, PHIL!
PLEEEEEEZE... JUST TURN AROUND.
I CAN'T... SEE ANYTHING!
MAN, POLITICS IS SO BORING.
LET'S GO.

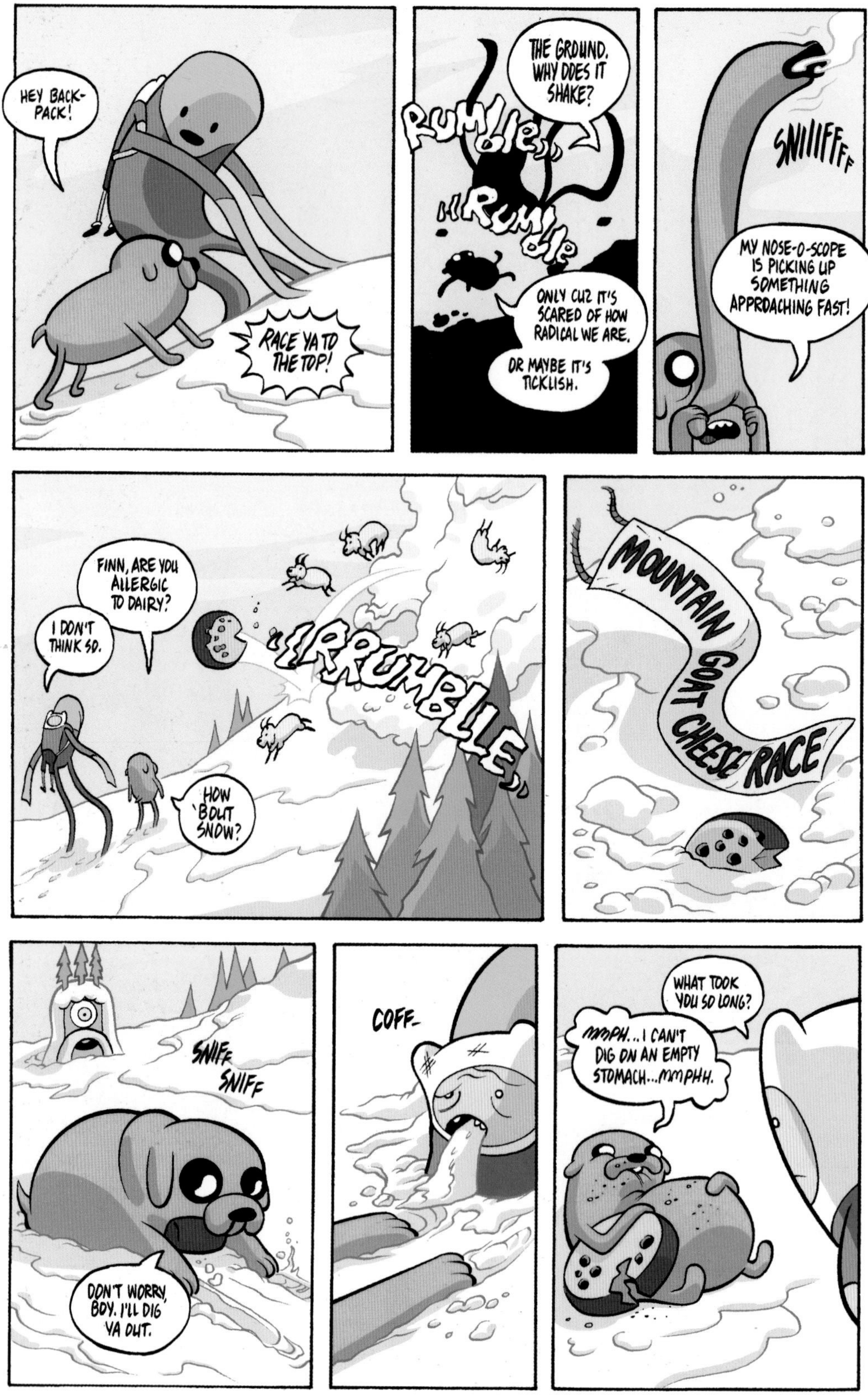
HEY BACK-PACK!
RACE YA TO THE TOP!
THE GROUND. WHY DOES IT SHAKE?
RUMBLE
RUMBLE
ONLY CUZ IT'S SCARED OF HOW RADICAL WE ARE.
OR MAYBE IT'S TICKLISH.
SNIIIFFFF
MY NOSE-O-SCOPE IS PICKING UP SOMETHING APPROACHING FAST!
FINN, ARE YOU ALLERGIC TO DAIRY?
I DON'T THINK SO.
RRUMBLLE
HOW 'BOUT SNOW?
MOUNTAIN GOAT CHEESE RACE
SNIFF SNIFF
DON'T WORRY, BOY. I'LL DIG YA OUT.
COFF
WHAT TOOK YOU SO LONG?
MMPH...I CAN'T DIG ON AN EMPTY STOMACH...MMPHH.

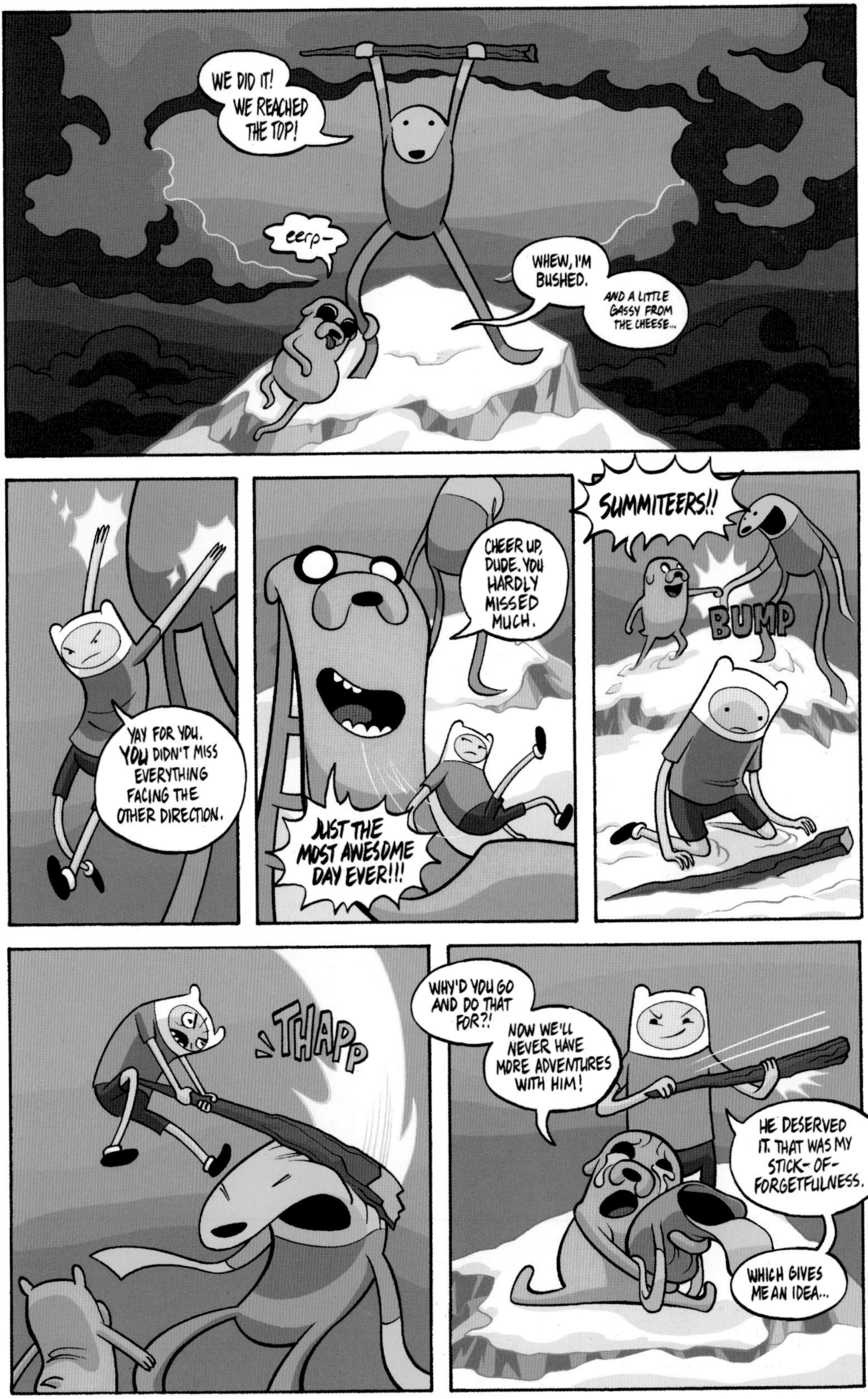
WE DID IT! WE REACHED THE TOP!
eerp-
WHEW, I'M BUSHED.
AND A LITTLE GASSY FROM THE CHEESE...
YAY FOR YOU. YOU DIDN'T MISS EVERYTHING FACING THE OTHER DIRECTION.
CHEER UP, DUDE. YOU HARDLY MISSED MUCH.
JUST THE MOST AWESOME DAY EVER!!!
SUMMITEERS!!
BUMP
THAPP
WHY'D YOU GO AND DO THAT FOR?!
NOW WE'LL NEVER HAVE MORE ADVENTURES WITH HIM!
HE DESERVED IT. THAT WAS MY STICK-OF-FORGETFULNESS.
WHICH GIVES ME AN IDEA...

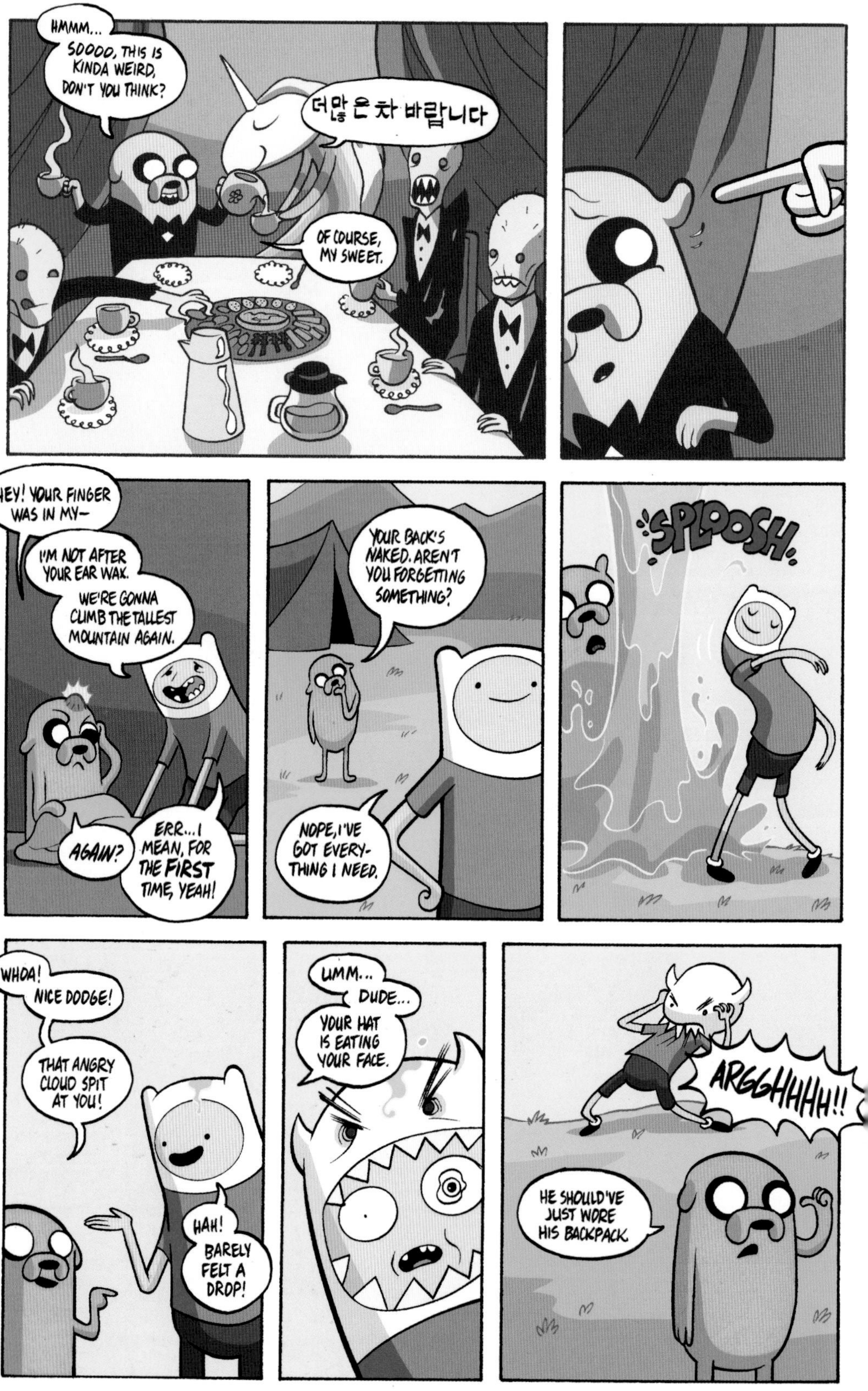
HMMM...
SOOOO, THIS IS KINDA WEIRD, DON'T YOU THINK?
더많은 차 바랍니다
OF COURSE, MY SWEET.
HEY! YOUR FINGER WAS IN MY—
I'M NOT AFTER YOUR EAR WAX.
WE'RE GONNA CLIMB THE TALLEST MOUNTAIN AGAIN.
AGAIN?
ERR...I MEAN, FOR THE FIRST TIME, YEAH!
YOUR BACK'S NAKED. AREN'T YOU FORGETTING SOMETHING?
NOPE, I'VE GOT EVERY-THING I NEED.
SPLOOSH
WHOA!
NICE DODGE!
THAT ANGRY CLOUD SPIT AT YOU!
HAH!
BARELY FELT A DROP!
UMM...
DUDE...
YOUR HAT IS EATING YOUR FACE.
ARGGHHHH!!
HE SHOULD'VE JUST WORE HIS BACKPACK.

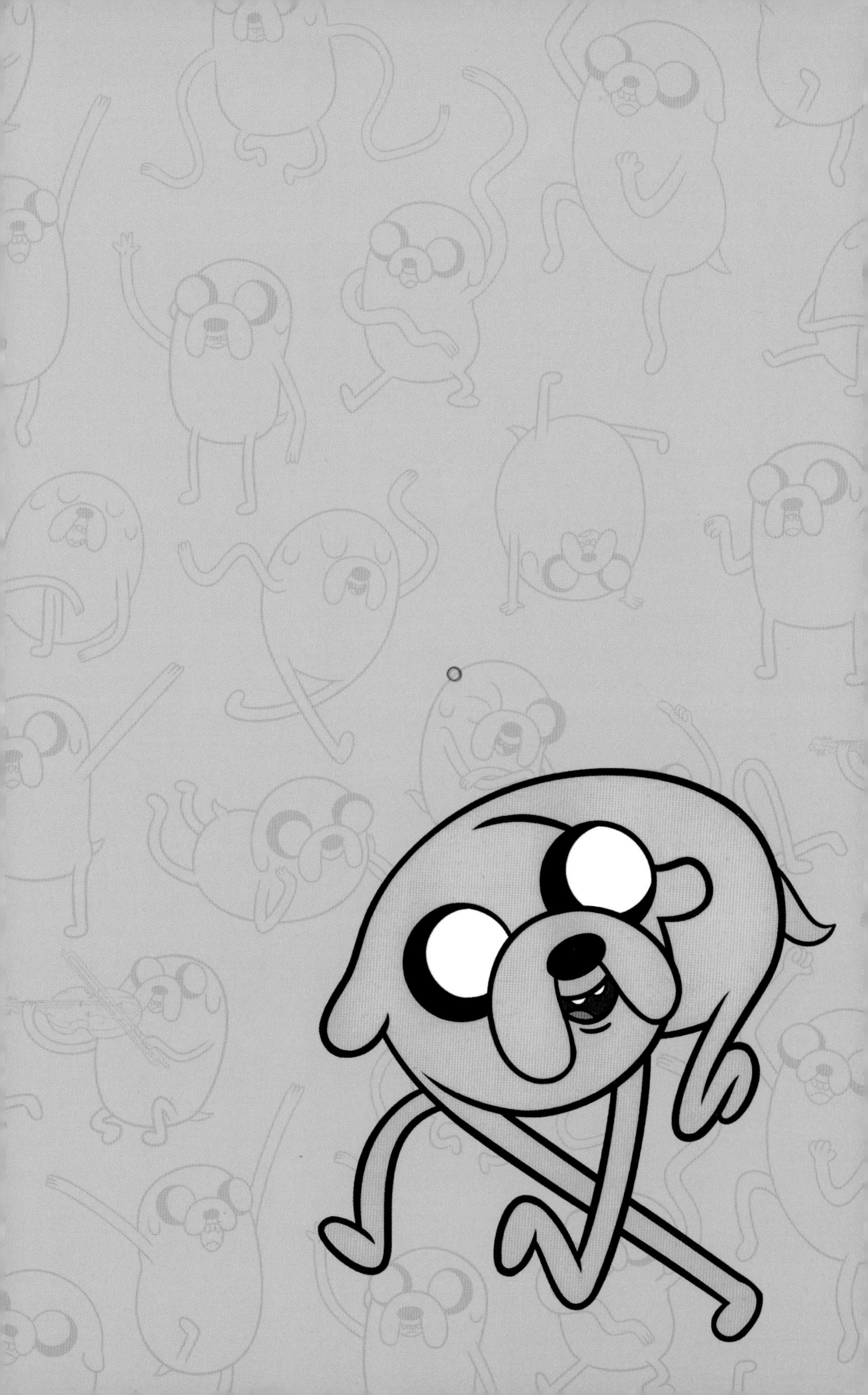

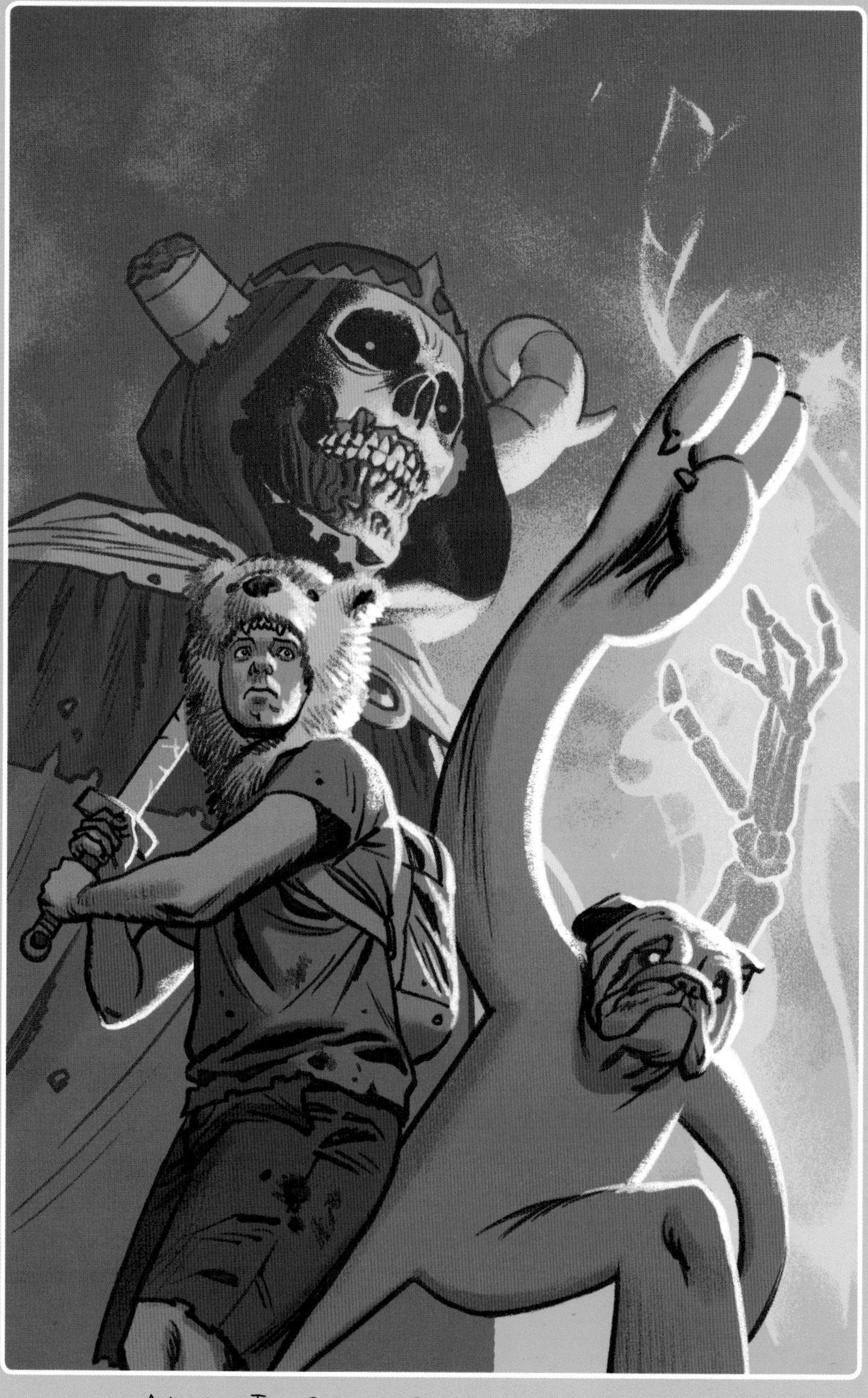

Adventure Time Comics #2 Cover by **Greg Smallwood**

"Dirty Dungeon"

Written and Illustrated by **Box Brown**

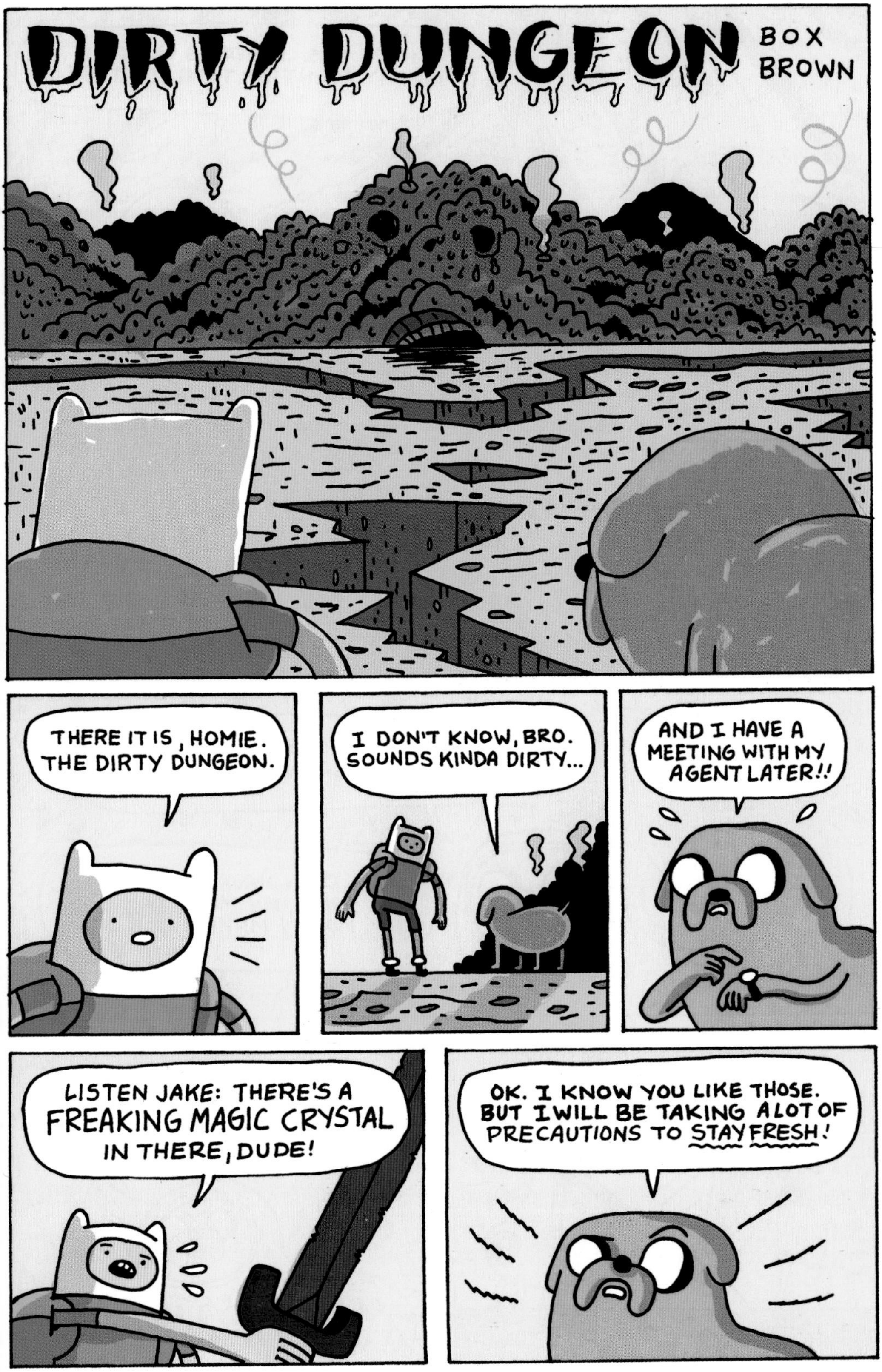
DIRTY DUNGEON
BOX BROWN
THERE IT IS, HOMIE. THE DIRTY DUNGEON.
I DON'T KNOW, BRO. SOUNDS KINDA DIRTY...
AND I HAVE A MEETING WITH MY AGENT LATER!!
LISTEN JAKE: THERE'S A FREAKING MAGIC CRYSTAL IN THERE, DUDE!
OK. I KNOW YOU LIKE THOSE. BUT I WILL BE TAKING A LOT OF PRECAUTIONS TO STAY FRESH!

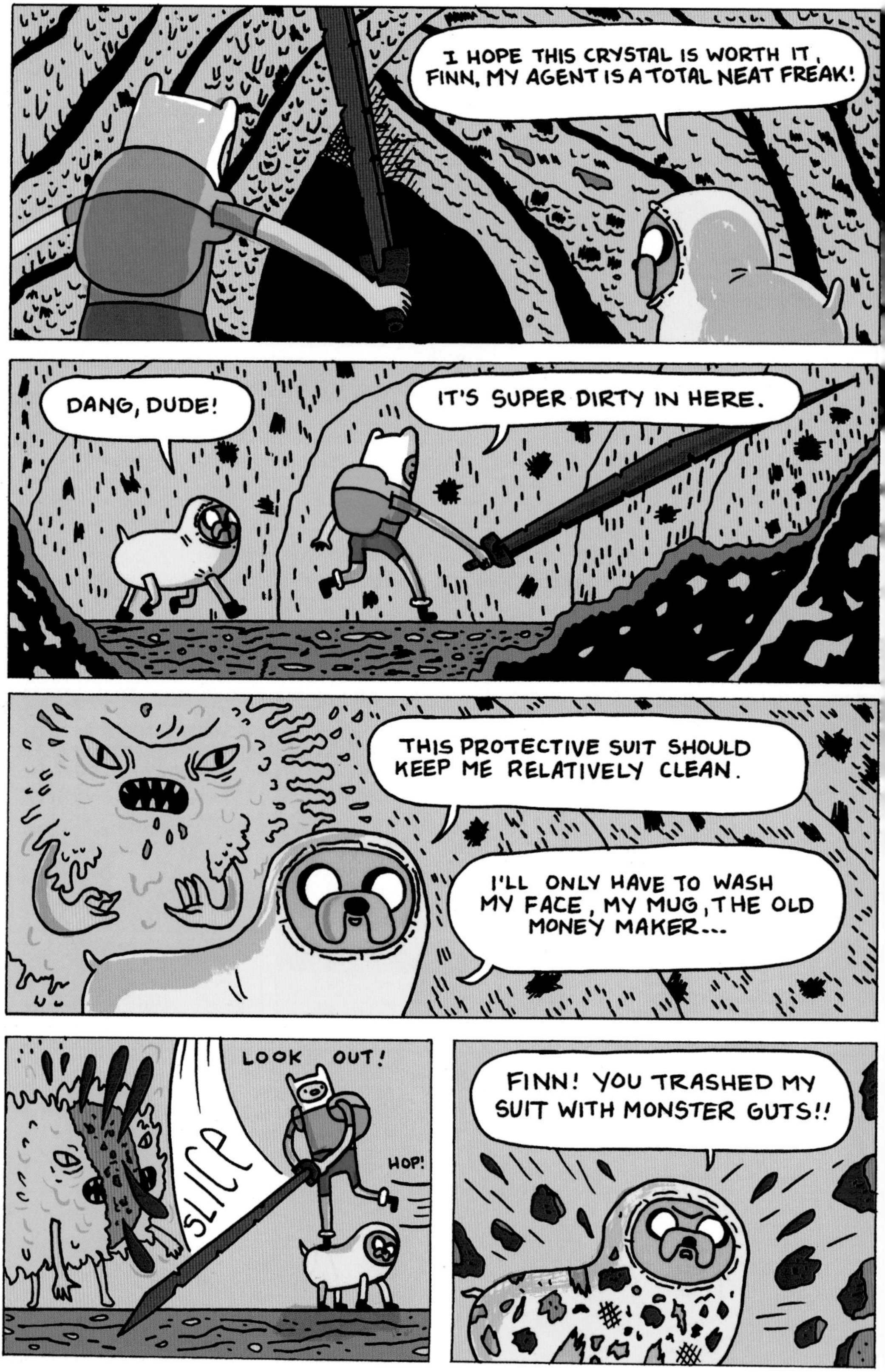
I HOPE THIS CRYSTAL IS WORTH IT, FINN, MY AGENT IS A TOTAL NEAT FREAK!
DANG, DUDE!
IT'S SUPER DIRTY IN HERE.
THIS PROTECTIVE SUIT SHOULD KEEP ME RELATIVELY CLEAN.
I'LL ONLY HAVE TO WASH MY FACE, MY MUG, THE OLD MONEY MAKER...
LOOK OUT!
SLICP
HOP!
FINN! YOU TRASHED MY SUIT WITH MONSTER GUTS!!

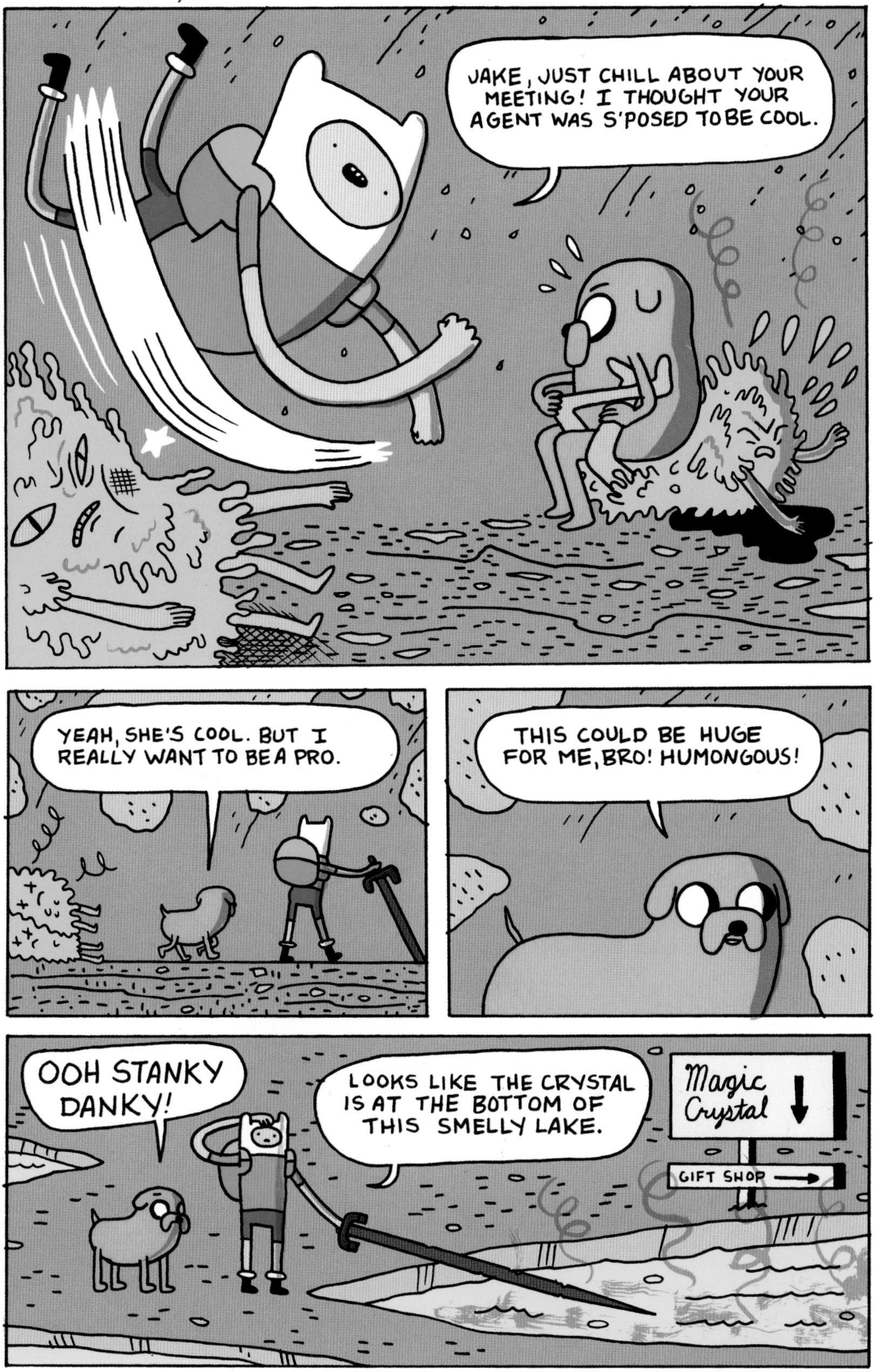
JAKE, JUST CHILL ABOUT YOUR MEETING! I THOUGHT YOUR AGENT WAS S'POSED TO BE COOL.
YEAH, SHE'S COOL. BUT I REALLY WANT TO BE A PRO.
THIS COULD BE HUGE FOR ME, BRO! HUMONGOUS!
OOH STANKY DANKY!
LOOKS LIKE THE CRYSTAL IS AT THE BOTTOM OF THIS SMELLY LAKE.
Magic Crystal
GIFT SHOP

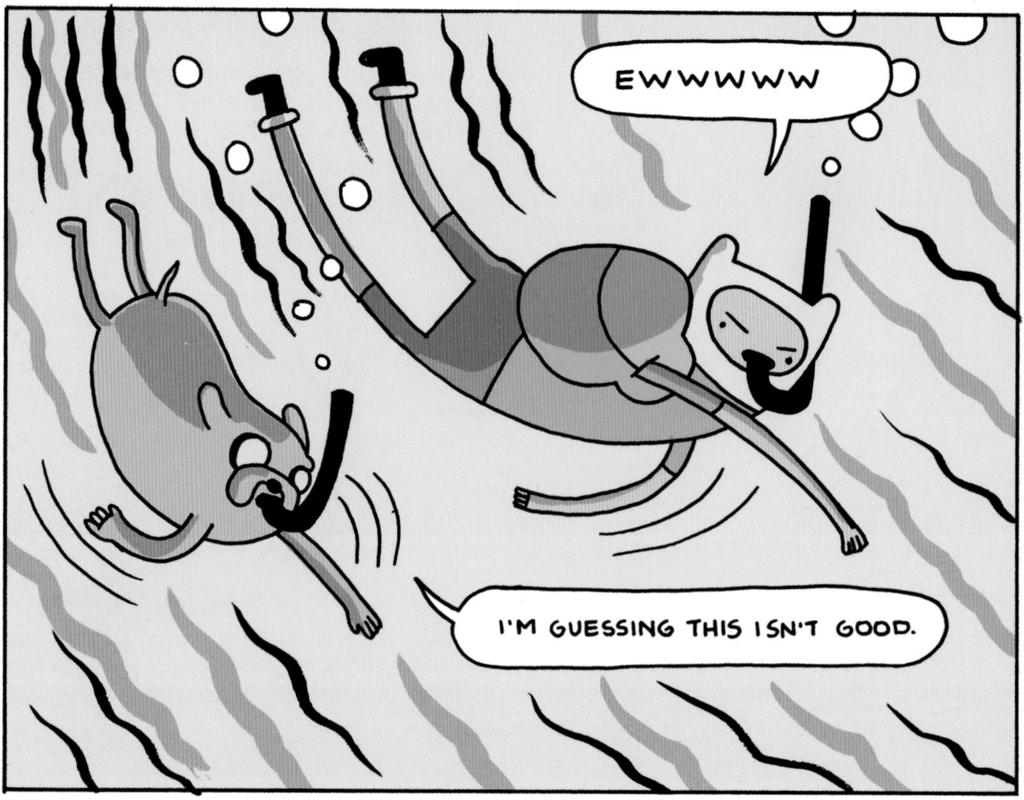
EWWWWW
I'M GUESSING THIS ISN'T GOOD.

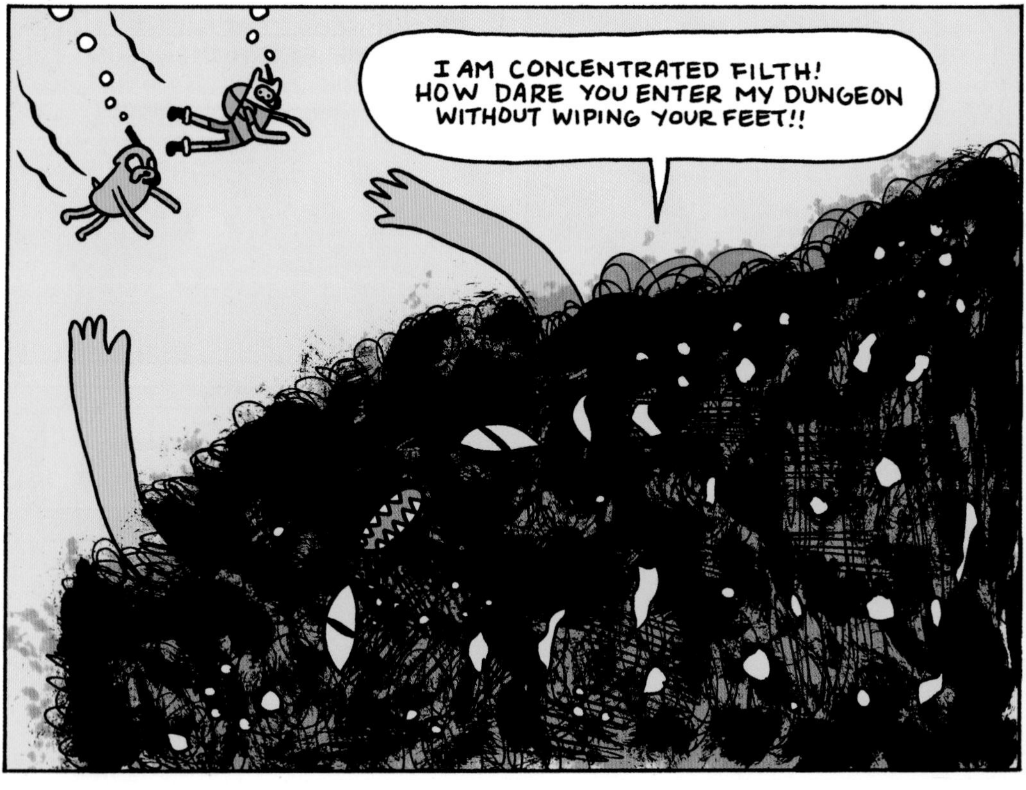
I AM CONCENTRATED FILTH! HOW DARE YOU ENTER MY DUNGEON WITHOUT WIPING YOUR FEET!!

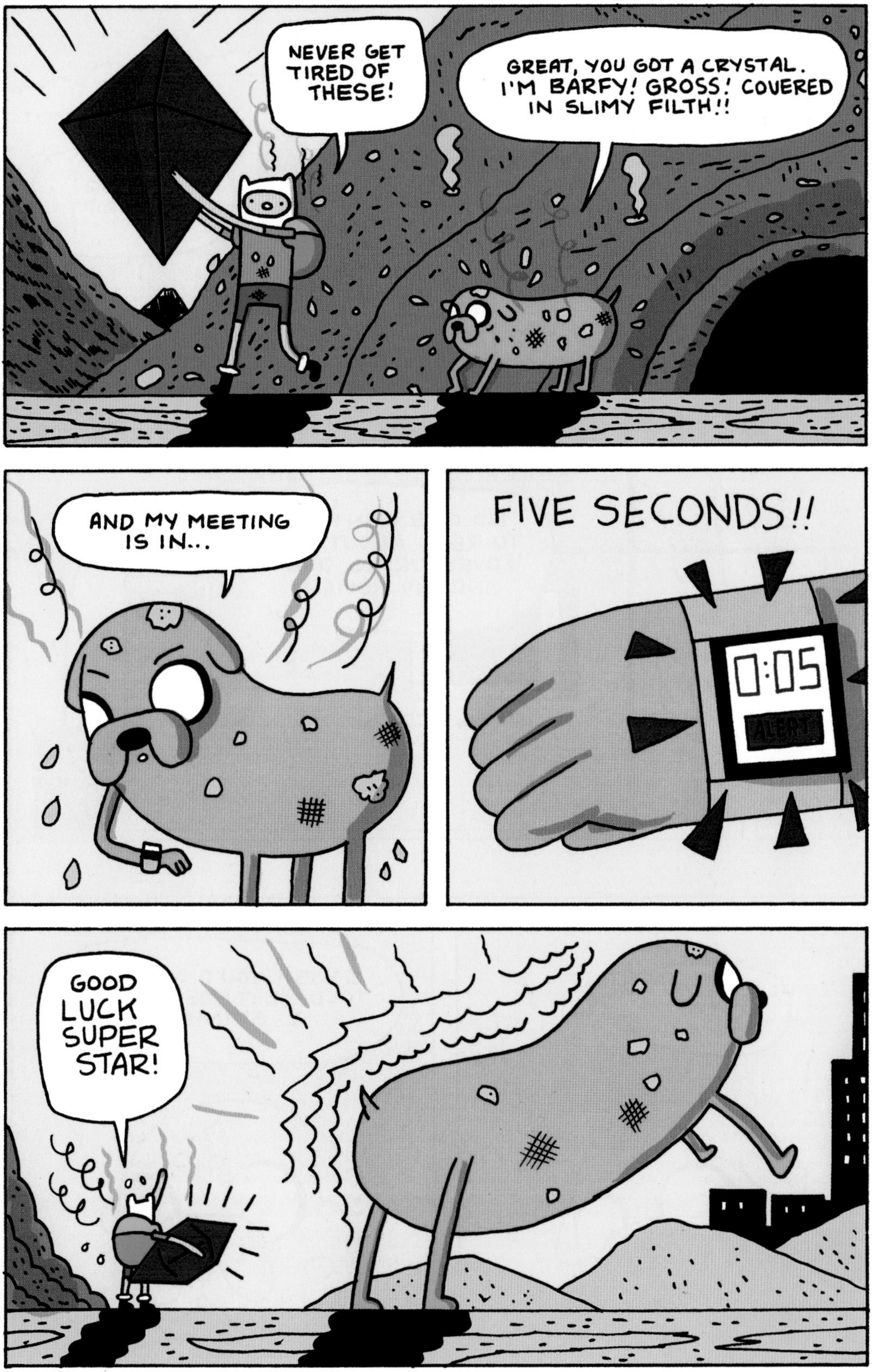
NEVER GET TIRED OF THESE!
GREAT, YOU GOT A CRYSTAL. I'M BARFY! GROSS! COVERED IN SLIMY FILTH!!
AND MY MEETING IS IN...
FIVE SECONDS!!
0:05
ALERT
GOOD LUCK SUPER STAR!

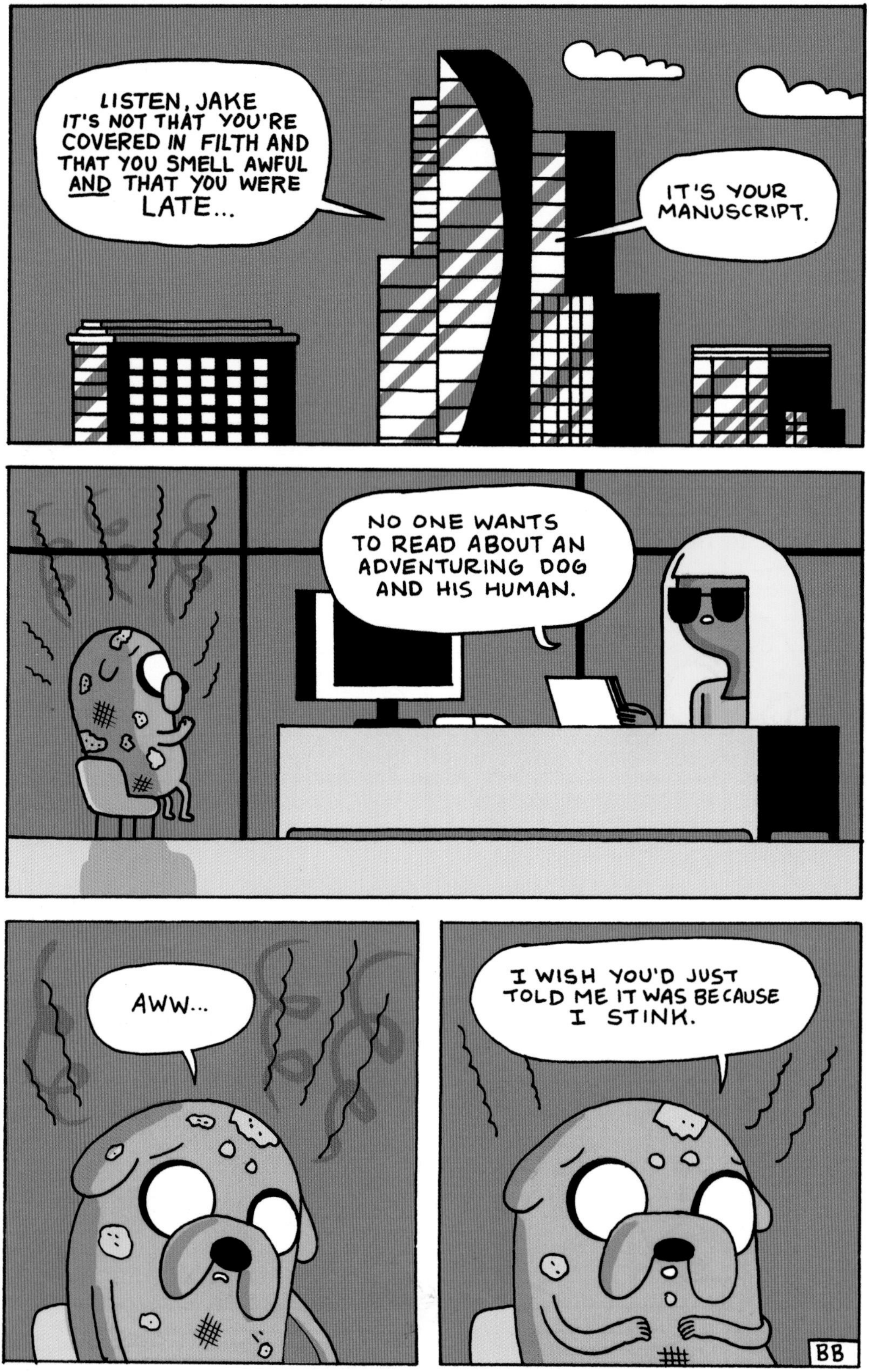
LISTEN, JAKE IT'S NOT THAT YOU'RE COVERED IN FILTH AND THAT YOU SMELL AWFUL AND THAT YOU WERE LATE...
IT'S YOUR MANUSCRIPT.
NO ONE WANTS TO READ ABOUT AN ADVENTURING DOG AND HIS HUMAN.
AWW...
I WISH YOU'D JUST TOLD ME IT WAS BECAUSE I STINK.
BB

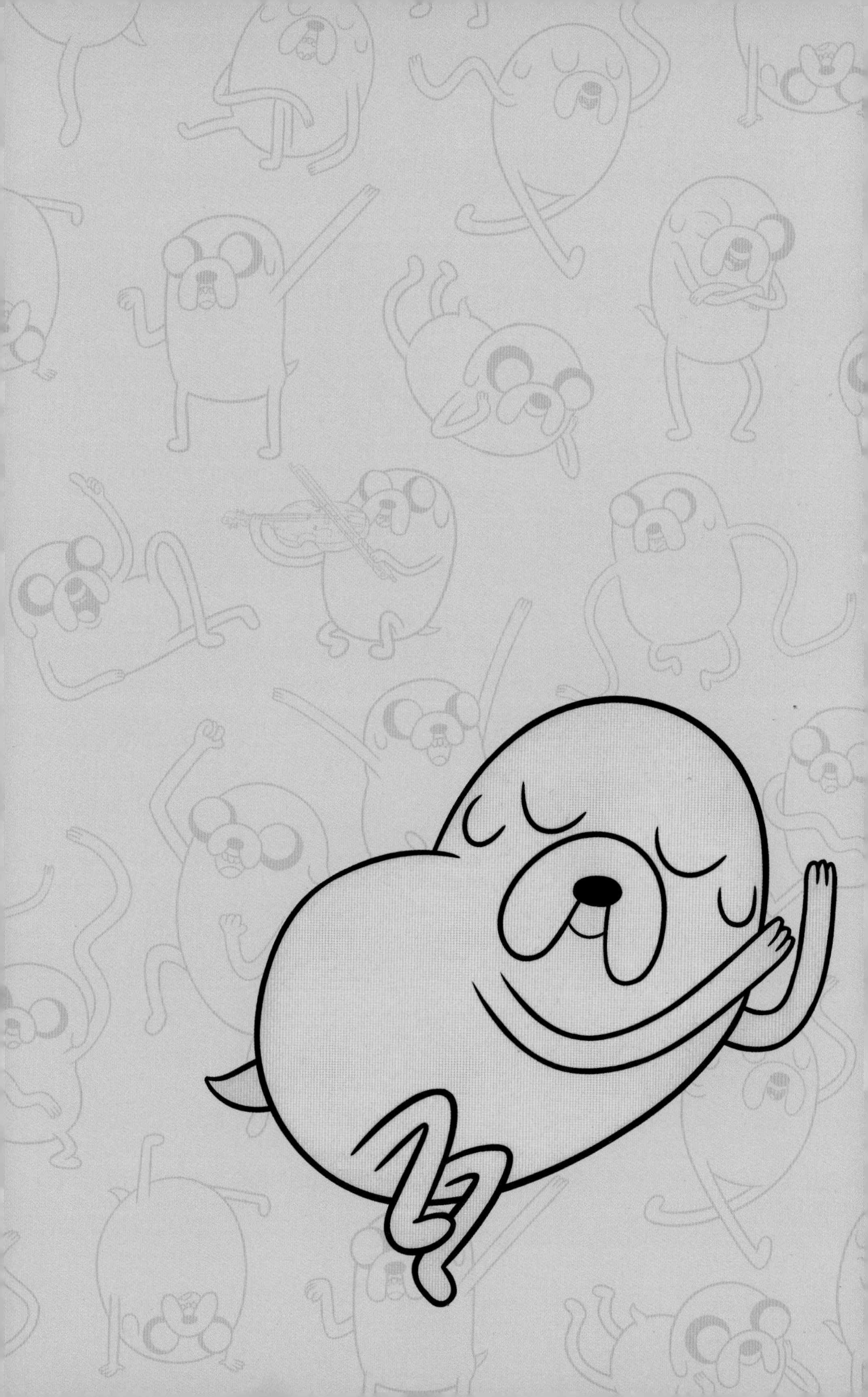

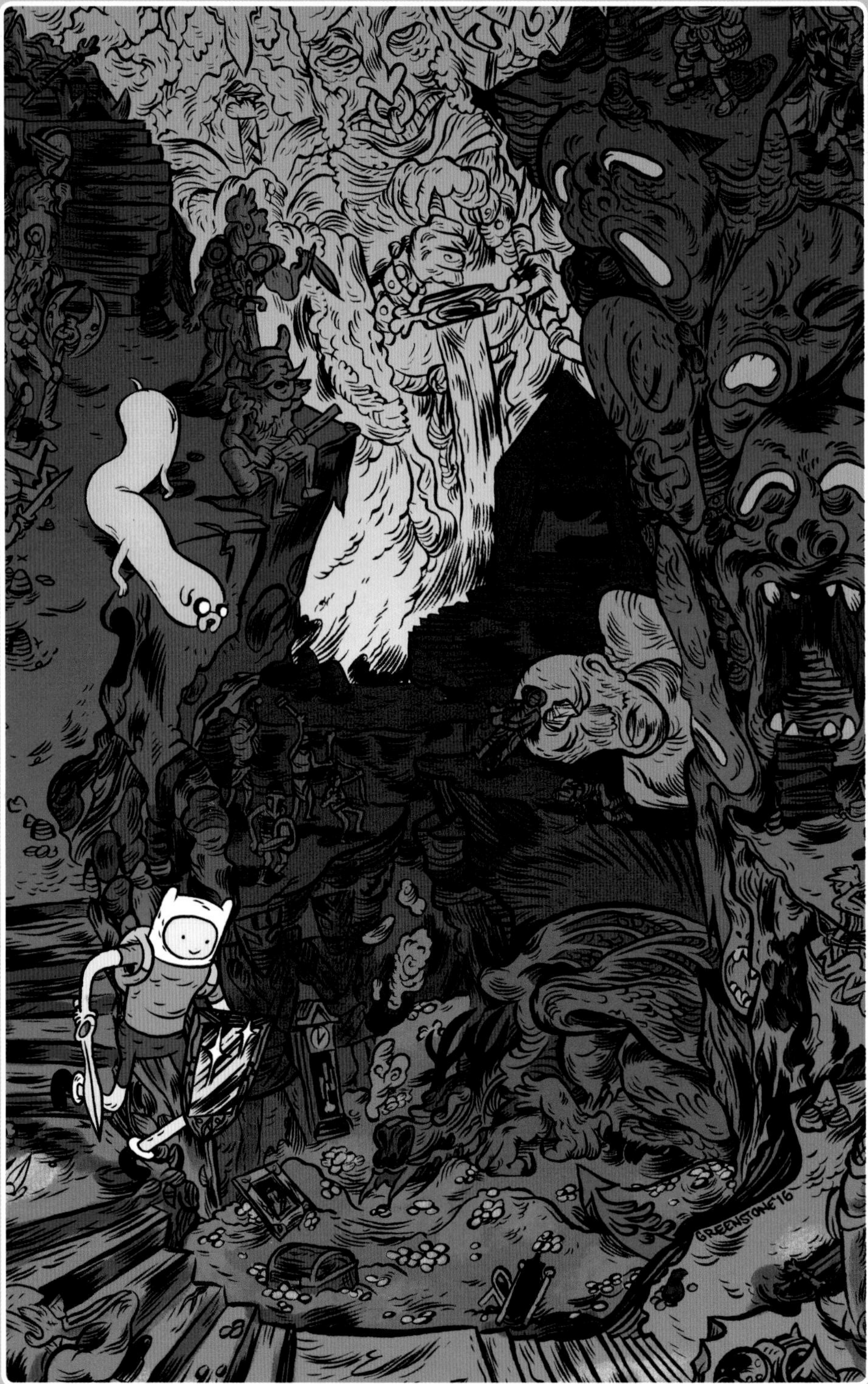
GREENSTONE'16

Adventure Time Comics #4 Subscription Cover by **Andrew Greenstone**

"To the North"

Written by **Nicole Andelfinger**

Illustrated by **Anissa Espinosa**

TO THE NORTH

WRITTEN BY: NICOLE ANDELFINGER
DRAWN BY: ANISSA ESPINOSA

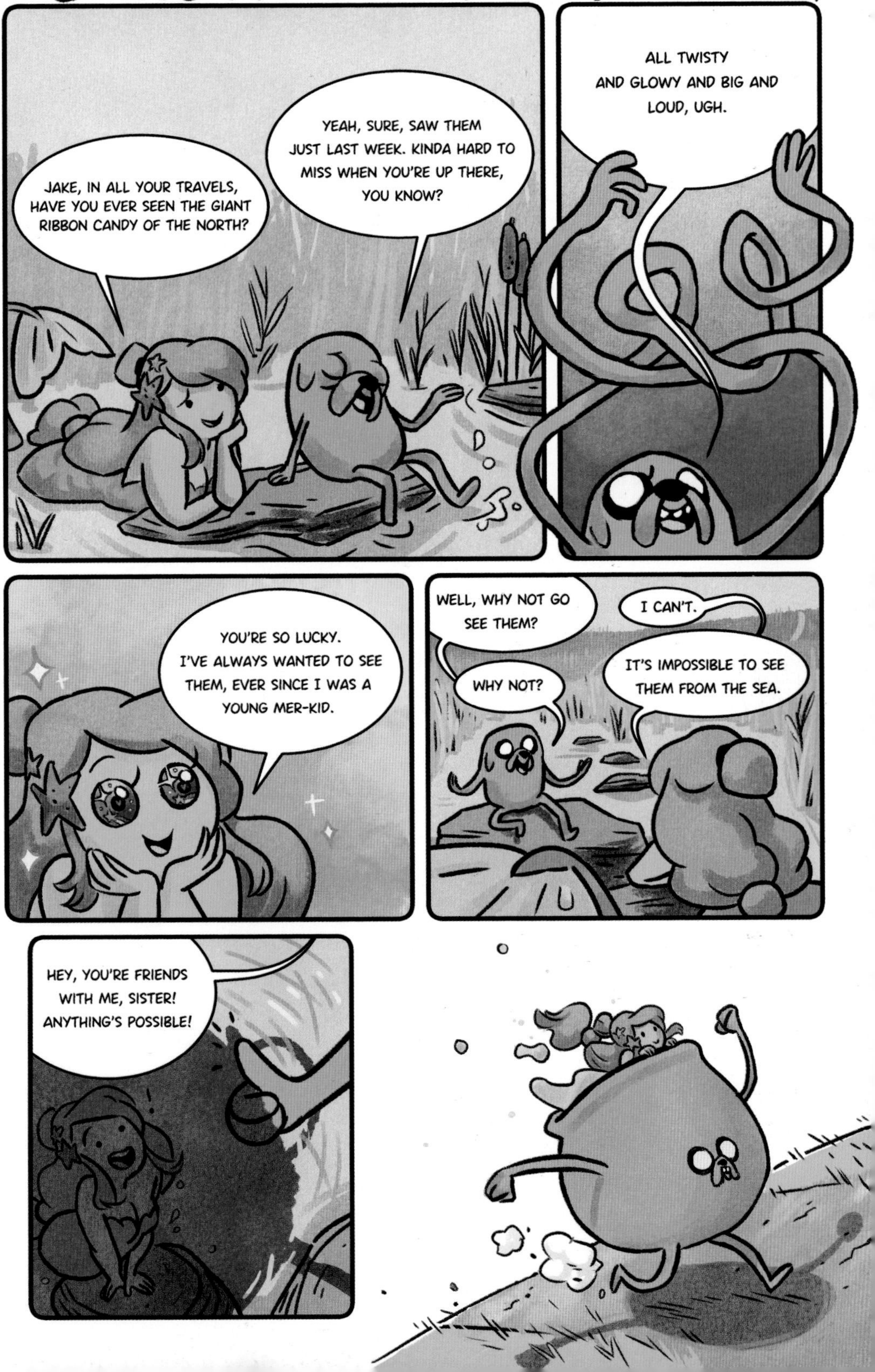
JAKE, IN ALL YOUR TRAVELS, HAVE YOU EVER SEEN THE GIANT RIBBON CANDY OF THE NORTH?
YEAH, SURE, SAW THEM JUST LAST WEEK. KINDA HARD TO MISS WHEN YOU'RE UP THERE, YOU KNOW?
ALL TWISTY AND GLOWY AND BIG AND LOUD, UGH.
YOU'RE SO LUCKY. I'VE ALWAYS WANTED TO SEE THEM, EVER SINCE I WAS A YOUNG MER-KID.
WELL, WHY NOT GO SEE THEM?
I CAN'T.
WHY NOT?
IT'S IMPOSSIBLE TO SEE THEM FROM THE SEA.
HEY, YOU'RE FRIENDS WITH ME, SISTER! ANYTHING'S POSSIBLE!

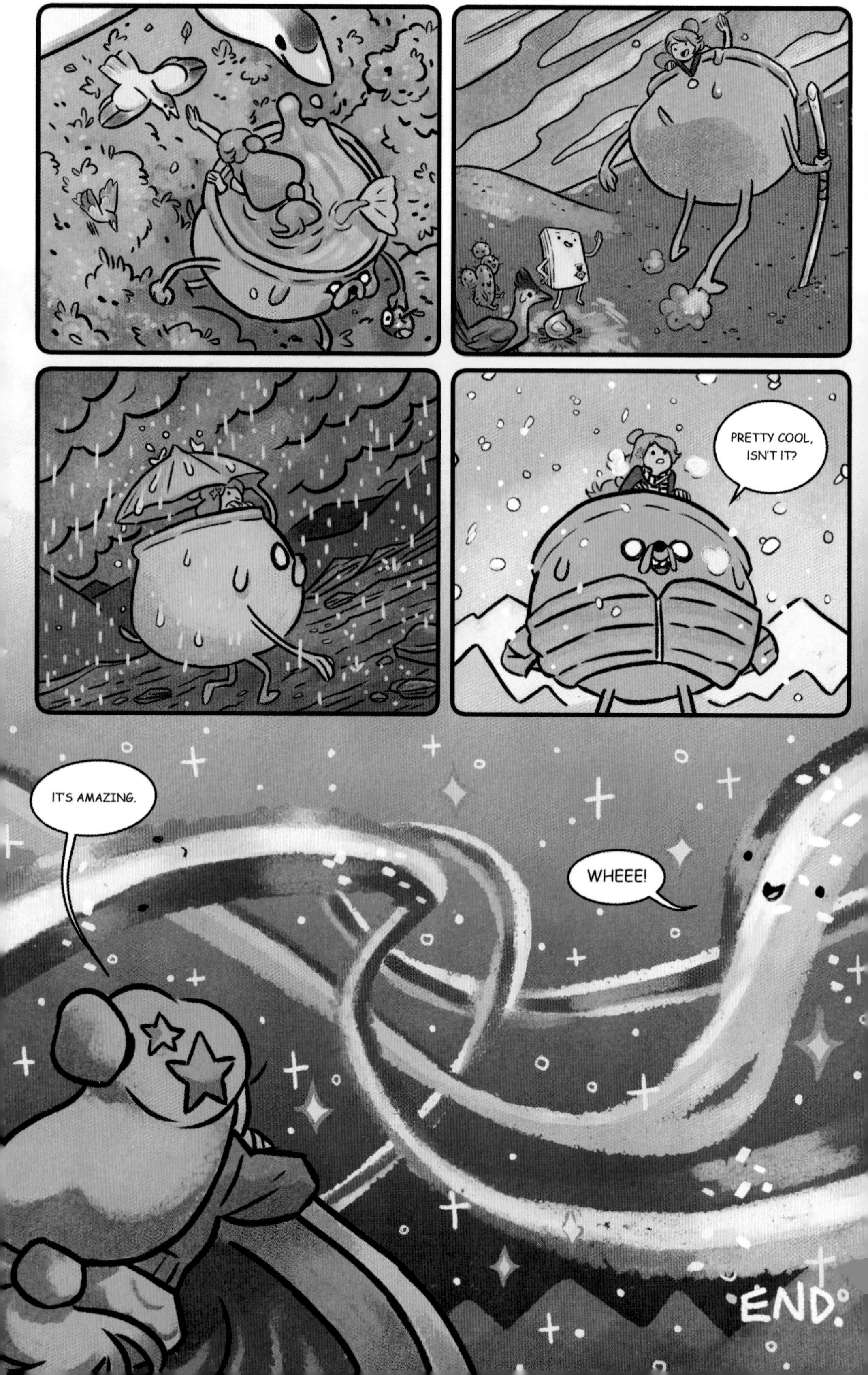
PRETTY COOL, ISN'T IT?
IT'S AMAZING.
WHEEE!
END.

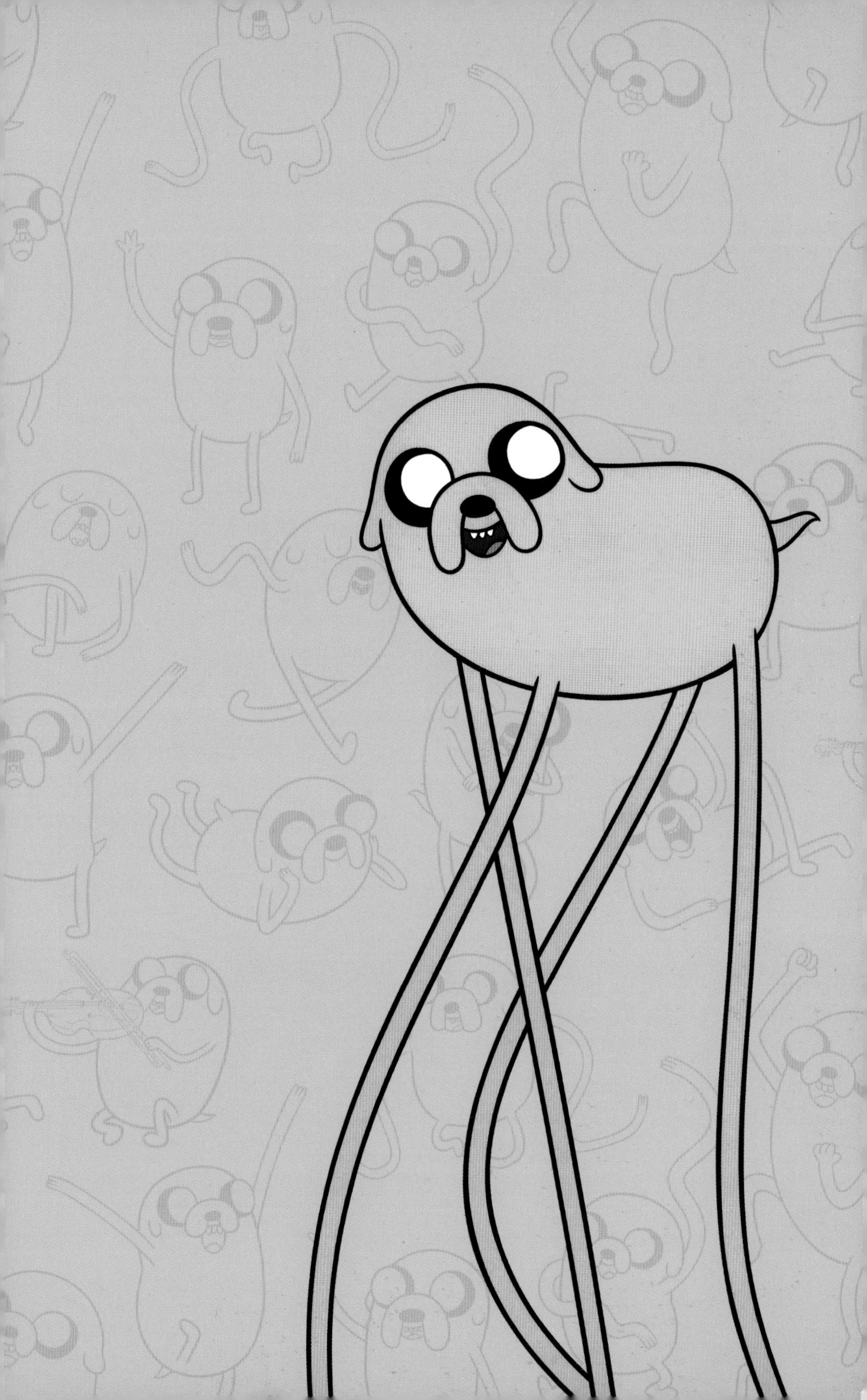

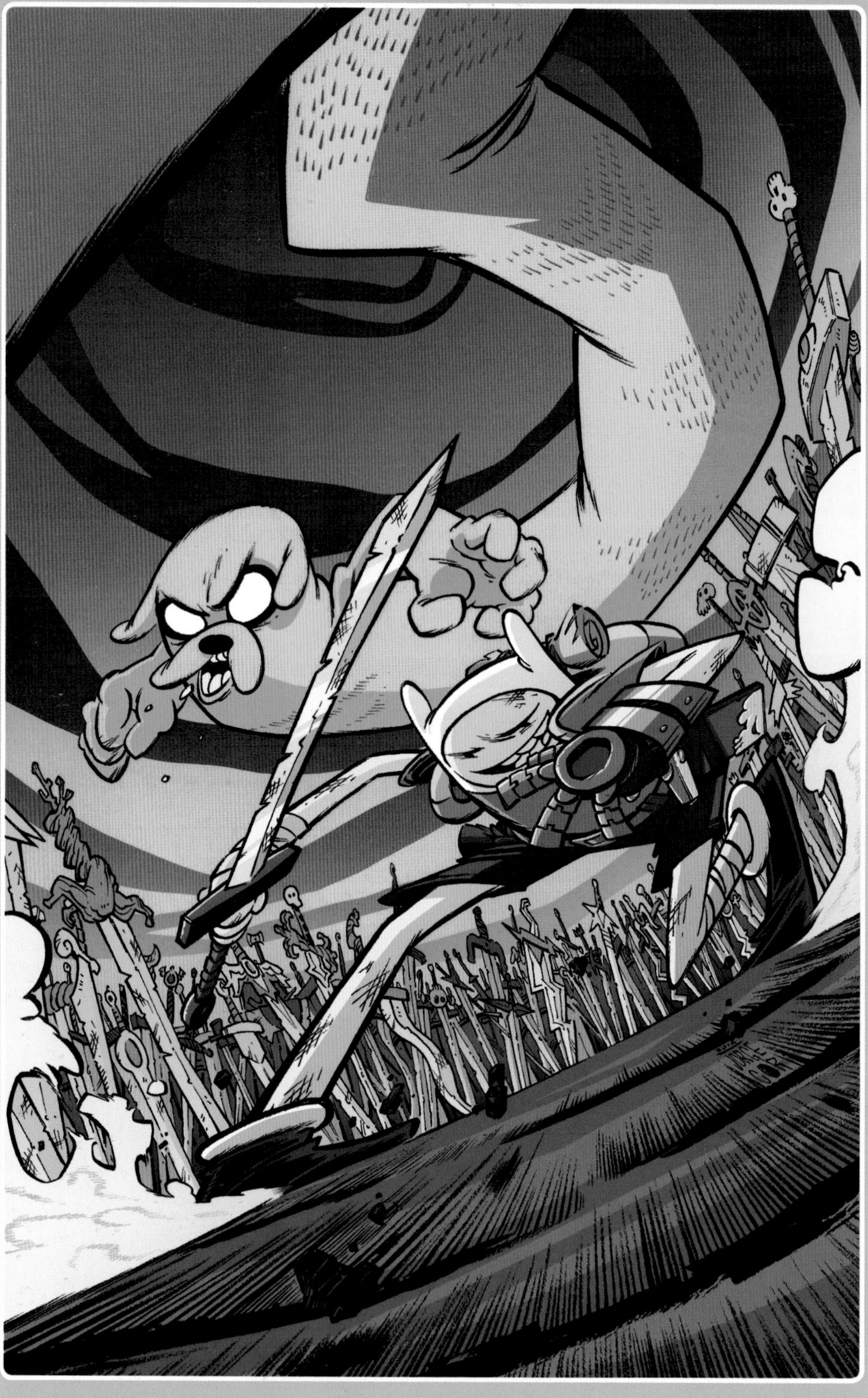

Adventure Time #50 Subscription Cover by **Jorge Corona**

"Stolen Youth"

Written by **Christopher Hastings** Illustrated by **Ian McGinty**

Colors by **Maarta Laiho** Letters by **Steve Wands**

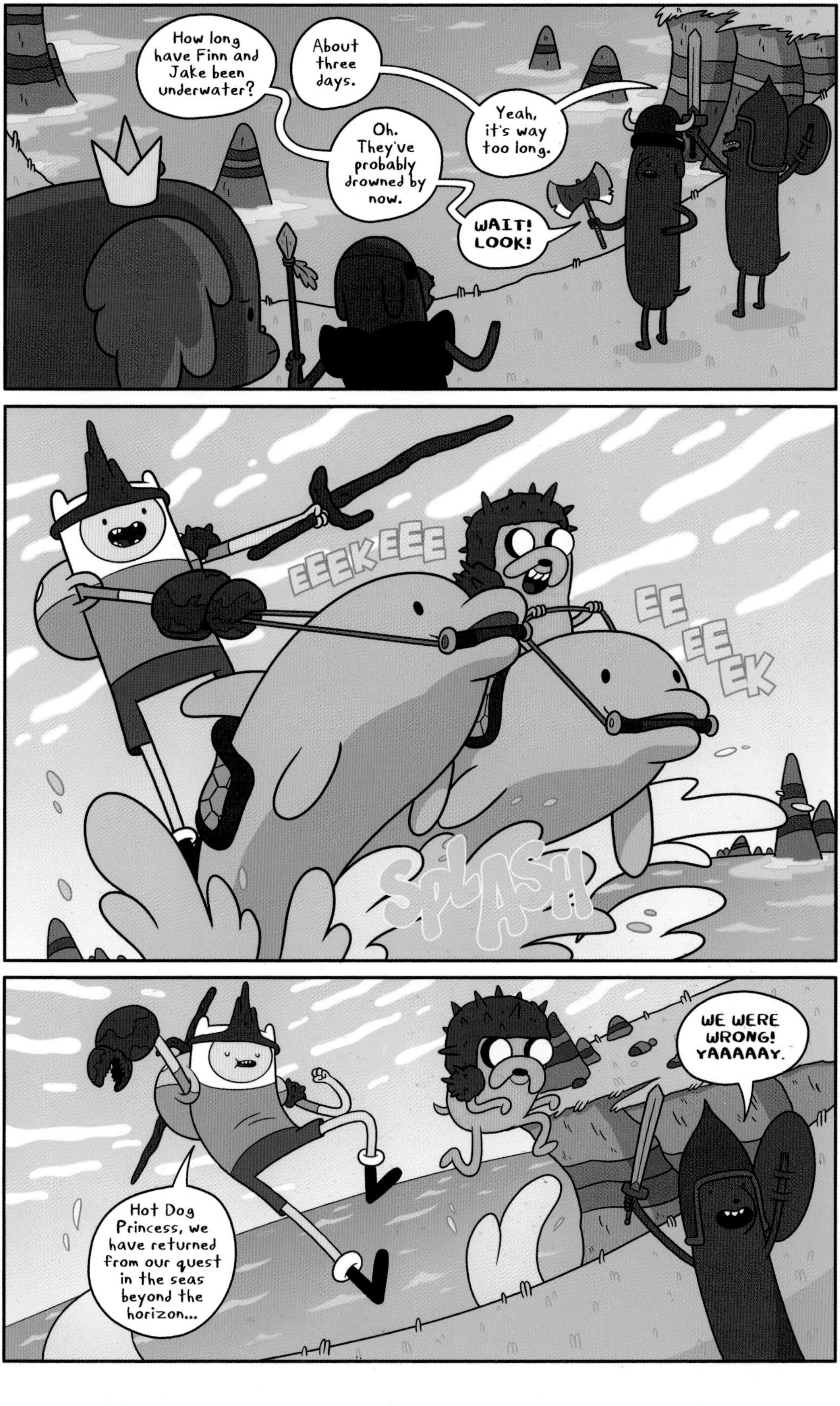
How long have Finn and Jake been underwater?
About three days.
Oh. They've probably drowned by now.
Yeah, it's way too long.
WAIT! LOOK!
EEEKEEE
EE EE EK
SPLASH
Hot Dog Princess, we have returned from our quest in the seas beyond the horizon...
WE WERE WRONG! YAAAAAY.

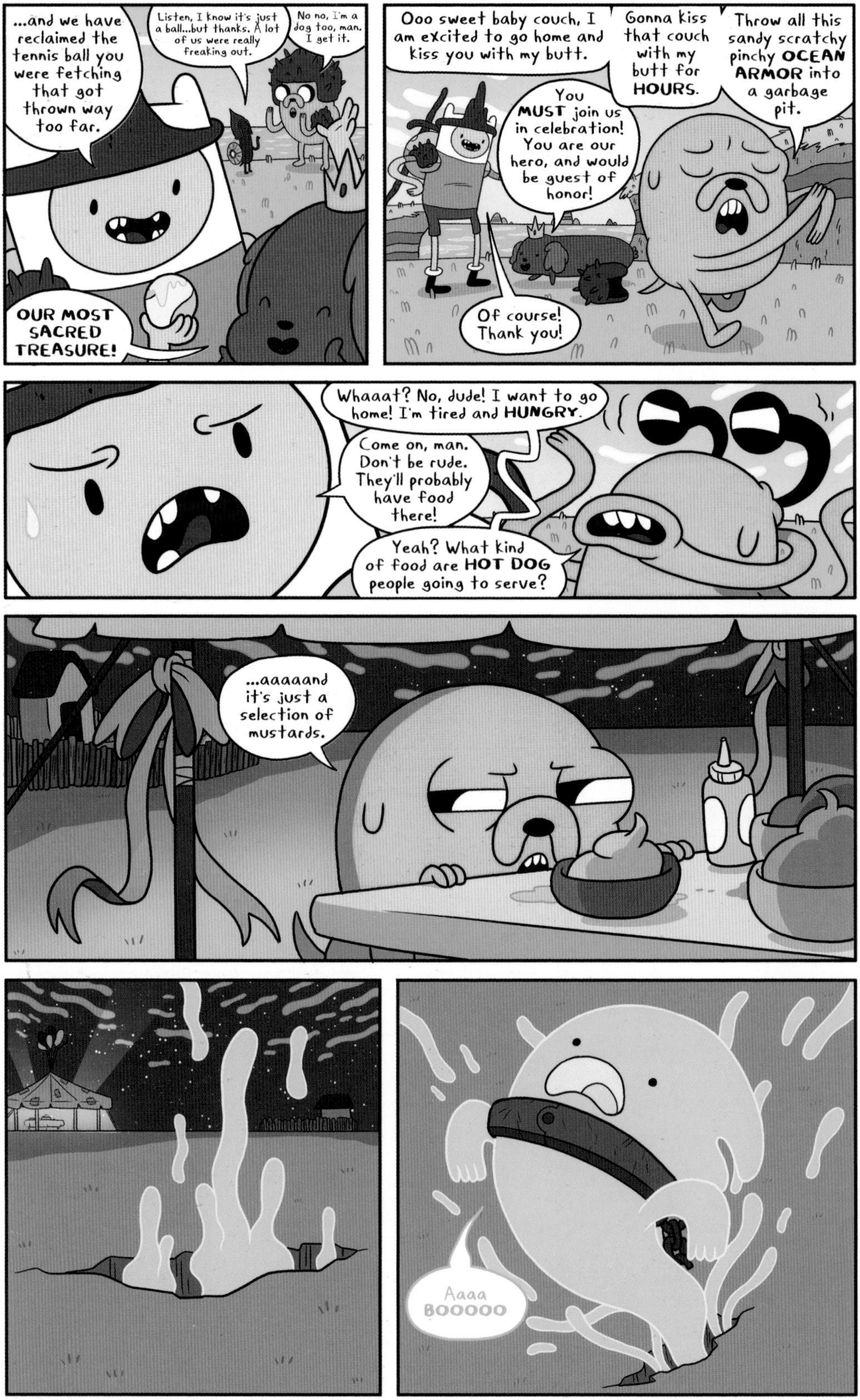
...and we have reclaimed the tennis ball you were fetching that got thrown way too far.
Listen, I know it's just a ball...but thanks. A lot of us were really freaking out.
No no, I'm a dog too, man. I get it.
OUR MOST SACRED TREASURE!
Ooo sweet baby couch, I am excited to go home and kiss you with my butt.
Gonna kiss that couch with my butt for HOURS.
Throw all this sandy scratchy pinchy OCEAN ARMOR into a garbage pit.
You MUST join us in celebration! You are our hero, and would be guest of honor!
Of course! Thank you!
Whaaat? No, dude! I want to go home! I'm tired and HUNGRY.
Come on, man. Don't be rude. They'll probably have food there!
Yeah? What kind of food are HOT DOG people going to serve?
...aaaaand it's just a selection of mustards.
Aaaa BOOOOO

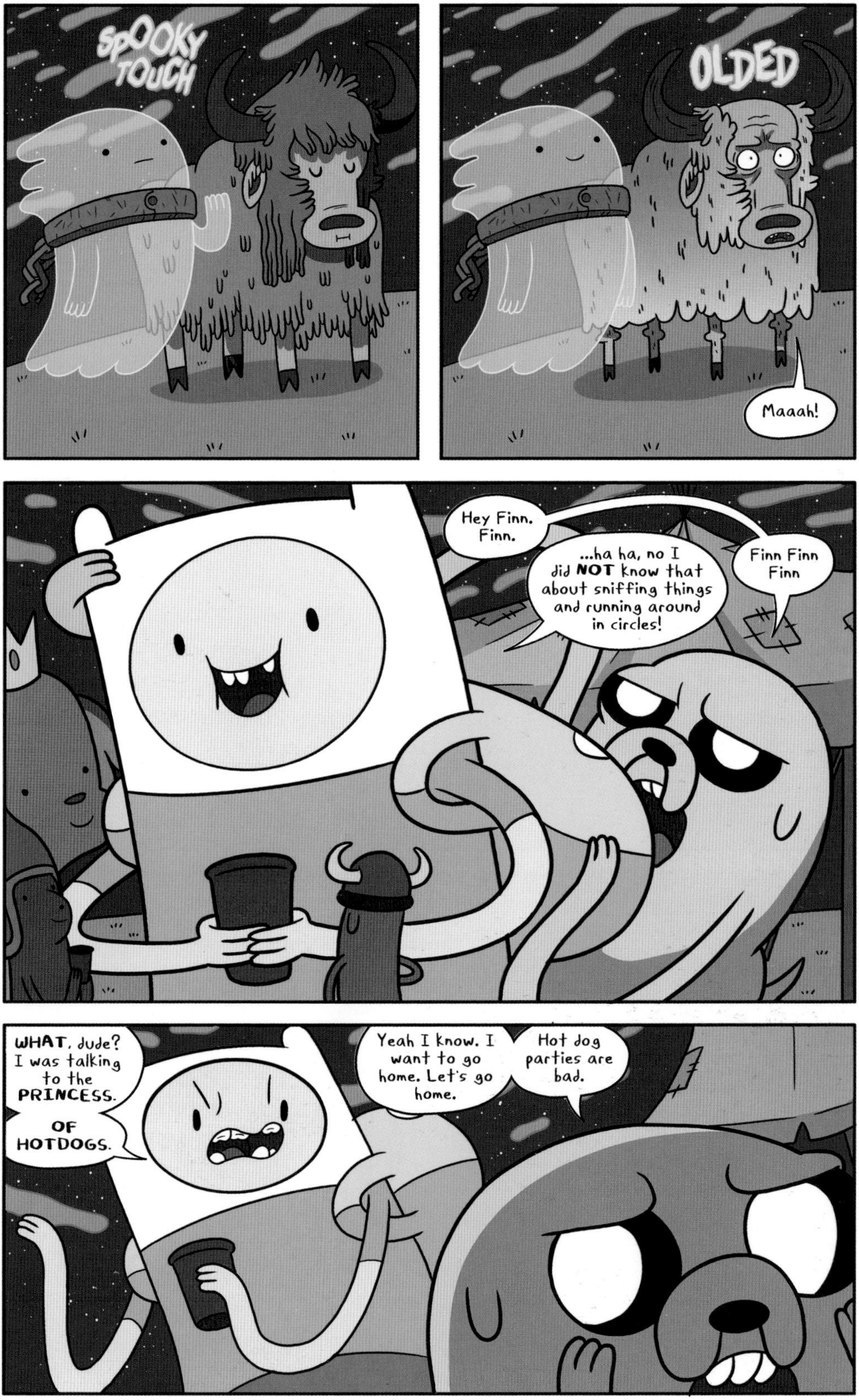
SPOOKY TOUCH
OLDED
Maaah!
Hey Finn. Finn.
...ha ha, no I did NOT know that about sniffing things and running around in circles!
Finn Finn Finn
WHAT, dude? I was talking to the PRINCESS.
OF HOTDOGS.
Yeah I know. I want to go home. Let's go home.
Hot dog parties are bad.

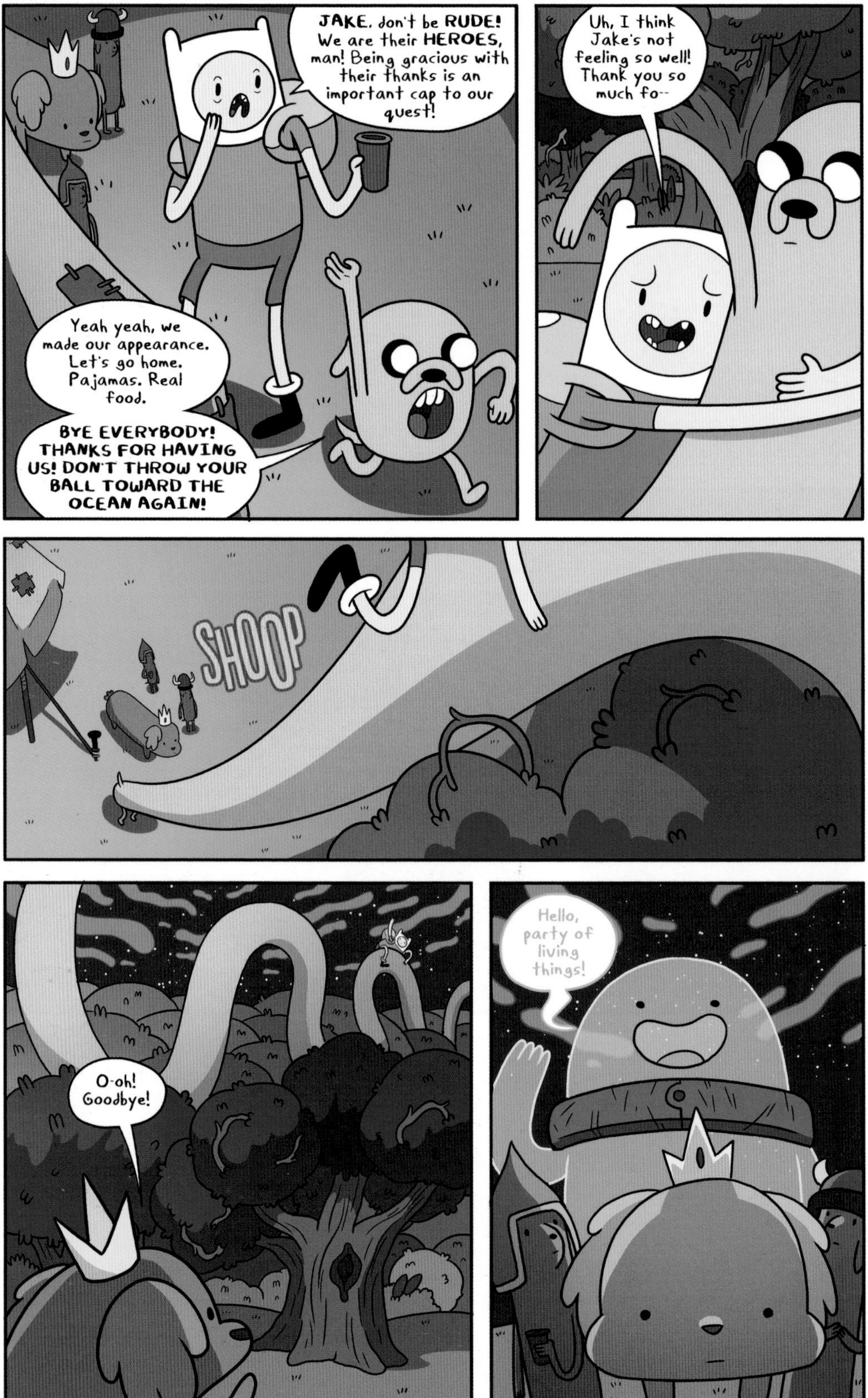
JAKE, don't be RUDE! We are their HEROES, man! Being gracious with their thanks is an important cap to our quest!
Yeah yeah, we made our appearance. Let's go home. Pajamas. Real food.
BYE EVERYBODY! THANKS FOR HAVING US! DON'T THROW YOUR BALL TOWARD THE OCEAN AGAIN!
Uh, I think Jake's not feeling so well! Thank you so much fo--
SHOOP
O-oh! Goodbye!
Hello, party of living things!

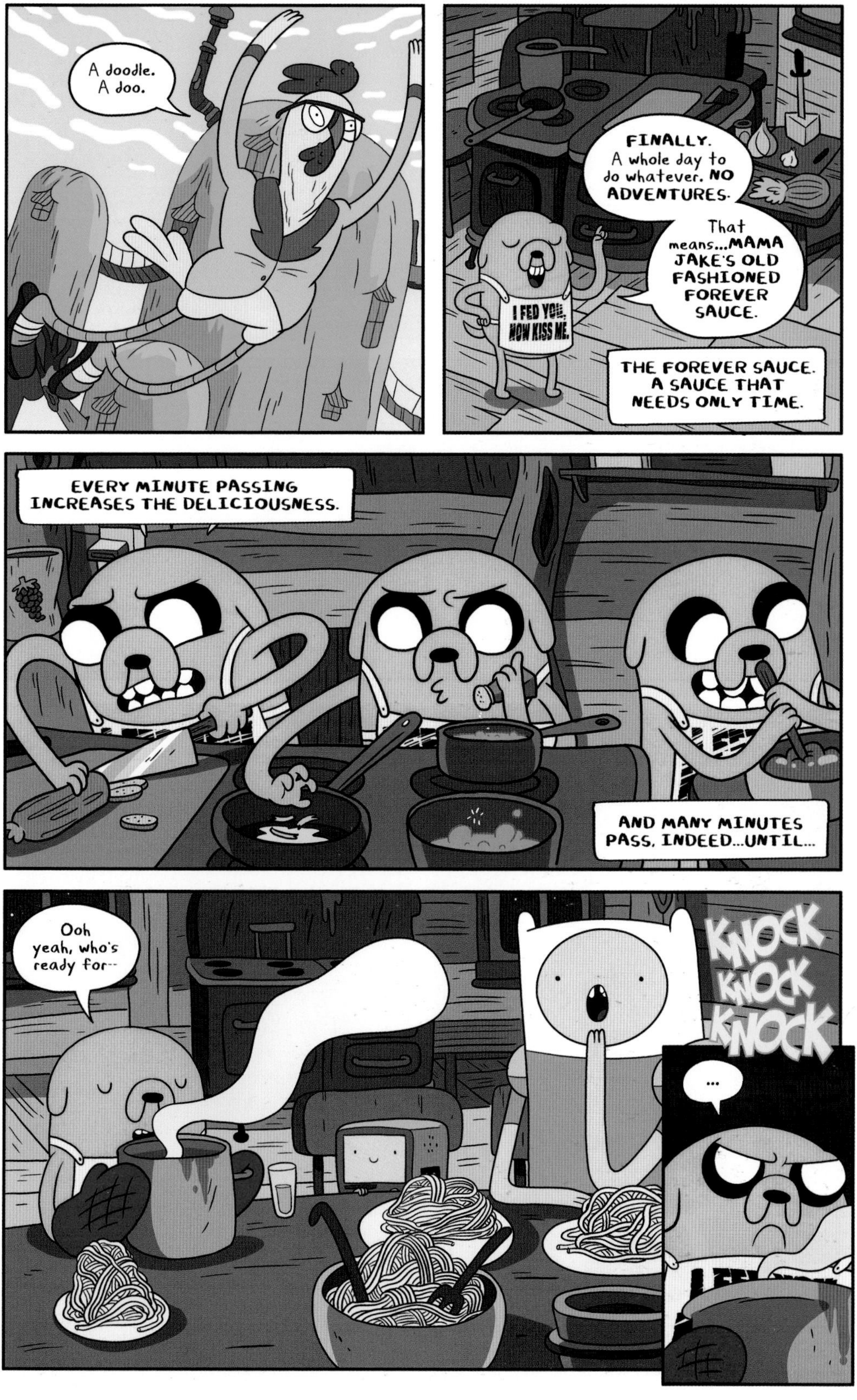
A doodle. A doo.
FINALLY. A whole day to do whatever. NO ADVENTURES.
That means...MAMA JAKE'S OLD FASHIONED FOREVER SAUCE.
I FED YOU, NOW KISS ME.
THE FOREVER SAUCE. A SAUCE THAT NEEDS ONLY TIME.
EVERY MINUTE PASSING INCREASES THE DELICIOUSNESS.
AND MANY MINUTES PASS, INDEED...UNTIL...
Ooh yeah, who's ready for--
KNOCK KNOCK KNOCK
...

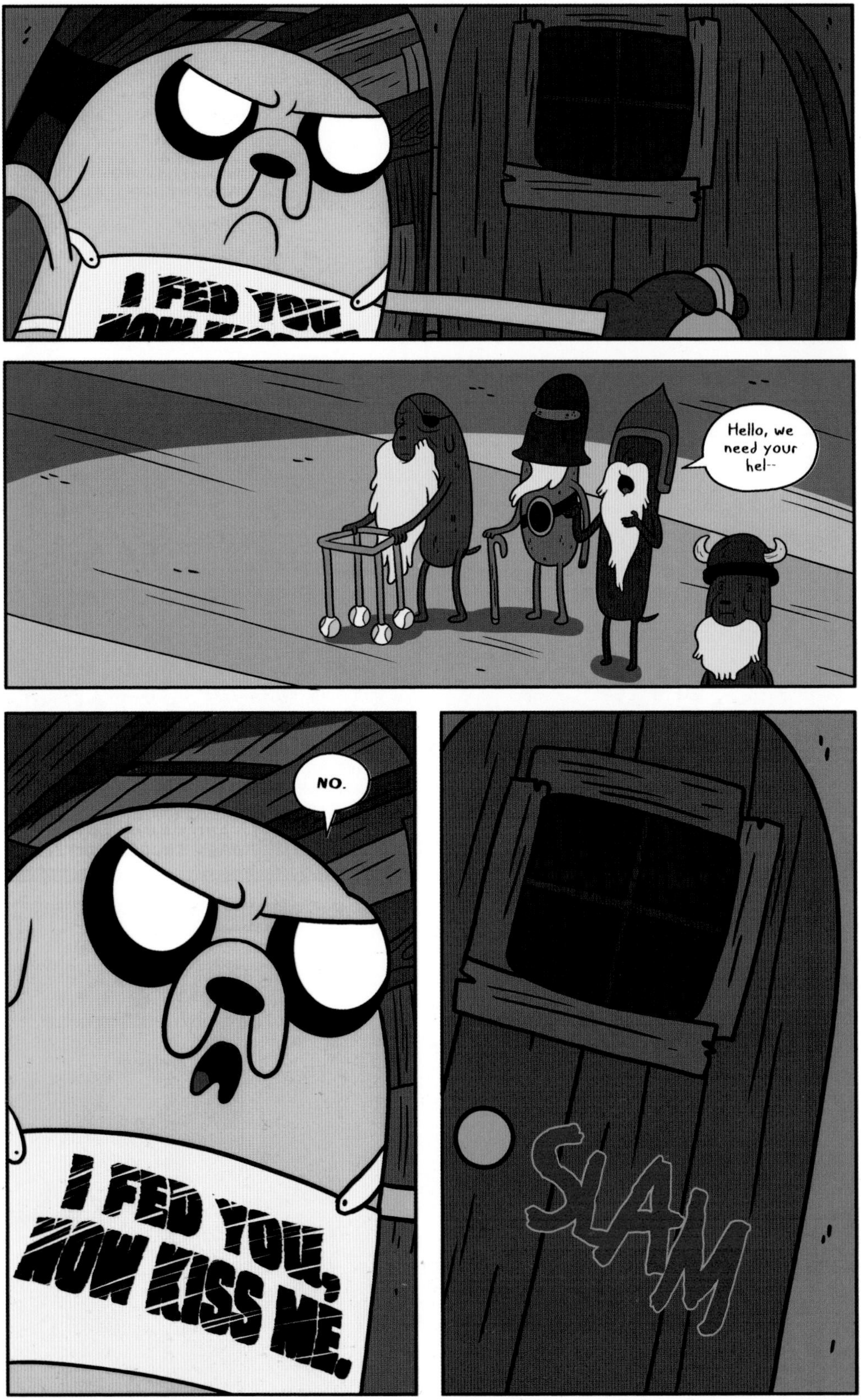
I FED YOU
Hello, we need your hel--
NO.
I FED YOU, NOW KISS ME.
SLAM

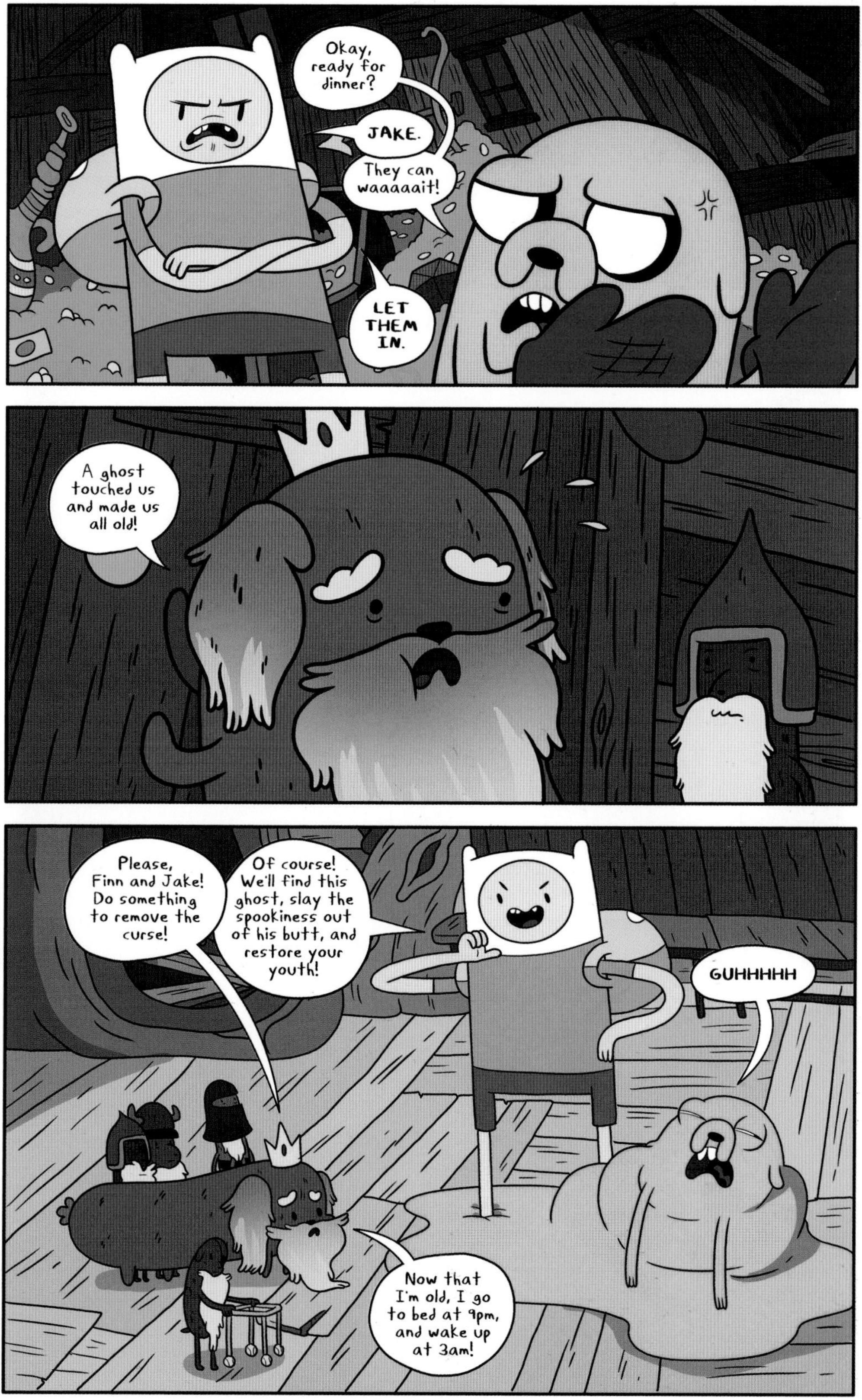
Okay, ready for dinner?
JAKE.
They can waaaaait!
LET THEM IN.
A ghost touched us and made us all old!
Please, Finn and Jake! Do something to remove the curse!
Of course! We'll find this ghost, slay the spookiness out of his butt, and restore your youth!
GUHHHHH
Now that I'm old, I go to bed at 9pm, and wake up at 3am!

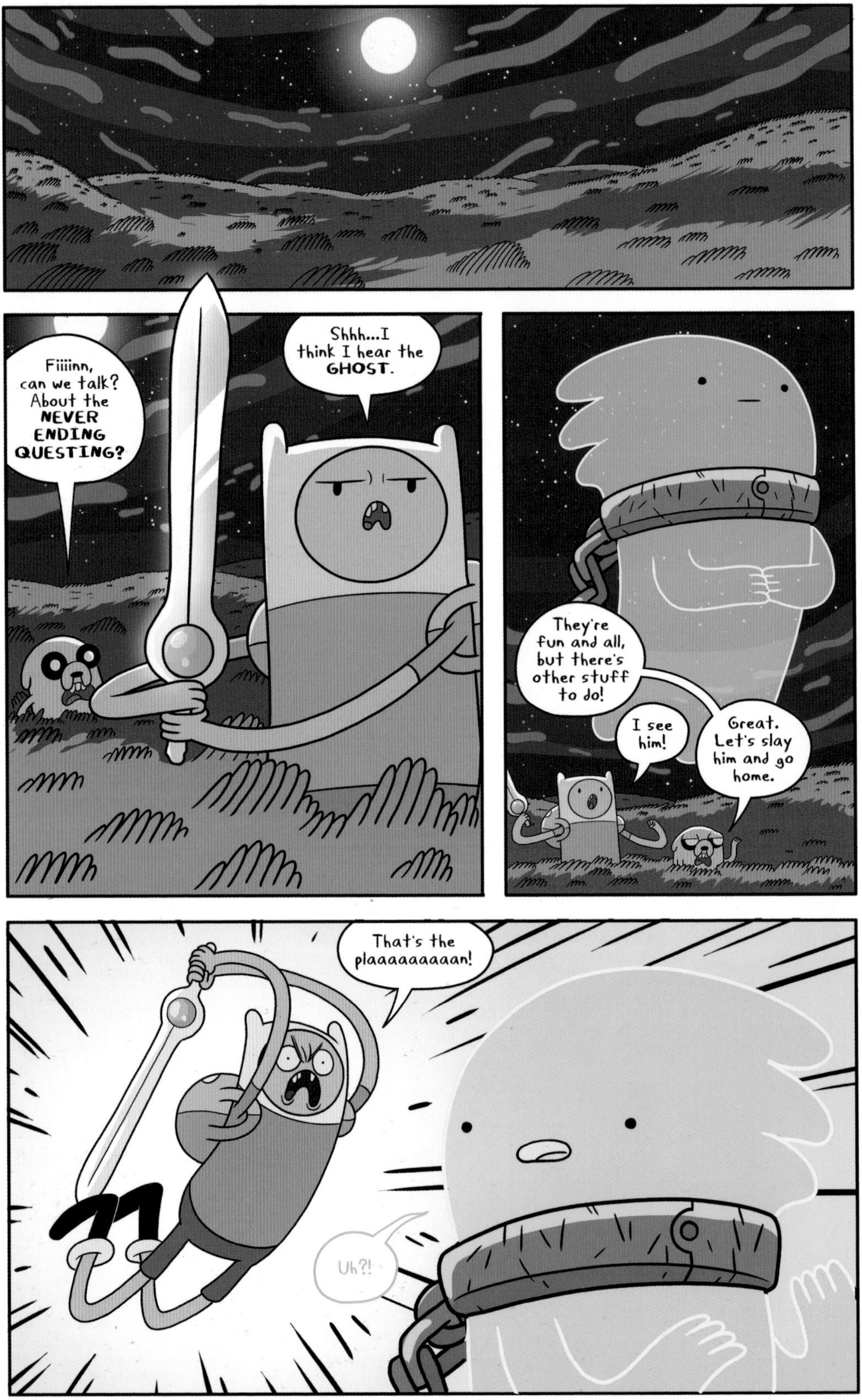
Fiiiinn, can we talk? About the NEVER ENDING QUESTING?
Shhh...I think I hear the GHOST.
They're fun and all, but there's other stuff to do!
I see him!
Great. Let's slay him and go home.
That's the plaaaaaaaaan!
Uh?!

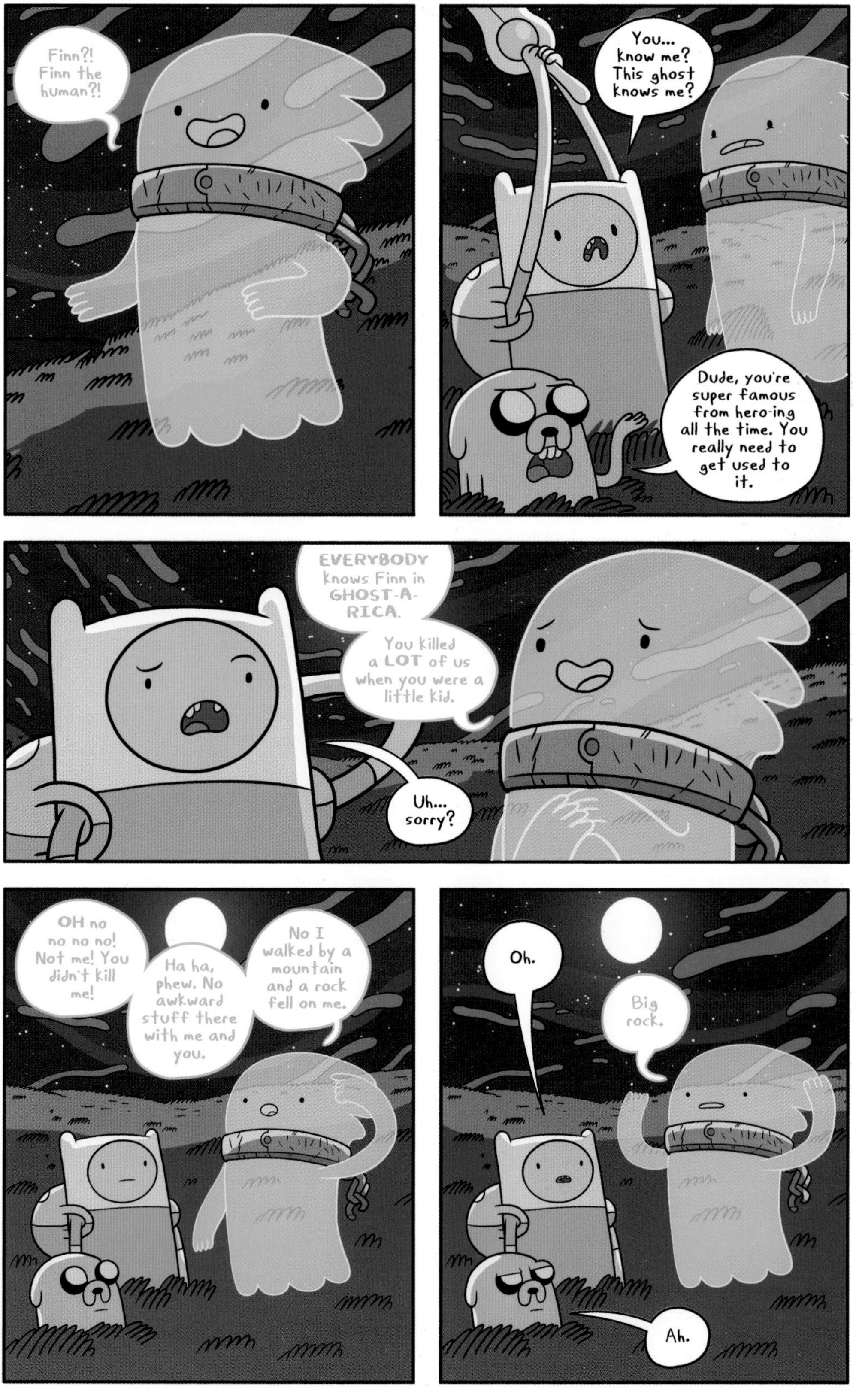

Finn?! Finn the human?!
You... know me? This ghost knows me?
Dude, you're super famous from hero-ing all the time. You really need to get used to it.
EVERYBODY knows Finn in GHOST-A-RICA.
You killed a LOT of us when you were a little kid.
Uh... sorry?
OH no no no no! Not me! You didn't kill me!
Ha ha, phew. No awkward stuff there with me and you.
No I walked by a mountain and a rock fell on me.
Oh.
Big rock.
Ah.

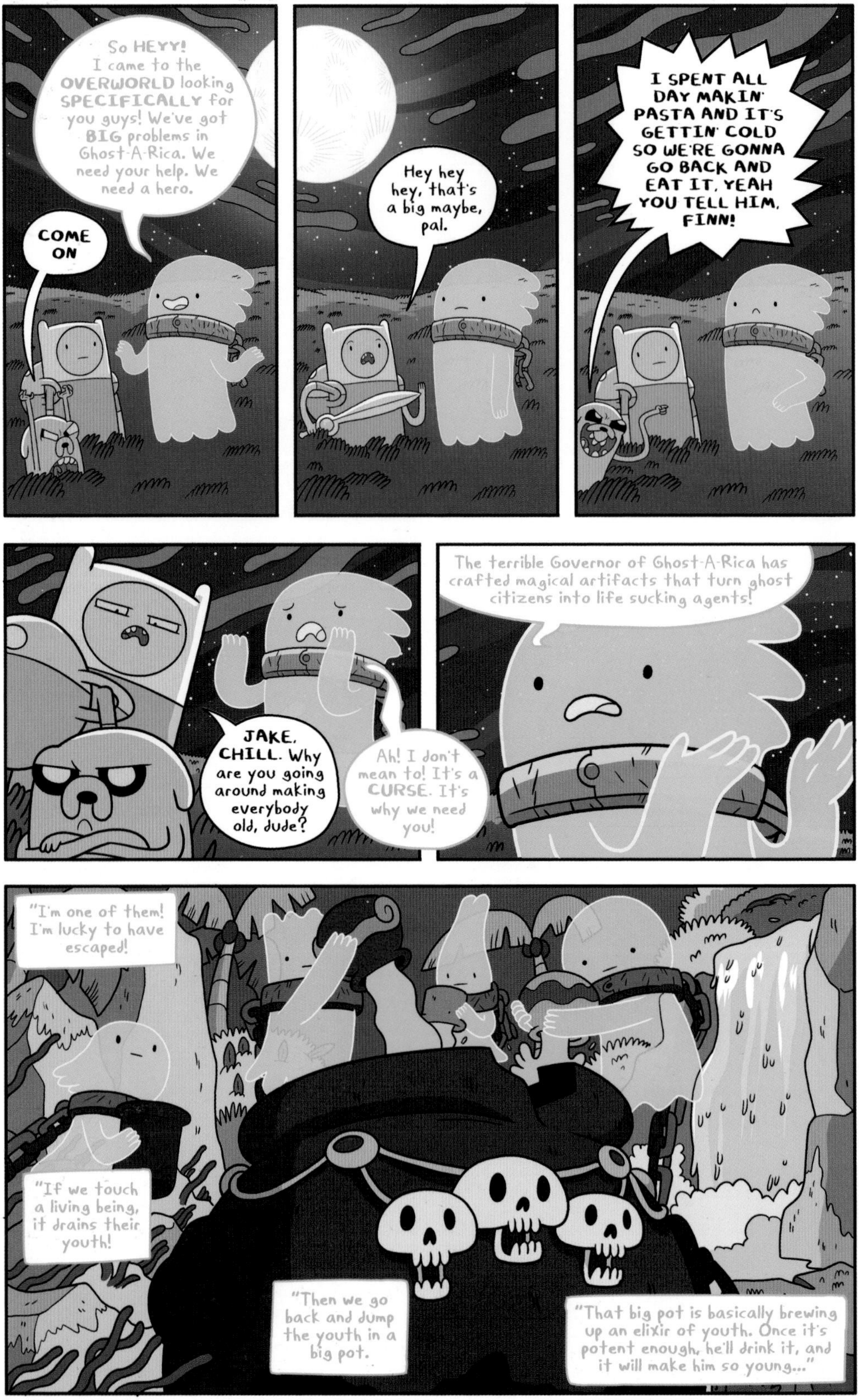

So HEYY! I came to the OVERWORLD looking SPECIFICALLY for you guys! We've got BIG problems in Ghost-A-Rica. We need your help. We need a hero.
COME ON
Hey hey hey, that's a big maybe, pal.
I SPENT ALL DAY MAKIN' PASTA AND IT'S GETTIN' COLD SO WE'RE GONNA GO BACK AND EAT IT. YEAH YOU TELL HIM, FINN!
JAKE. CHILL. Why are you going around making everybody old, dude?
Ah! I don't mean to! It's a CURSE. It's why we need you!
The terrible Governor of Ghost-A-Rica has crafted magical artifacts that turn ghost citizens into life sucking agents!
"I'm one of them! I'm lucky to have escaped!
"If we touch a living being, it drains their youth!
"Then we go back and dump the youth in a big pot.
"That big pot is basically brewing up an elixir of youth. Once it's potent enough, he'll drink it, and it will make him so young..."

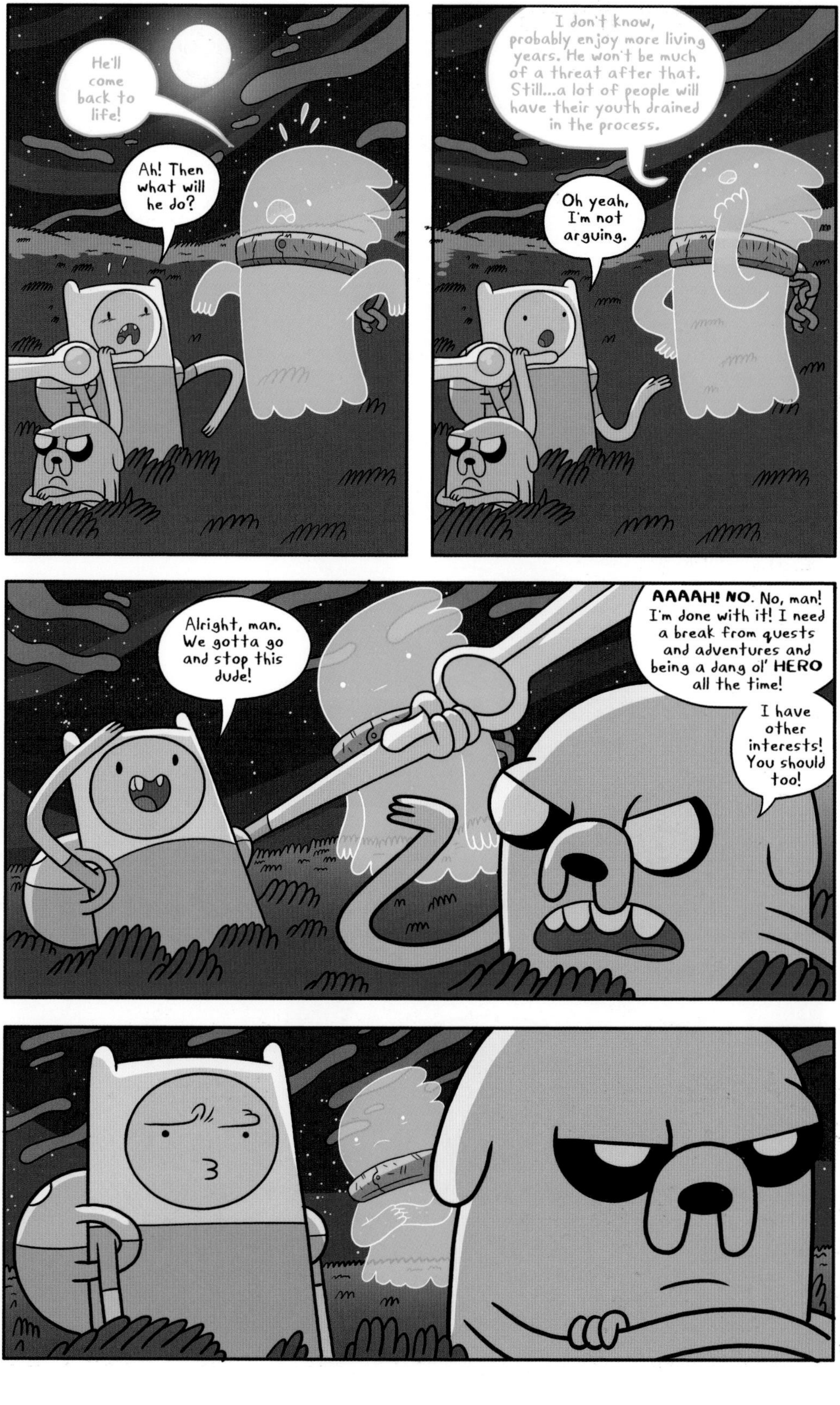
He'll come back to life!
Ah! Then what will he do?
I don't know, probably enjoy more living years. He won't be much of a threat after that. Still...a lot of people will have their youth drained in the process.
Oh yeah, I'm not arguing.
Alright, man. We gotta go and stop this dude!
AAAAH! NO. No, man! I'm done with it! I need a break from quests and adventures and being a dang ol' HERO all the time!
I have other interests! You should too!

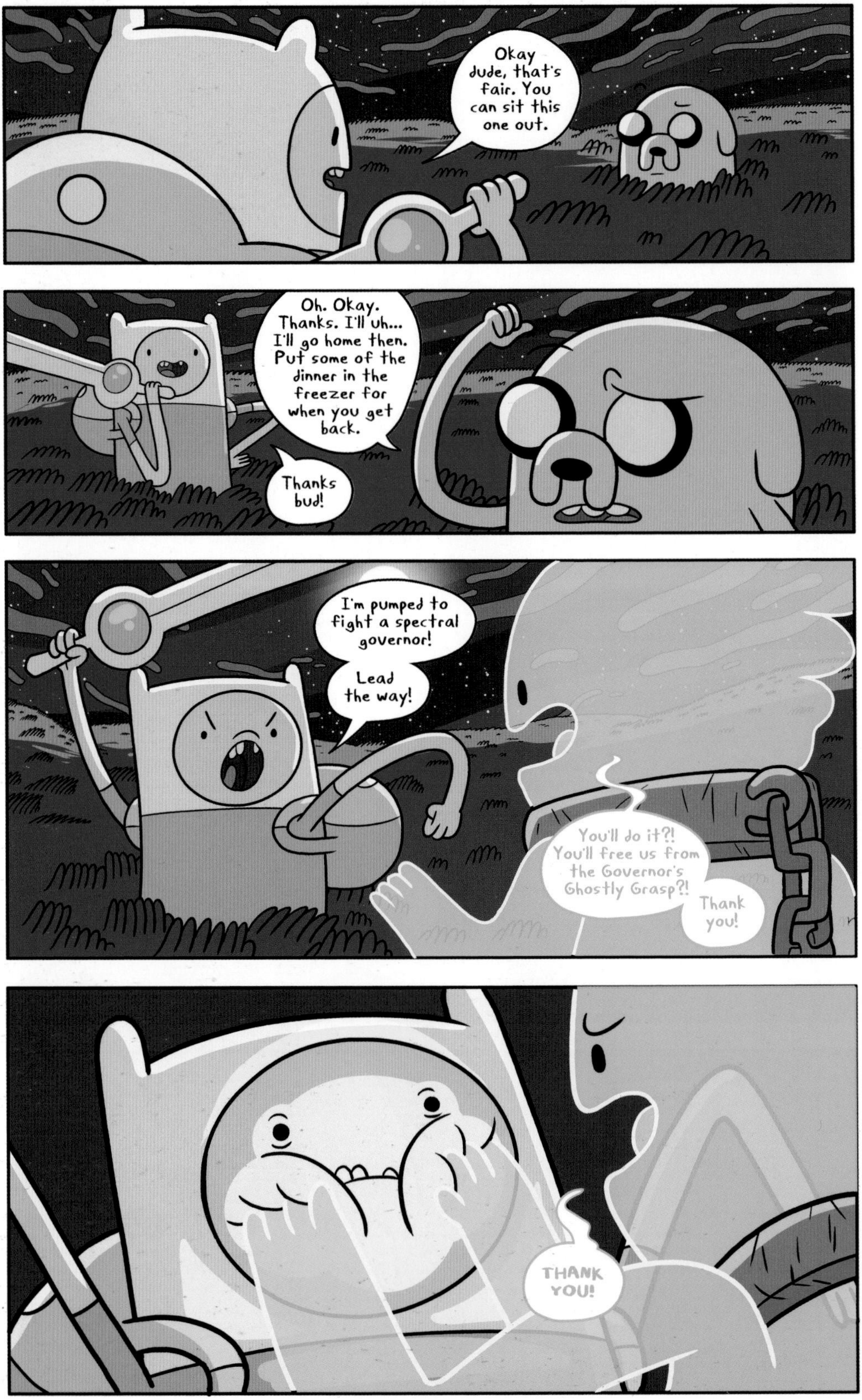
Okay dude, that's fair. You can sit this one out.
Oh. Okay. Thanks. I'll uh... I'll go home then. Put some of the dinner in the freezer for when you get back.
Thanks bud!
I'm pumped to fight a spectral governor!
Lead the way!
You'll do it?! You'll free us from the Governor's Ghostly Grasp?!
Thank you!
THANK YOU!

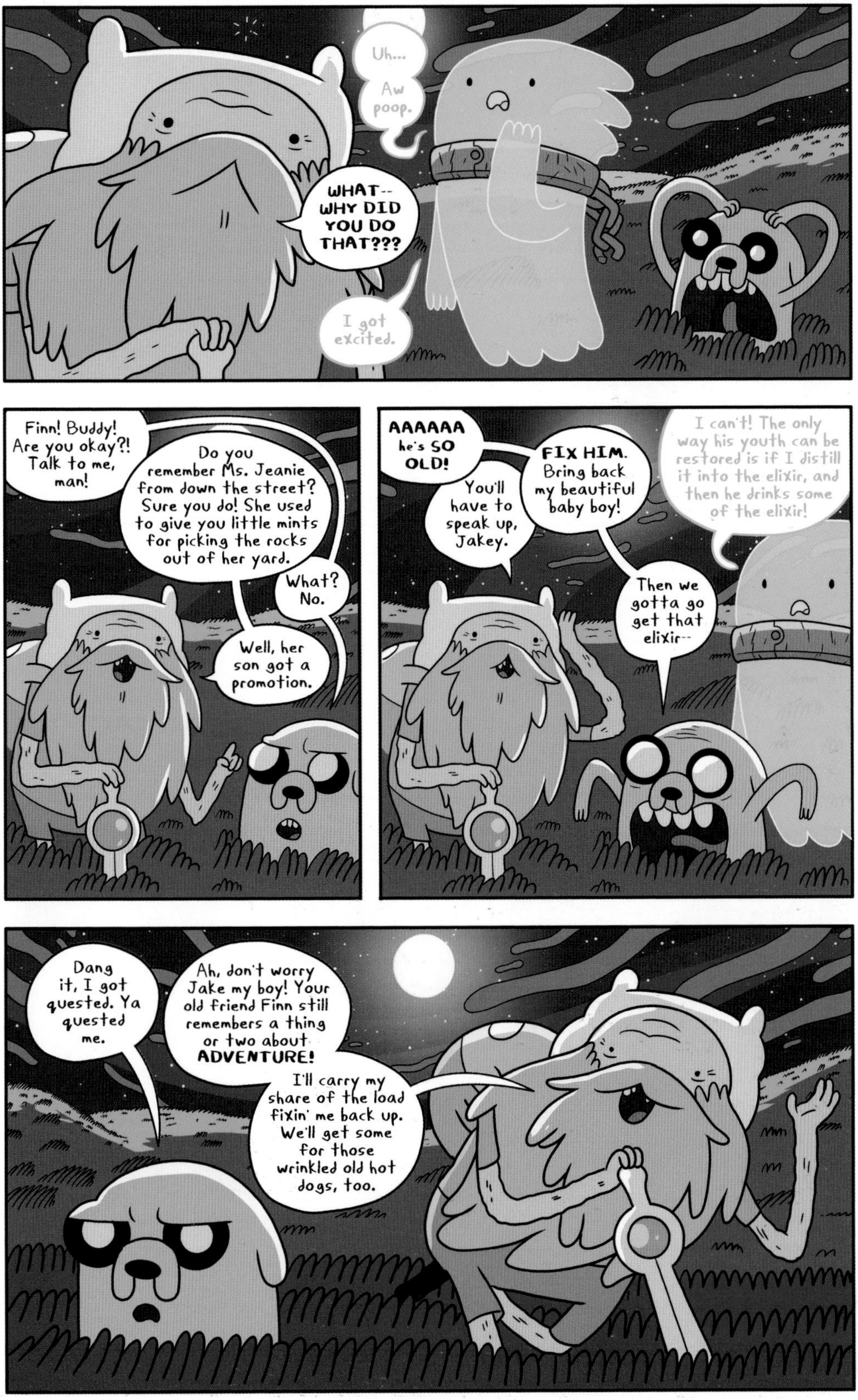
Uh...
Aw poop.
WHAT-- WHY DID YOU DO THAT???
I got excited.
Finn! Buddy! Are you okay?! Talk to me, man!
Do you remember Ms. Jeanie from down the street? Sure you do! She used to give you little mints for picking the rocks out of her yard.
What? No.
Well, her son got a promotion.
AAAAAA he's SO OLD!
You'll have to speak up, Jakey.
FIX HIM. Bring back my beautiful baby boy!
I can't! The only way his youth can be restored is if I distill it into the elixir, and then he drinks some of the elixir!
Then we gotta go get that elixir--
Dang it, I got quested. Ya quested me.
Ah, don't worry Jake my boy! Your old friend Finn still remembers a thing or two about ADVENTURE!
I'll carry my share of the load fixin' me back up. We'll get some for those wrinkled old hot dogs, too.

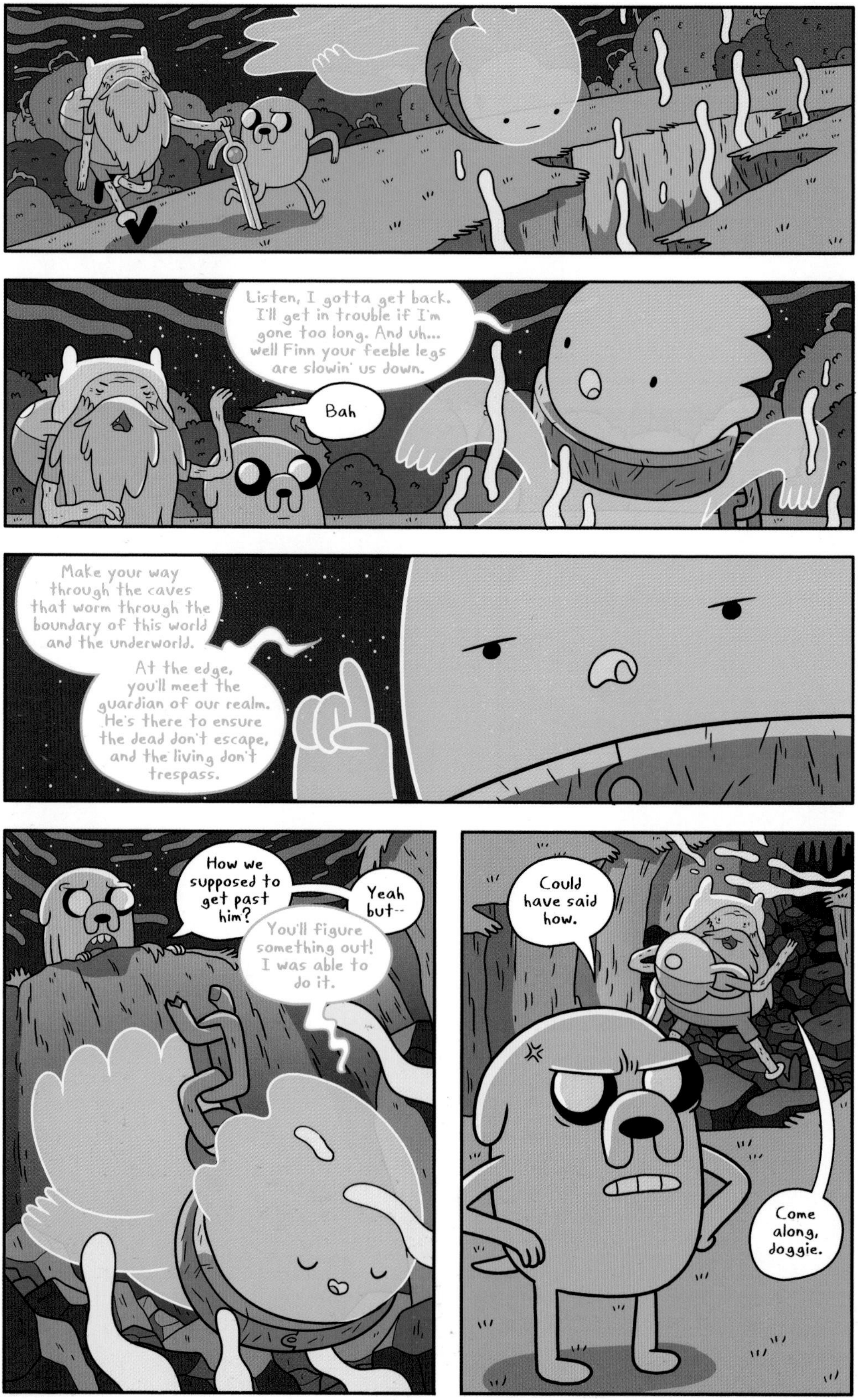

Listen, I gotta get back. I'll get in trouble if I'm gone too long. And uh... well Finn your feeble legs are slowin' us down.
Bah
Make your way through the caves that worm through the boundary of this world and the underworld.
At the edge, you'll meet the guardian of our realm. He's there to ensure the dead don't escape, and the living don't trespass.
How we supposed to get past him?
Yeah but--
You'll figure something out! I was able to do it.
Could have said how.
Come along, doggie.

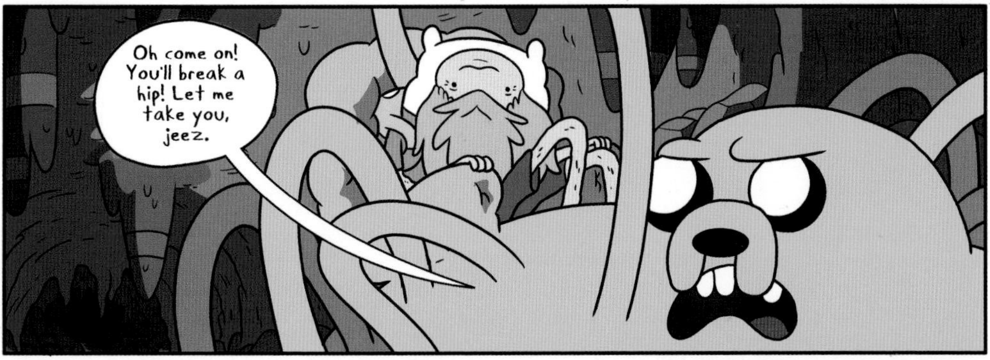
Oh come on! You'll break a hip! Let me take you, jeez.

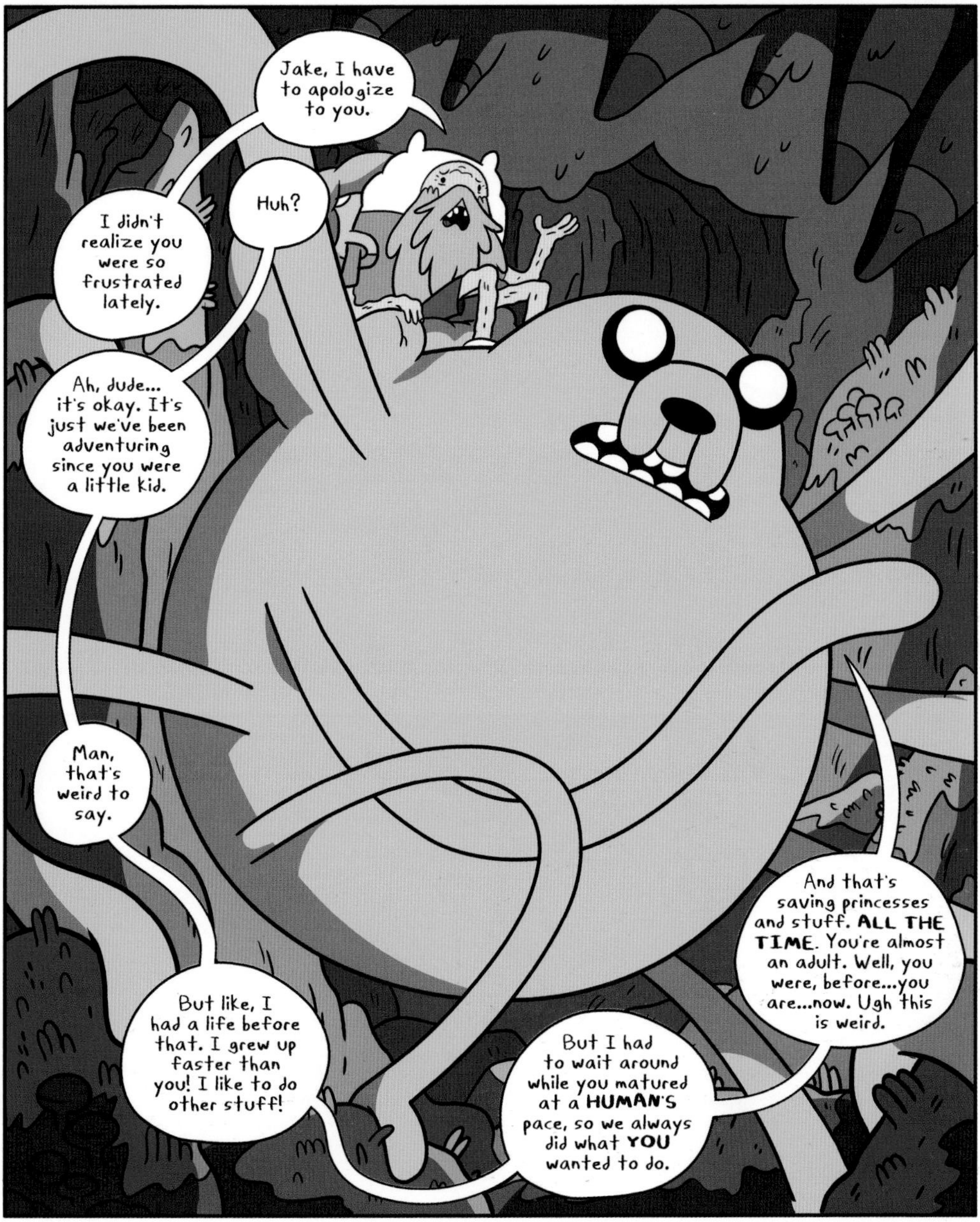
Jake, I have to apologize to you.
Huh?
I didn't realize you were so frustrated lately.
Ah, dude... it's okay. It's just we've been adventuring since you were a little kid.
Man, that's weird to say.
But like, I had a life before that. I grew up faster than you! I like to do other stuff!
But I had to wait around while you matured at a HUMAN'S pace, so we always did what YOU wanted to do.
And that's saving princesses and stuff. ALL THE TIME. You're almost an adult. Well, you were, before...you are...now. Ugh this is weird.

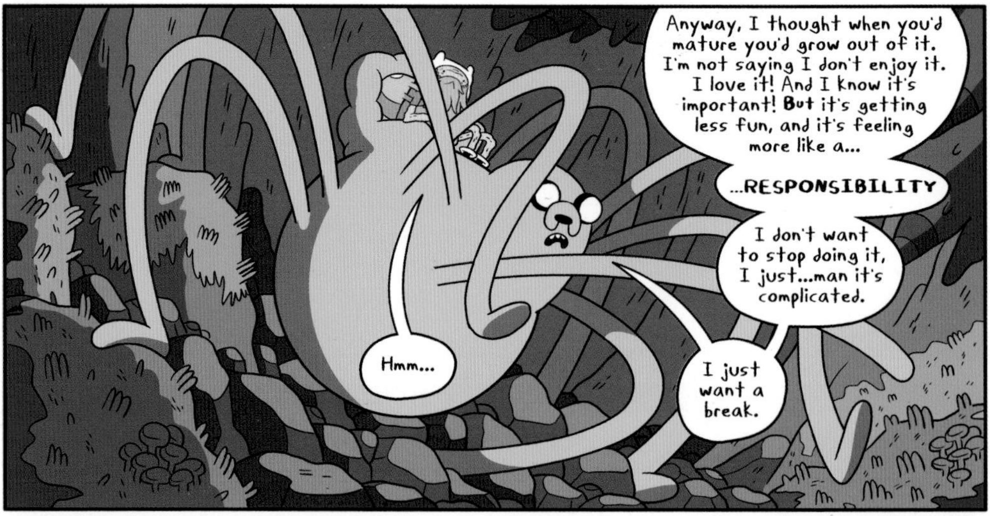
Anyway, I thought when you'd mature you'd grow out of it. I'm not saying I don't enjoy it. I love it! And I know it's important! But it's getting less fun, and it's feeling more like a...
...RESPONSIBILITY
I don't want to stop doing it, I just...man it's complicated.
I just want a break.
Hmm...

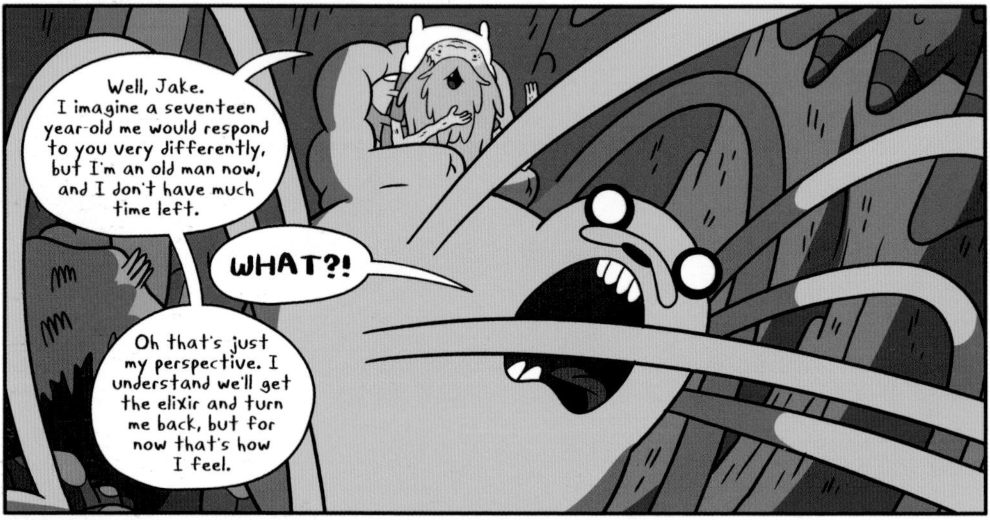
Well, Jake. I imagine a seventeen year-old me would respond to you very differently, but I'm an old man now, and I don't have much time left.
WHAT?!
Oh that's just my perspective. I understand we'll get the elixir and turn me back, but for now that's how I feel.

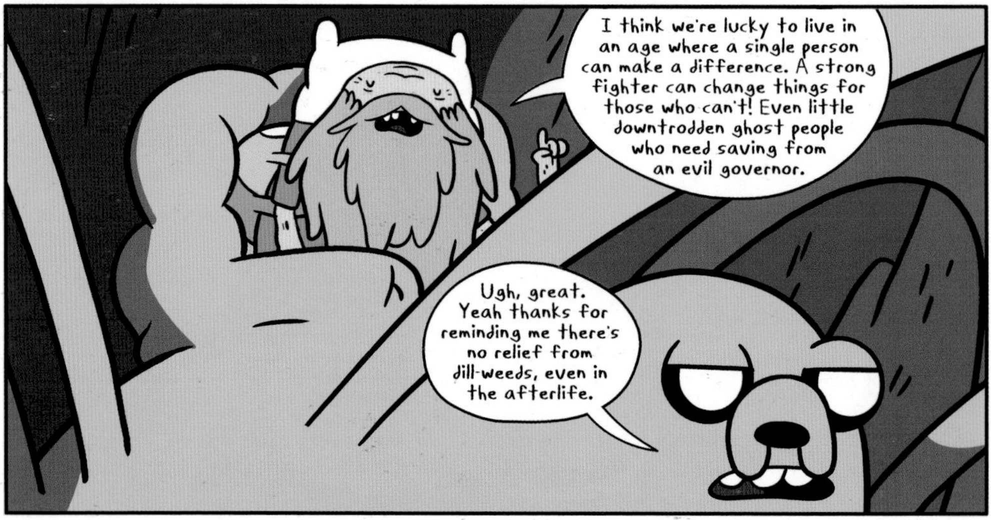
I think we're lucky to live in an age where a single person can make a difference. A strong fighter can change things for those who can't! Even little downtrodden ghost people who need saving from an evil governor.
Ugh, great. Yeah thanks for reminding me there's no relief from dill-weeds, even in the afterlife.

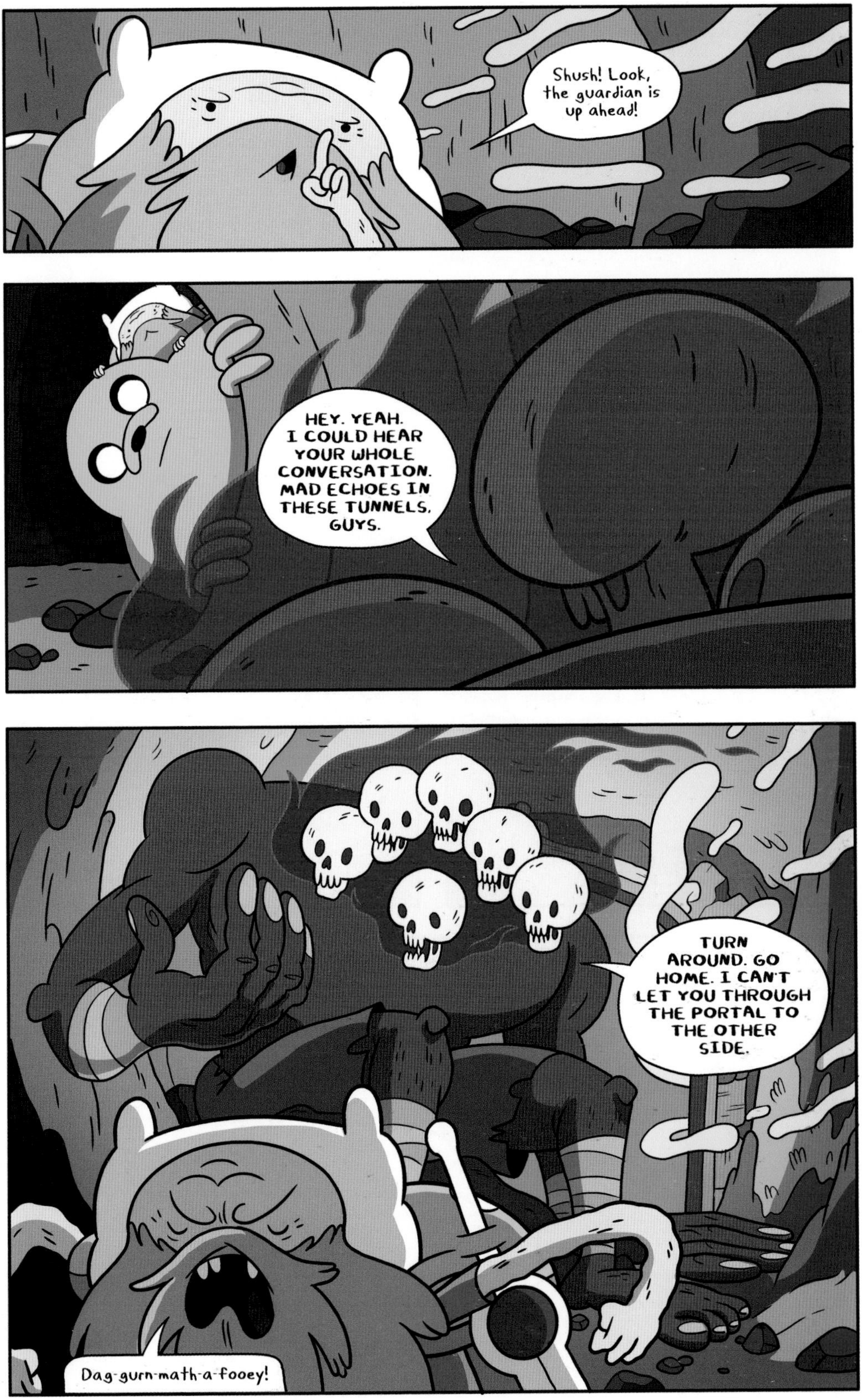
Shush! Look, the guardian is up ahead!
HEY. YEAH. I COULD HEAR YOUR WHOLE CONVERSATION. MAD ECHOES IN THESE TUNNELS, GUYS.
TURN AROUND. GO HOME. I CAN'T LET YOU THROUGH THE PORTAL TO THE OTHER SIDE.
Dag-gurn-math-a-fooey!

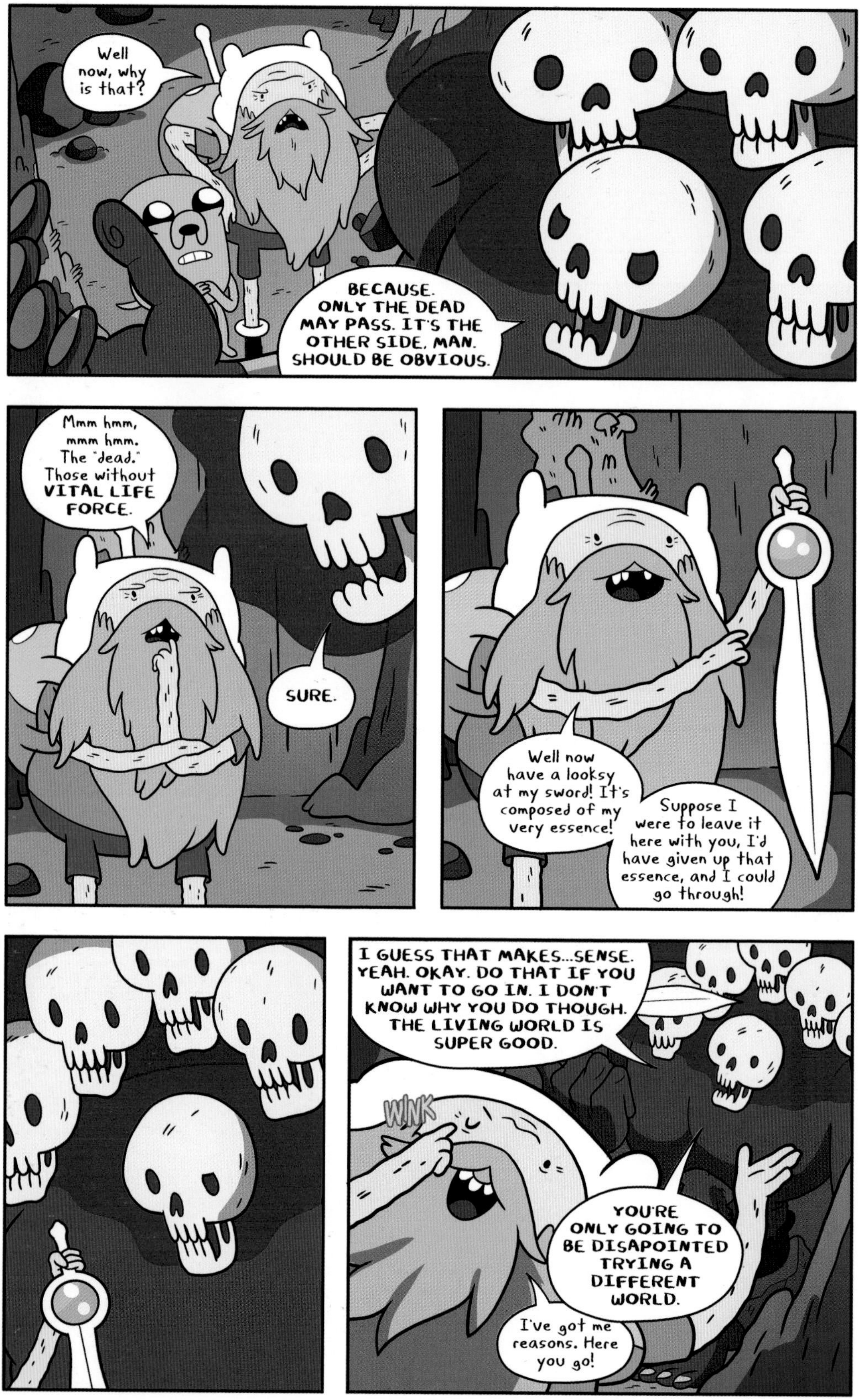
Well now, why is that?
BECAUSE. ONLY THE DEAD MAY PASS. IT'S THE OTHER SIDE, MAN. SHOULD BE OBVIOUS.
Mmm hmm, mmm hmm. The "dead." Those without VITAL LIFE FORCE.
SURE.
Well now have a looksy at my sword! It's composed of my very essence!
Suppose I were to leave it here with you, I'd have given up that essence, and I could go through!
I GUESS THAT MAKES...SENSE. YEAH. OKAY. DO THAT IF YOU WANT TO GO IN. I DON'T KNOW WHY YOU DO THOUGH. THE LIVING WORLD IS SUPER GOOD.
WINK
YOU'RE ONLY GOING TO BE DISAPOINTED TRYING A DIFFERENT WORLD.
I've got me reasons. Here you go!

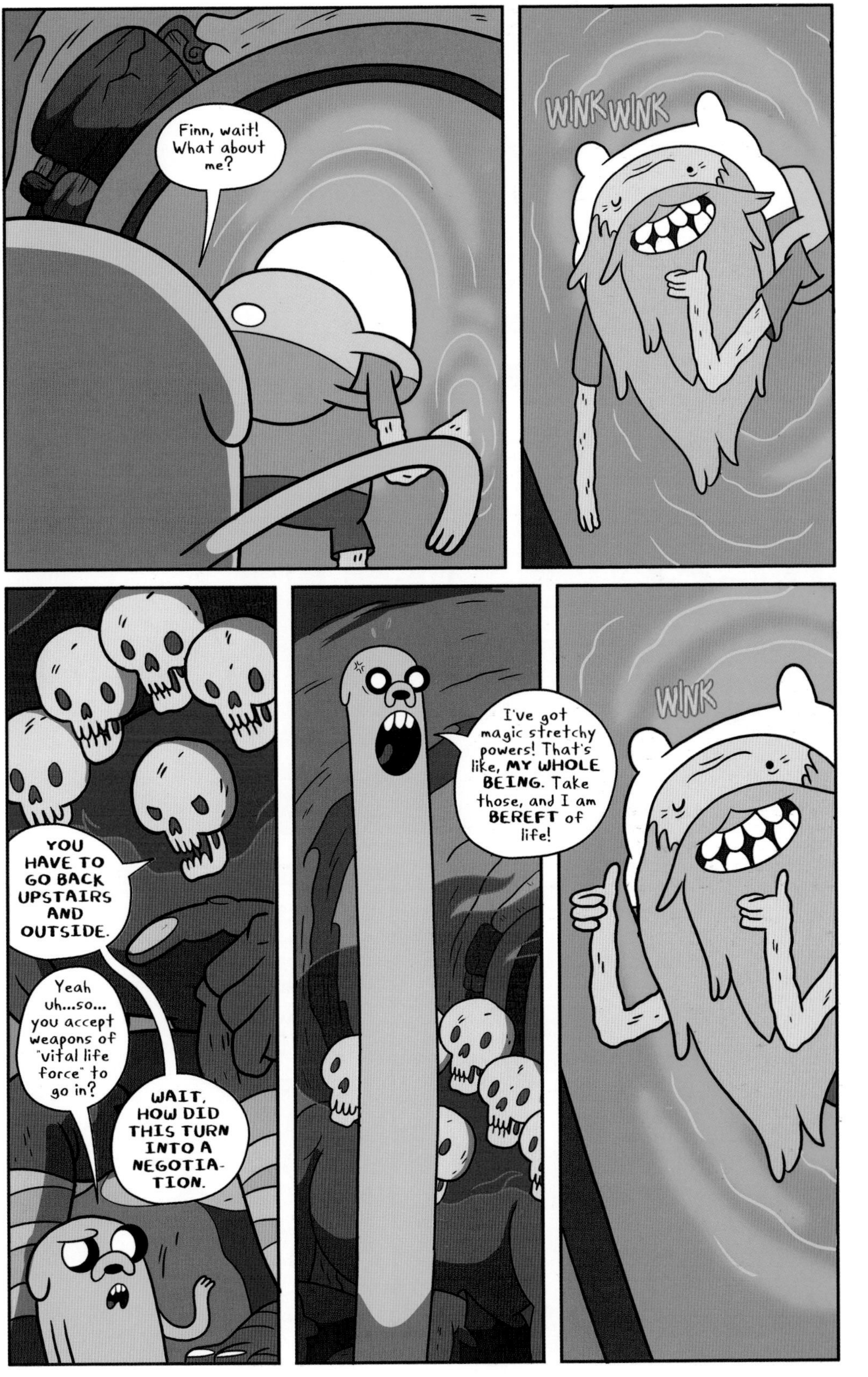
Finn, wait! What about me?
WINK WINK
YOU HAVE TO GO BACK UPSTAIRS AND OUTSIDE.
Yeah uh...so... you accept weapons of "vital life force" to go in?
WAIT, HOW DID THIS TURN INTO A NEGOTIATION.
I've got magic stretchy powers! That's like, MY WHOLE BEING. Take those, and I am BEREFT of life!
WINK

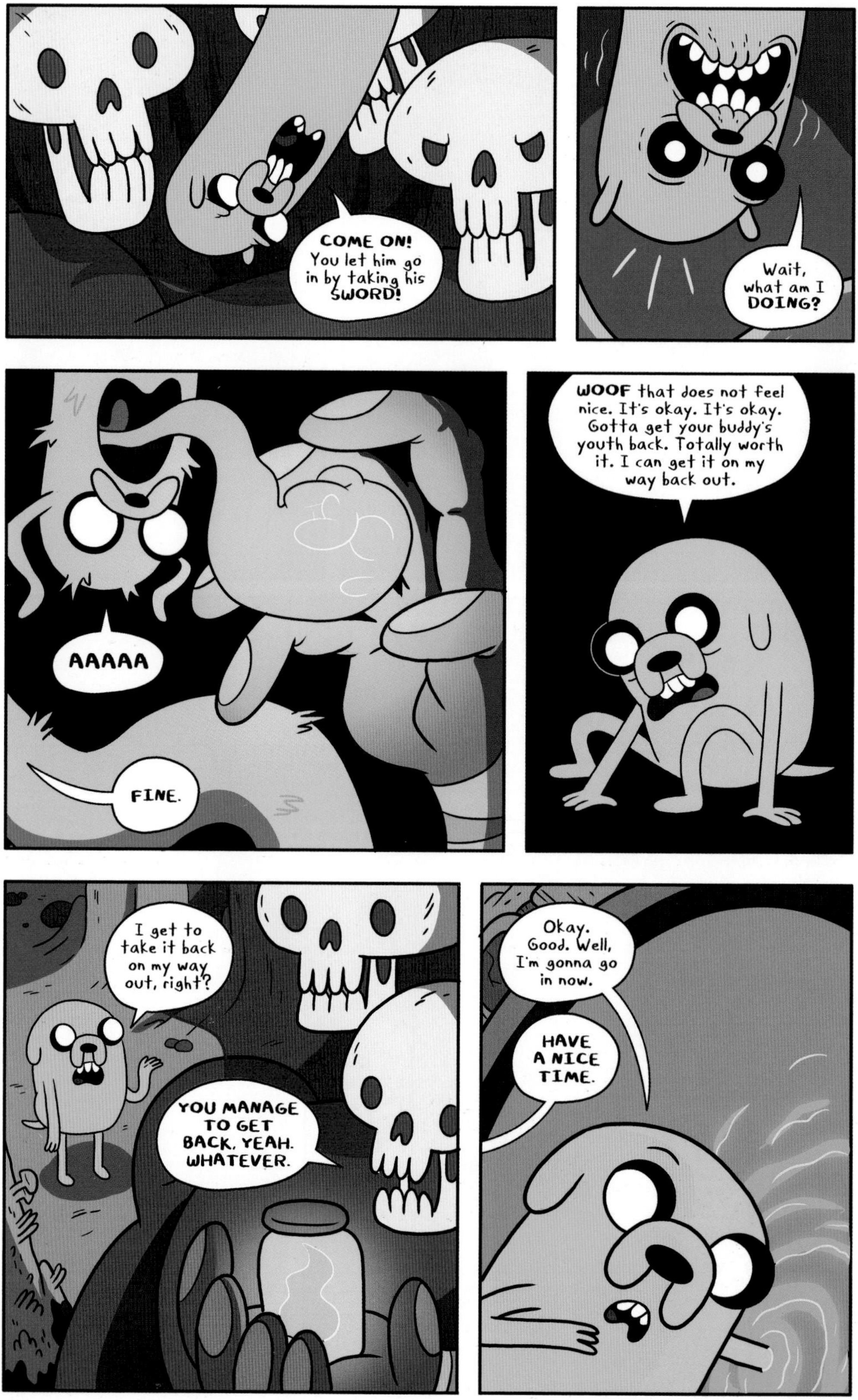
COME ON! You let him go in by taking his SWORD!
Wait, what am I DOING?
AAAAA
FINE.
WOOF that does not feel nice. It's okay. It's okay. Gotta get your buddy's youth back. Totally worth it. I can get it on my way back out.
I get to take it back on my way out, right?
YOU MANAGE TO GET BACK, YEAH. WHATEVER.
Okay. Good. Well, I'm gonna go in now.
HAVE A NICE TIME.

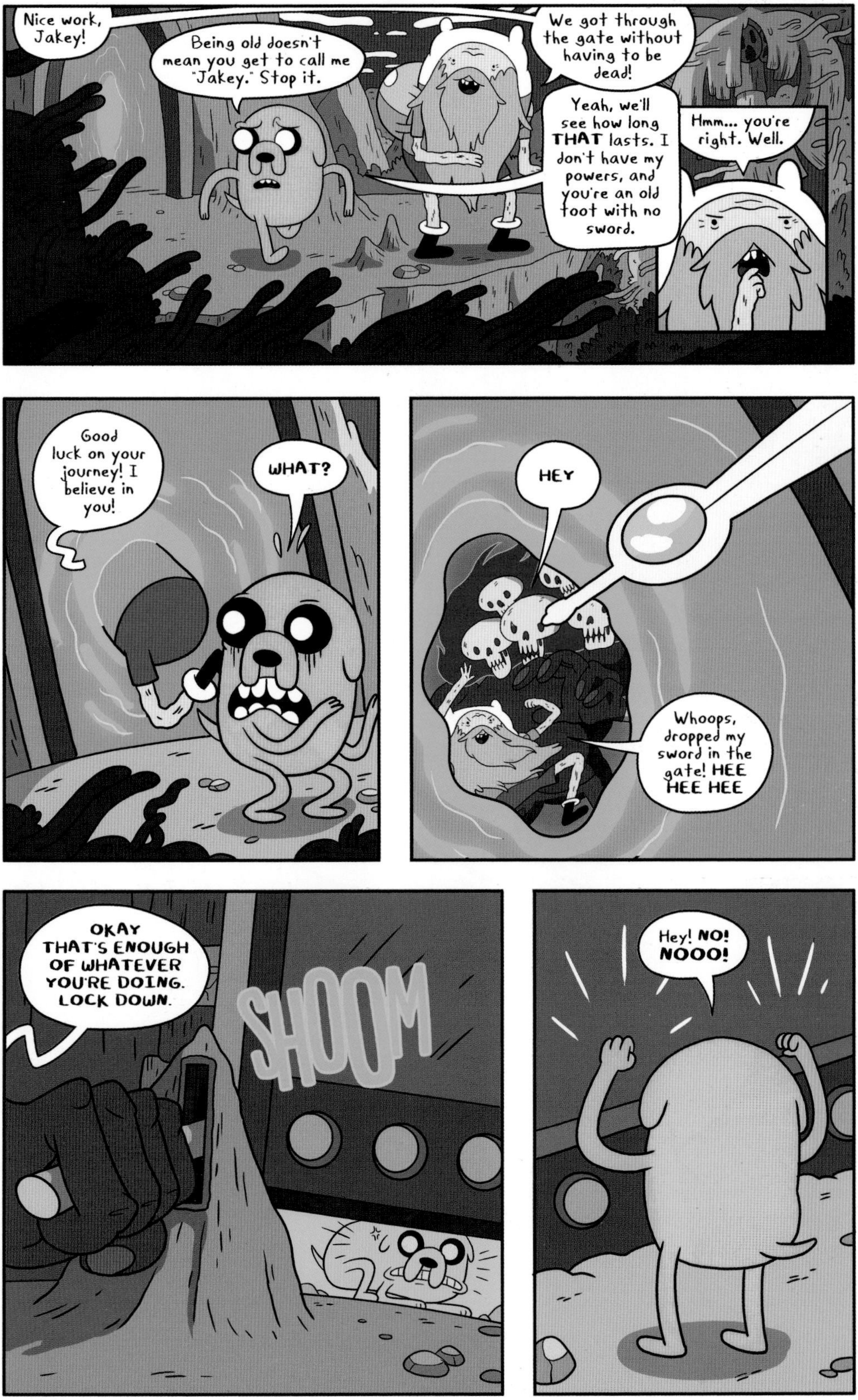
Nice work, Jakey!
Being old doesn't mean you get to call me "Jakey." Stop it.
We got through the gate without having to be dead!
Yeah, we'll see how long THAT lasts. I don't have my powers, and you're an old foot with no sword.
Hmm... you're right. Well.
Good luck on your journey! I believe in you!
WHAT?
HEY
Whoops, dropped my sword in the gate! HEE HEE HEE
OKAY THAT'S ENOUGH OF WHATEVER YOU'RE DOING. LOCK DOWN.
SHOOM
Hey! NO! NOOO!

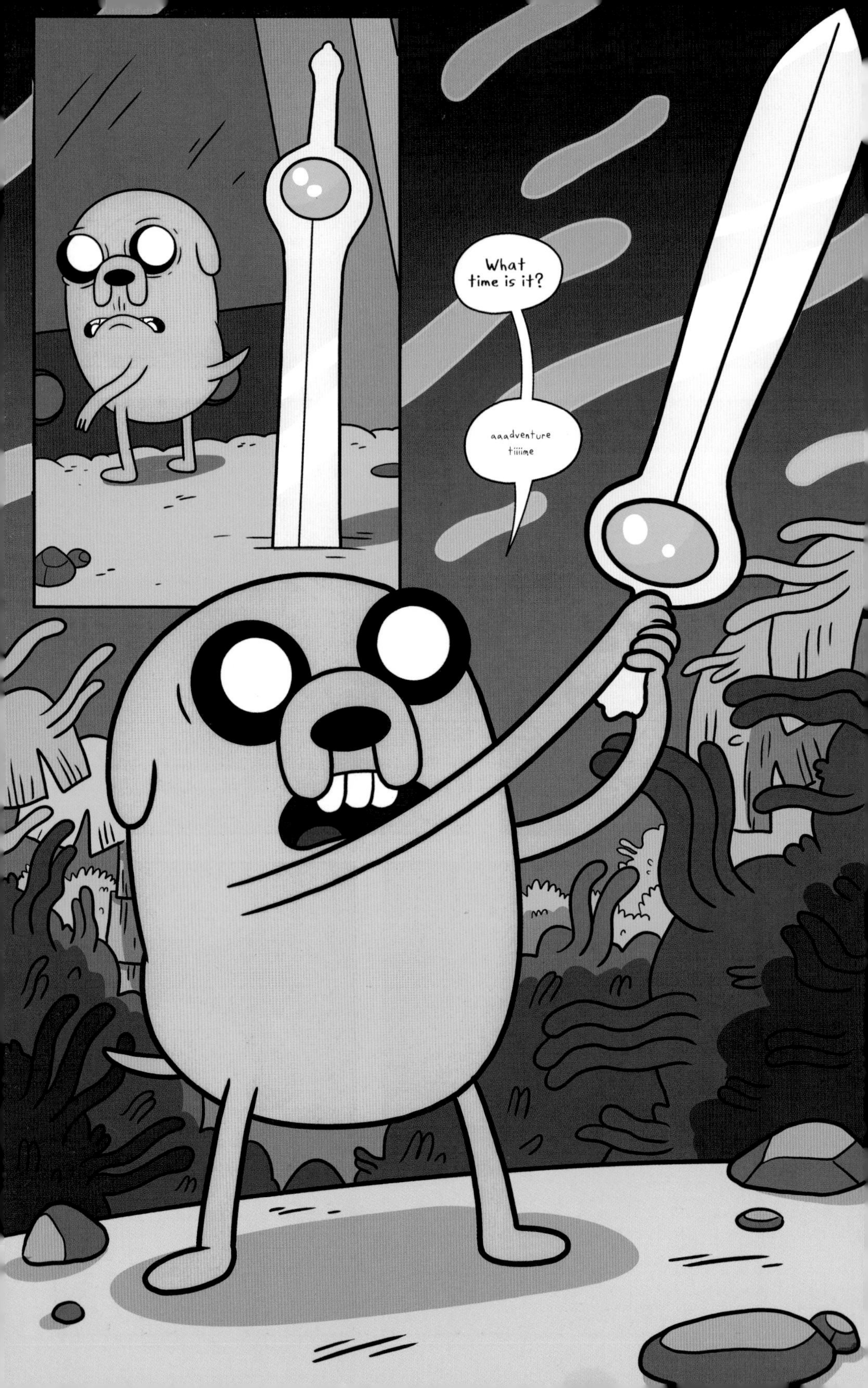
What time is it?
aaadventure tiiiime

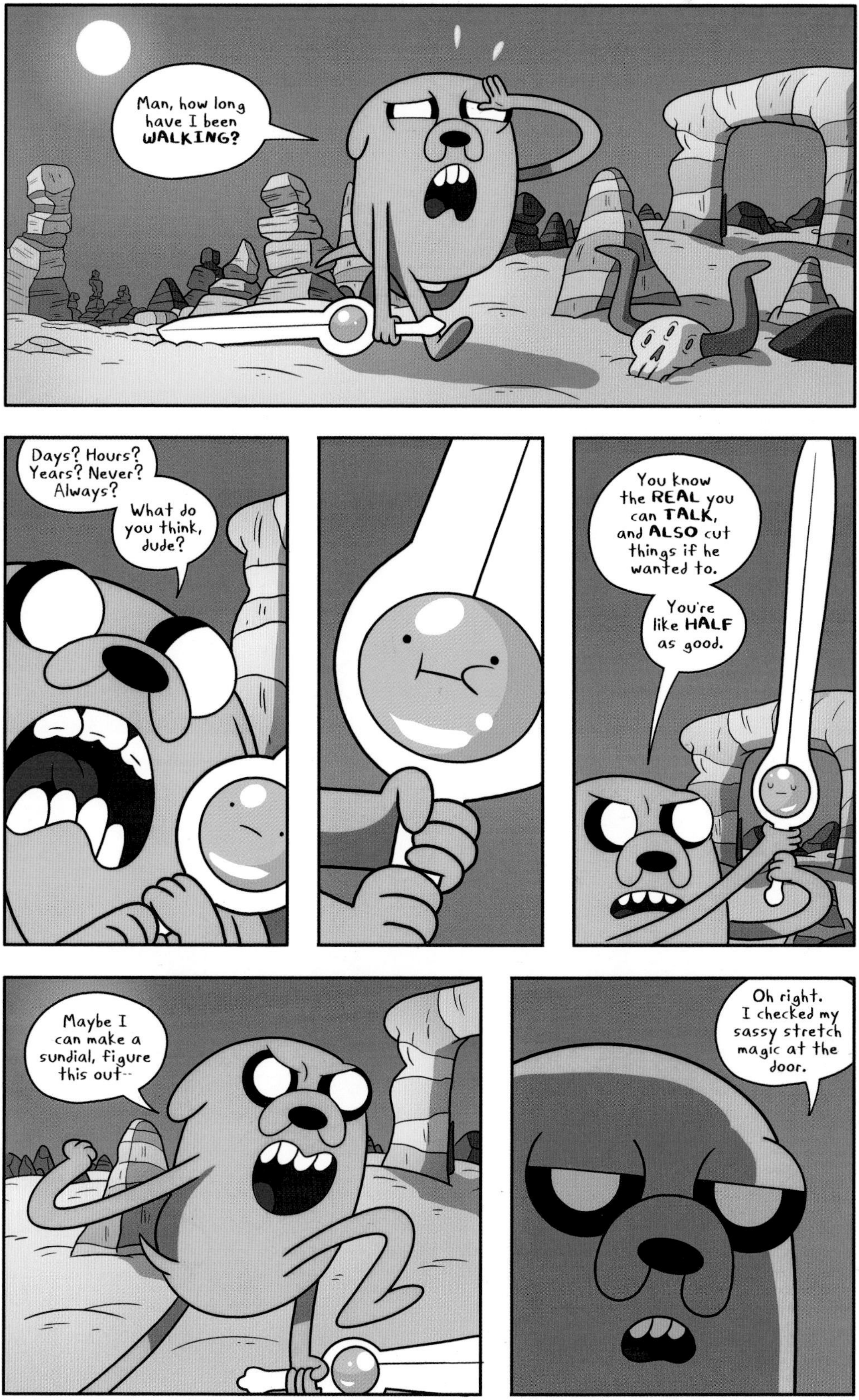
Man, how long have I been WALKING?
Days? Hours? Years? Never? Always?
What do you think, dude?
You know the REAL you can TALK, and ALSO cut things if he wanted to.
You're like HALF as good.
Maybe I can make a sundial, figure this out--
Oh right. I checked my sassy stretch magic at the door.

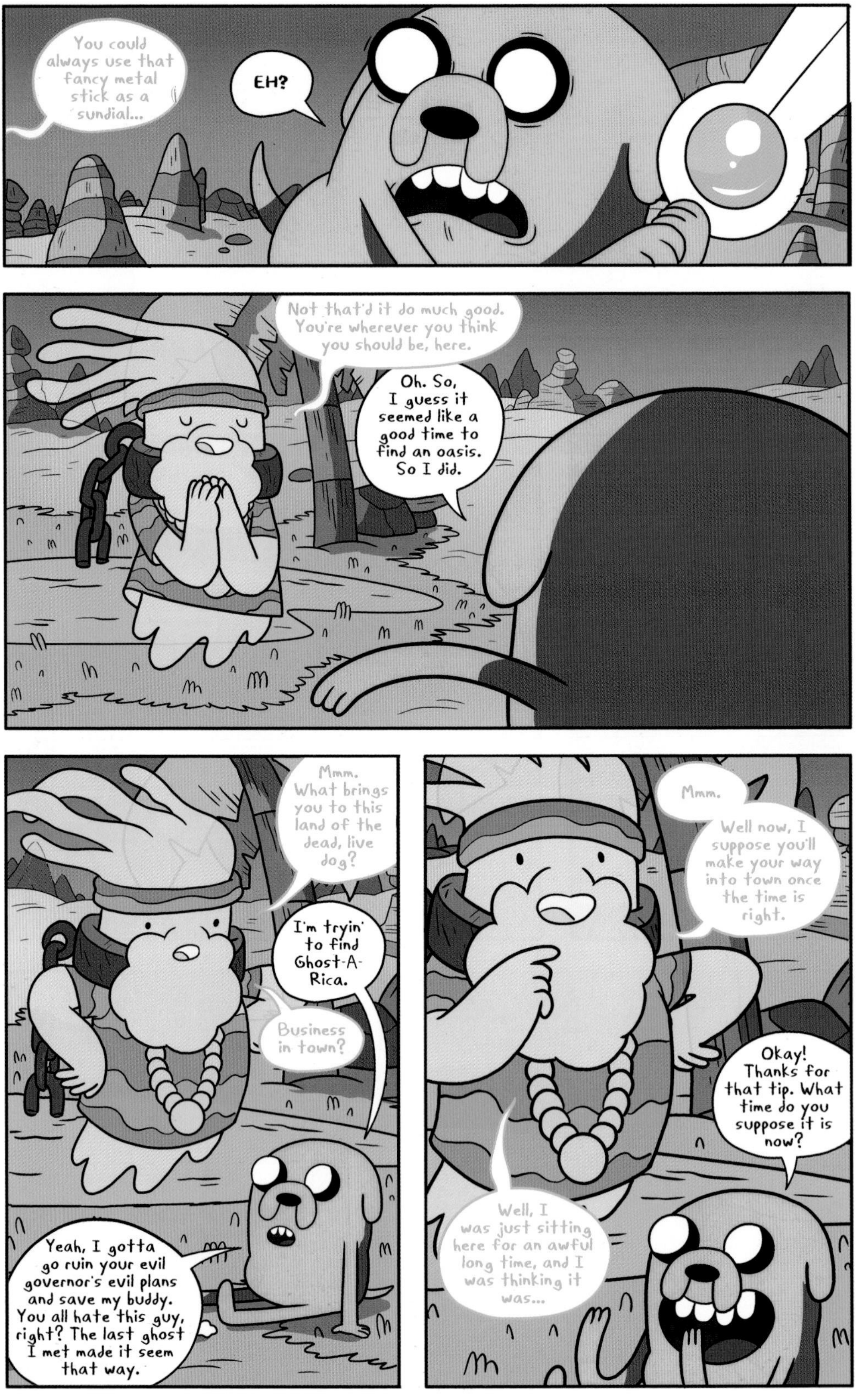

You could always use that fancy metal stick as a sundial...
EH?
Not that'd it do much good. You're wherever you think you should be, here.
Oh. So, I guess it seemed like a good time to find an oasis. So I did.
Mmm. What brings you to this land of the dead, live dog?
I'm tryin' to find Ghost-A-Rica.
Business in town?
Yeah, I gotta go ruin your evil governor's evil plans and save my buddy. You all hate this guy, right? The last ghost I met made it seem that way.
Mmm.
Well now, I suppose you'll make your way into town once the time is right.
Okay! Thanks for that tip. What time do you suppose it is now?
Well, I was just sitting here for an awful long time, and I was thinking it was...

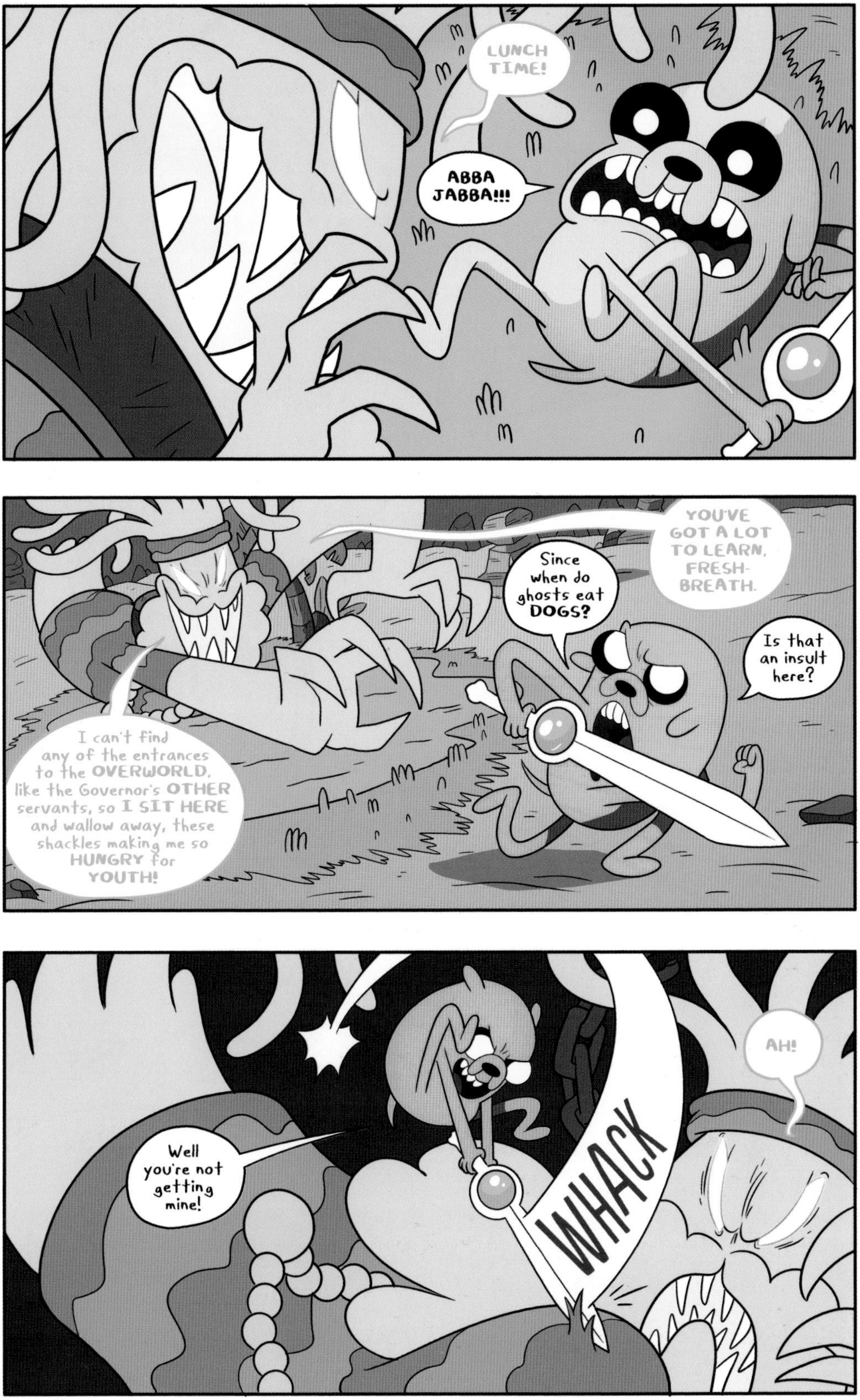
LUNCH TIME!
ABBA JABBA!!!
YOU'VE GOT A LOT TO LEARN, FRESH-BREATH.
Since when do ghosts eat DOGS?
Is that an insult here?
I can't find any of the entrances to the OVERWORLD, like the Governor's OTHER servants, so I SIT HERE and wallow away, these shackles making me so HUNGRY for YOUTH!
AH!
Well you're not getting mine!
WHACK

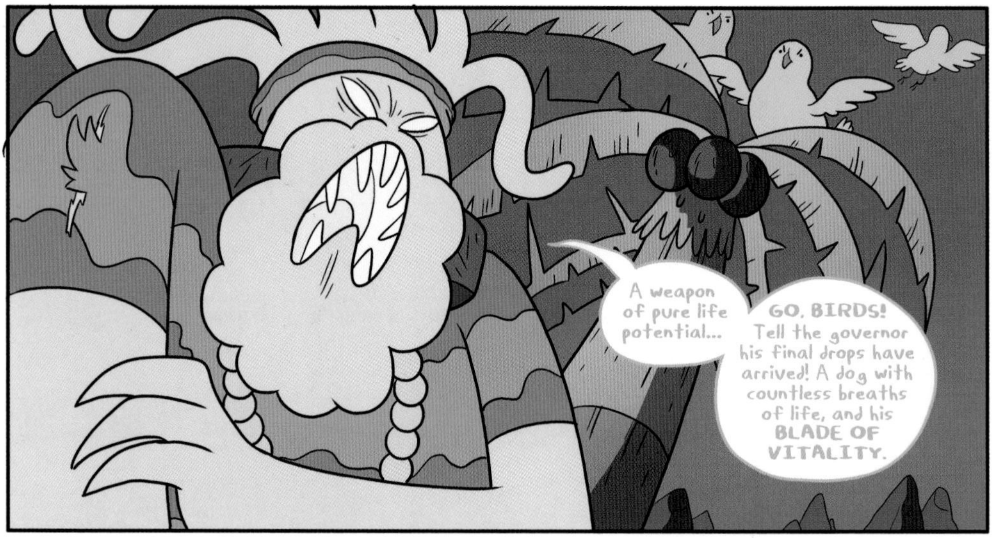
A weapon of pure life potential...
GO, BIRDS! Tell the governor his final drops have arrived! A dog with countless breaths of life, and his BLADE OF VITALITY.

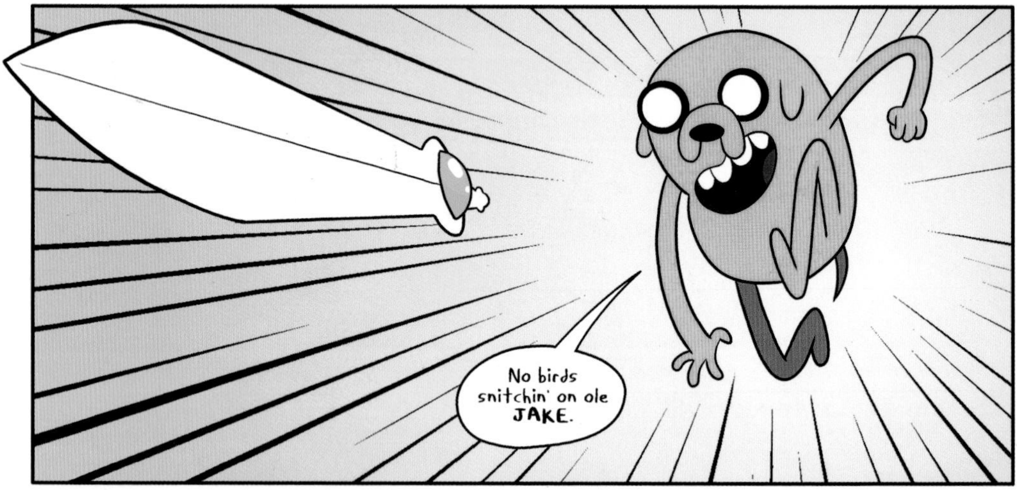
No birds snitchin' on ole JAKE.

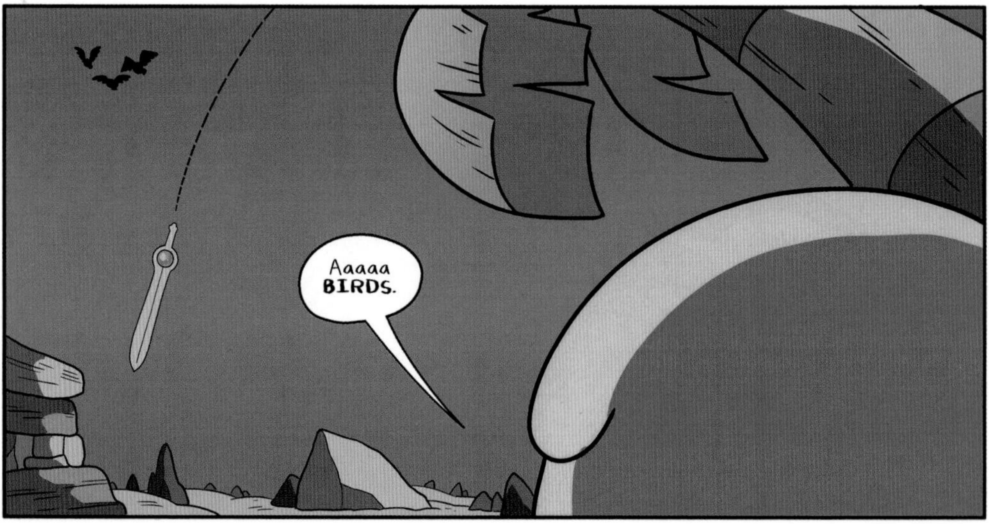
Aaaaa BIRDS.

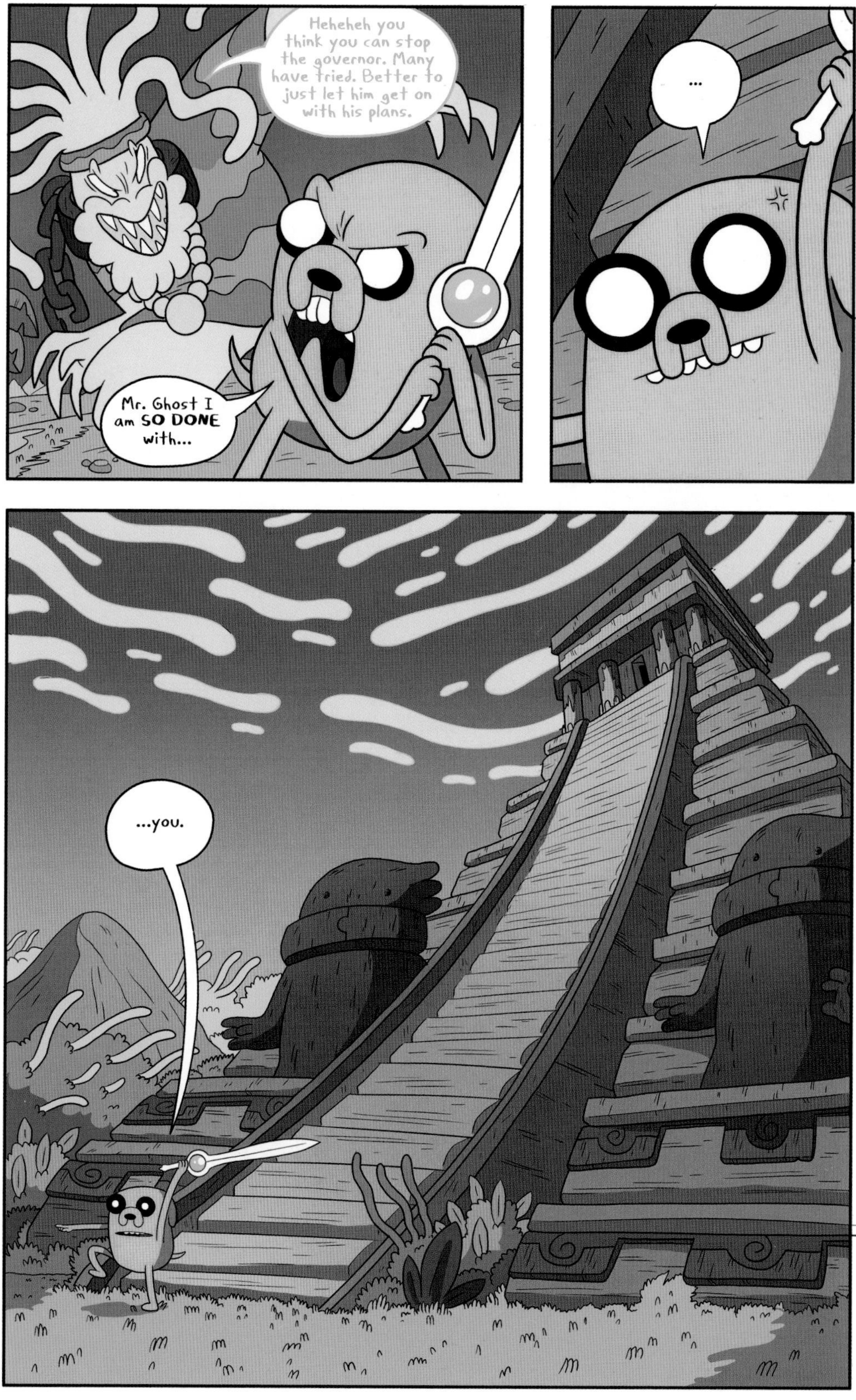
Heheheh you think you can stop the governor. Many have tried. Better to just let him get on with his plans.
Mr. Ghost I am **SO DONE** with...
...
...you.

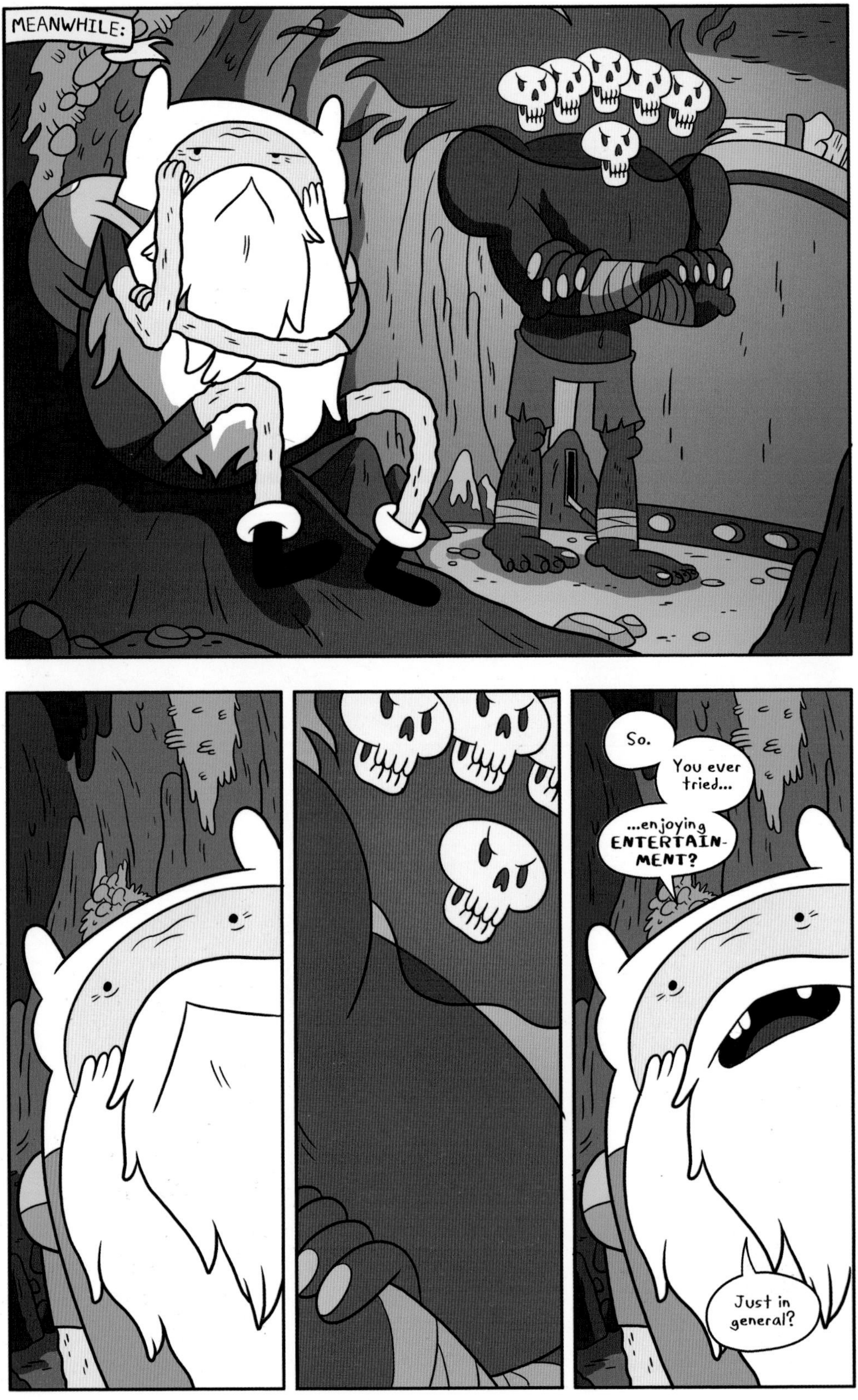
MEANWHILE:
So.
You ever tried...
...enjoying ENTERTAIN-MENT?
Just in general?

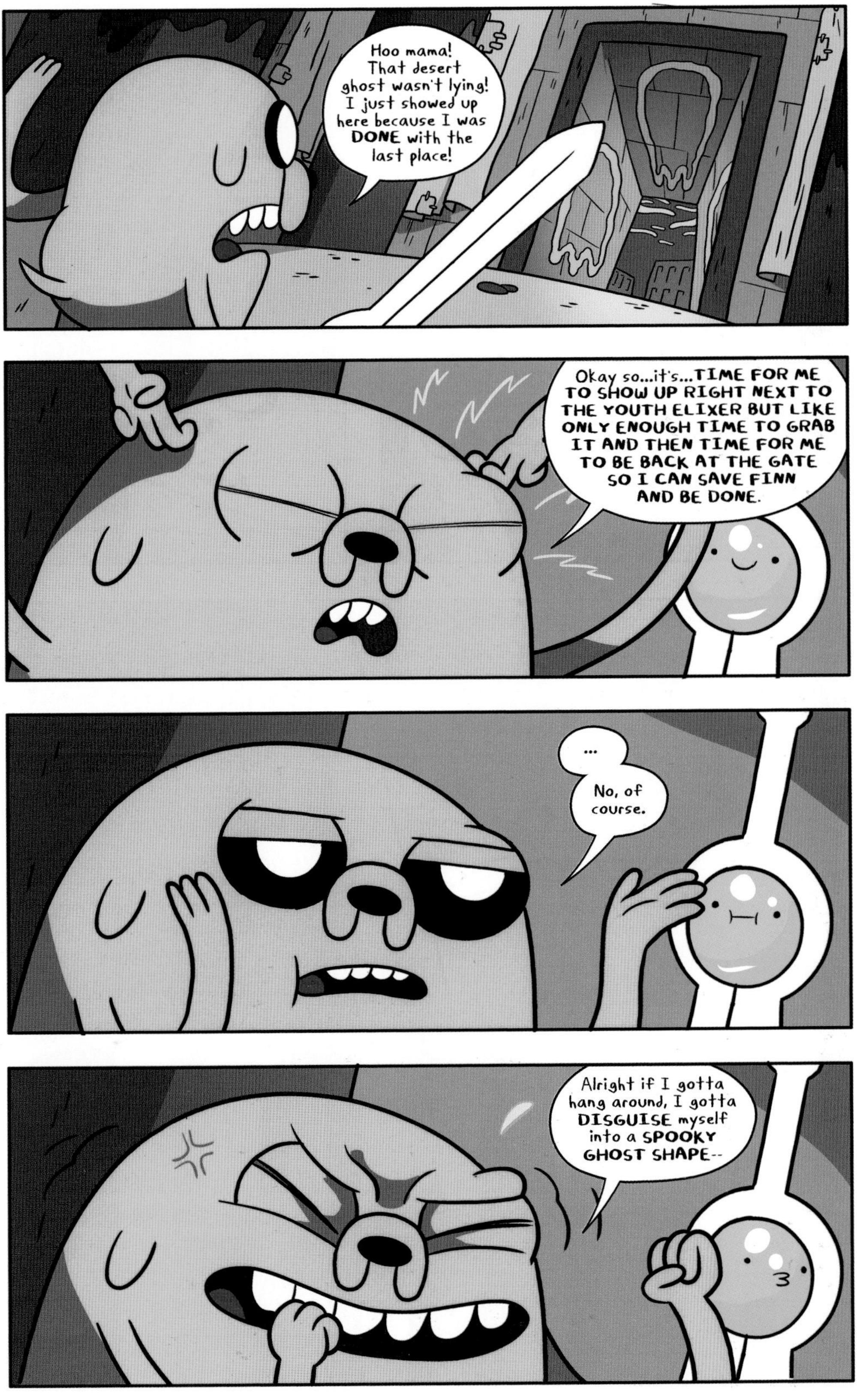
Hoo mama! That desert ghost wasn't lying! I just showed up here because I was **DONE** with the last place!
Okay so...it's...TIME FOR ME TO SHOW UP RIGHT NEXT TO THE YOUTH ELIXER BUT LIKE ONLY ENOUGH TIME TO GRAB IT AND THEN TIME FOR ME TO BE BACK AT THE GATE SO I CAN SAVE FINN AND BE DONE.
...
No, of course.
Alright if I gotta hang around, I gotta **DISGUISE** myself into a **SPOOKY GHOST SHAPE**--

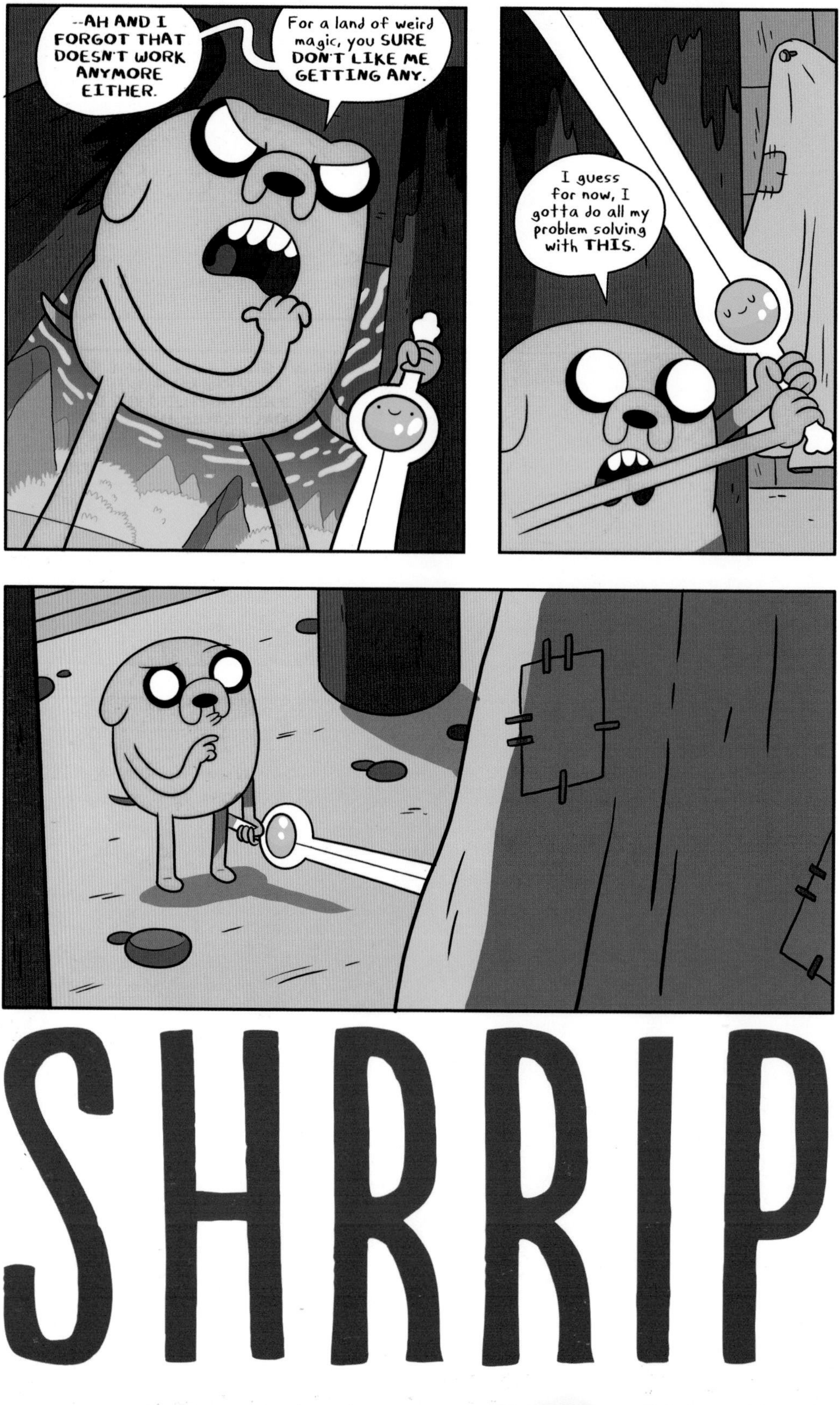
--AH AND I FORGOT THAT DOESN'T WORK ANYMORE EITHER.
For a land of weird magic, you SURE DON'T LIKE ME GETTING ANY.
I guess for now, I gotta do all my problem solving with THIS.
SHRRIP

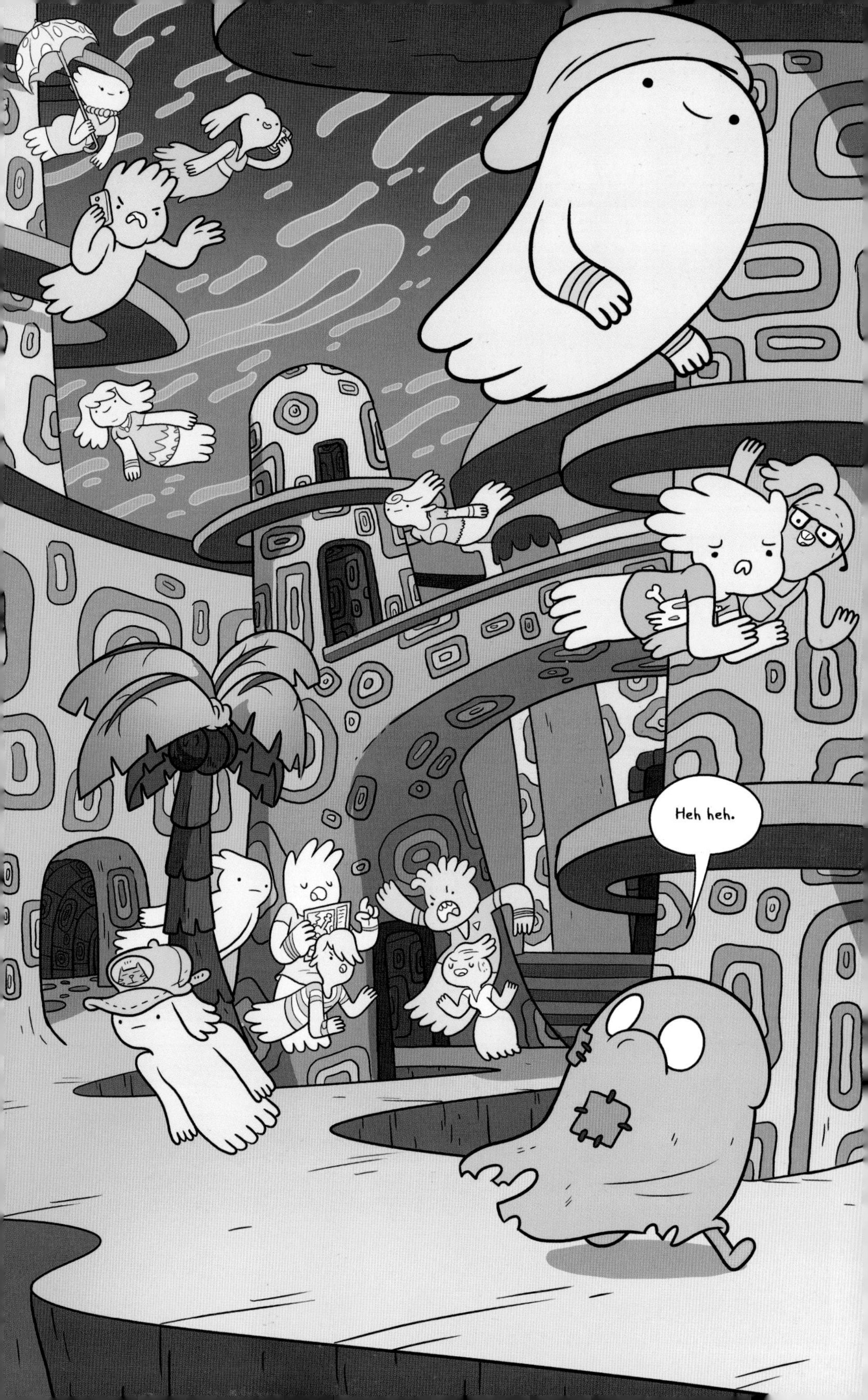
Heh heh.

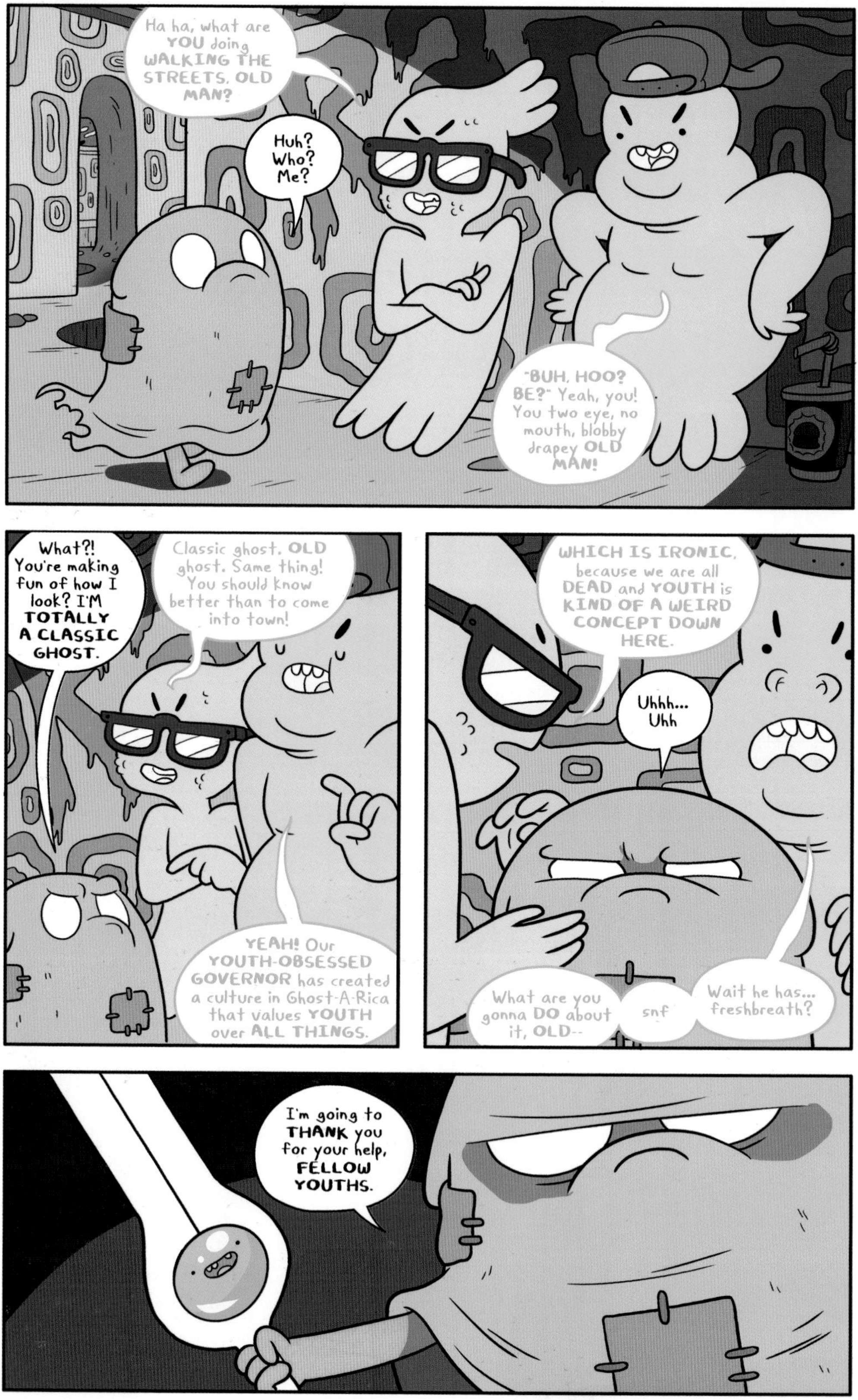
Ha ha, what are YOU doing WALKING THE STREETS, OLD MAN?
Huh? Who? Me?
"BUH, HOO? BE?" Yeah, you! You two eye, no mouth, blobby drapey OLD MAN!
What?! You're making fun of how I look? I'M TOTALLY A CLASSIC GHOST.
Classic ghost. OLD ghost. Same thing! You should know better than to come into town!
YEAH! Our YOUTH-OBSESSED GOVERNOR has created a culture in Ghost-A-Rica that values YOUTH over ALL THINGS.
WHICH IS IRONIC, because we are all DEAD and YOUTH is KIND OF A WEIRD CONCEPT DOWN HERE.
Uhhh... Uhh
What are you gonna DO about it, OLD--
snf
Wait he has... freshbreath?
I'm going to THANK you for your help, FELLOW YOUTHS.

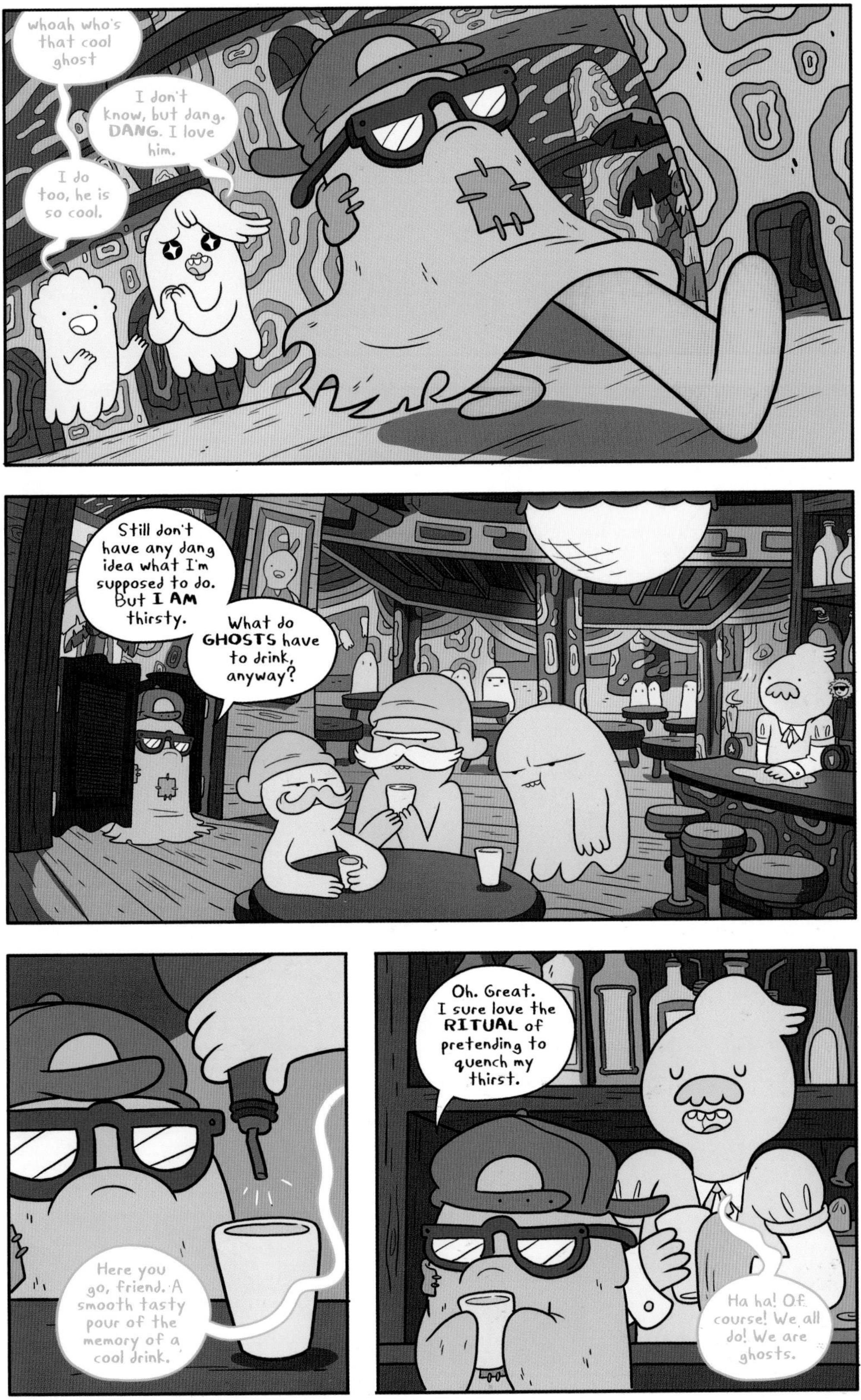
whoah who's that cool ghost
I don't know, but dang. DANG. I love him.
I do too, he is so cool.
Still don't have any dang idea what I'm supposed to do. But I AM thirsty.
What do GHOSTS have to drink, anyway?
Here you go, friend. A smooth tasty pour of the memory of a cool drink.
Oh. Great. I sure love the RITUAL of pretending to quench my thirst.
Ha ha! Of course! We all do! We are ghosts.

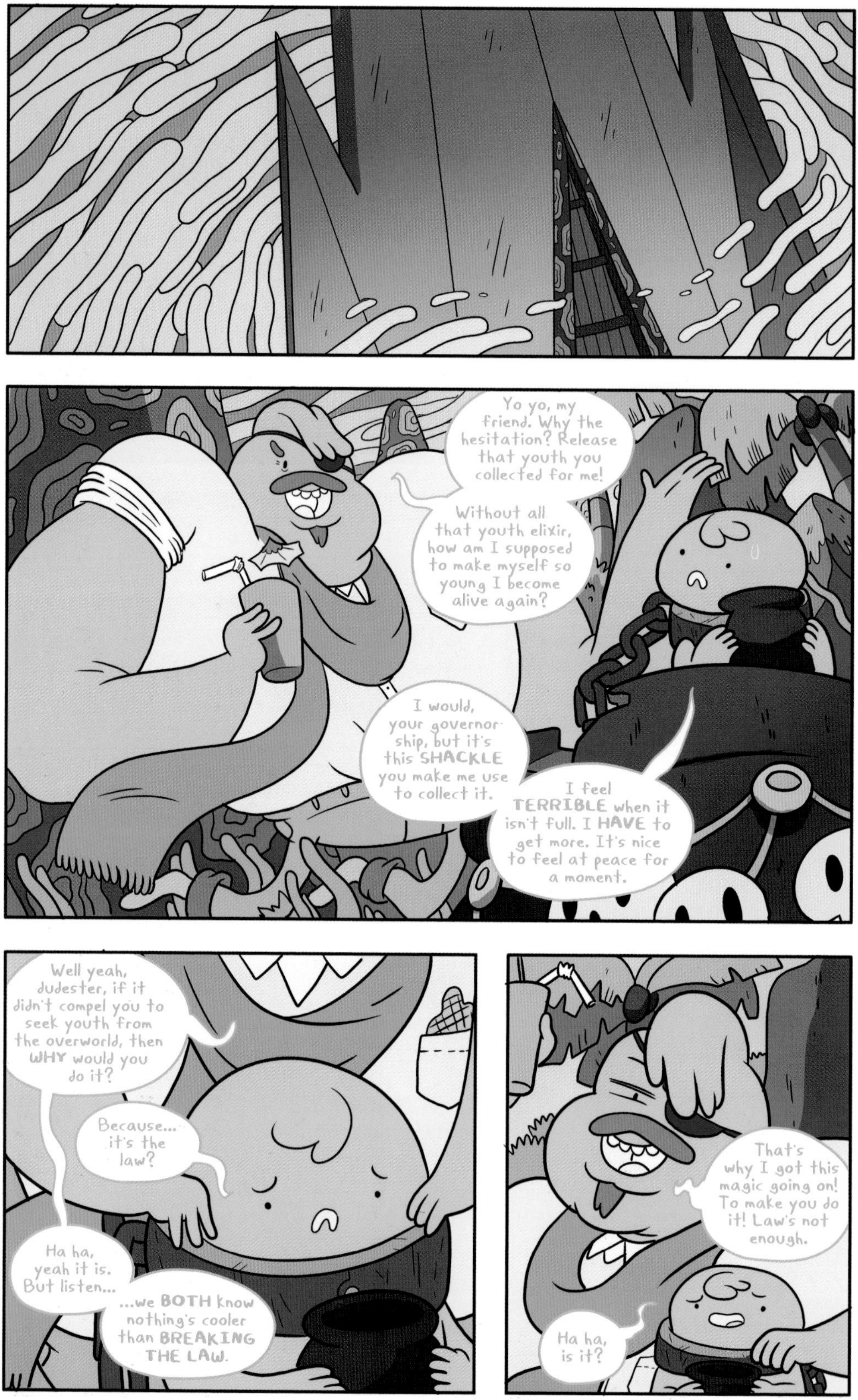

Yo yo, my friend. Why the hesitation? Release that youth you collected for me!
Without all that youth elixir, how am I supposed to make myself so young I become alive again?
I would, your governorship, but it's this SHACKLE you make me use to collect it.
I feel TERRIBLE when it isn't full. I HAVE to get more. It's nice to feel at peace for a moment.
Well yeah, dudester, if it didn't compel you to seek youth from the overworld, then WHY would you do it?
Because... it's the law?
Ha ha, yeah it is. But listen...
...we BOTH know nothing's cooler than BREAKING THE LAW.
That's why I got this magic going on! To make you do it! Law's not enough.
Ha ha, is it?

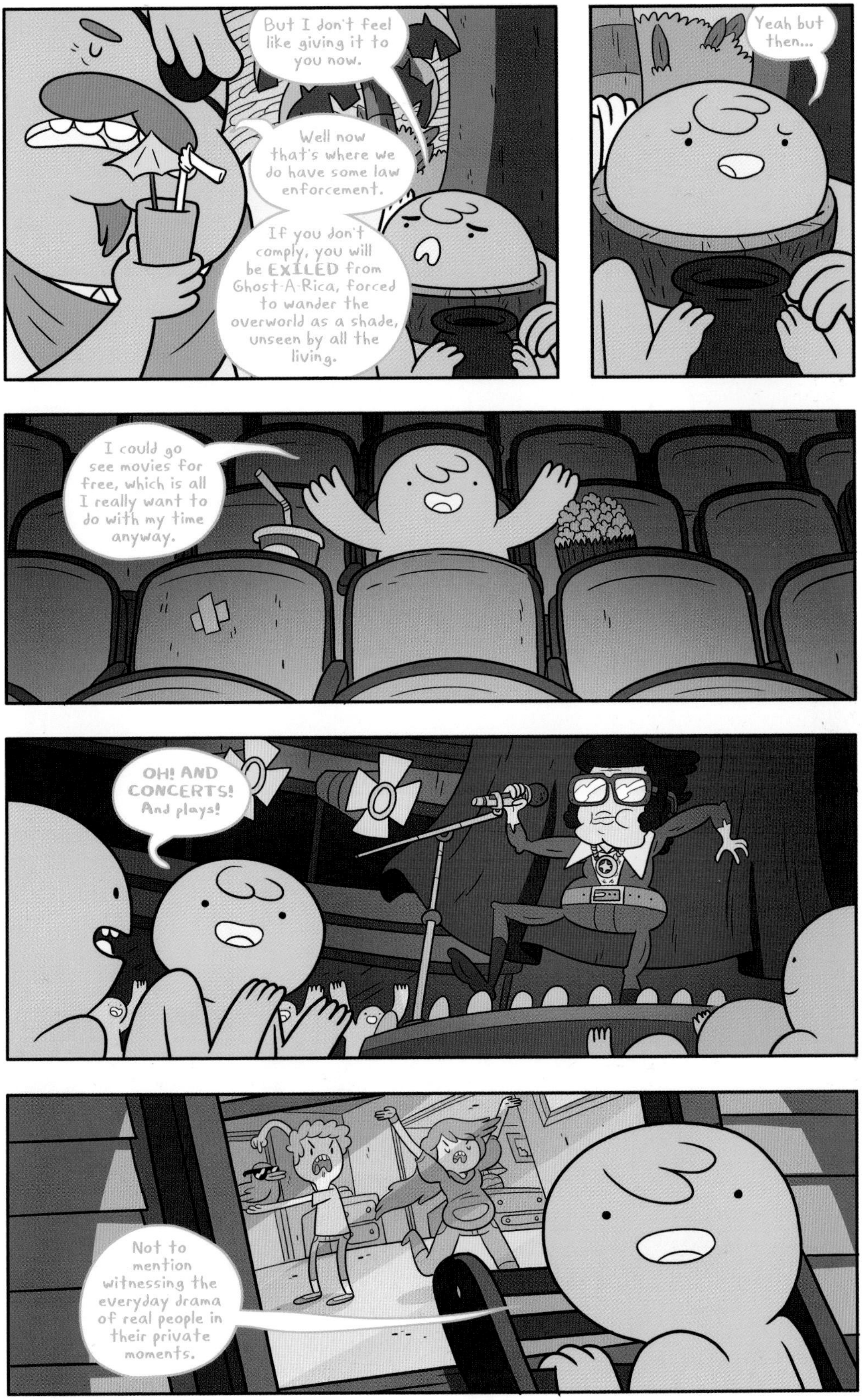
But I don't feel like giving it to you now.
Well now that's where we do have some law enforcement.
If you don't comply, you will be EXILED from Ghost-A-Rica, forced to wander the overworld as a shade, unseen by all the living.
Yeah but then...
I could go see movies for free, which is all I really want to do with my time anyway.
OH! AND CONCERTS! And plays!
Not to mention witnessing the everyday drama of real people in their private moments.

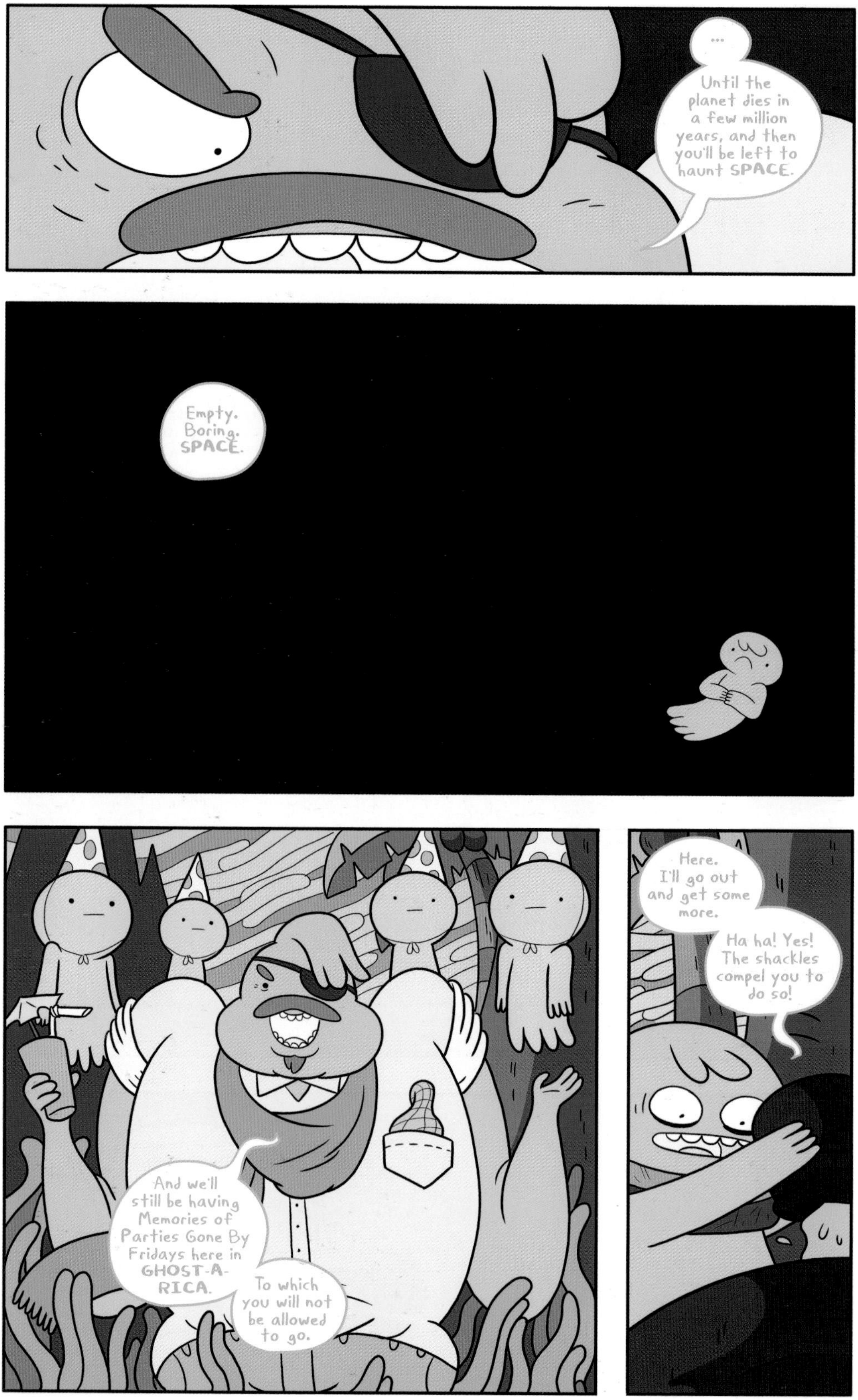
...
Until the planet dies in a few million years, and then you'll be left to haunt SPACE.
Empty. Boring. SPACE.
And we'll still be having Memories of Parties Gone By Fridays here in GHOST-A-RICA.
To which you will not be allowed to go.
Here. I'll go out and get some more.
Ha ha! Yes! The shackles compel you to do so!

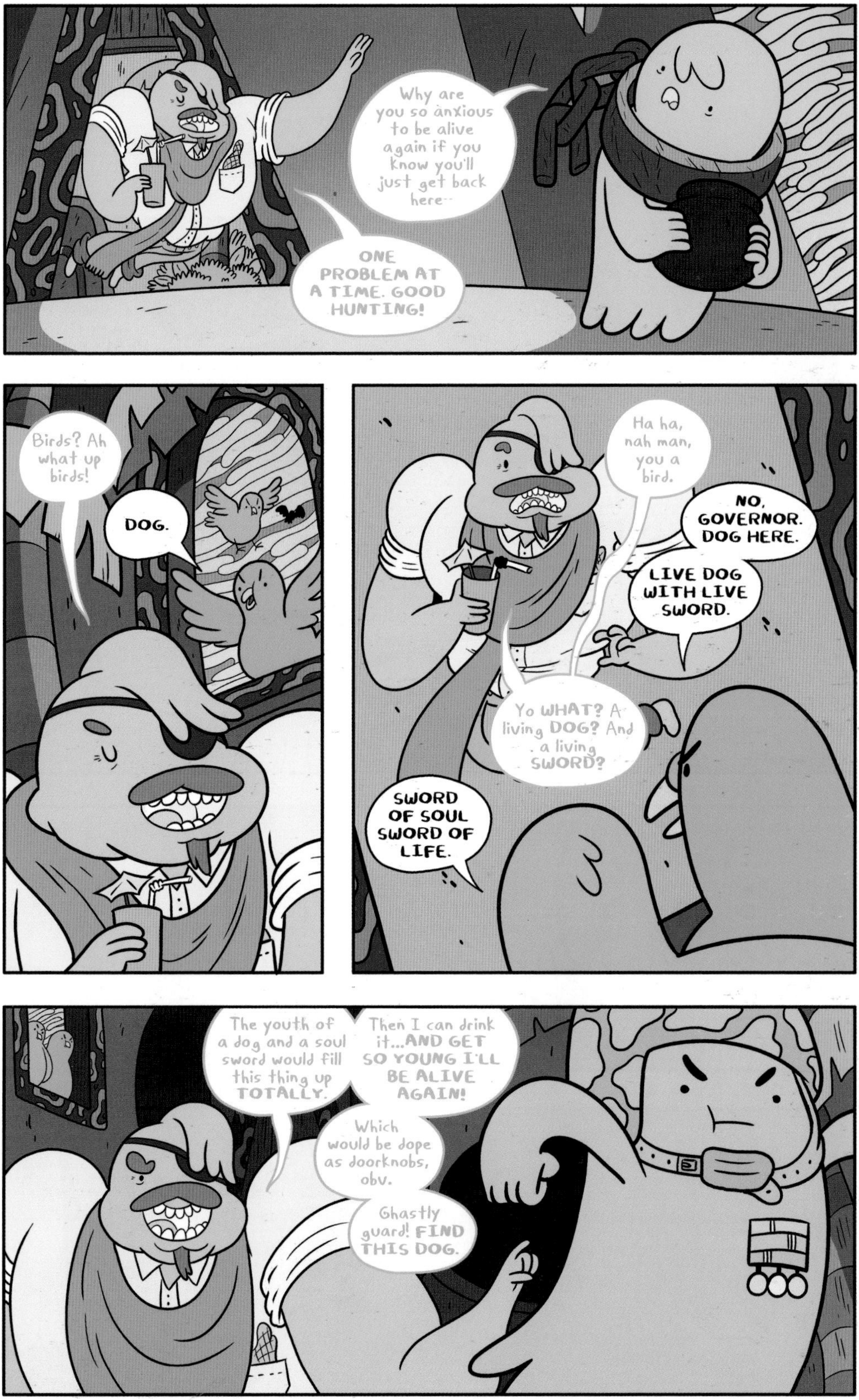

Why are you so anxious to be alive again if you know you'll just get back here--
ONE PROBLEM AT A TIME. GOOD HUNTING!
Birds? Ah what up birds!
DOG.
Ha ha, nah man, you a bird.
NO, GOVERNOR. DOG HERE.
LIVE DOG WITH LIVE SWORD.
Yo WHAT? A living DOG? And a living SWORD?
SWORD OF SOUL SWORD OF LIFE.
The youth of a dog and a soul sword would fill this thing up TOTALLY.
Then I can drink it...AND GET SO YOUNG I'LL BE ALIVE AGAIN!
Which would be dope as doorknobs, obv.
Ghastly guard! FIND THIS DOG.

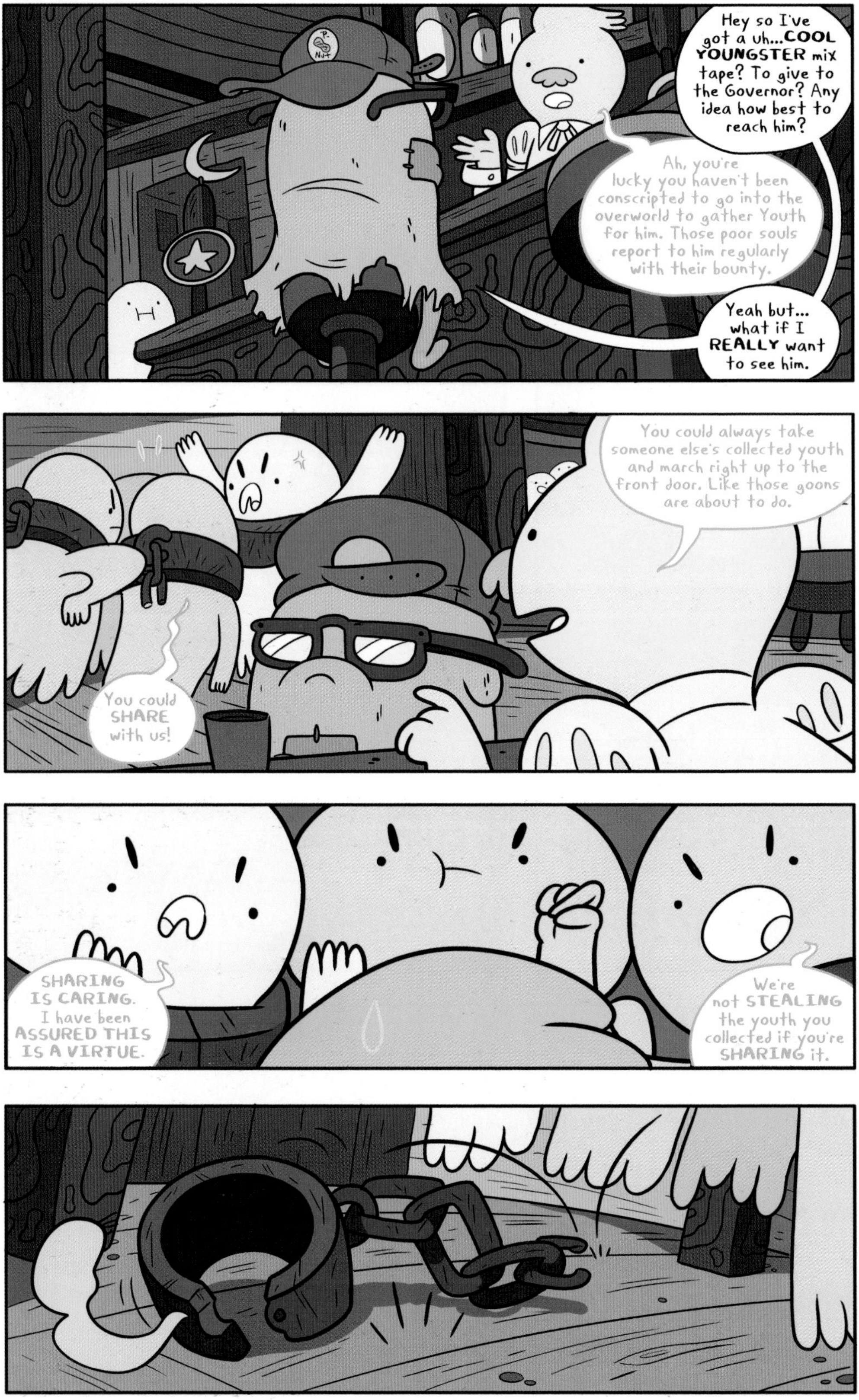
Hey so I've got a uh...COOL YOUNGSTER mix tape? To give to the Governor? Any idea how best to reach him?
Ah, you're lucky you haven't been conscripted to go into the overworld to gather Youth for him. Those poor souls report to him regularly with their bounty.
Yeah but... what if I REALLY want to see him.
You could always take someone else's collected youth and march right up to the front door. Like those goons are about to do.
You could SHARE with us!
SHARING IS CARING. I have been ASSURED THIS IS A VIRTUE.
We're not STEALING the youth you collected if you're SHARING it.

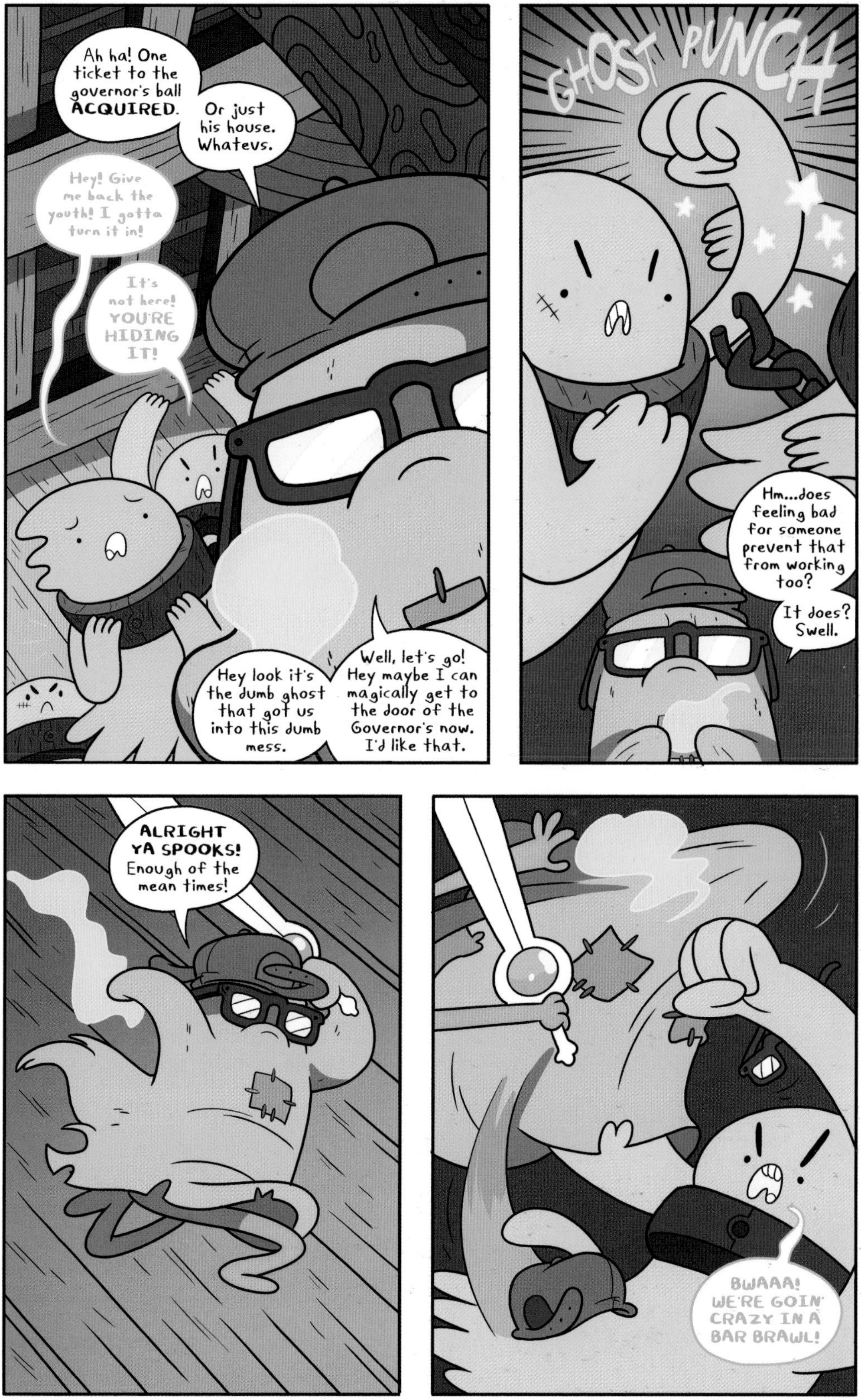
Ah ha! One ticket to the governor's ball ACQUIRED.
Or just his house. Whatevs.
Hey! Give me back the youth! I gotta turn it in!
It's not here! YOU'RE HIDING IT!
Hey look it's the dumb ghost that got us into this dumb mess.
Well, let's go! Hey maybe I can magically get to the door of the Governor's now. I'd like that.
GHOST PUNCH
Hm...does feeling bad for someone prevent that from working too?
It does? Swell.
ALRIGHT YA SPOOKS! Enough of the mean times!
BWAAA! WE'RE GOIN' CRAZY IN A BAR BRAWL!

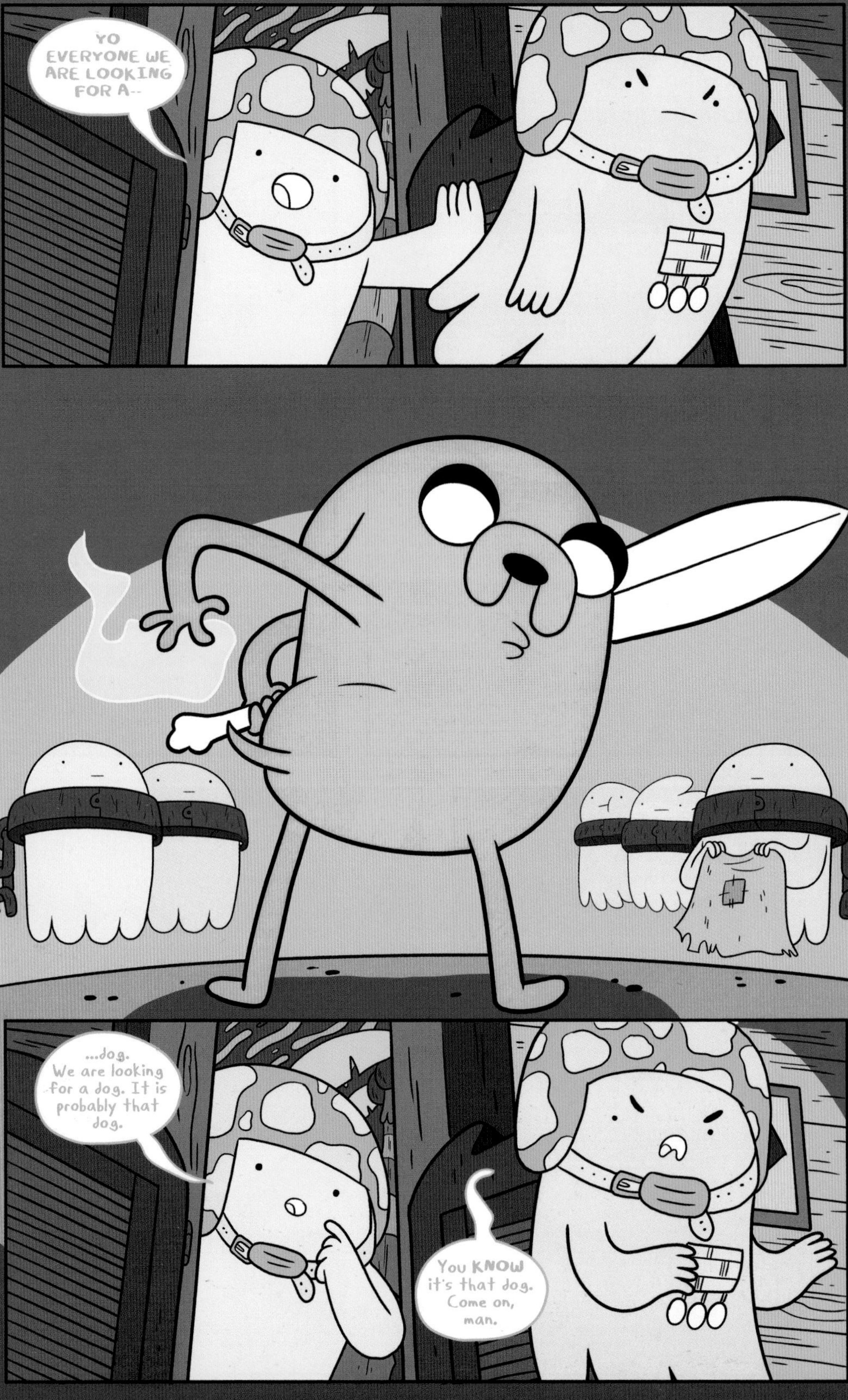
YO EVERYONE WE ARE LOOKING FOR A--
...dog. We are looking for a dog. It is probably that dog.
You KNOW it's that dog. Come on, man.

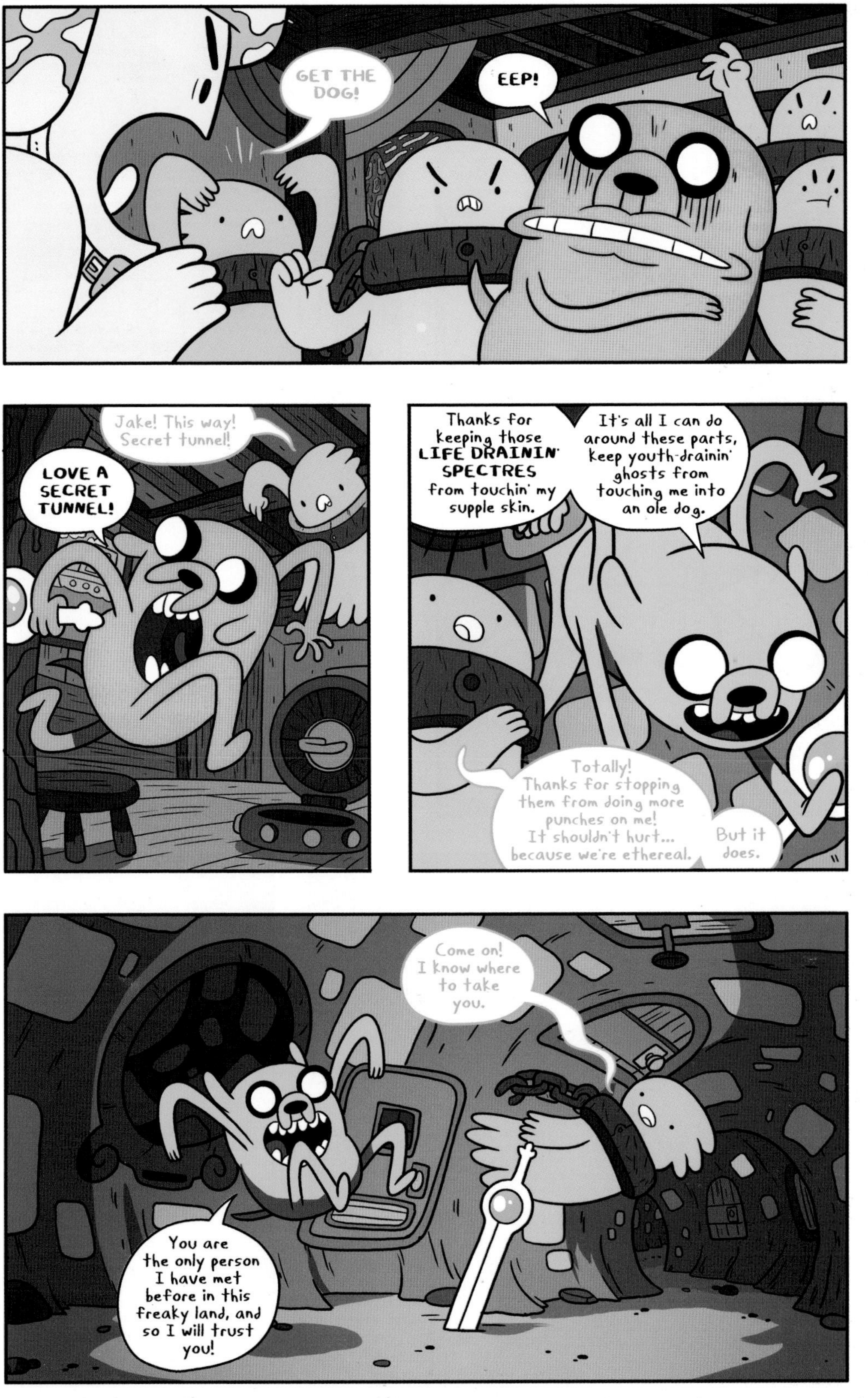

GET THE DOG!
EEP!
Jake! This way! Secret tunnel!
LOVE A SECRET TUNNEL!
Thanks for keeping those LIFE DRAININ' SPECTRES from touchin' my supple skin.
It's all I can do around these parts, keep youth-drainin' ghosts from touching me into an ole dog.
Totally! Thanks for stopping them from doing more punches on me! It shouldn't hurt... because we're ethereal.
But it does.
Come on! I know where to take you.
You are the only person I have met before in this freaky land, and so I will trust you!

Hey, so that guardian in between my world and yours seemed **PRETTY** serious about keeping anybody from crossing either way.

Oh he is SO serious about that. That's like his number one thing.

Yeah, but it looks like there is a small army of ghosts going to Ooo to drain youth and come back. How are they getting past him?

Oh, not just Ooo! Oh no no! There are doors and paths to hundreds of spaces and places. Not all are "official" doors.

Couldn't find a hero to fix your mess in one of those hundred other spaces, huh?

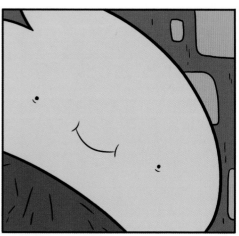

Right. Man, these tunnels are **SPOOKY**. Like, wasn't there A LOT more space behind us just a second ago?

That's just how it is in this particular deadworld. You may have noticed but you're only really where you want to be when--

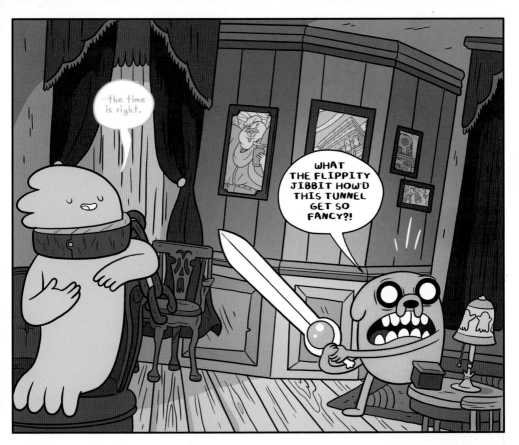

--the time is right.

WHAT THE FLIPPITY JIBBIT HOW'D THIS TUNNEL GET SO FANCY?!

This is where you need to be, Jake! You're all the closer to the HEART of our WICKED GOVERNOR'S lair!

Oh YEAH? And where might THAT--

SPHH oh glob even the cookies are dead here.

WHERE MIGHT THAT BE?

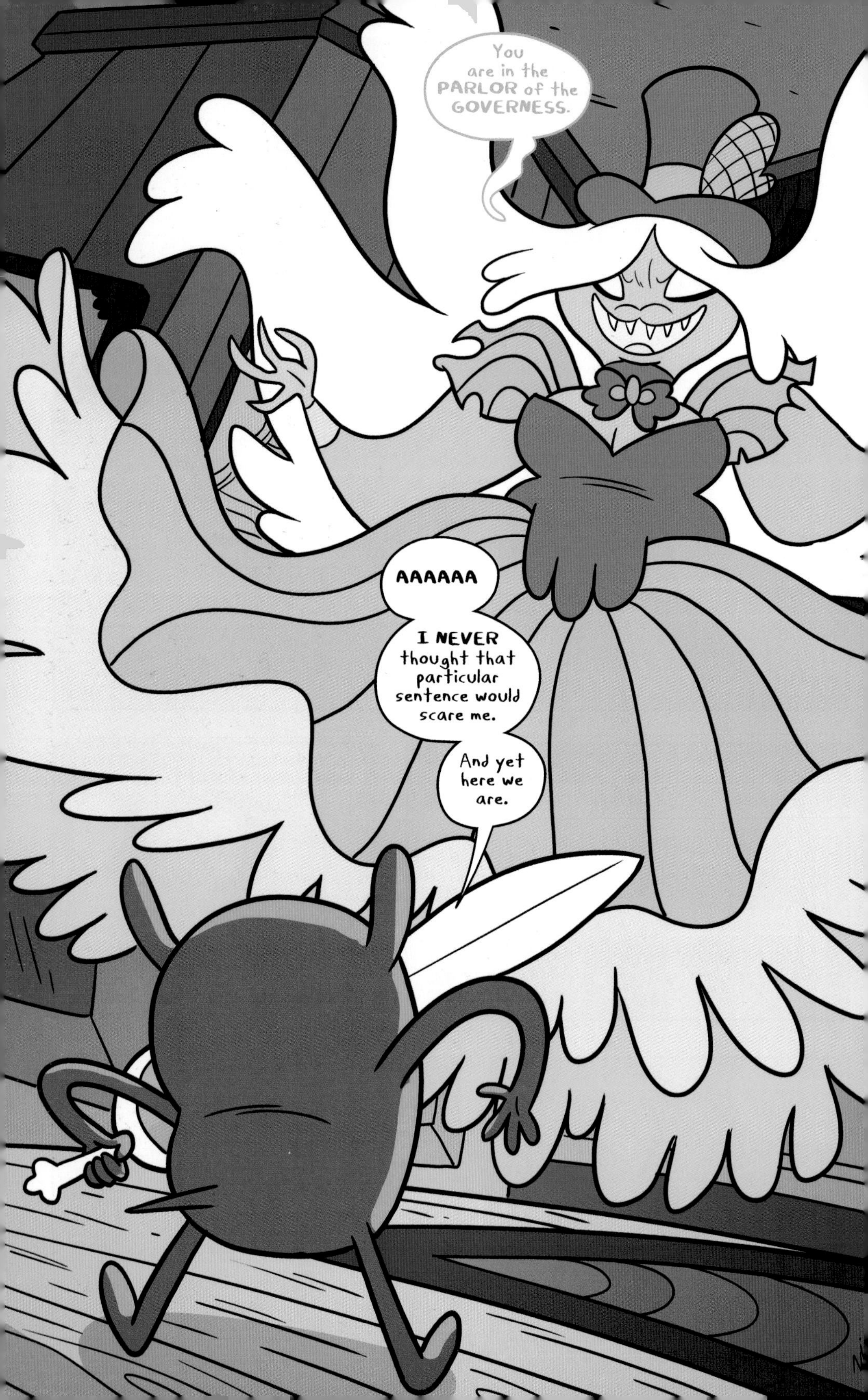
You are in the PARLOR of the GOVERNESS.
AAAAAA
I NEVER thought that particular sentence would scare me.
And yet here we are.

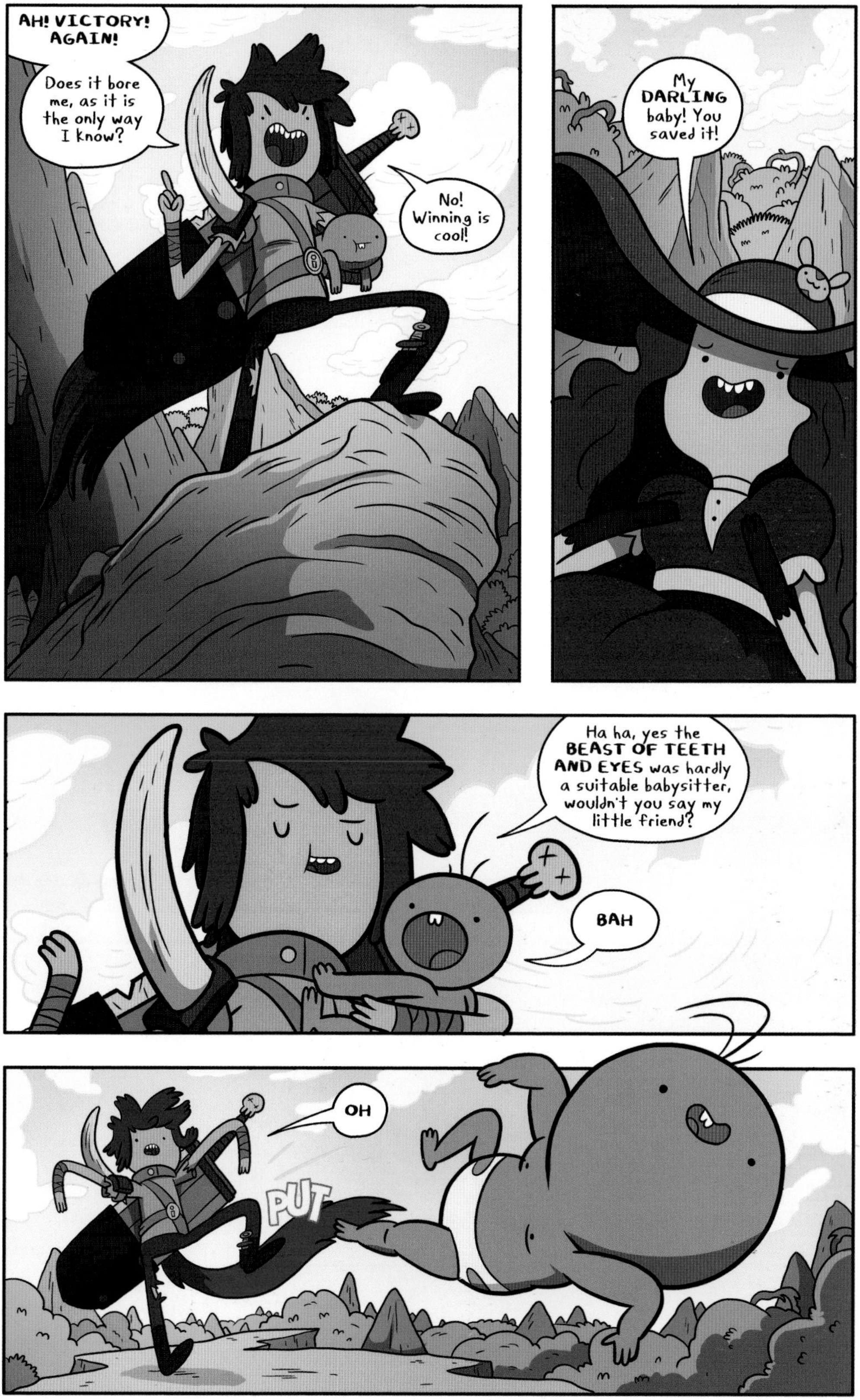
AH! VICTORY! AGAIN!
Does it bore me, as it is the only way I know?
No! Winning is cool!
My DARLING baby! You saved it!
Ha ha, yes the BEAST OF TEETH AND EYES was hardly a suitable babysitter, wouldn't you say my little friend?
BAH
OH
PUT

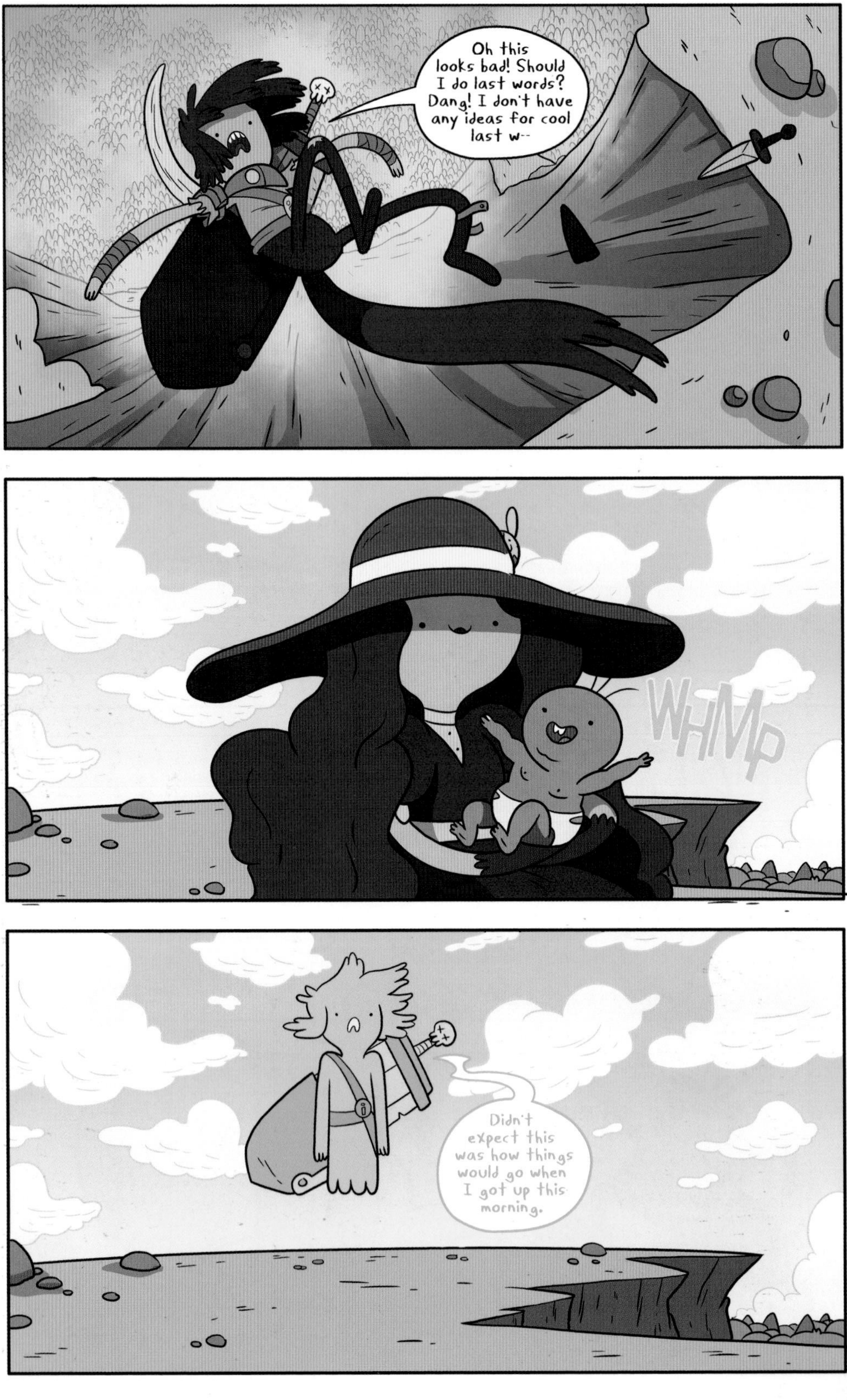
Oh this looks bad! Should I do last words? Dang! I don't have any ideas for cool last w--
WHMP
Didn't expect this was how things would go when I got up this morning.

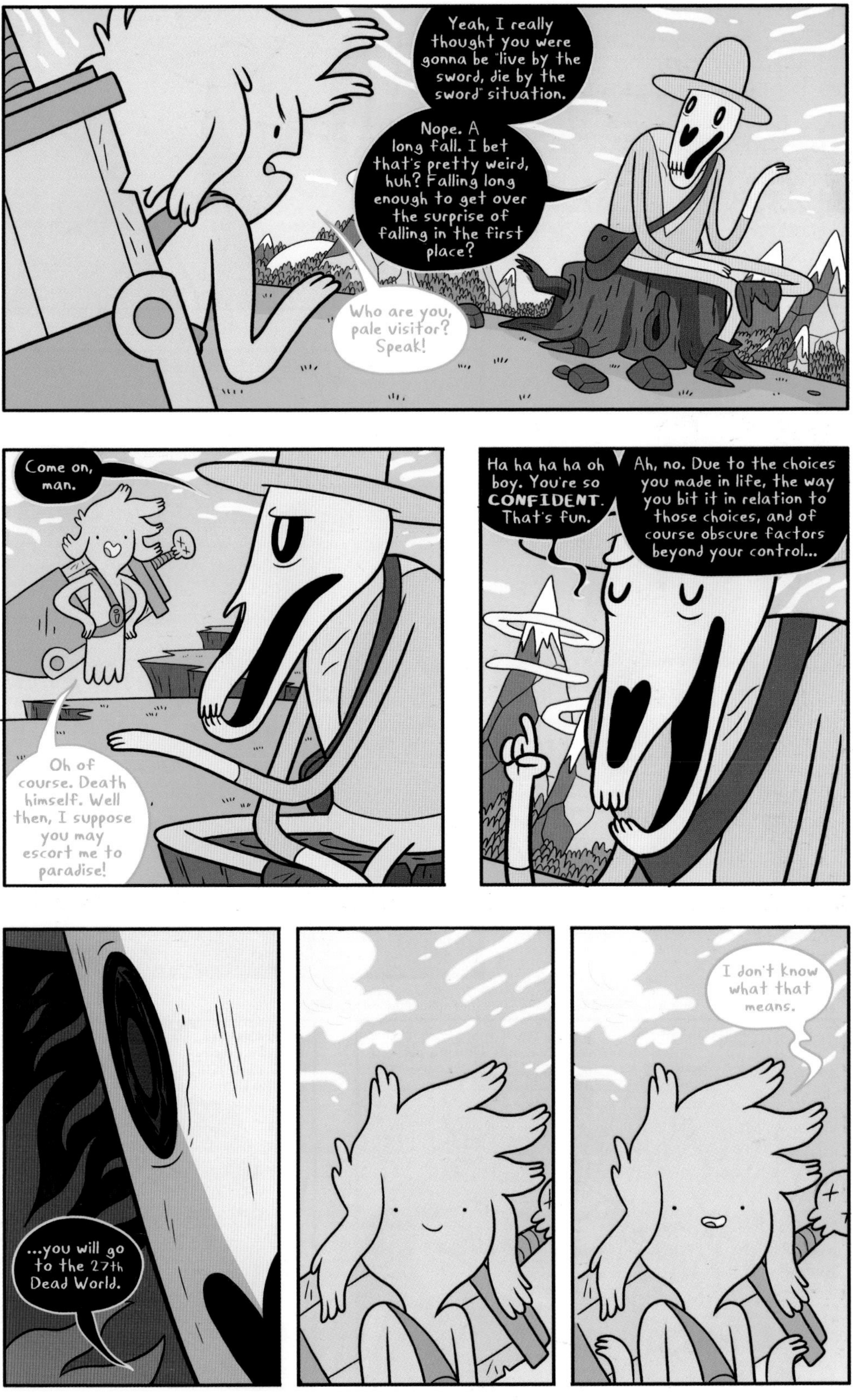
Yeah, I really thought you were gonna be "live by the sword, die by the sword" situation.
Nope. A long fall. I bet that's pretty weird, huh? Falling long enough to get over the surprise of falling in the first place?
Who are you, pale visitor? Speak!
Come on, man.
Oh of course. Death himself. Well then, I suppose you may escort me to paradise!
Ha ha ha ha oh boy. You're so CONFIDENT. That's fun.
Ah, no. Due to the choices you made in life, the way you bit it in relation to those choices, and of course obscure factors beyond your control...
...you will go to the 27th Dead World.
I don't know what that means.

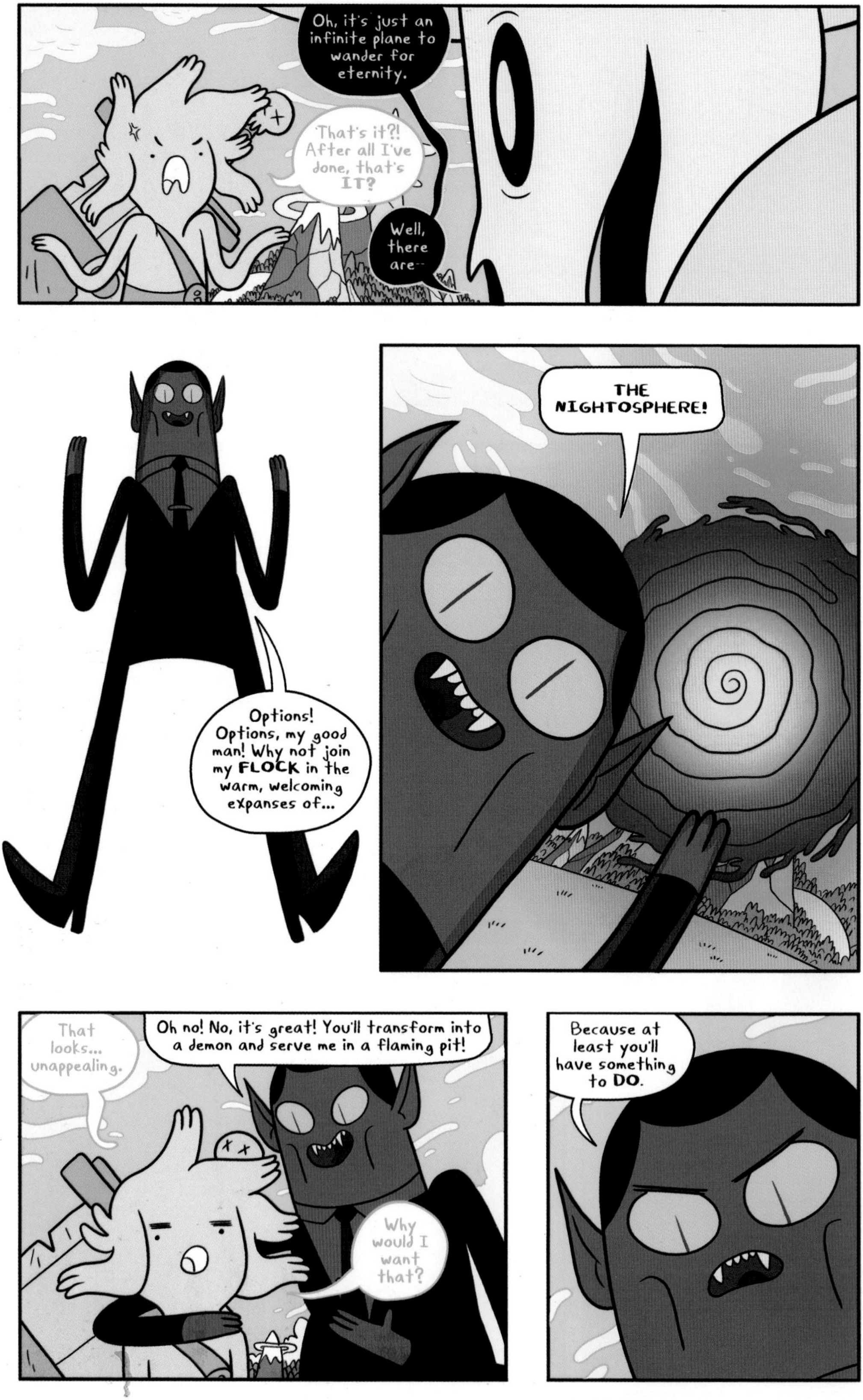

Oh, it's just an infinite plane to wander for eternity.
That's it?! After all I've done, that's IT?
Well, there are--
Options! Options, my good man! Why not join my FLOCK in the warm, welcoming expanses of...
THE NIGHTOSPHERE!
That looks... unappealing.
Oh no! No, it's great! You'll transform into a demon and serve me in a flaming pit!
Why would I want that?
Because at least you'll have something to DO.

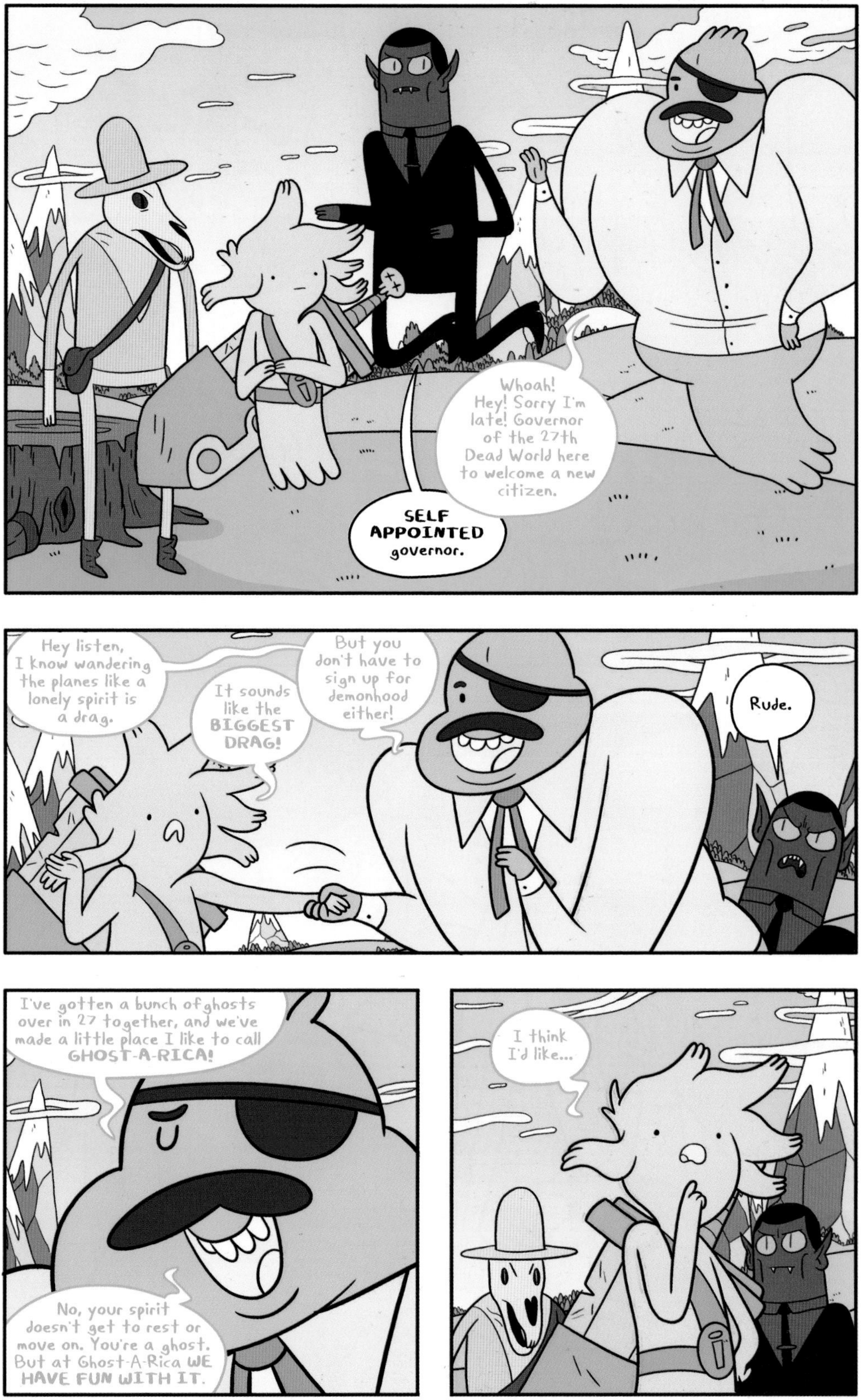

Whoah! Hey! Sorry I'm late! Governor of the 27th Dead World here to welcome a new citizen.
SELF APPOINTED governor.
Hey listen, I know wandering the planes like a lonely spirit is a drag.
It sounds like the BIGGEST DRAG!
But you don't have to sign up for demonhood either!
Rude.
I've gotten a bunch of ghosts over in 27 together, and we've made a little place I like to call GHOST-A-RICA!
No, your spirit doesn't get to rest or move on. You're a ghost. But at Ghost-A-Rica WE HAVE FUN WITH IT.
I think I'd like...

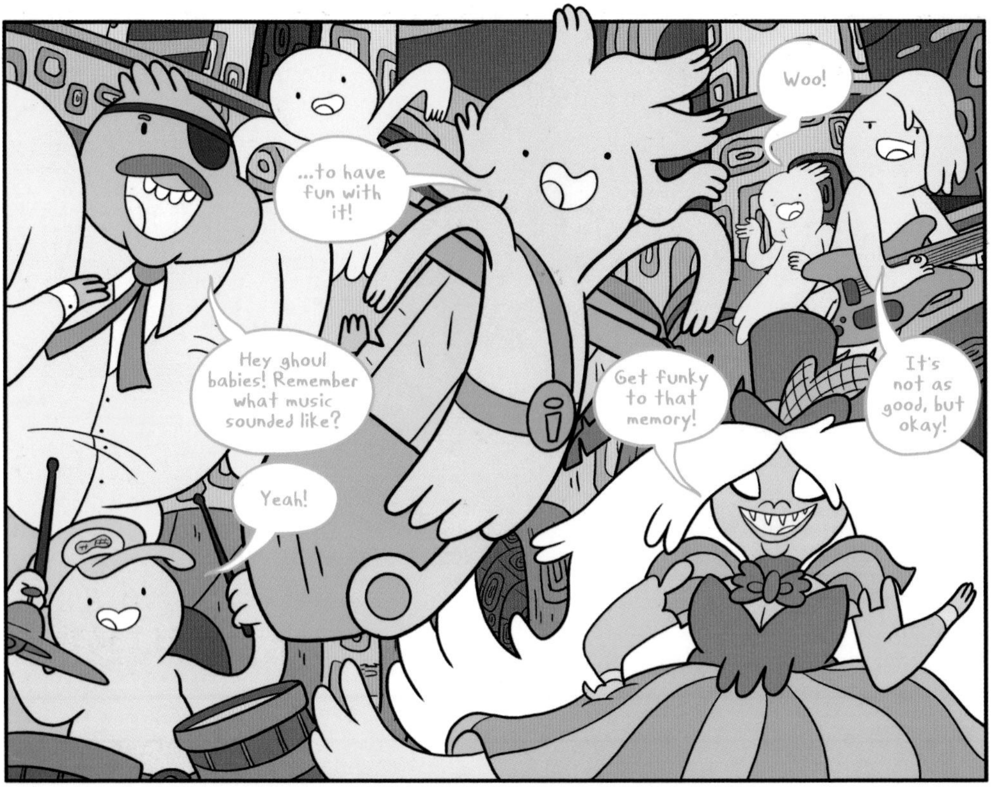
...to have fun with it!
Woo!
Hey ghoul babies! Remember what music sounded like?
Get funky to that memory!
It's not as good, but okay!
Yeah!

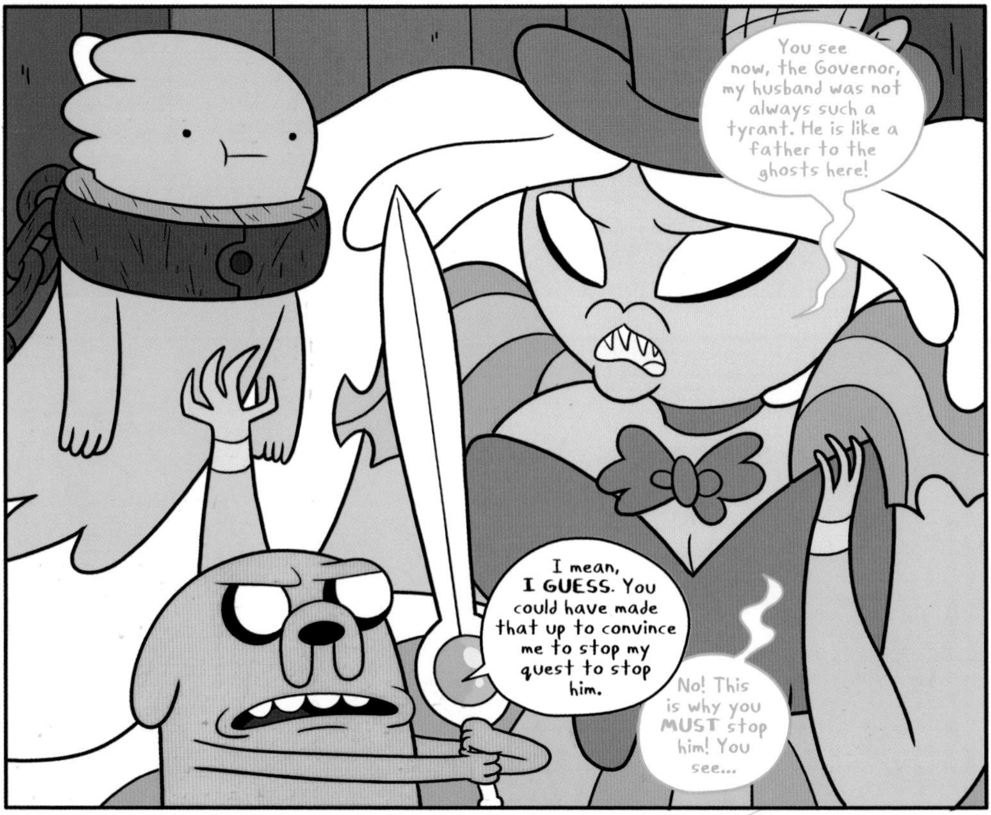
You see now, the Governor, my husband was not always such a tyrant. He is like a father to the ghosts here!
I mean, **I GUESS**. You could have made that up to convince me to stop my quest to stop him.
No! This is why you **MUST** stop him! You see...

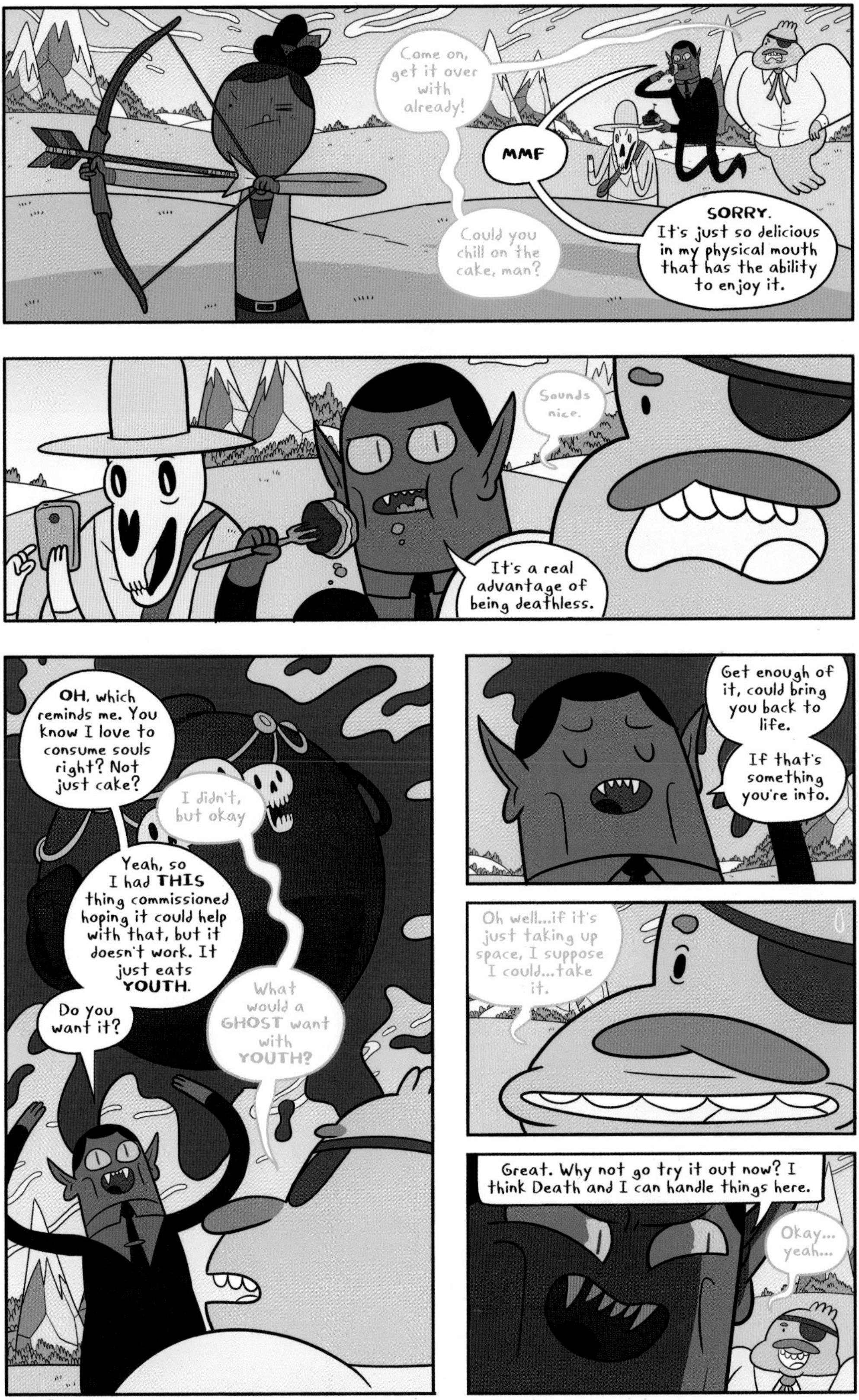
Come on, get it over with already!
MMF
Could you chill on the cake, man?
SORRY. It's just so delicious in my physical mouth that has the ability to enjoy it.
Sounds nice.
It's a real advantage of being deathless.
OH, which reminds me. You know I love to consume souls right? Not just cake?
I didn't, but okay
Yeah, so I had THIS thing commissioned hoping it could help with that, but it doesn't work. It just eats YOUTH.
Do you want it?
What would a GHOST want with YOUTH?
Get enough of it, could bring you back to life.
If that's something you're into.
Oh well...if it's just taking up space, I suppose I could...take it.
Great. Why not go try it out now? I think Death and I can handle things here.
Okay... yeah...

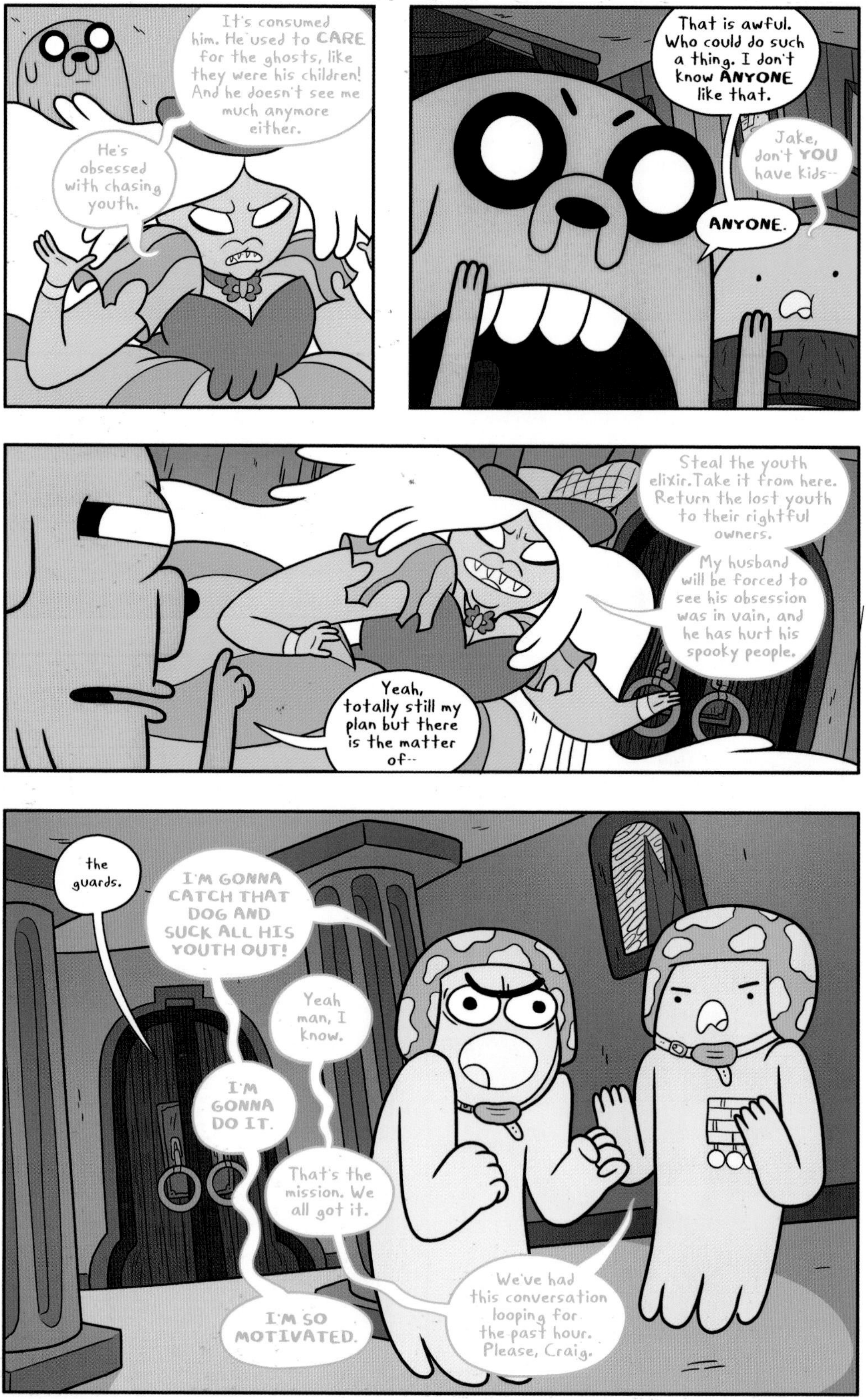
It's consumed him. He used to CARE for the ghosts, like they were his children! And he doesn't see me much anymore either.
He's obsessed with chasing youth.
That is awful. Who could do such a thing. I don't know ANYONE like that.
Jake, don't YOU have kids--
ANYONE.
Steal the youth elixir. Take it from here. Return the lost youth to their rightful owners.
My husband will be forced to see his obsession was in vain, and he has hurt his spooky people.
Yeah, totally still my plan but there is the matter of--
the guards.
I'M GONNA CATCH THAT DOG AND SUCK ALL HIS YOUTH OUT!
Yeah man, I know.
I'M GONNA DO IT.
That's the mission. We all got it.
I'M SO MOTIVATED.
We've had this conversation looping for the past hour. Please, Craig.

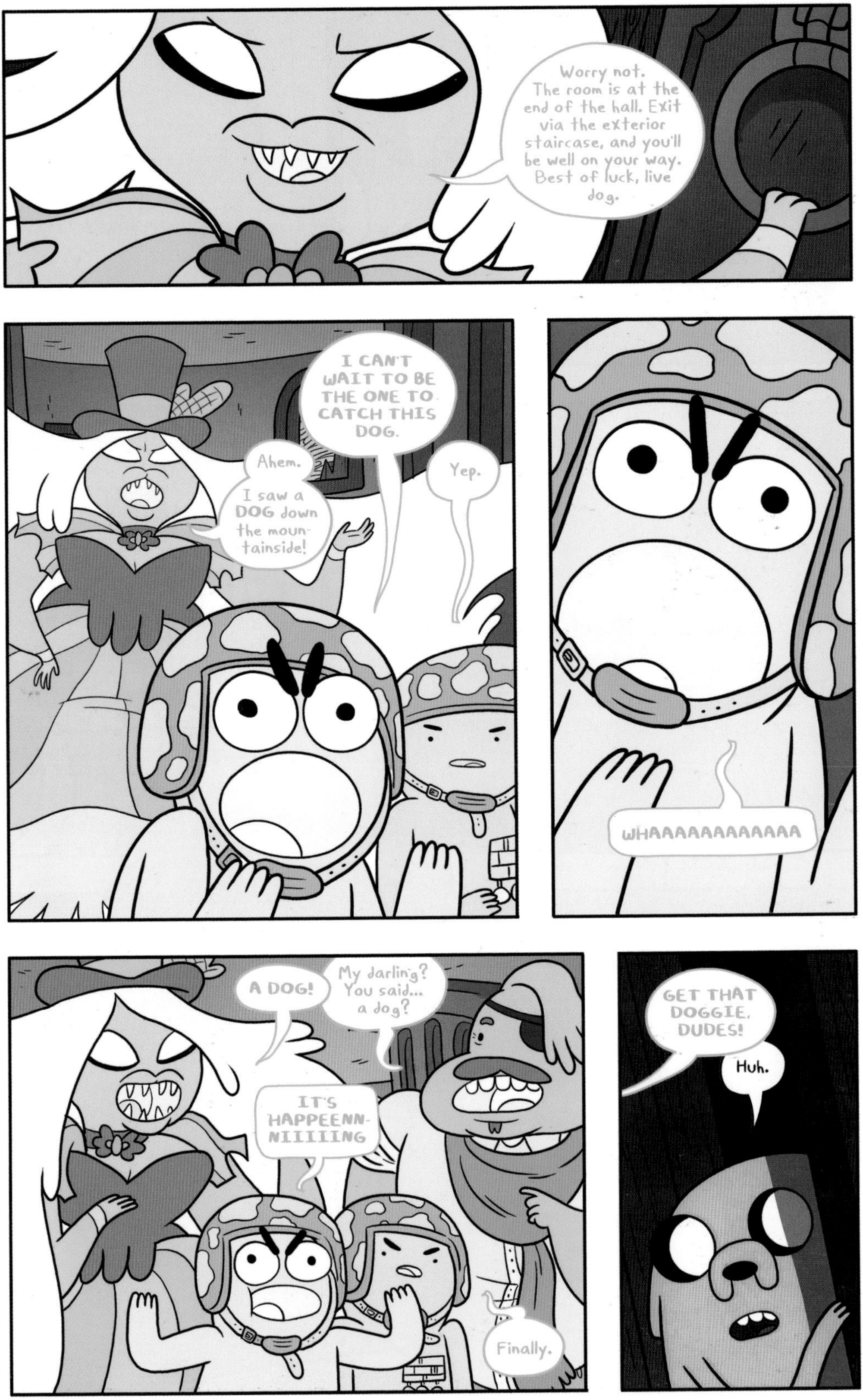
Worry not. The room is at the end of the hall. Exit via the exterior staircase, and you'll be well on your way. Best of luck, live dog.
Ahem.
I saw a DOG down the moun-tainside!
I CAN'T WAIT TO BE THE ONE TO CATCH THIS DOG.
Yep.
WHAAAAAAAAAAAA
A DOG!
My darling? You said... a dog?
IT'S HAPPEENN-NIIIIING
Finally.
GET THAT DOGGIE, DUDES!
Huh.

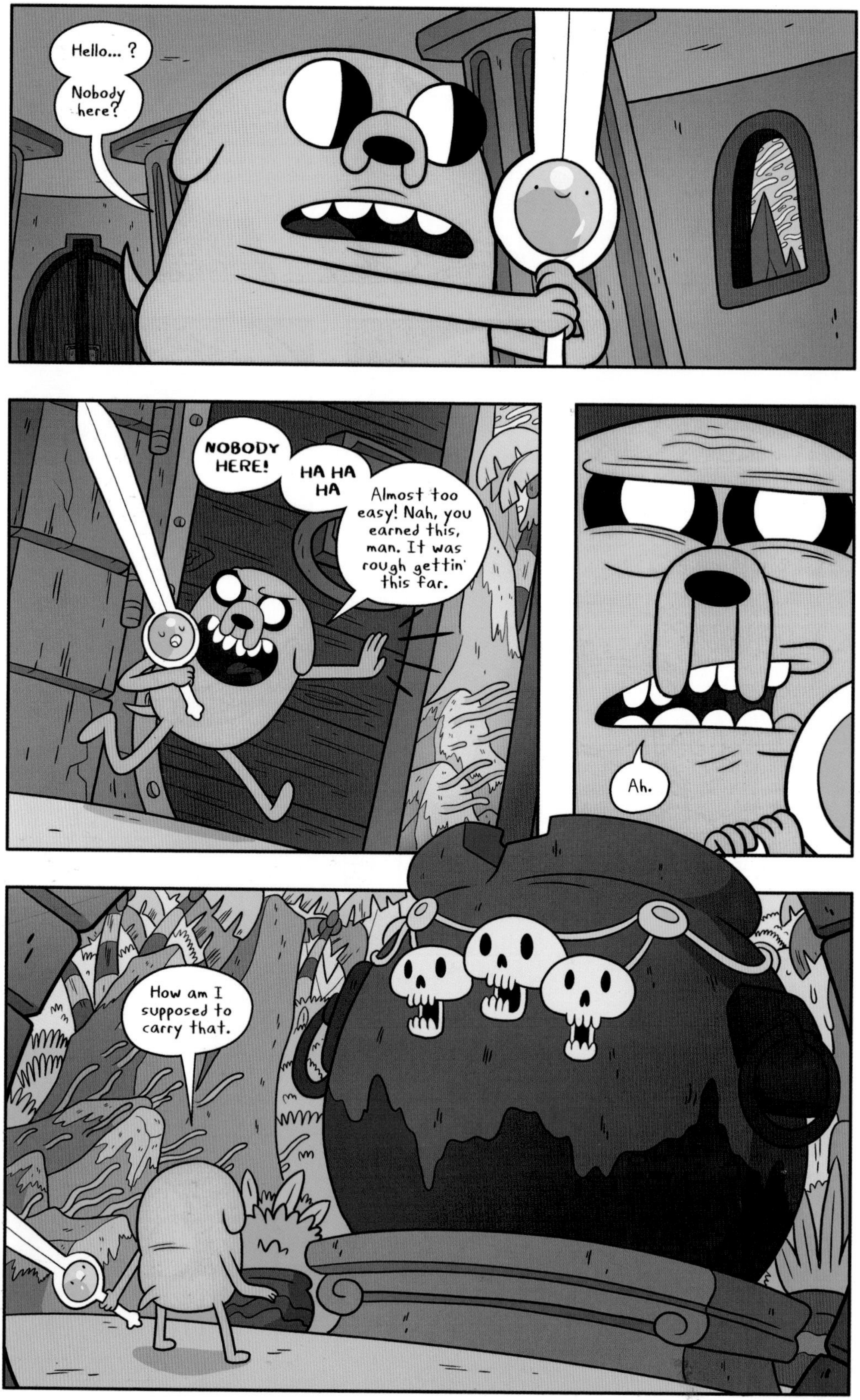
Hello... ?
Nobody here?
NOBODY HERE!
HA HA HA
Almost too easy! Nah, you earned this, man. It was rough gettin' this far.
Ah.
How am I supposed to carry that.

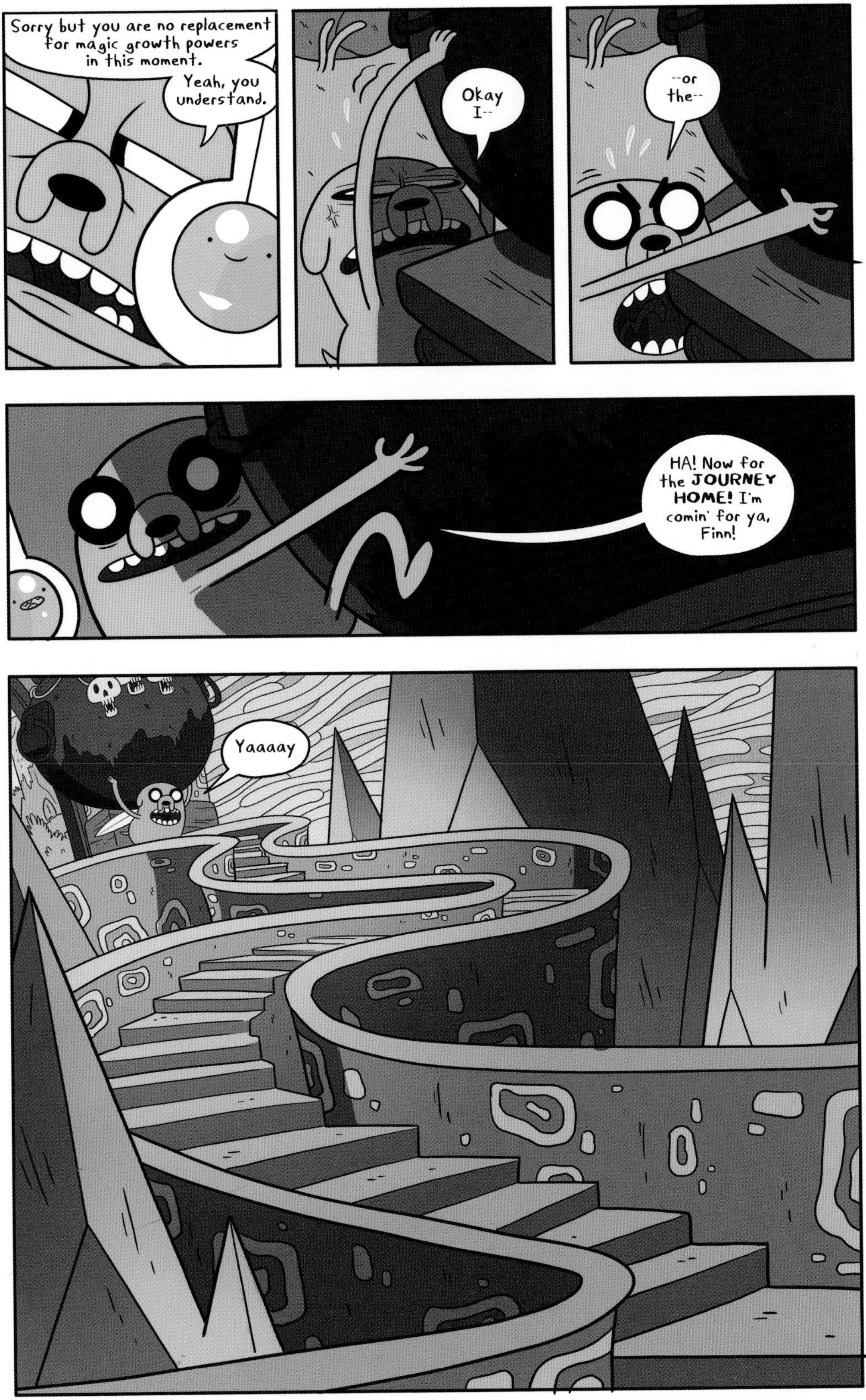
Sorry but you are no replacement for magic growth powers in this moment.
Yeah, you understand.
Okay I--
--or the--
HA! Now for the JOURNEY HOME! I'm comin' for ya, Finn!
Yaaaay

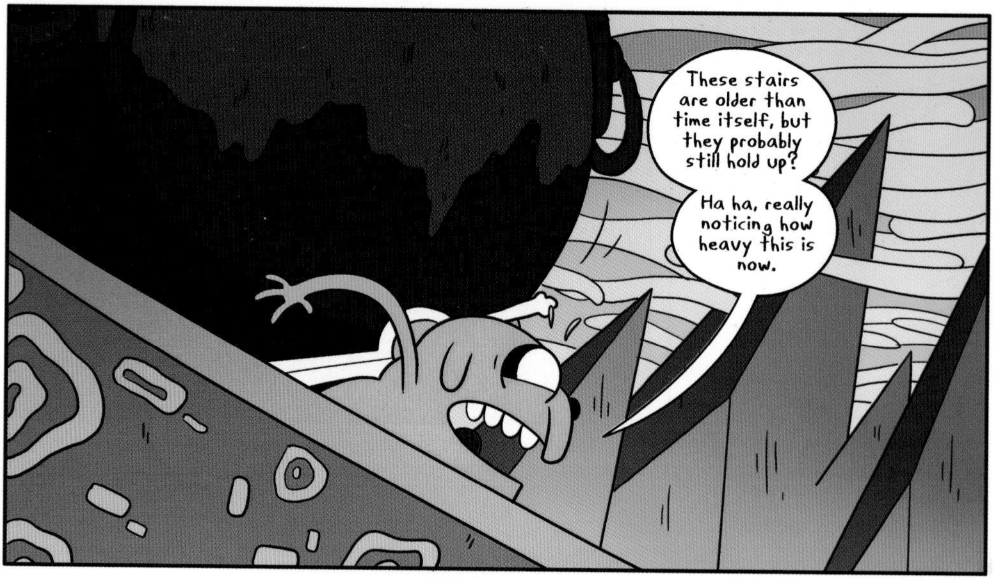
These stairs are older than time itself, but they probably still hold up?
Ha ha, really noticing how heavy this is now.

SHOCKINGLY, HE MADE IT. TOTALLY FINE.

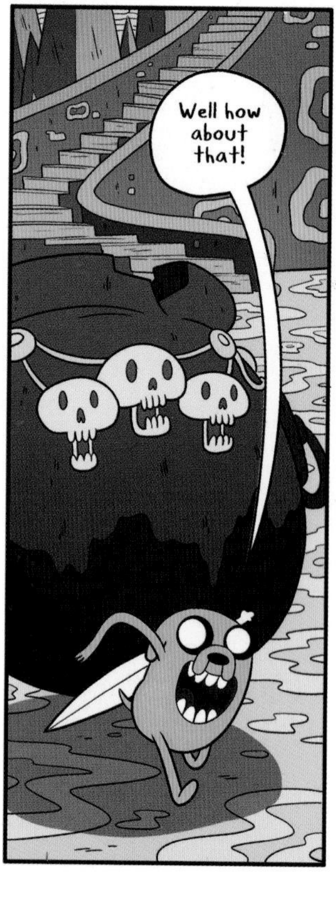
Well how about that!

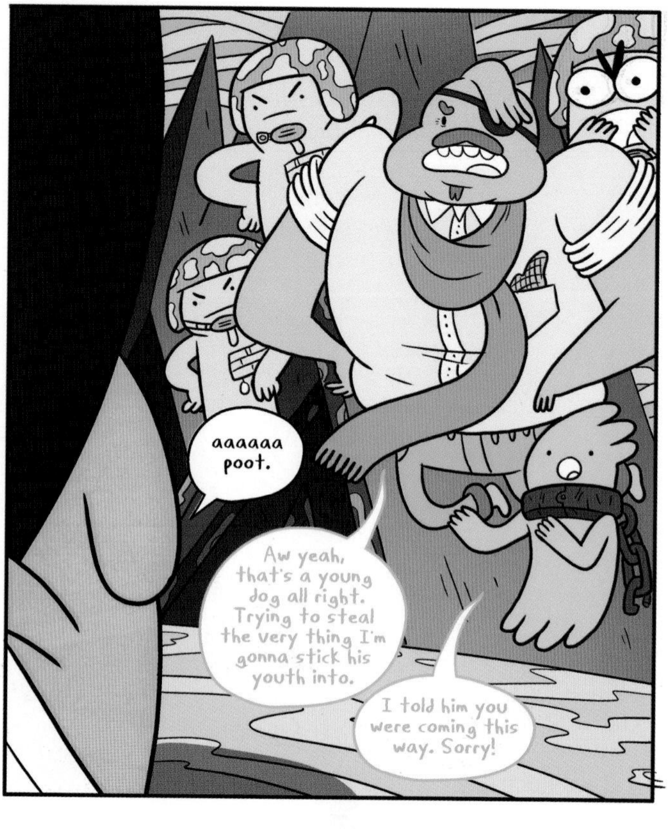
aaaaaa poot.
Aw yeah, that's a young dog all right. Trying to steal the very thing I'm gonna stick his youth into.
I told him you were coming this way. Sorry!

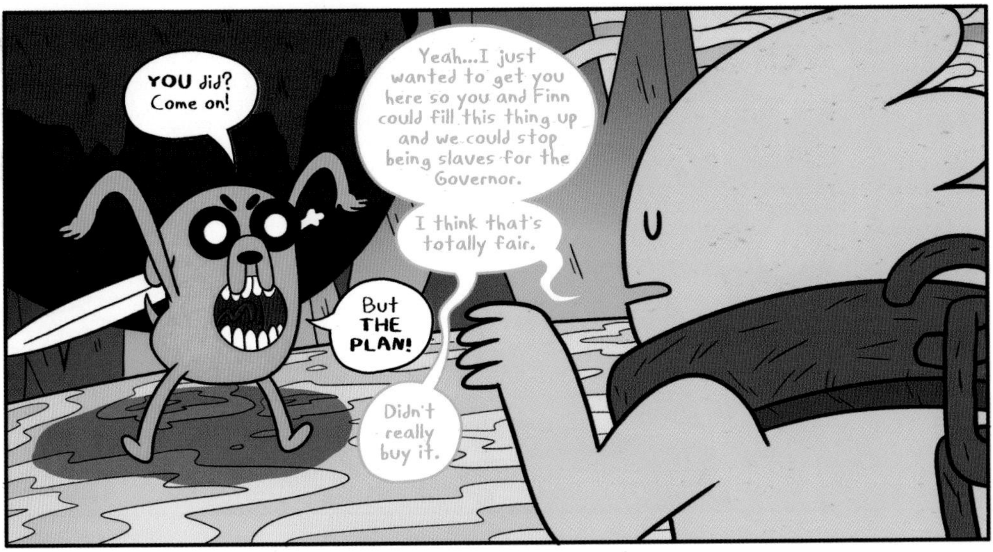
YOU did? Come on!
Yeah...I just wanted to get you here so you and Finn could fill this thing up and we could stop being slaves for the Governor.
I think that's totally fair.
But THE PLAN!
Didn't really buy it.

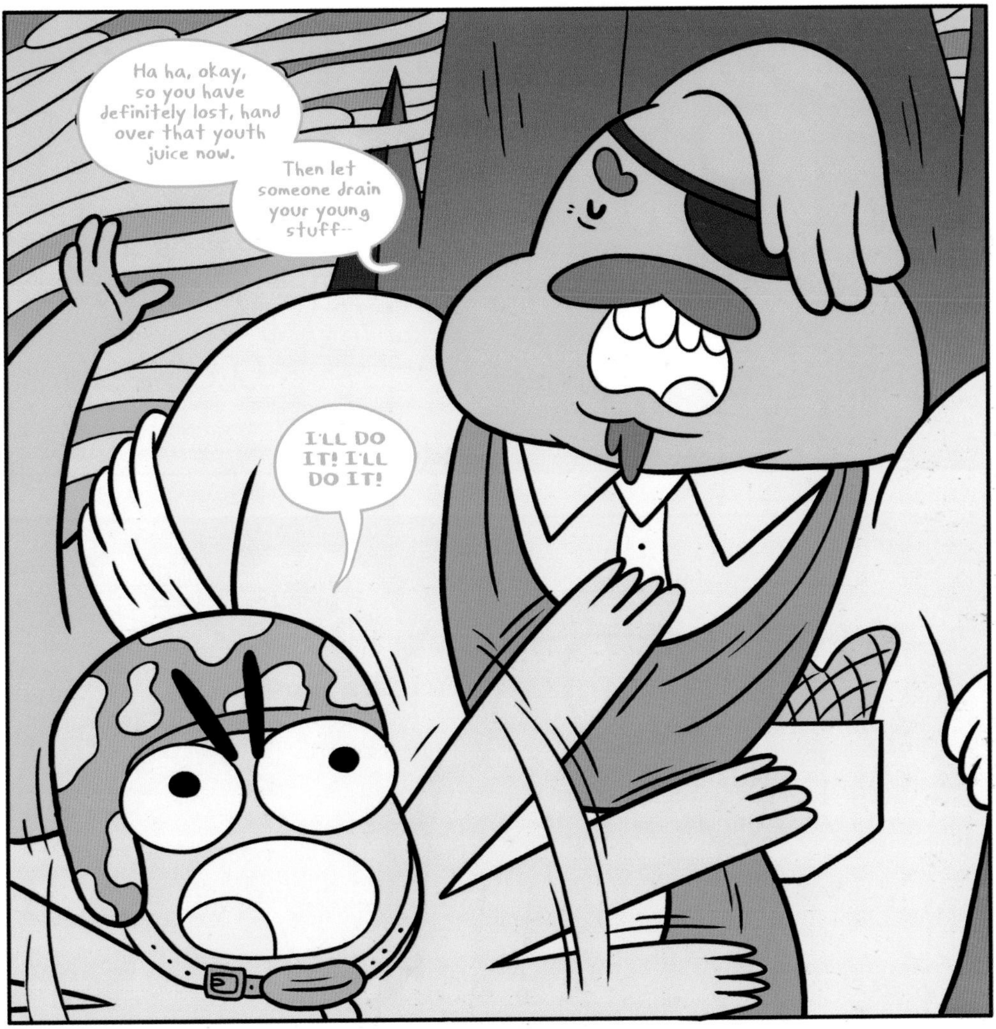
Ha ha, okay, so you have definitely lost, hand over that youth juice now.
Then let someone drain your young stuff--
I'LL DO IT! I'LL DO IT!

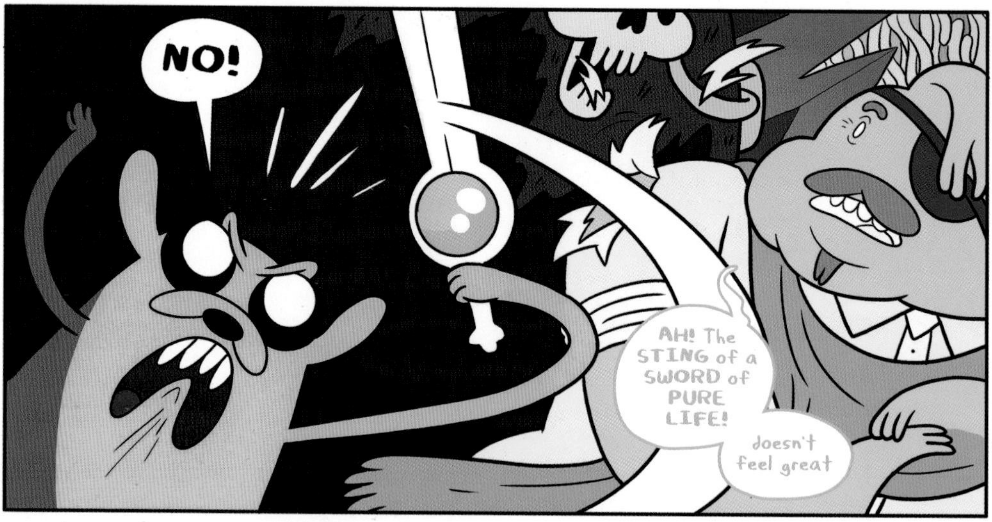
NO!
AH! The STING of a SWORD of PURE LIFE!
doesn't feel great

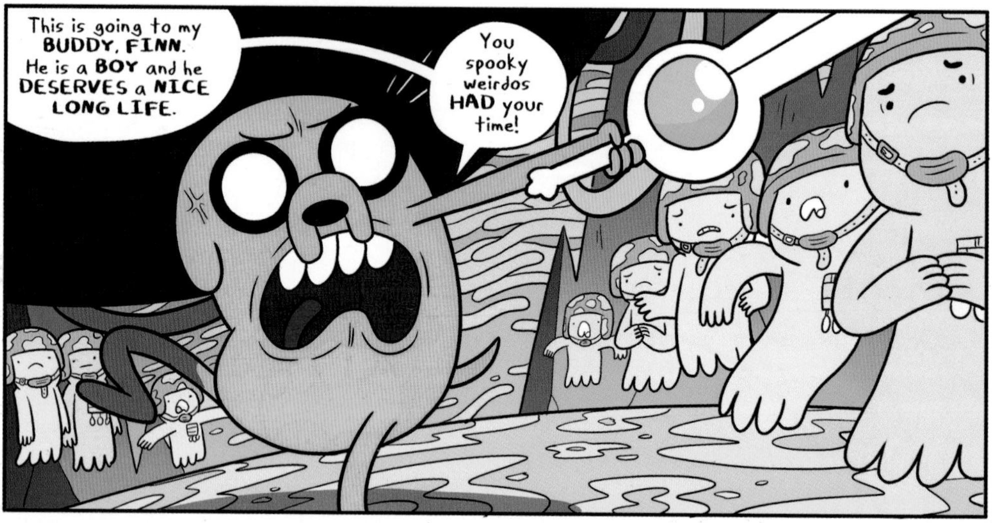
This is going to my BUDDY, FINN. He is a BOY and he DESERVES a NICE LONG LIFE.
You spooky weirdos HAD your time!

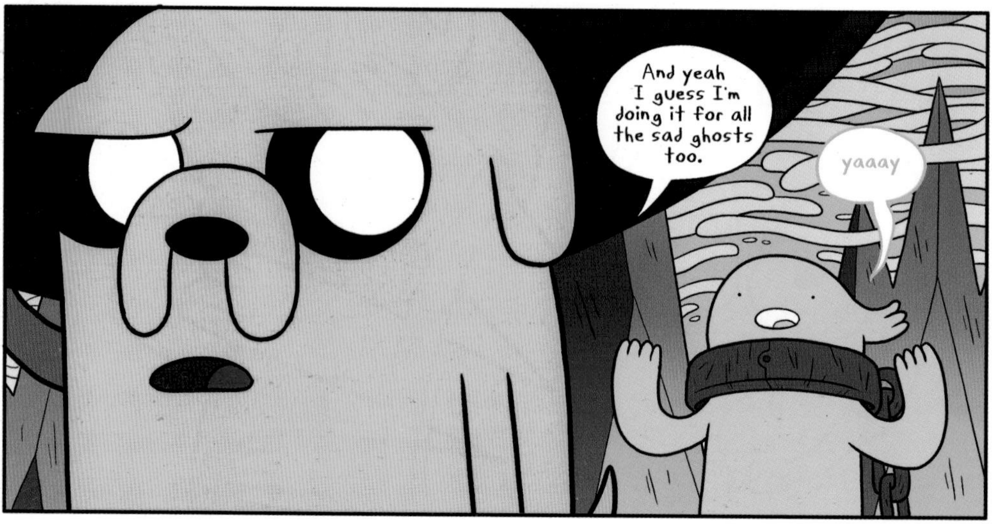
And yeah I guess I'm doing it for all the sad ghosts too.
yaaay

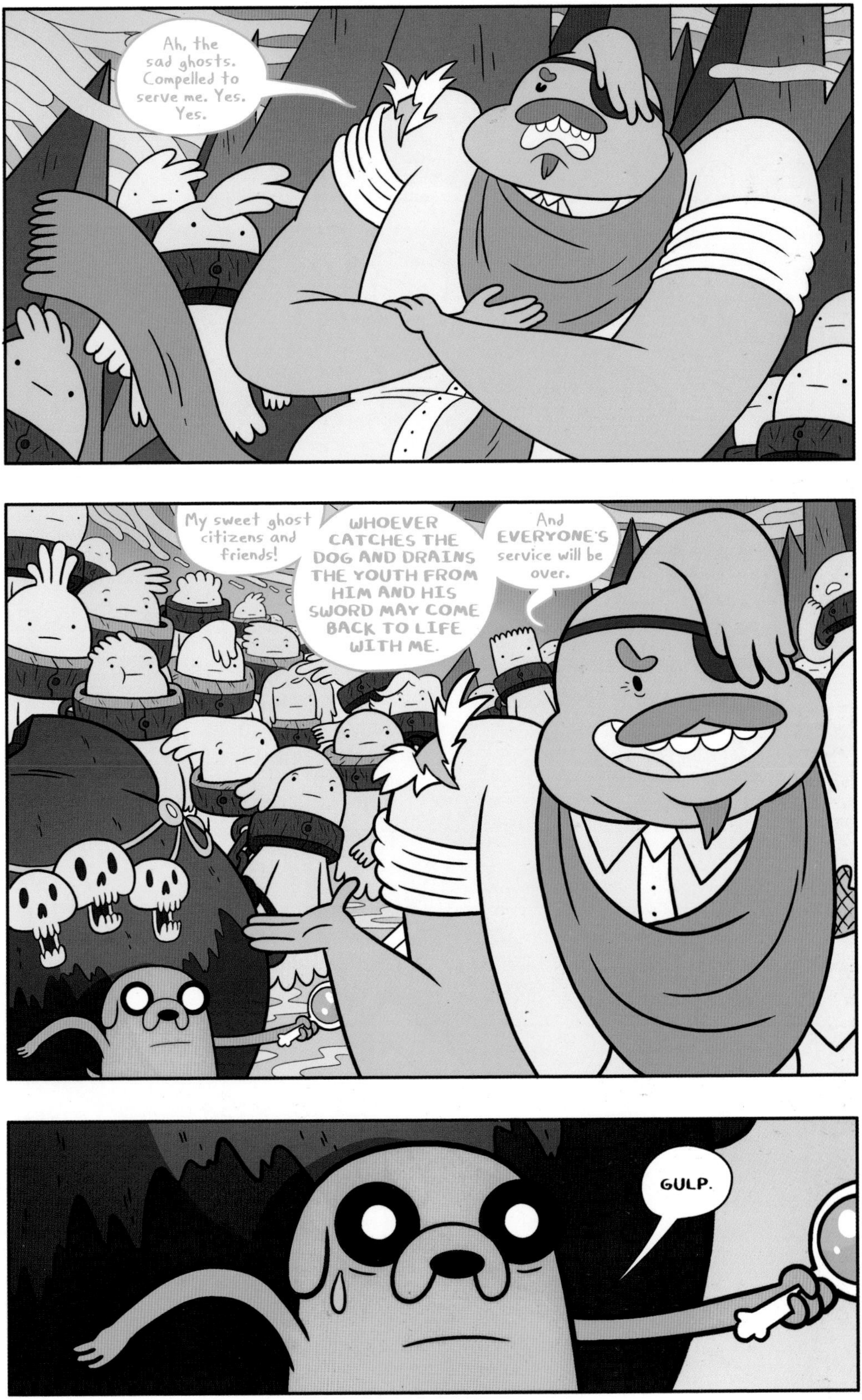
Ah, the sad ghosts. Compelled to serve me. Yes. Yes.
My sweet ghost citizens and friends!
WHOEVER CATCHES THE DOG AND DRAINS THE YOUTH FROM HIM AND HIS SWORD MAY COME BACK TO LIFE WITH ME.
And EVERYONE'S service will be over.
GULP.

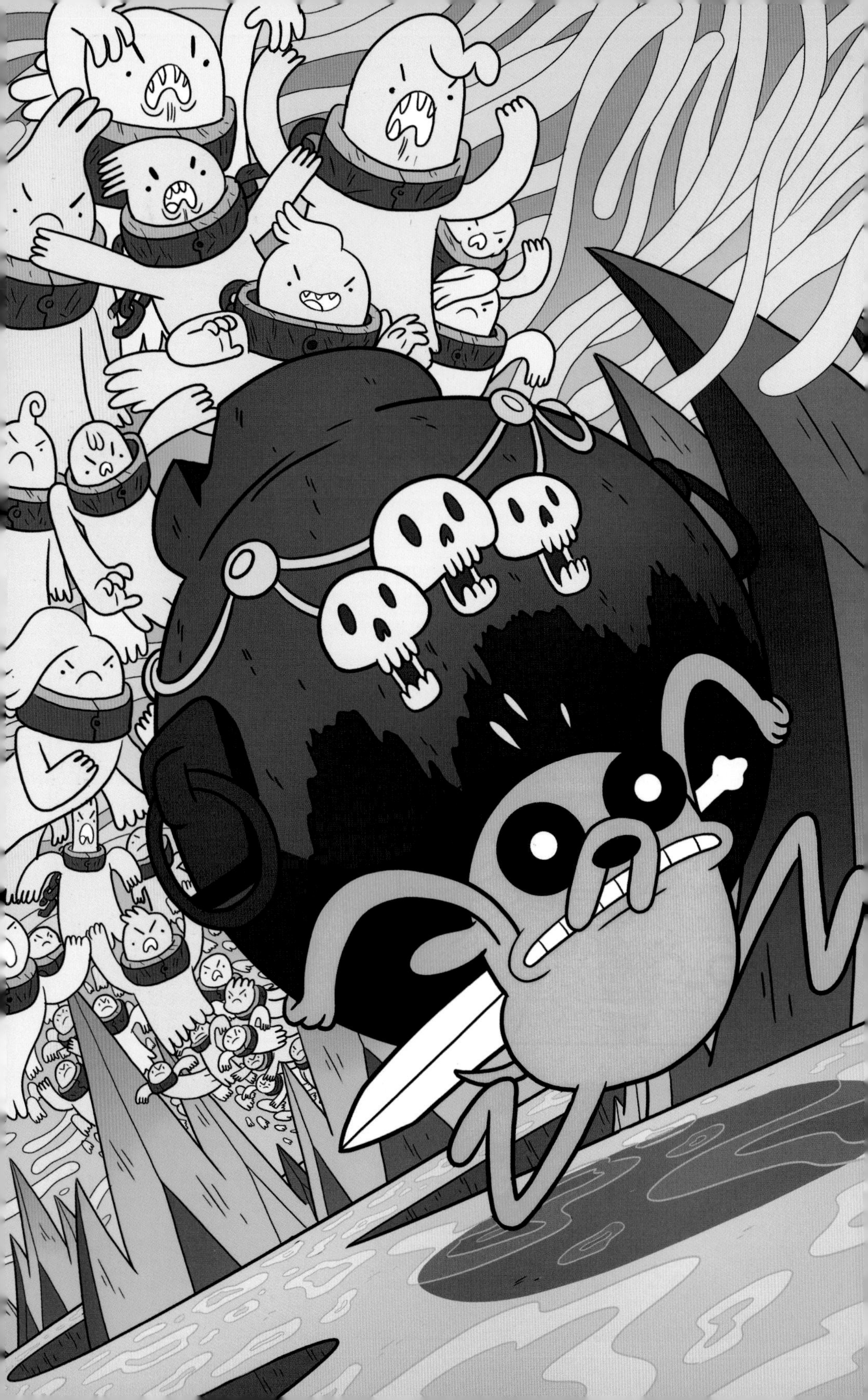

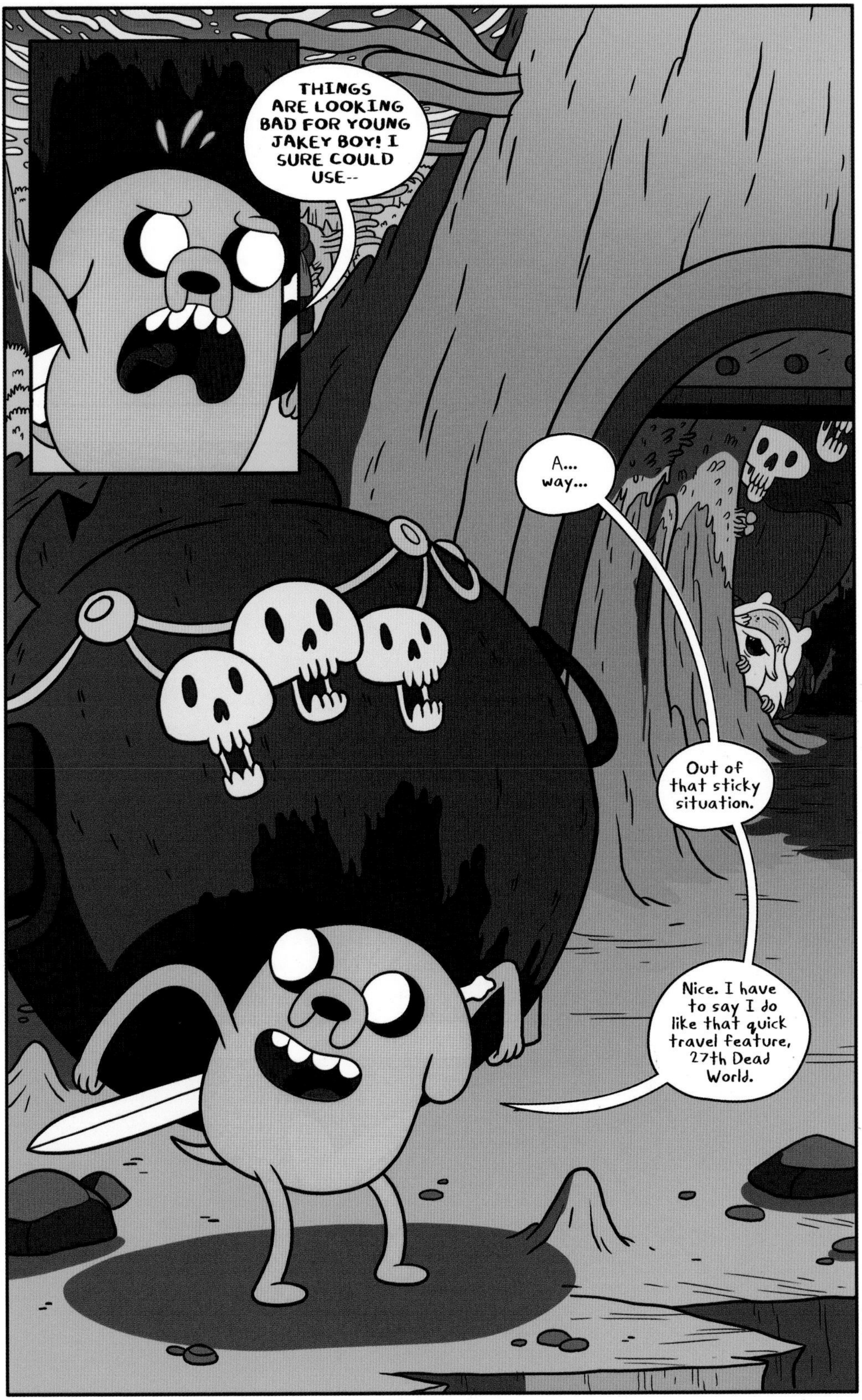
THINGS ARE LOOKING BAD FOR YOUNG JAKEY BOY! I SURE COULD USE--
A... way...
Out of that sticky situation.
Nice. I have to say I do like that quick travel feature, 27th Dead World.

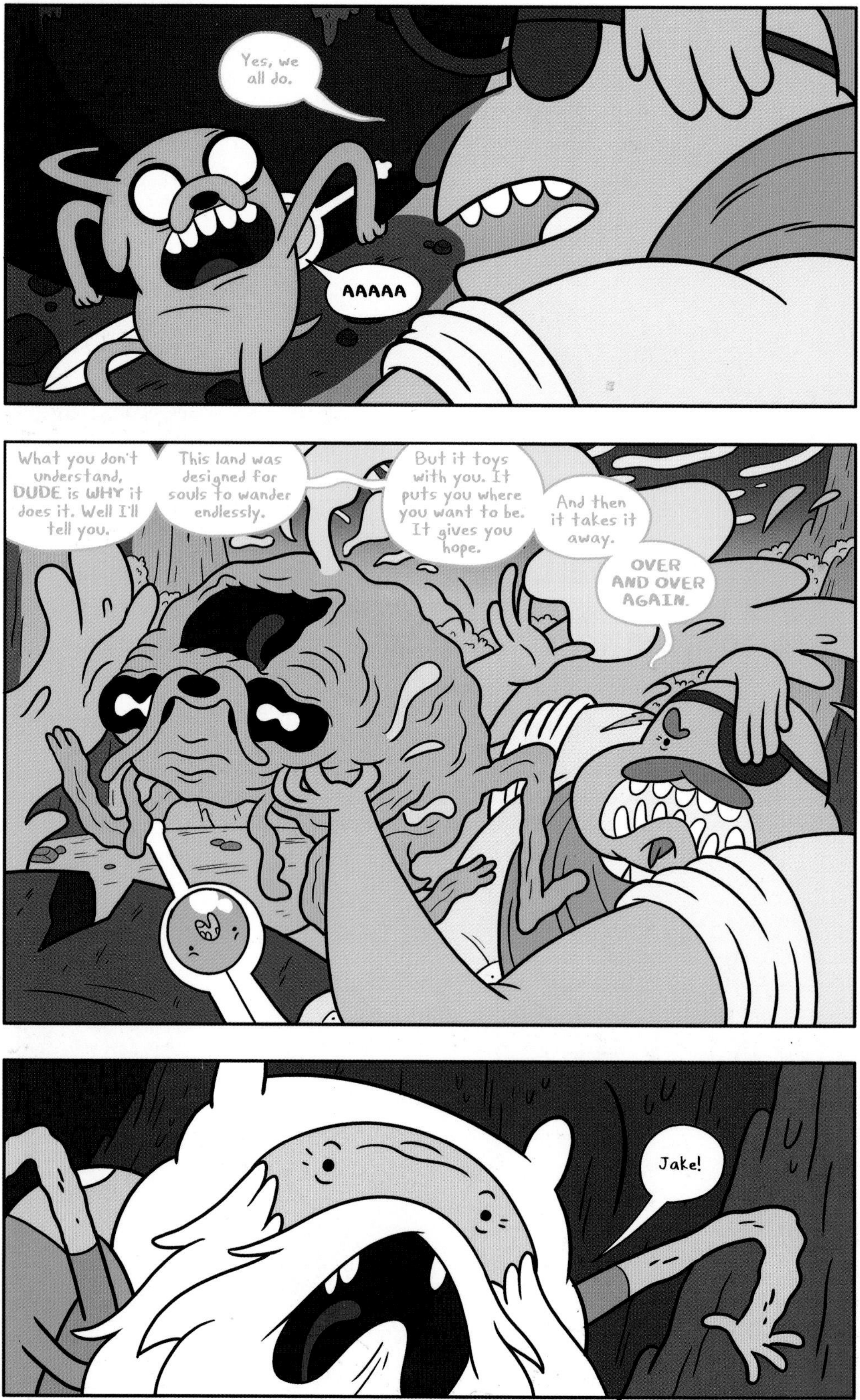
Yes, we all do.
AAAAA
What you don't understand, DUDE is WHY it does it. Well I'll tell you.
This land was designed for souls to wander endlessly.
But it toys with you. It puts you where you want to be. It gives you hope.
And then it takes it away.
OVER AND OVER AGAIN.
Jake!

And that should do it! Rad! Hey gatekeeper, got a soon to be living coming through in a minute.

I DON'T CARE. FINE.

Hey man... you enjoy it.

I'm old and wise now.

Thanks! That's pretty sportsmanlike of you.

You know, I started this quest when I thought I was **SUPER TIRED** of doing quests.

Uh huh.

But the thing was, I was still doing them! And I didn't have to!

yeah

I could have been spending that time with my family.

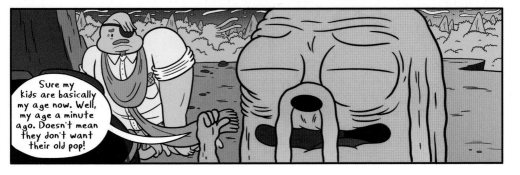

Sure my kids are basically my age now. Well, my age a minute ago. Doesn't mean they don't want their old pop!

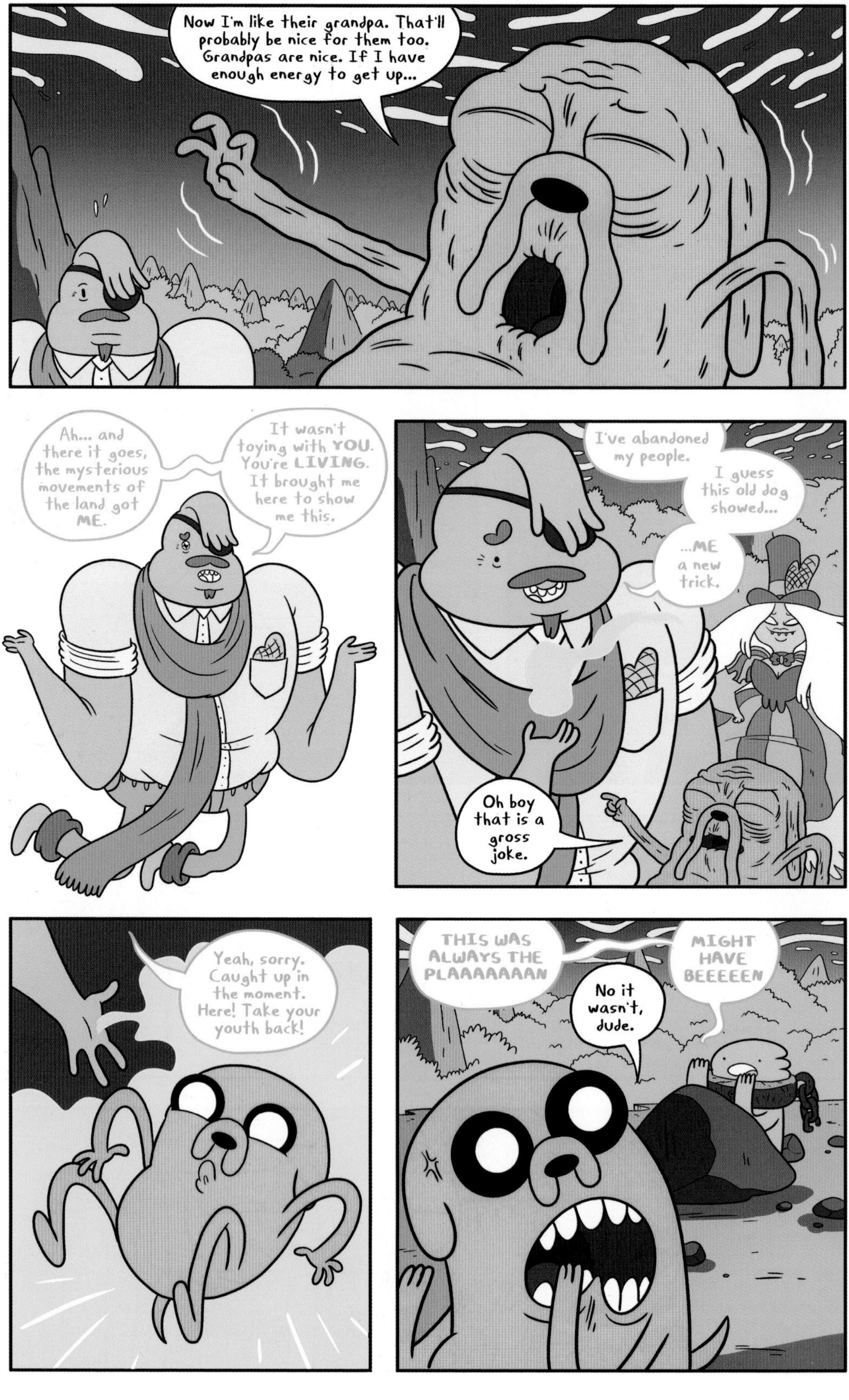

Now I'm like their grandpa. That'll probably be nice for them too. Grandpas are nice. If I have enough energy to get up...
Ah... and there it goes, the mysterious movements of the land got ME.
It wasn't toying with YOU. You're LIVING. It brought me here to show me this.
I've abandoned my people.
I guess this old dog showed...
...ME a new trick.
Oh boy that is a gross joke.
Yeah, sorry. Caught up in the moment. Here! Take your youth back!
THIS WAS ALWAYS THE PLAAAAAAAN
MIGHT HAVE BEEEEEN
No it wasn't, dude.

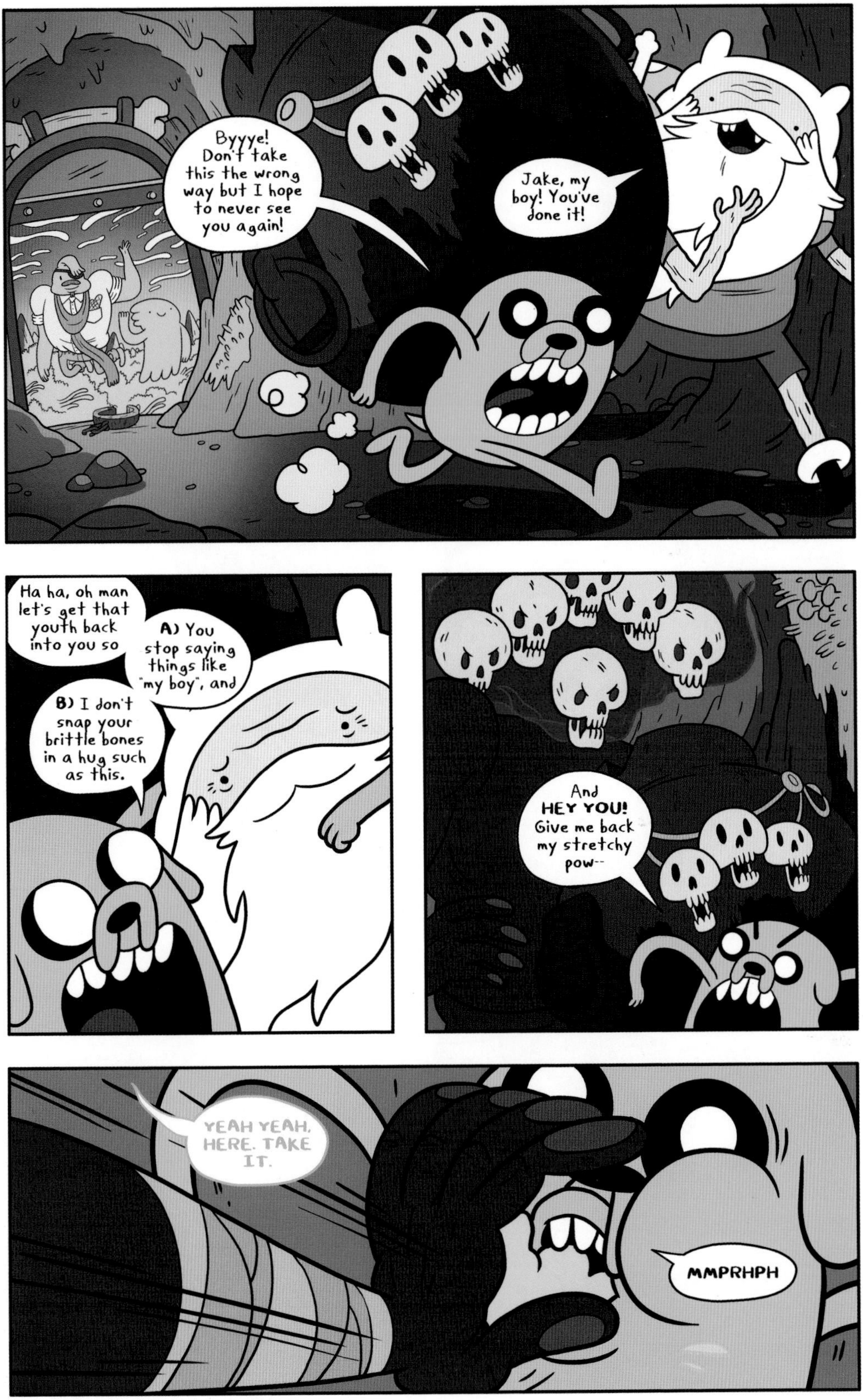
Byyye! Don't take this the wrong way but I hope to never see you again!
Jake, my boy! You've done it!
Ha ha, oh man let's get that youth back into you so
A) You stop saying things like "my boy", and
B) I don't snap your brittle bones in a hug such as this.
And HEY YOU! Give me back my stretchy pow--
YEAH YEAH. HERE. TAKE IT.
MMPRHPH

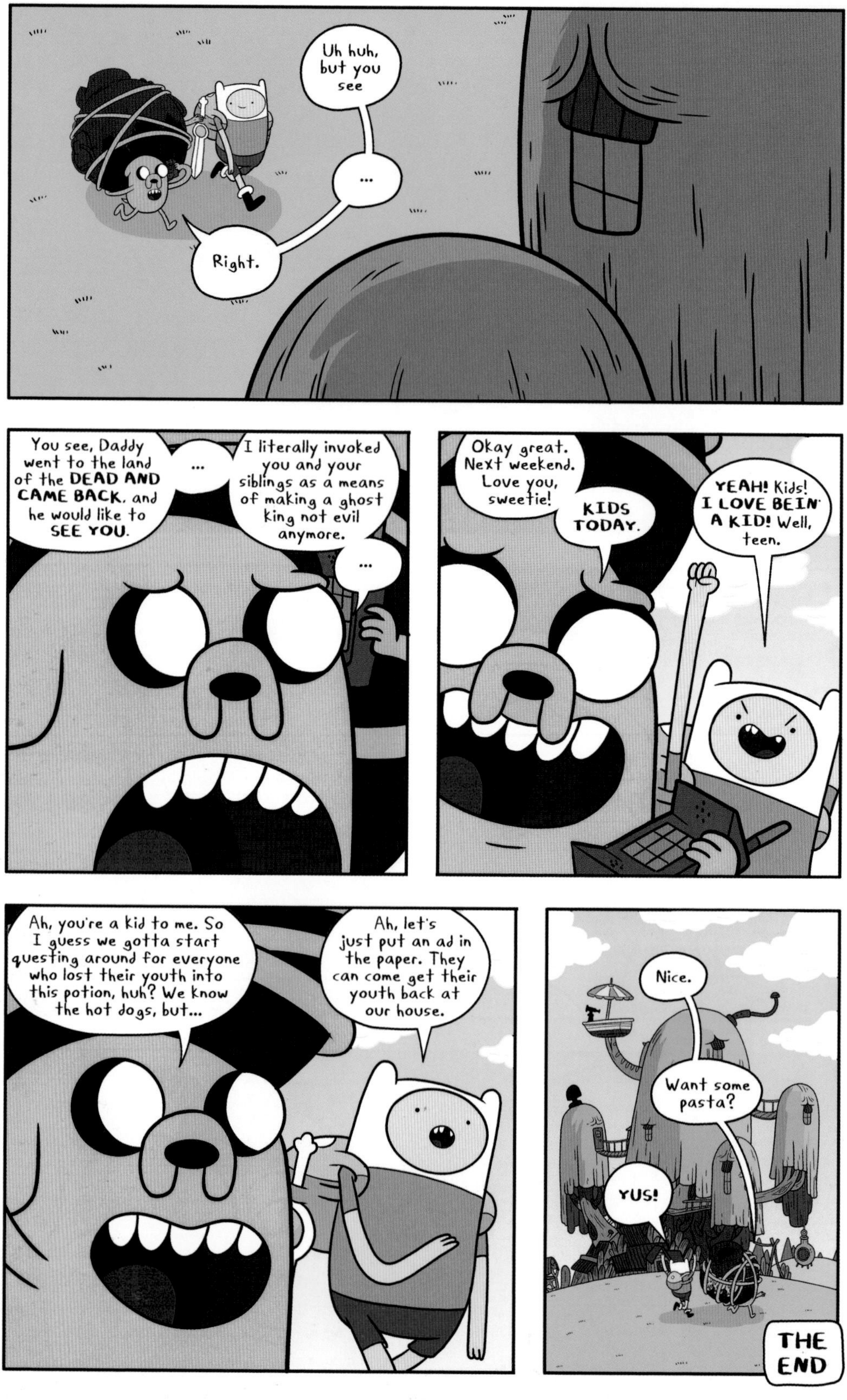
Uh huh, but you see
...
Right.
You see, Daddy went to the land of the DEAD AND CAME BACK, and he would like to SEE YOU.
...
I literally invoked you and your siblings as a means of making a ghost king not evil anymore.
...
Okay great. Next weekend. Love you, sweetie!
KIDS TODAY.
YEAH! Kids! I LOVE BEIN' A KID! Well, teen.
Ah, you're a kid to me. So I guess we gotta start questing around for everyone who lost their youth into this potion, huh? We know the hot dogs, but...
Ah, let's just put an ad in the paper. They can come get their youth back at our house.
Nice.
Want some pasta?
YUS!
THE END

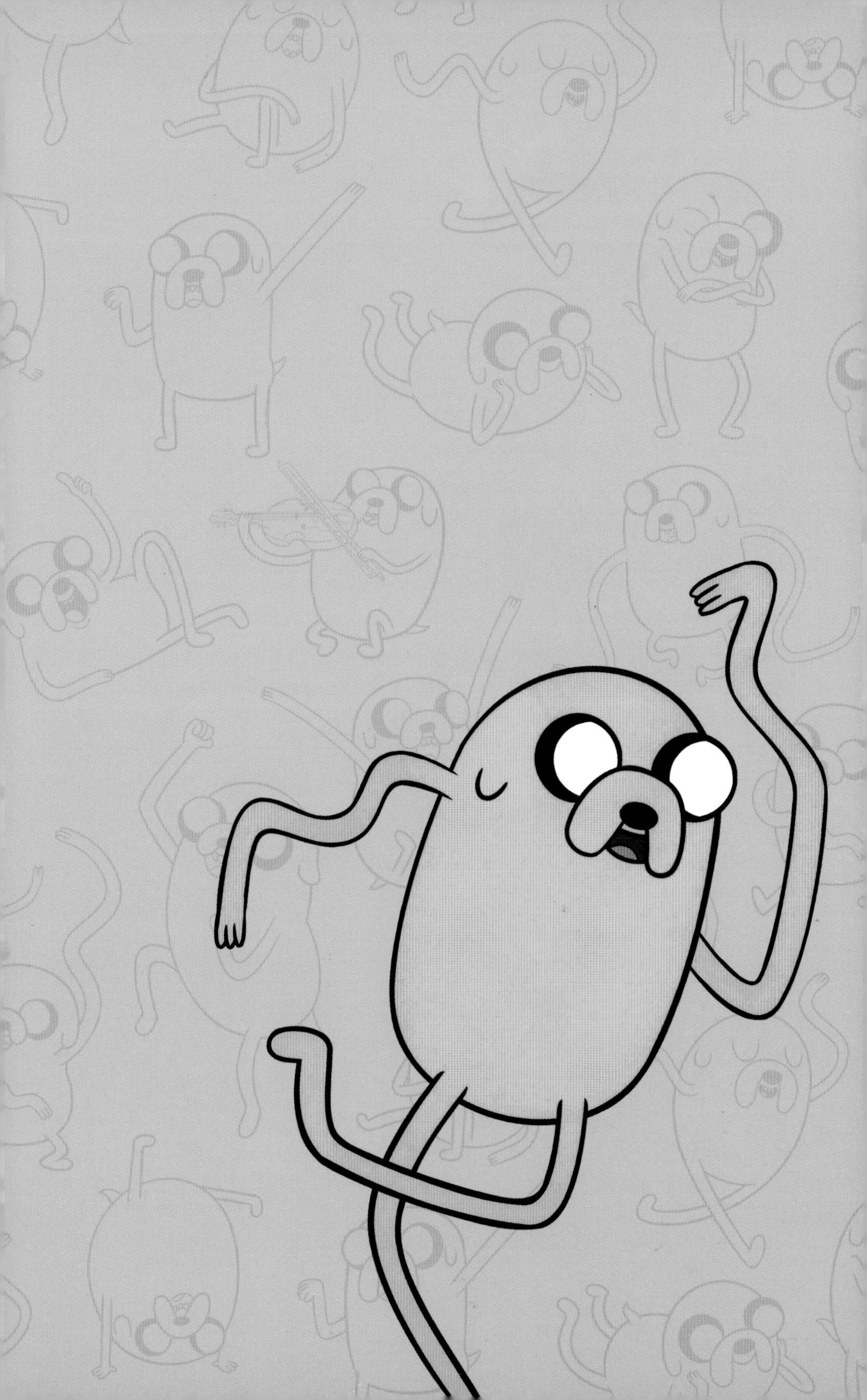

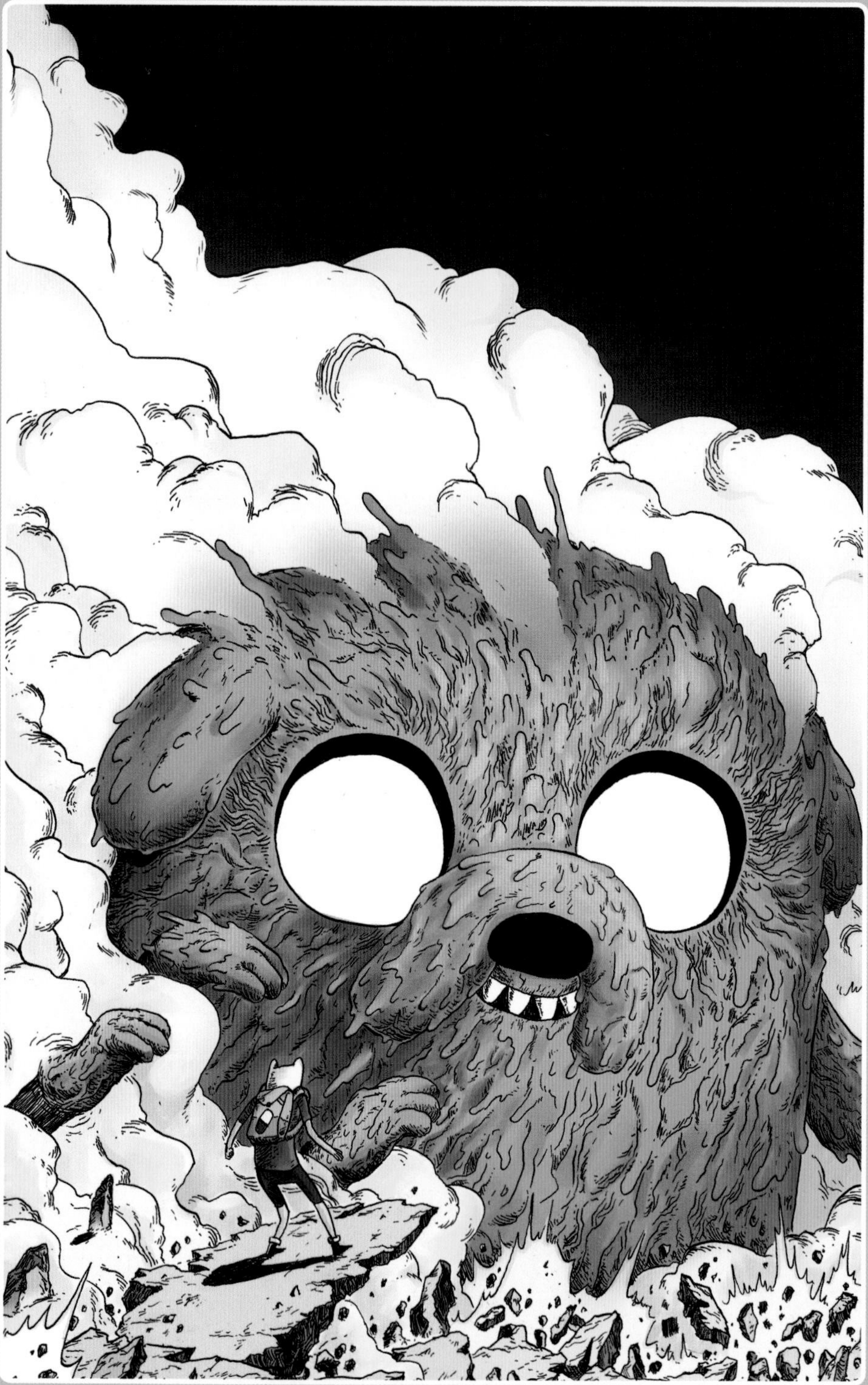

Adventure Time: Flip Side #3 Cover D by Sloane Leong

"Body by Jake"

Written by Max Davison Illustrated by Luca Claretti

Colors by Eleonora Bruni Letters by Taylor Esposito

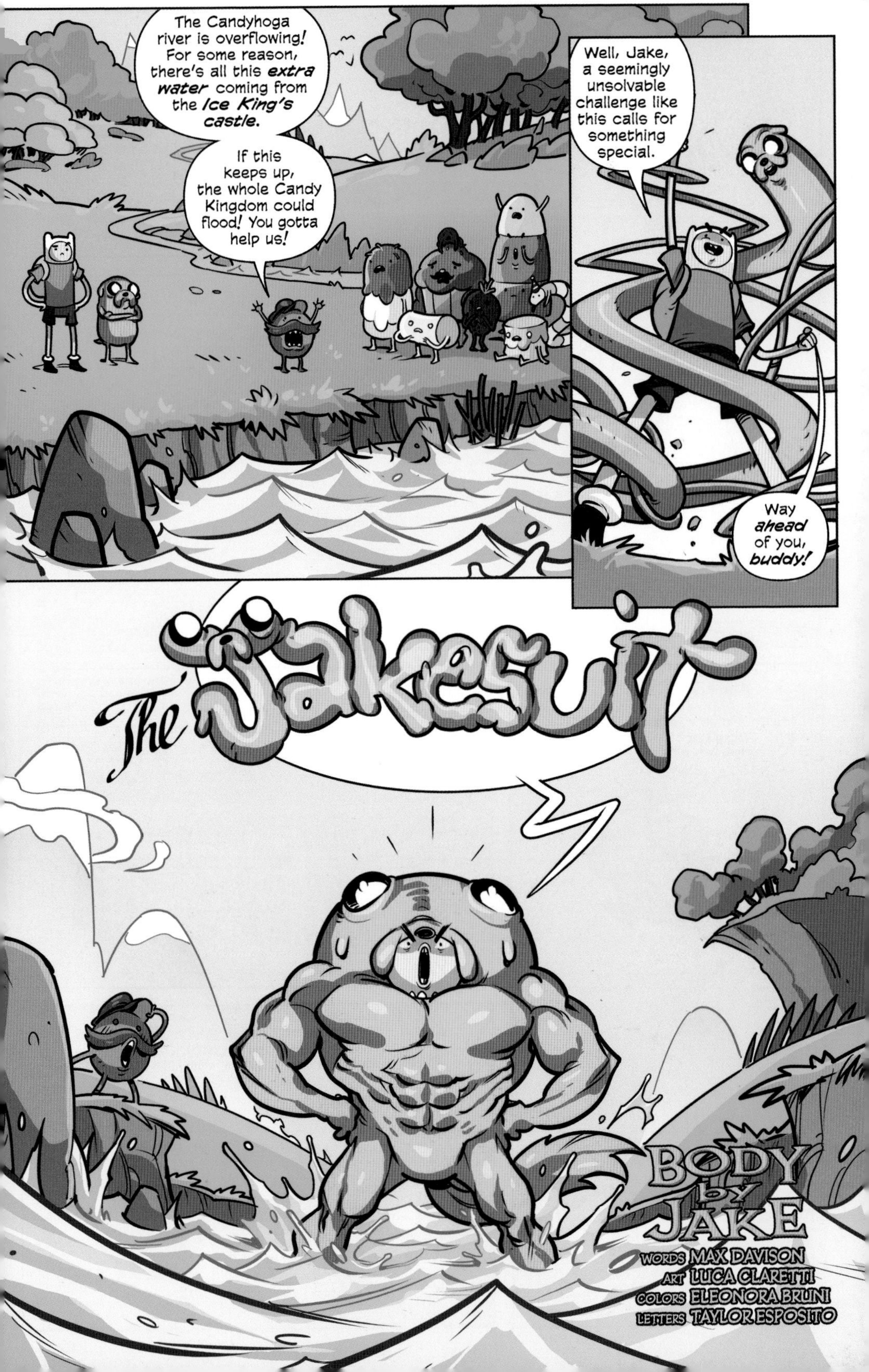
The Candyhoga river is overflowing! For some reason, there's all this extra water coming from the Ice King's castle.
If this keeps up, the whole Candy Kingdom could flood! You gotta help us!
Well, Jake, a seemingly unsolvable challenge like this calls for something special.
Way ahead of you, buddy!
The Jakesuit
BODY by JAKE
WORDS MAX DAVISON
ART LUCA CLARETTI
COLORS ELEONORA BRUNI
LETTERS TAYLOR ESPOSITO

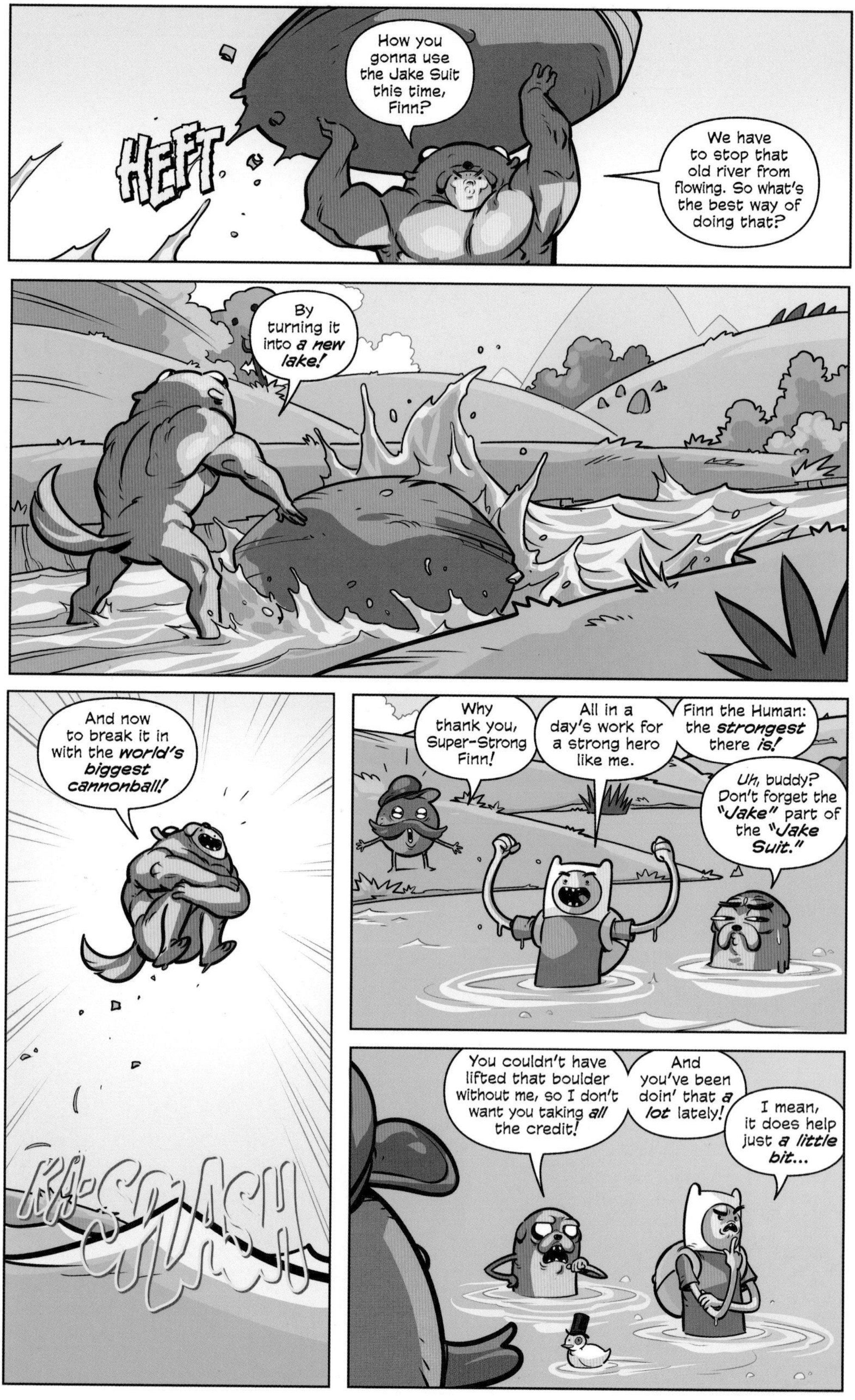
How you gonna use the Jake Suit this time, Finn?
HEFT
We have to stop that old river from flowing. So what's the best way of doing that?
By turning it into *a new lake!*
And now to break it in with the *world's biggest cannonball!*
KA-SPLASH
Why thank you, Super-Strong Finn!
All in a day's work for a strong hero like me.
Finn the Human: the *strongest* there *is!*
Uh, buddy? Don't forget the *"Jake"* part of the *"Jake Suit."*
You couldn't have lifted that boulder without me, so I don't want you taking *all* the credit!
And you've been doin' that *a lot* lately!
I mean, it does help just *a little bit...*

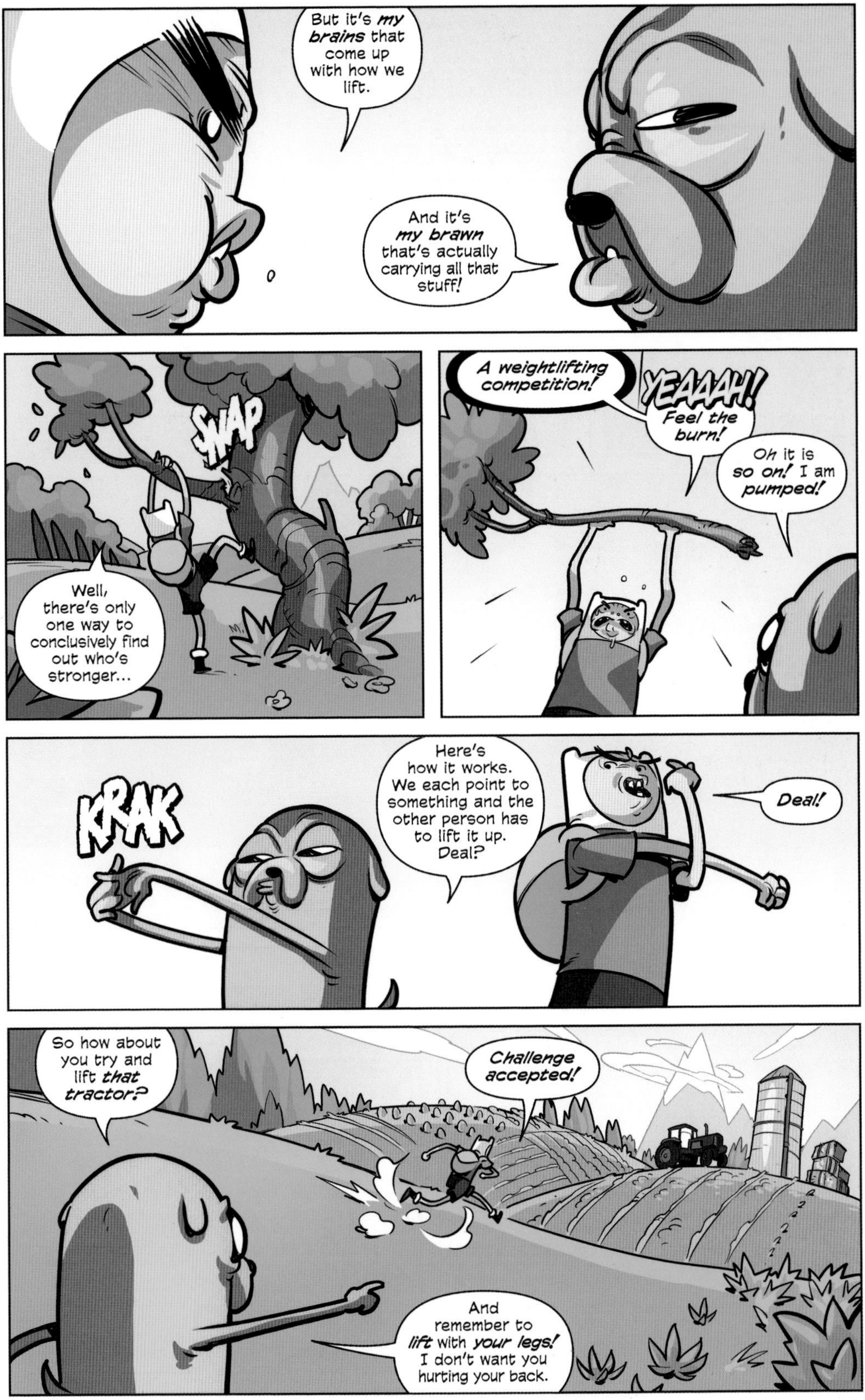

But it's *my brains* that come up with how we lift.
And it's *my brawn* that's actually carrying all that stuff!
SNAP
Well, there's only one way to conclusively find out who's stronger...
A weightlifting competition!
YEAAAH!
Feel the burn!
Oh it is *so on!* I am *pumped!*
KRAK
Here's how it works. We each point to something and the other person has to lift it up. Deal?
Deal!
So how about you try and lift *that tractor?*
Challenge accepted!
And remember to *lift* with *your legs!* I don't want you hurting your back.

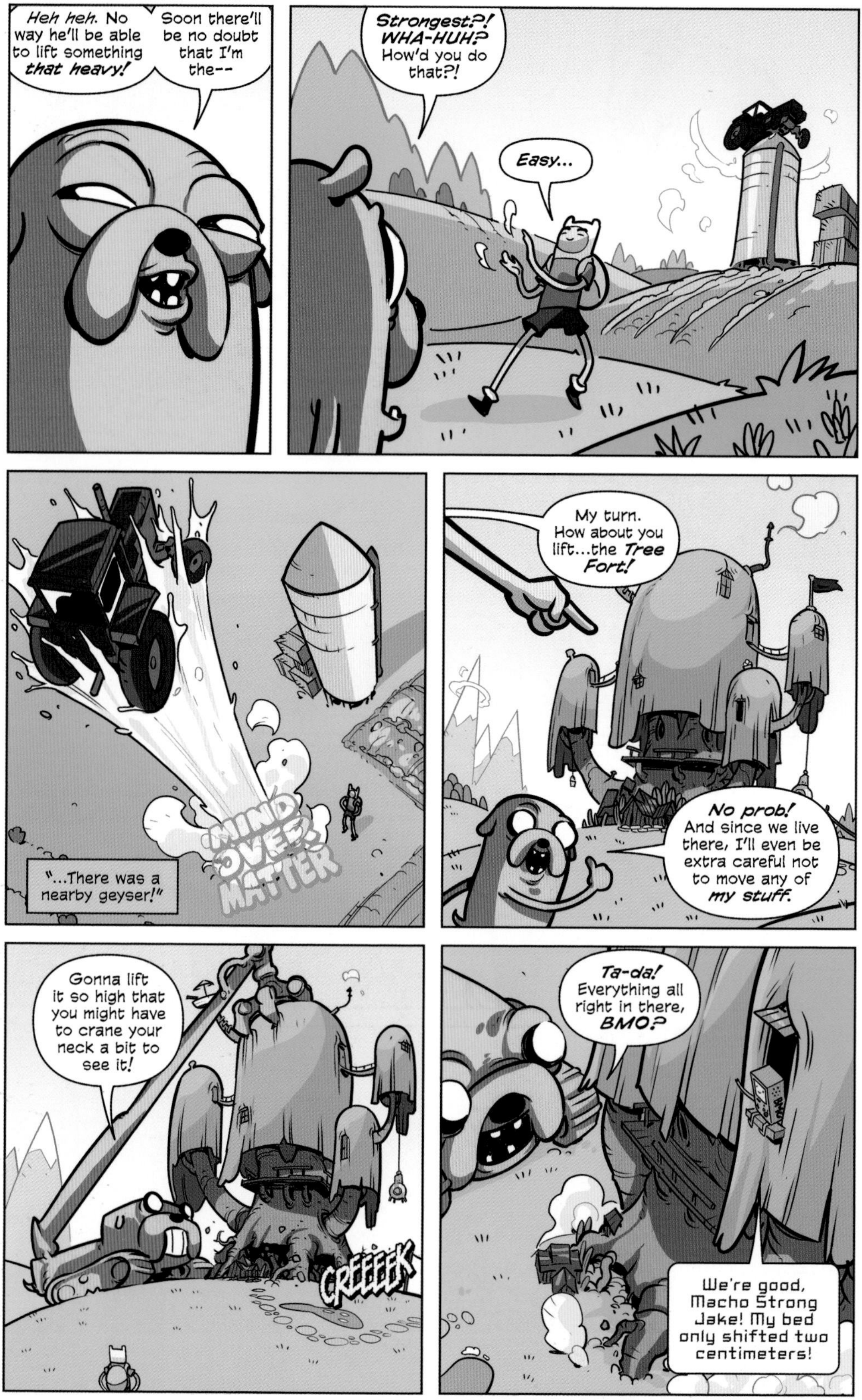
Heh heh. No way he'll be able to lift something that heavy!
Soon there'll be no doubt that I'm the--
Strongest?! WHA-HUH? How'd you do that?!
Easy...
"...There was a nearby geyser!"
MIND OVER MATTER
My turn. How about you lift...the Tree Fort!
No prob! And since we live there, I'll even be extra careful not to move any of my stuff.
Gonna lift it so high that you might have to crane your neck a bit to see it!
CREEEEK
Ta-da! Everything all right in there, BMO?
We're good, Macho Strong Jake! My bed only shifted two centimeters!

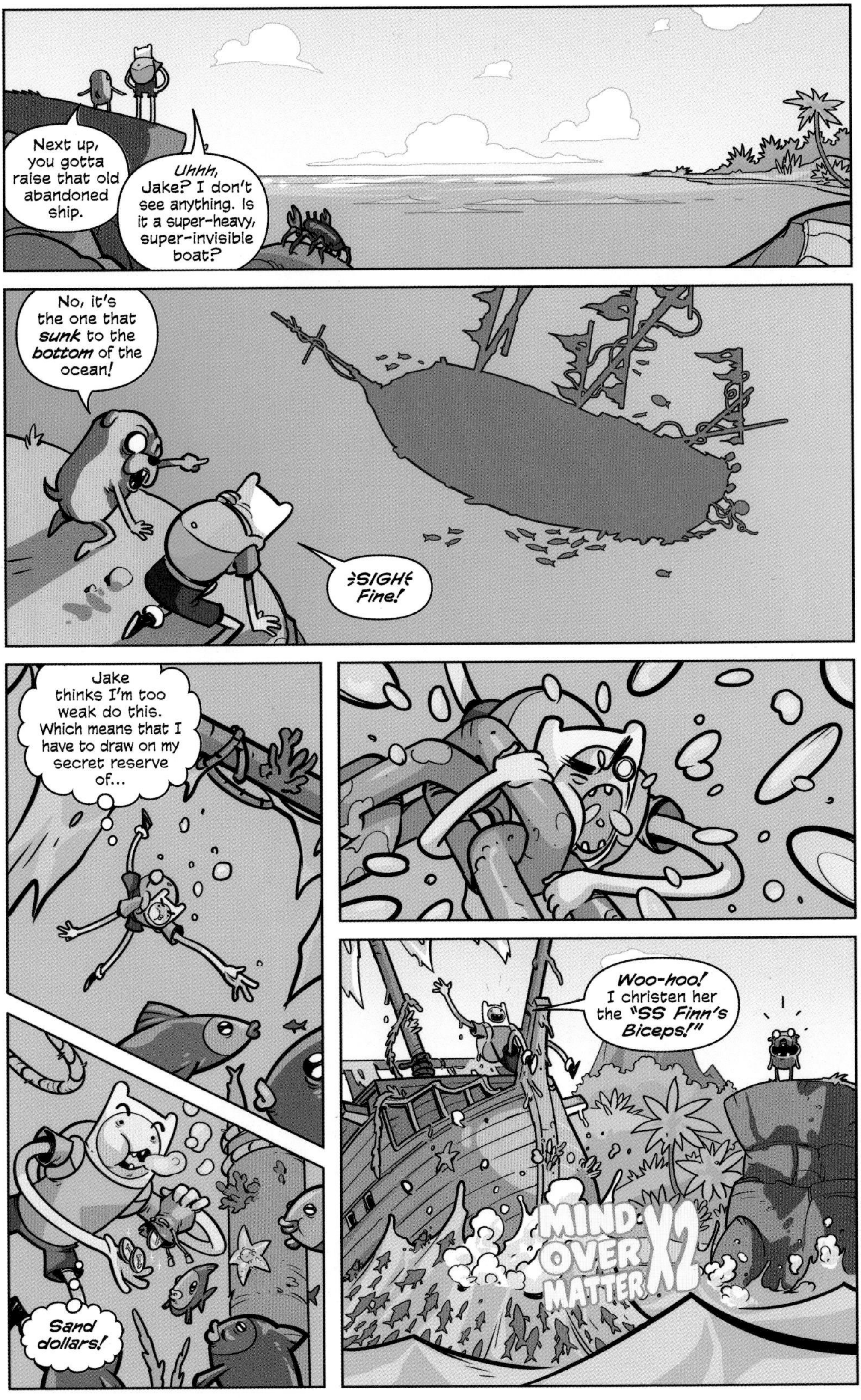
Next up, you gotta raise that old abandoned ship.
Uhhh, Jake? I don't see anything. Is it a super-heavy, super-invisible boat?
No, it's the one that sunk to the bottom of the ocean!
SIGH Fine!
Jake thinks I'm too weak do this. Which means that I have to draw on my secret reserve of...
Sand dollars!
Woo-hoo! I christen her the "SS Finn's Biceps!"
MIND OVER MATTER X2

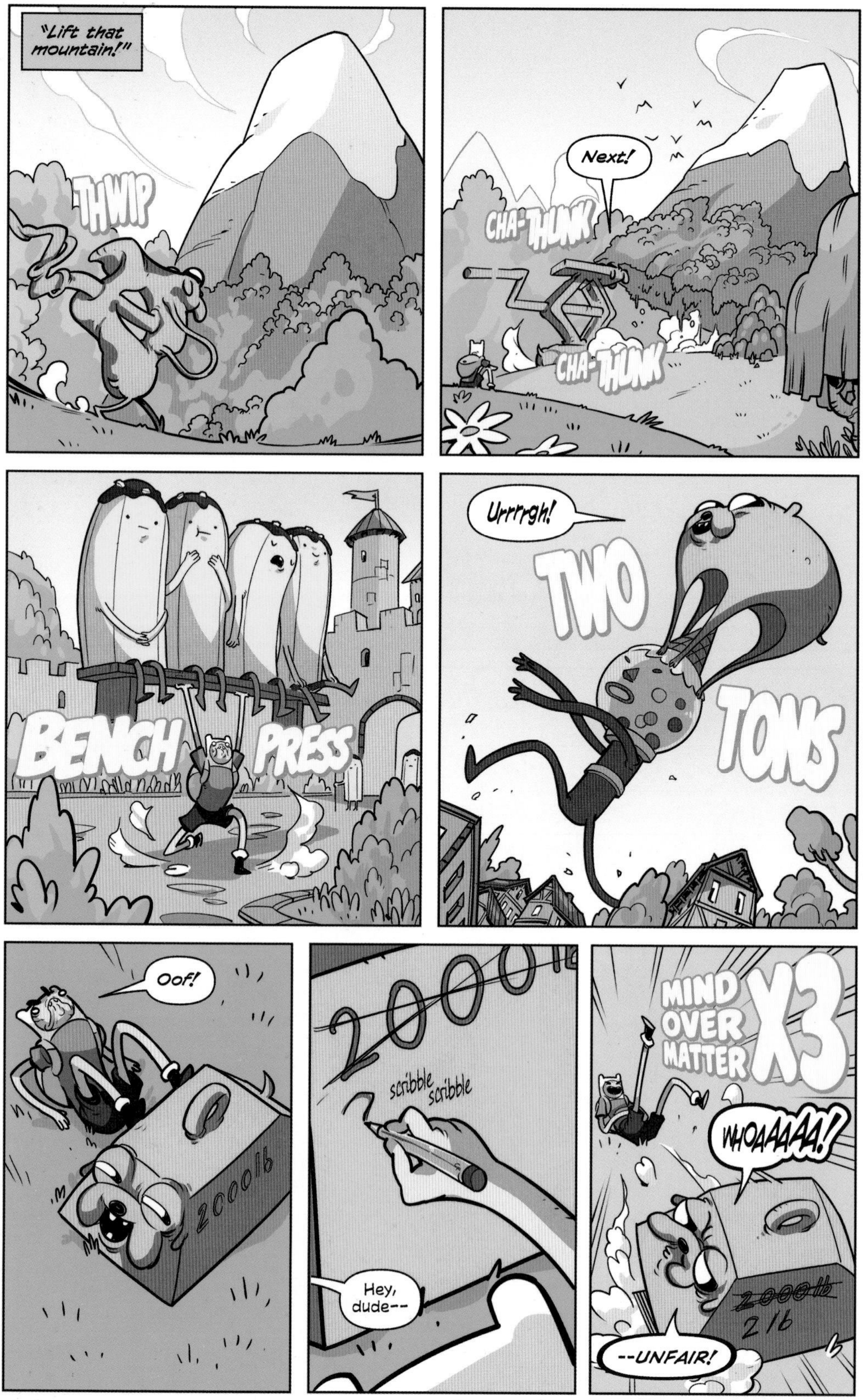
"Lift that mountain!"
THWIP
Next!
CHA-THUNK
CHA-THUNK
BENCH PRESS
Urrrrgh!
TWO TONS
Oof!
2000lb
2000lb
scribble scribble
Hey, dude--
MIND OVER MATTER X3
WHOAAAAA!
2000lb
2lb
--UNFAIR!

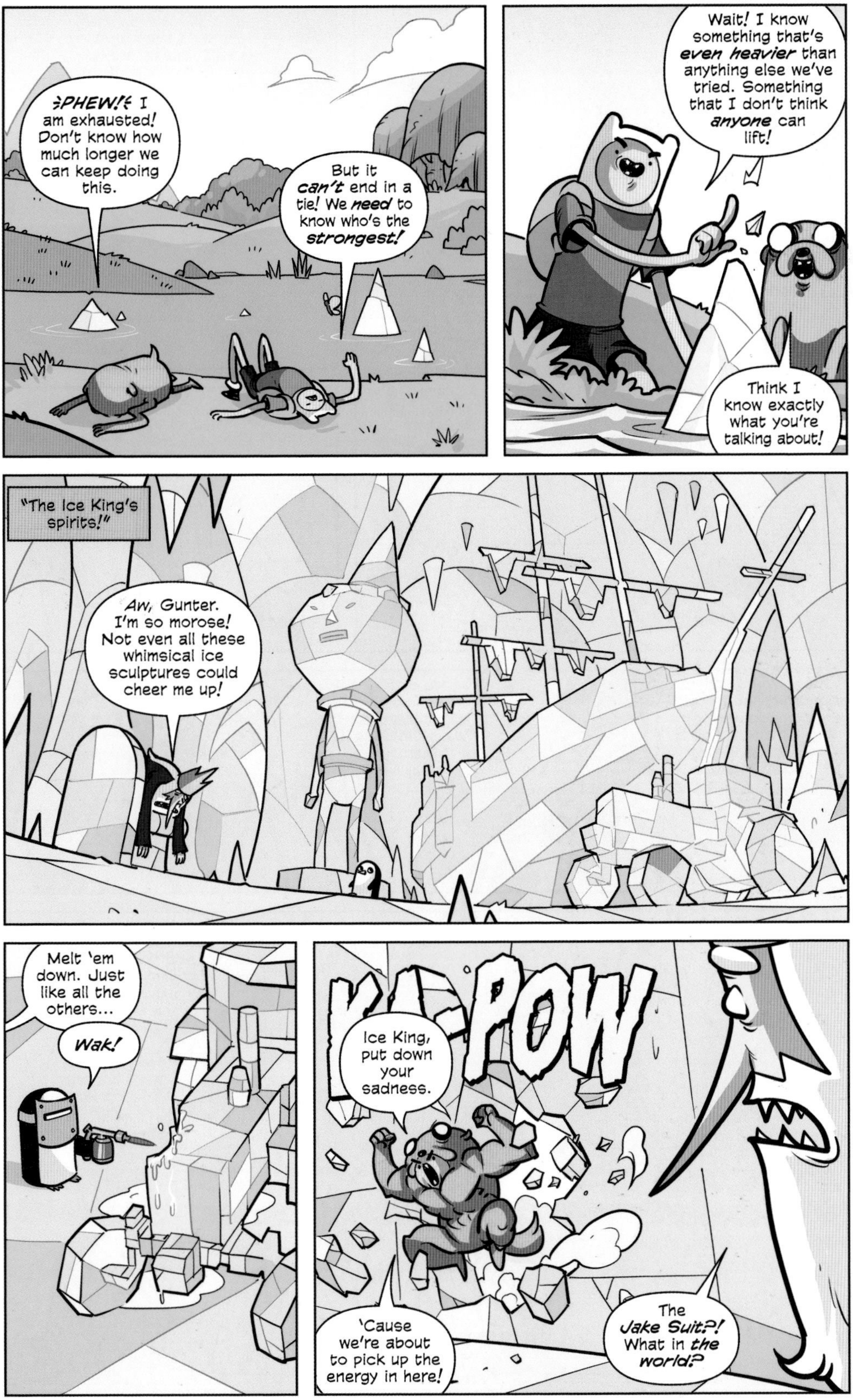

PHEW! I am exhausted! Don't know how much longer we can keep doing this.
But it can't end in a tie! We need to know who's the strongest!
Wait! I know something that's even heavier than anything else we've tried. Something that I don't think anyone can lift!
Think I know exactly what you're talking about!
"The Ice King's spirits!"
Aw, Gunter. I'm so morose! Not even all these whimsical ice sculptures could cheer me up!
Melt 'em down. Just like all the others...
Wak!
KA-POW
Ice King, put down your sadness.
'Cause we're about to pick up the energy in here!
The Jake Suit?! What in the world?

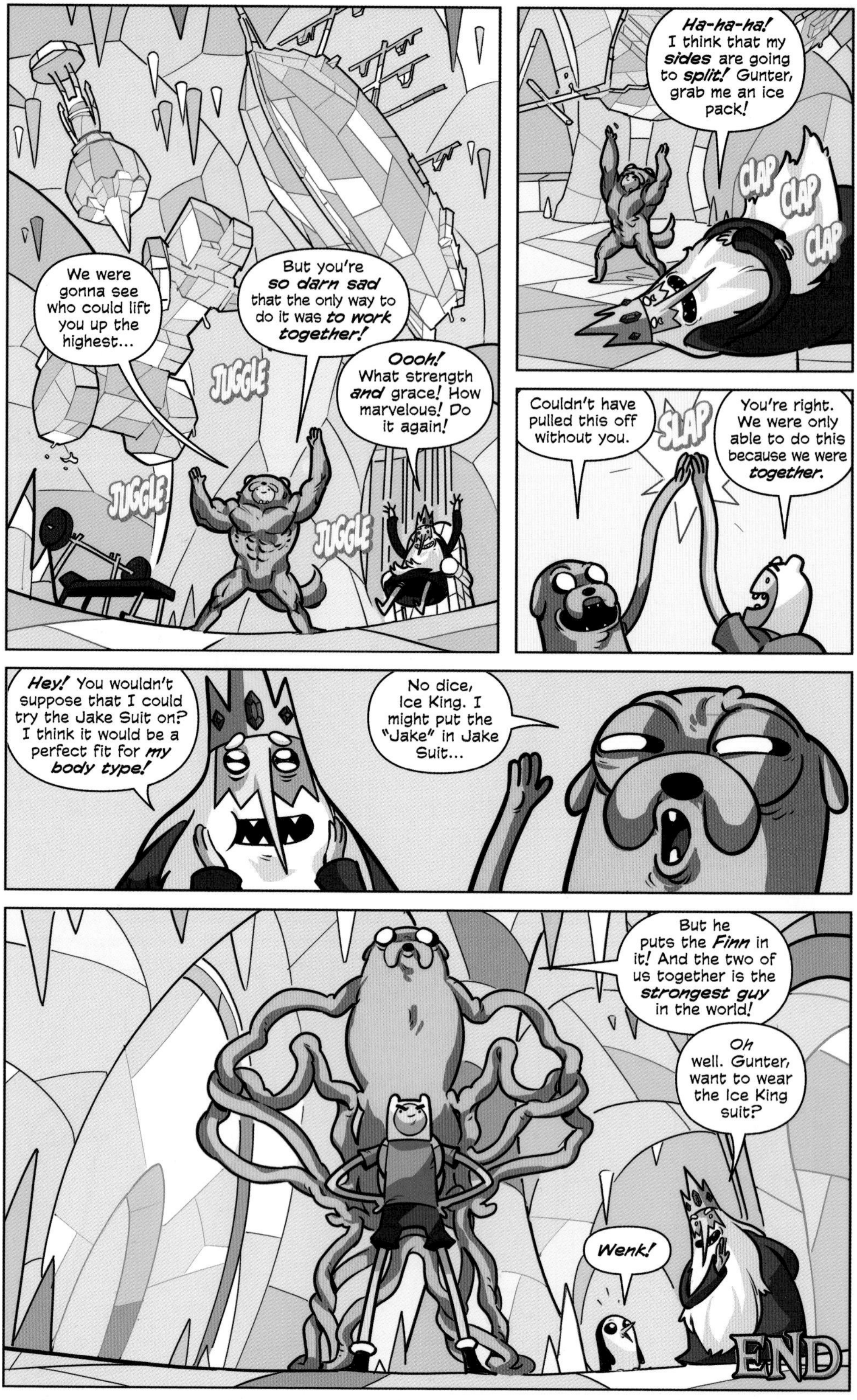
We were gonna see who could lift you up the highest...
But you're *so darn sad* that the only way to do it was *to work together!*
JUGGLE
JUGGLE
JUGGLE
Oooh! What strength *and* grace! How marvelous! Do it again!
Ha-ha-ha! I think that my *sides* are going to *split!* Gunter, grab me an ice pack!
CLAP
CLAP
CLAP
Couldn't have pulled this off without you.
SLAP
You're right. We were only able to do this because we were *together.*
Hey! You wouldn't suppose that I could try the Jake Suit on? I think it would be a perfect fit for *my body type!*
No dice, Ice King. I might put the "Jake" in Jake Suit...
But he puts the *Finn* in it! And the two of us together is the *strongest guy* in the world!
Oh well. Gunter, want to wear the Ice King suit?
Wenk!
END

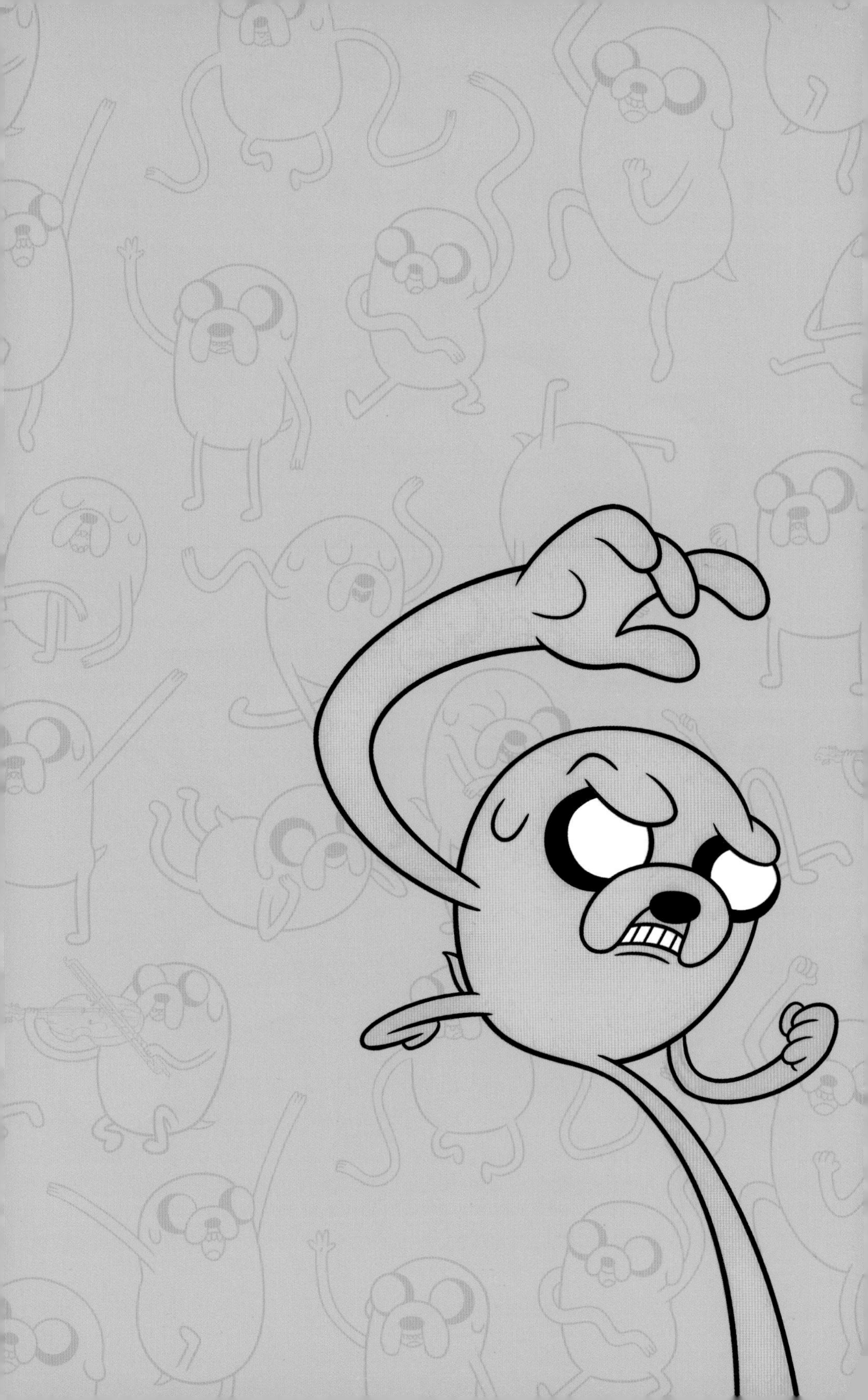

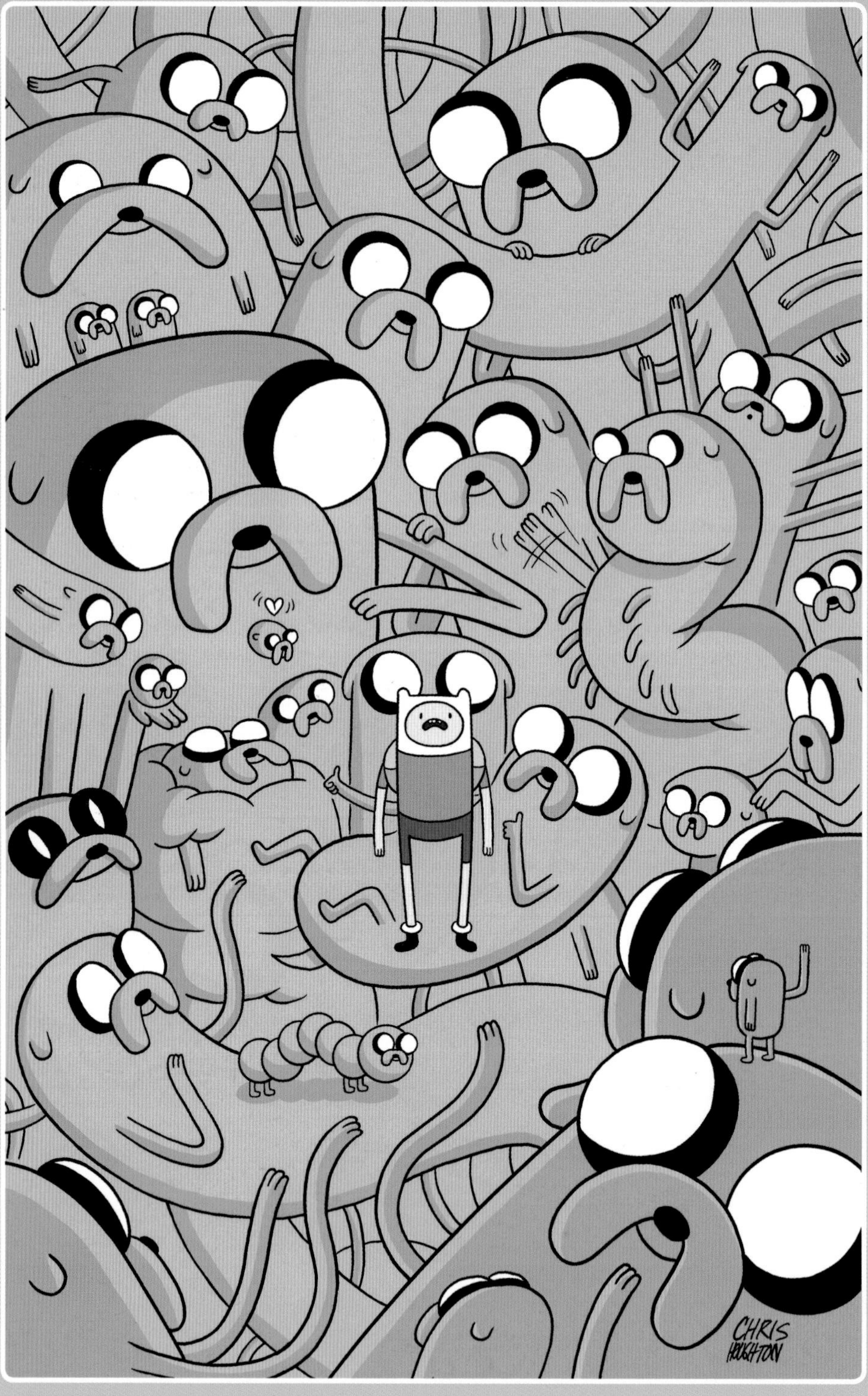
CHRIS HOUGHTON

Adventure Time #8 Cover A by **Chris Houghton**

"Chock Full O' Stuff"

Written and Illustrated by **David DeGrand**

Colors by **Kassandra Heller**

FINN AND JAKE IN "CHOCK FULL O' STUFF" BY DAVID DEGRAND

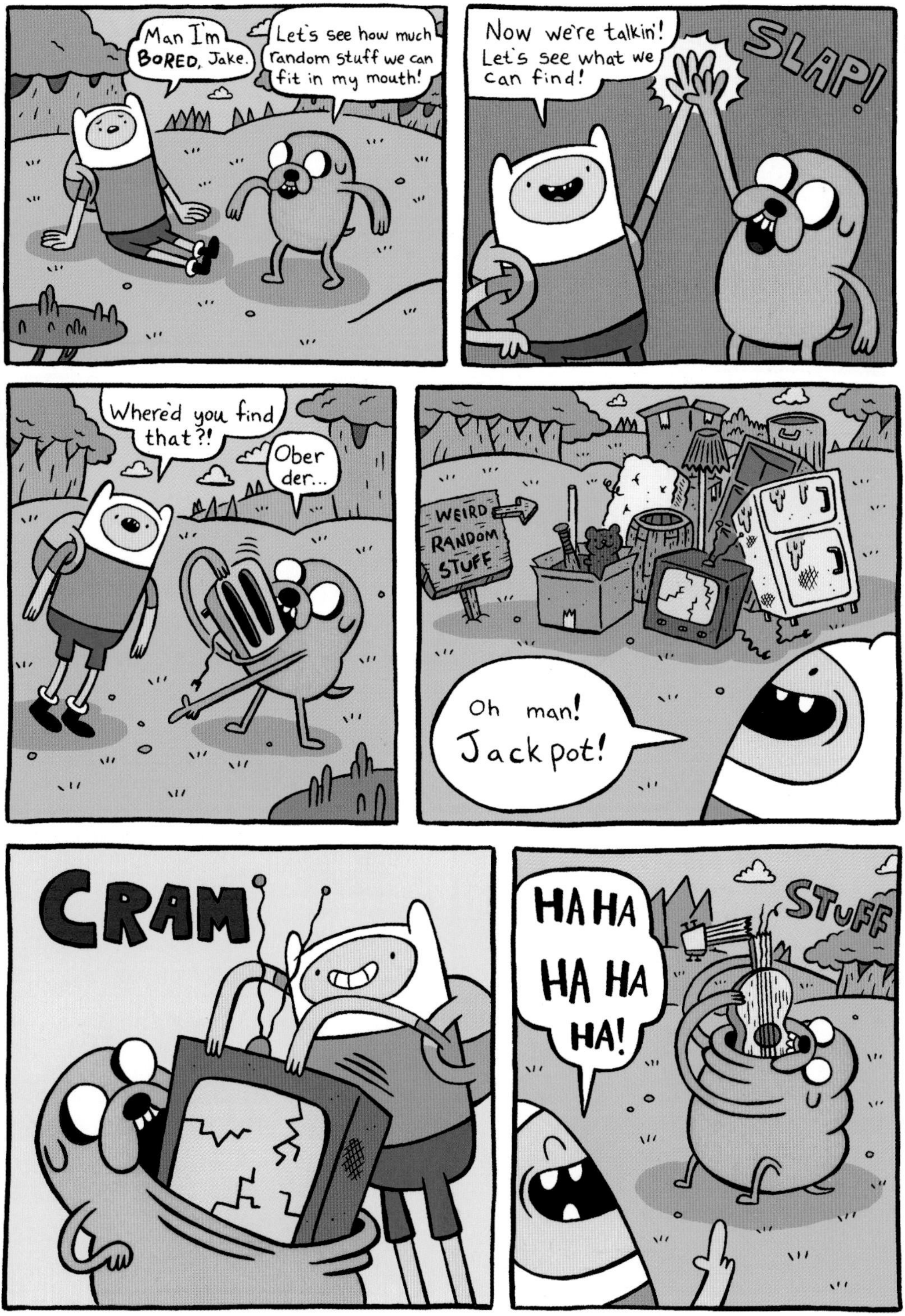

Man I'm BORED, Jake.
Let's see how much random stuff we can fit in my mouth!
Now we're talkin'! Let's see what we can find!
SLAP!
Where'd you find that?!
Ober der...
WEIRD RANDOM STUFF
Oh man! Jackpot!
CRAM
HA HA HA HA HA!
STUFF

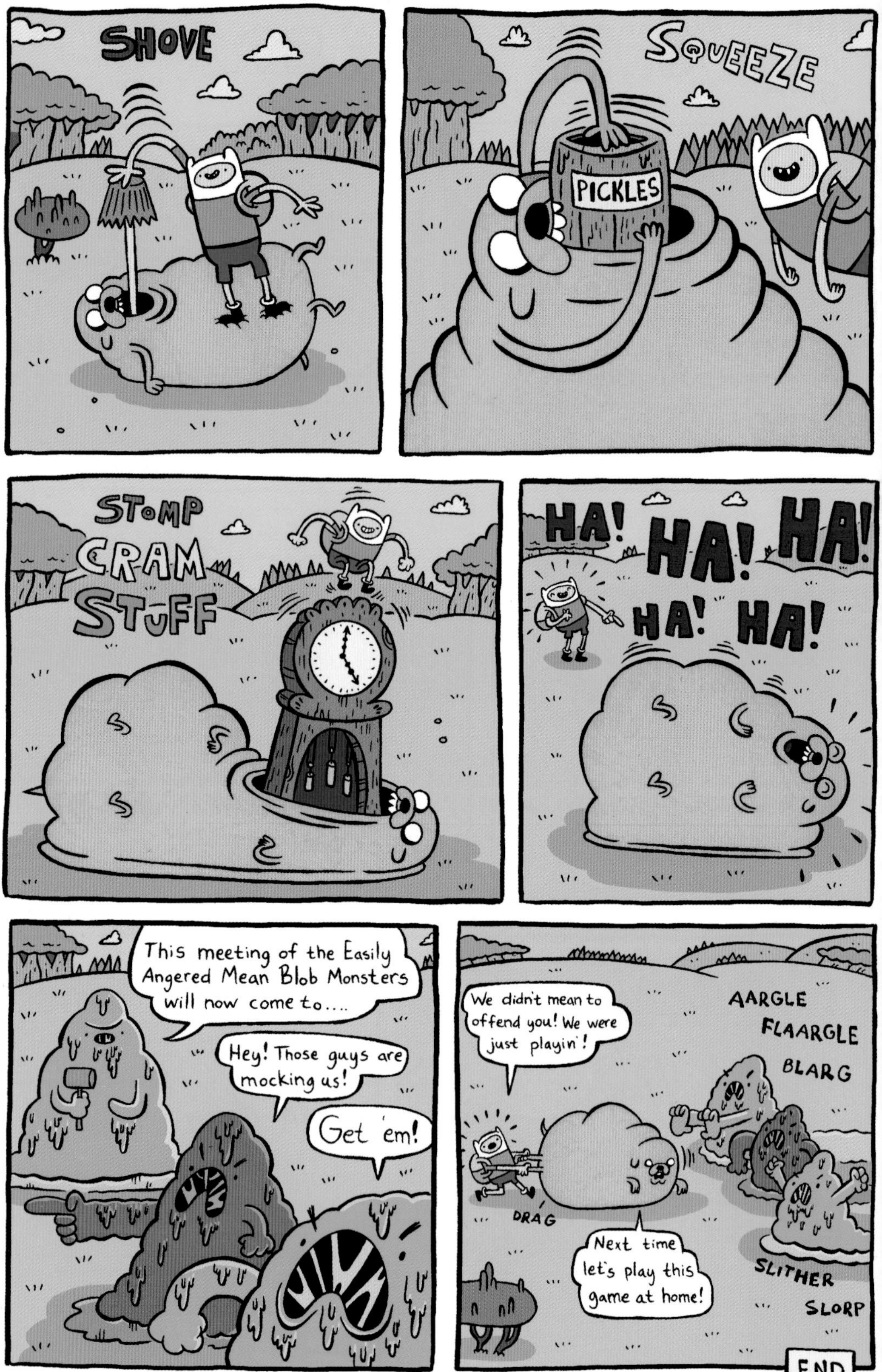

SHOVE
SQUEEZE
PICKLES
STOMP
CRAM
STUFF
HA! HA! HA!
HA! HA!
This meeting of the Easily Angered Mean Blob Monsters will now come to....
Hey! Those guys are mocking us!
Get 'em!
We didn't mean to offend you! We were just playin'!
AARGLE
FLAARGLE
BLARG
DRAG
Next time let's play this game at home!
SLITHER
SLORP
END

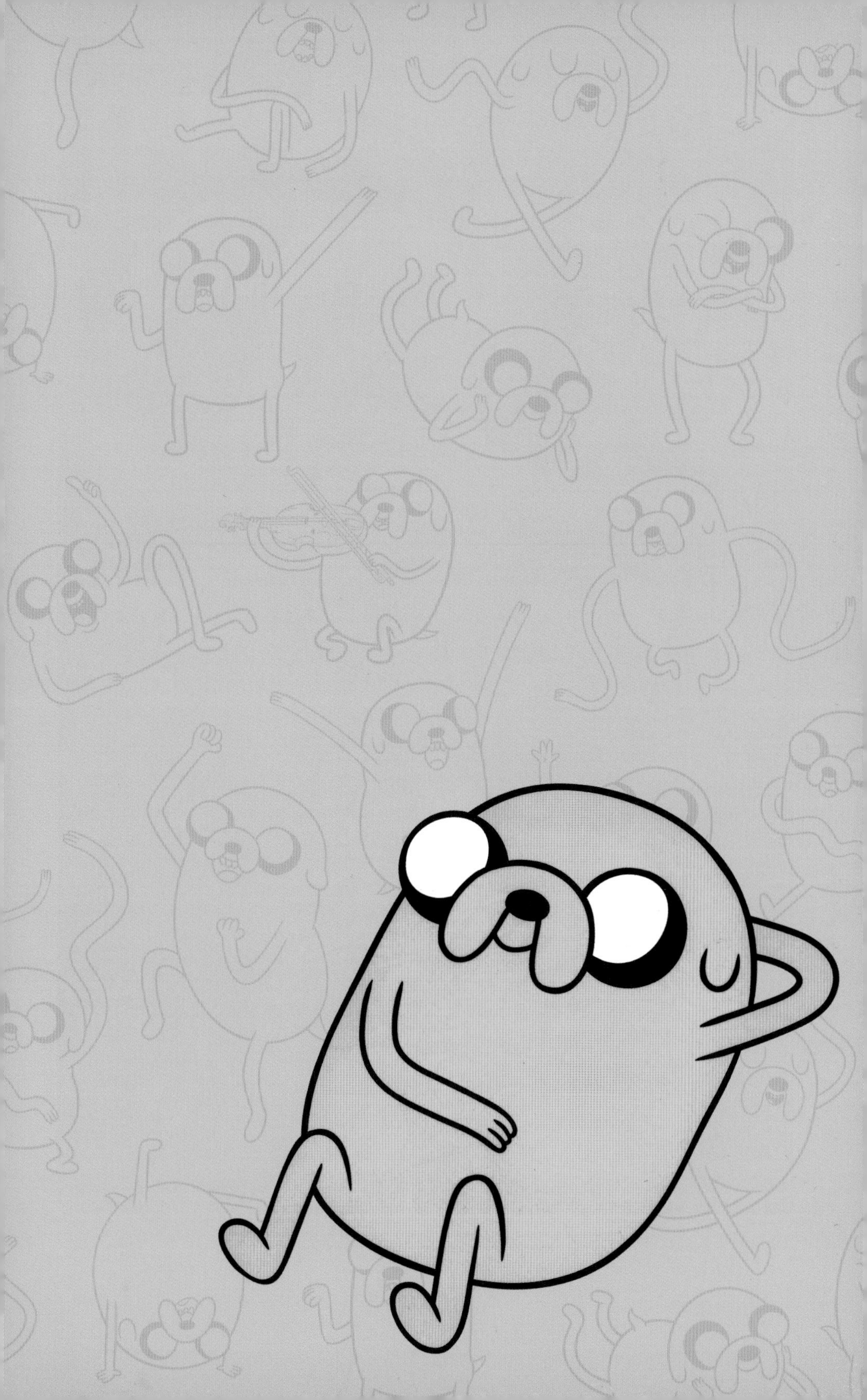

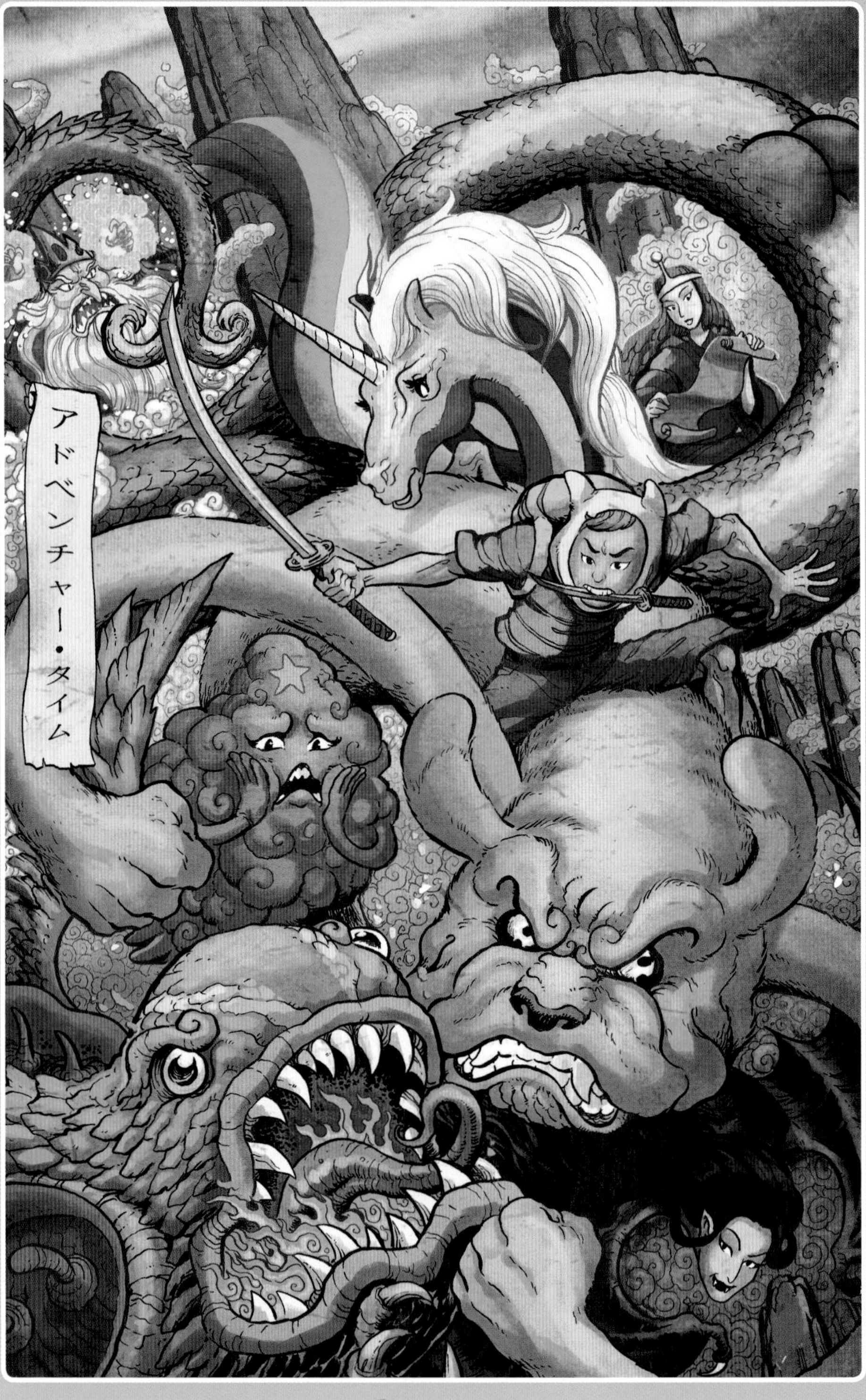
アドベンチャー・タイム

Adventure time Comics #20 Subscription Cover by **Matt Frank**

"Epic Yard Sale"

Written by **James Asmus** Illustrated by **Cristina Rose Chua**

Letters by **Mike Fiorentino**

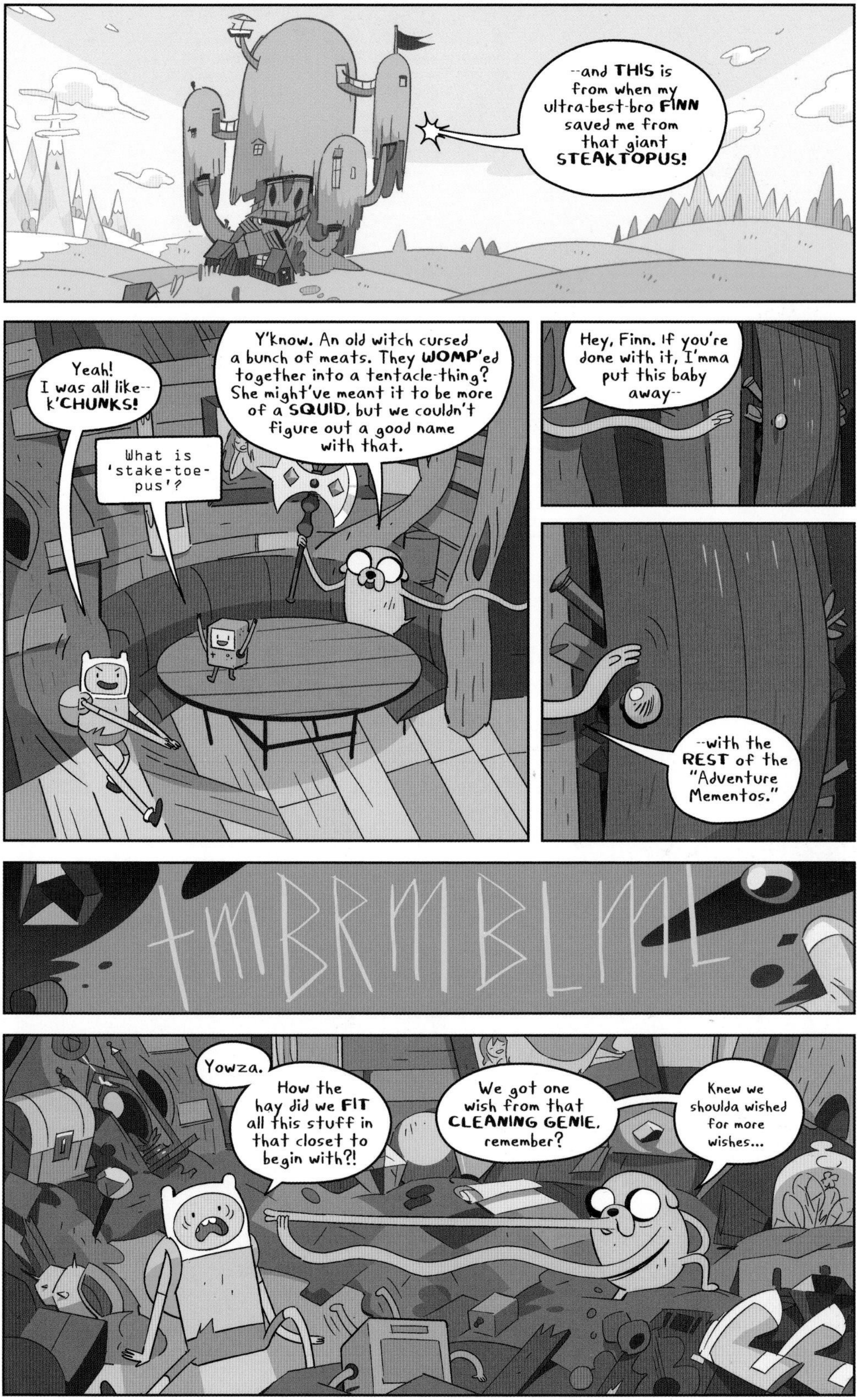
--and THIS is from when my ultra-best-bro FINN saved me from that giant STEAKTOPUS!
Yeah! I was all like-- k'CHUNKS!
What is 'stake-toe-pus'?
Y'know. An old witch cursed a bunch of meats. They WOMP'ed together into a tentacle-thing? She might've meant it to be more of a SQUID, but we couldn't figure out a good name with that.
Hey, Finn. If you're done with it, I'mma put this baby away--
--with the REST of the "Adventure Mementos."
TMBRMBLML
Yowza.
How the hay did we FIT all this stuff in that closet to begin with?!
We got one wish from that CLEANING GENIE, remember?
Knew we shoulda wished for more wishes...

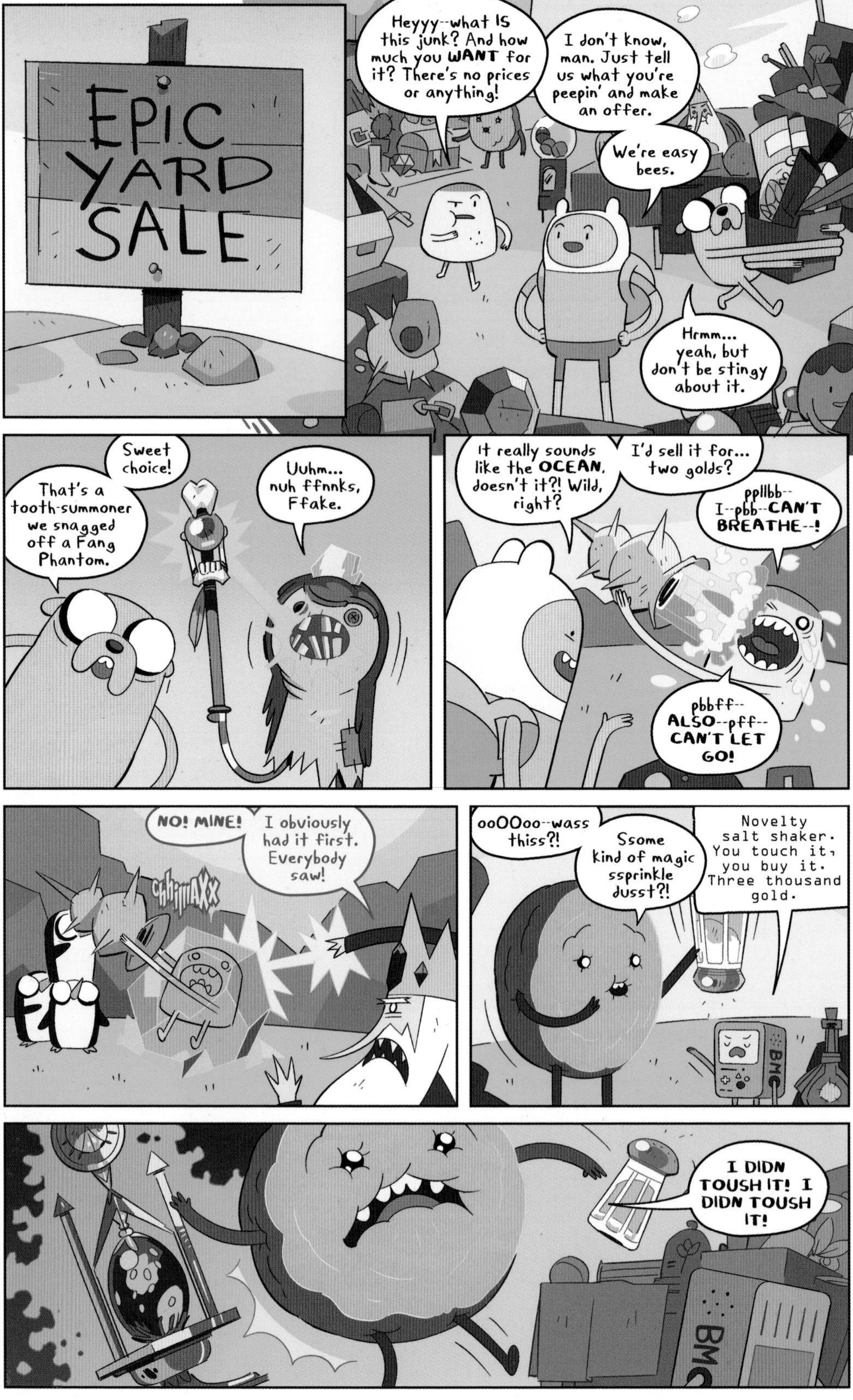
EPIC YARD SALE
Heyyy--what IS this junk? And how much you WANT for it? There's no prices or anything!
I don't know, man. Just tell us what you're peepin' and make an offer.
We're easy bees.
Hrmm... yeah, but don't be stingy about it.
Sweet choice!
That's a tooth-summoner we snagged off a Fang Phantom.
Uuhm... nuh ffnnks, Ffake.
It really sounds like the OCEAN, doesn't it?! Wild, right?
I'd sell it for... two golds?
ppllbb-- I--pbb--CAN'T BREATHE--!
pbbff-- ALSO--pff-- CAN'T LET GO!
NO! MINE!
I obviously had it first. Everybody saw!
CHHIIIAXX
oo0Ooo--wass thiss?!
Ssome kind of magic ssprinkle dusst?!
Novelty salt shaker. You touch it, you buy it. Three thousand gold.
BMO
I DIDN TOUSH IT! I DIDN TOUSH IT!
BMO

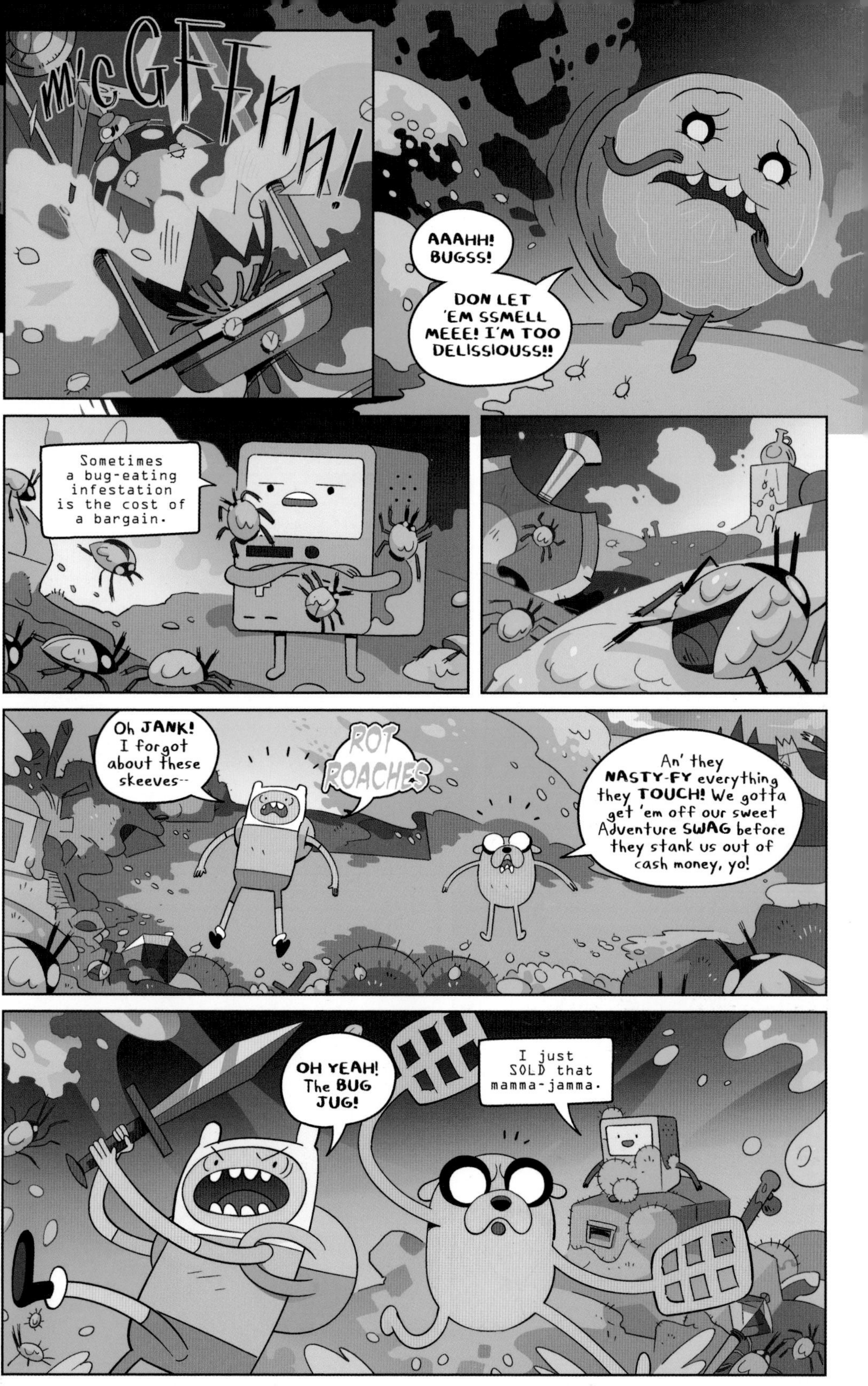
M'GGFFnn!
AAAHH! BUGSS!
DON LET 'EM SSMELL MEEE! I'M TOO DELISSIOUSS!!
Sometimes a bug-eating infestation is the cost of a bargain.
Oh JANK! I forgot about these skeeves--
ROT ROACHES
An' they NASTY-FY everything they TOUCH! We gotta get 'em off our sweet Adventure SWAG before they stank us out of cash money, yo!
OH YEAH! The BUG JUG!
I just SOLD that mamma-jamma.

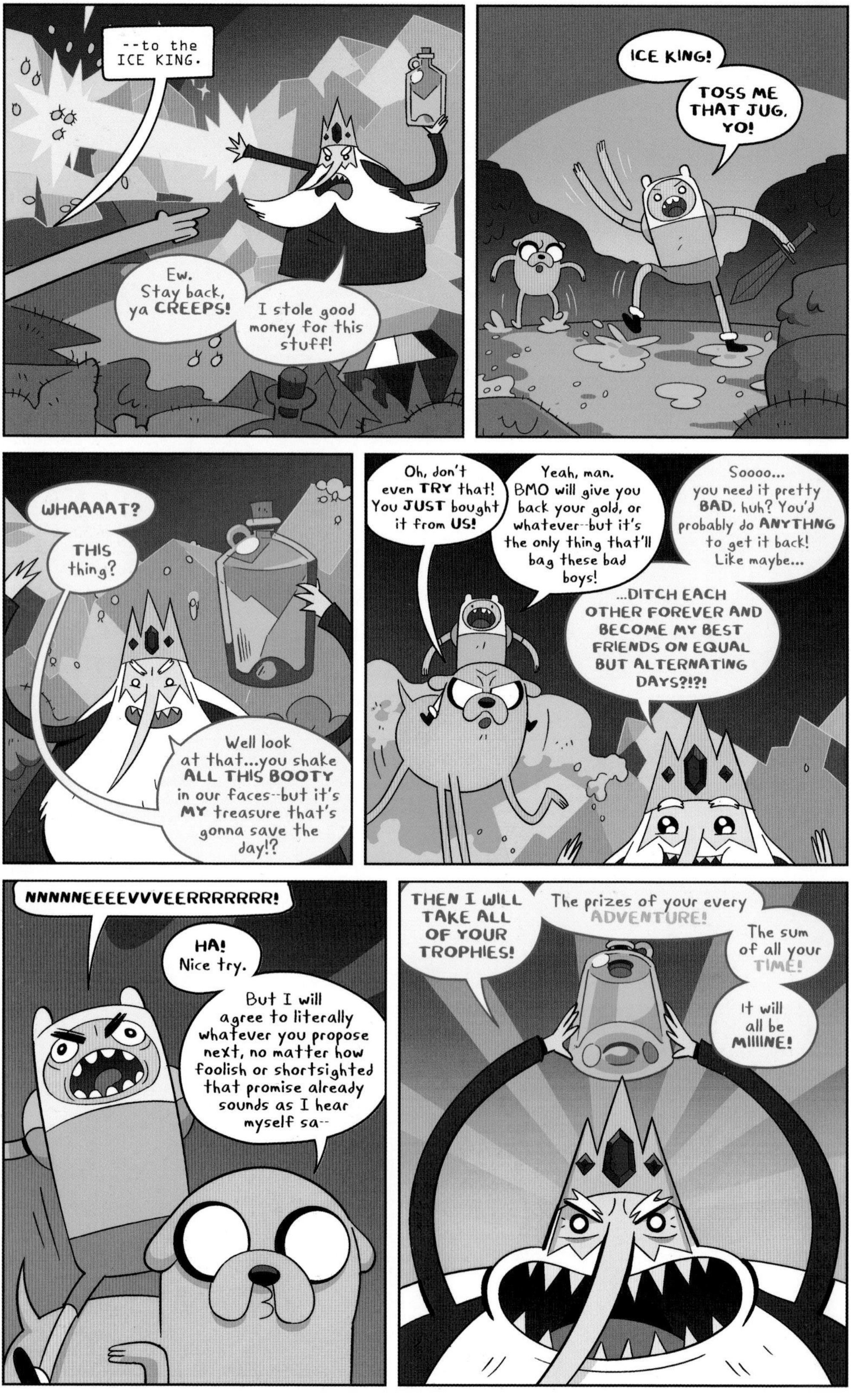
--to the ICE KING.
Ew. Stay back, ya CREEPS!
I stole good money for this stuff!
ICE KING!
TOSS ME THAT JUG, YO!
WHAAAAT?
THIS thing?
Well look at that...you shake ALL THIS BOOTY in our faces--but it's MY treasure that's gonna save the day!?
Oh, don't even TRY that! You JUST bought it from US!
Yeah, man. BMO will give you back your gold, or whatever--but it's the only thing that'll bag these bad boys!
Soooo... you need it pretty BAD, huh? You'd probably do ANYTHNG to get it back! Like maybe...
...DITCH EACH OTHER FOREVER AND BECOME MY BEST FRIENDS ON EQUAL BUT ALTERNATING DAYS?!?!
NNNNNEEEEVVVEERRRRRRRR!
HA! Nice try.
But I will agree to literally whatever you propose next, no matter how foolish or shortsighted that promise already sounds as I hear myself sa--
THEN I WILL TAKE ALL OF YOUR TROPHIES!
The prizes of your every ADVENTURE!
The sum of all your TIME!
It will all be MIIIINE!

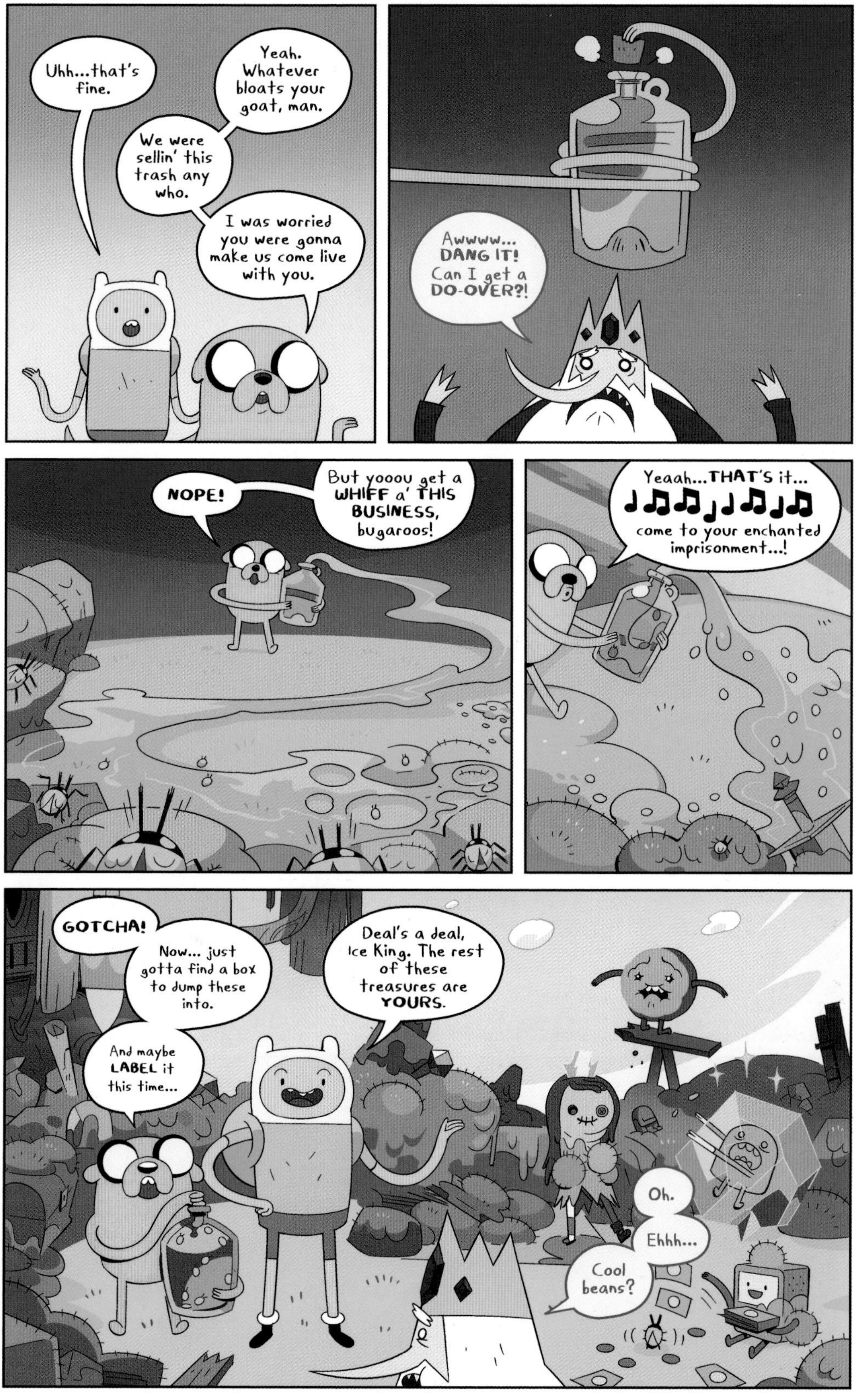
Uhh...that's fine.
Yeah. Whatever bloats your goat, man.
We were sellin' this trash any who.
I was worried you were gonna make us come live with you.
Awwww... DANG IT! Can I get a DO-OVER?!
NOPE!
But yooou get a WHIFF a' THIS BUSINESS, bugaroos!
Yeaah...THAT'S it... ♩♫♫♩♩♫♩♫ come to your enchanted imprisonment...!
GOTCHA!
Now... just gotta find a box to dump these into.
And maybe LABEL it this time...
Deal's a deal, Ice King. The rest of these treasures are YOURS.
Oh.
Ehhh...
Cool beans?

There we go!

Minimalistic!

Hey--it's cool how after that zim-zam today, this ONE li'l memento will probably remind us of all those OTHER mementos and THEIR adventures!

Yeah! That'll make for some SUPES EFFICIENT reminiscing.

But...what happened to all the ROT ROACHES, man?

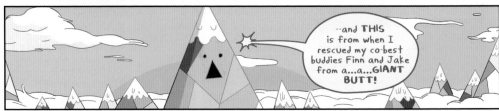

--and THIS is from when I rescued my co-best buddies Finn and Jake from a...a...GIANT BUTT!

Heh. Yeah. A big, beautiful butt...

weh.

It did TOO happen! If I didn't have all those adventures with my BEST FRIENDS--then how would I have all THESE KEEPSAKES, HUH?!

One for every time I CHOPPED A BUTT!

DEFINITELY NOT BUGS

Like-- WHAM!

DEFINITELY NOT BUGS

END

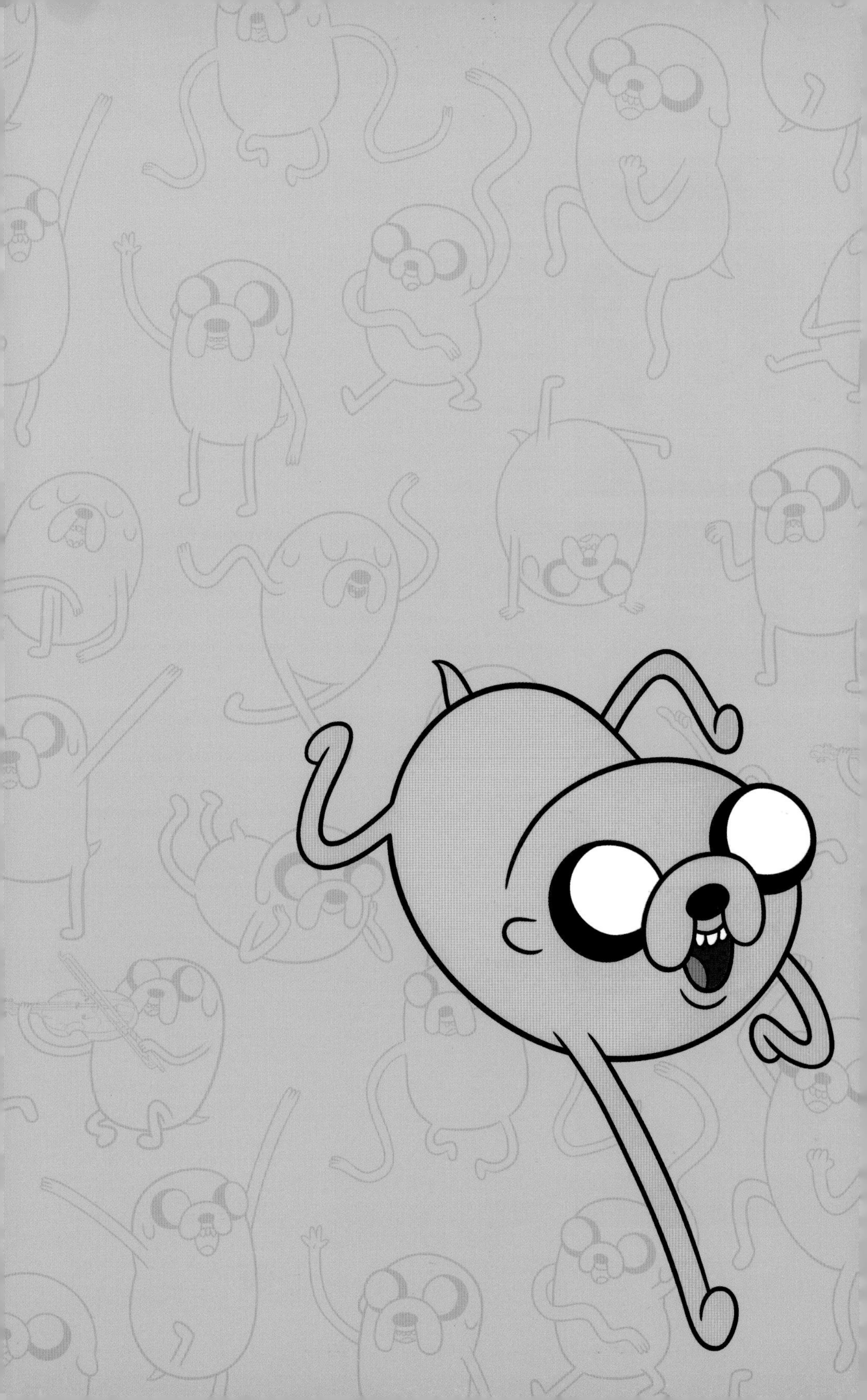

DISCOVER MORE ADVENTURE TIME

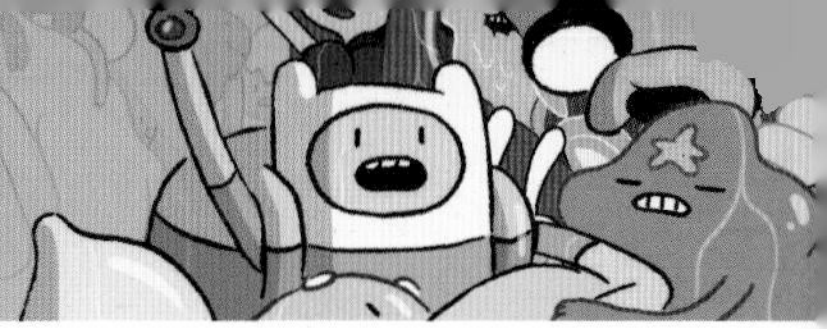

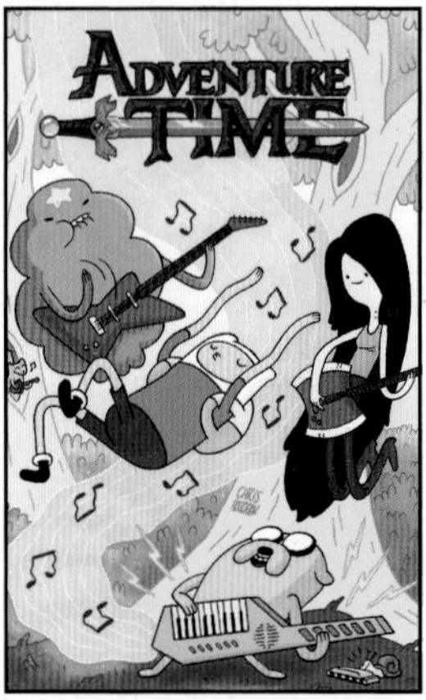
ADVENTURE TIME

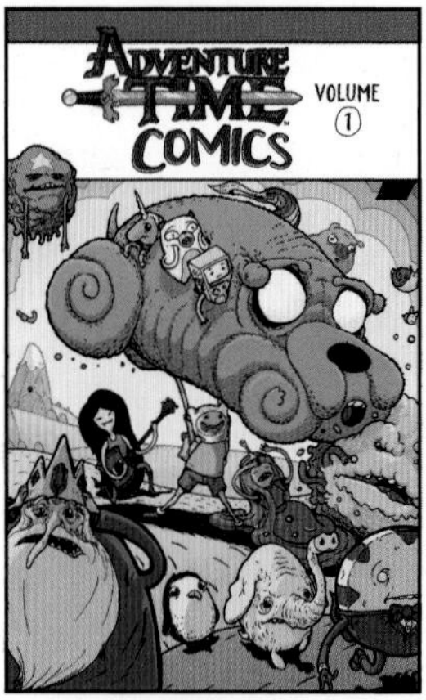
ADVENTURE TIME
COMICS
VOLUME 1

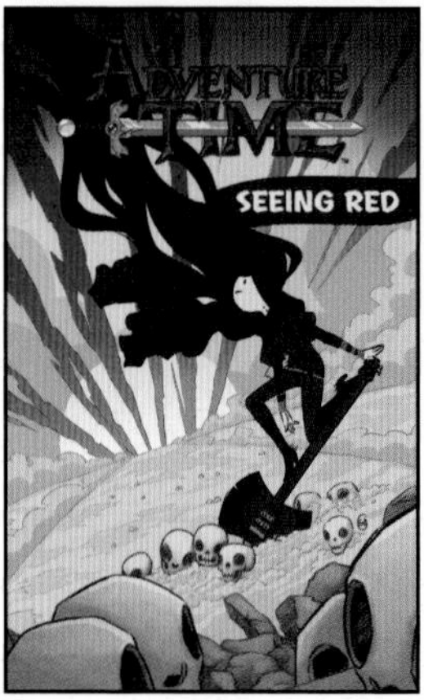
ADVENTURE TIME
SEEING RED

Adventure Time

Volume 1
ISBN: 978-1-60886-280-1 | $14.99 US

Volume 2
ISBN: 978-1-60886-323-5 | $14.99 US

Volume 3
ISBN: 978-1-60886-317-4 | $14.99

Volume 4
ISBN: 978-1-60886-351-8 | $14.99

Volume 5
ISBN: 978-1-60886-401-0 | $14.99

Volume 6
ISBN: 978-1-60886-482-9 | $14.99

Volume 7
ISBN: 978-1-60886-746-2 | $14.99

Volume 8
ISBN: 978-1-60886-795-0 | $14.99

Volume 9
ISBN: 978-1-60886-843-8 | $14.99

Volume 10
ISBN: 978-1-60886-909-1 | $14.99

Volume 11
ISBN: 978-1-60886-946-6 | $14.99

Volume 12
ISBN: 978-1-68415-005-2 | $14.99

Volume 13
ISBN: 978-1-68415-051-9 | $14.99

Volume 14
ISBN: 978-1-68415-144-8 | $14.99

Volume 15
ISBN: 978-1-68415-203-2 | $14.99

Volume 16
ISBN: 978-1-68415-272-8 | $14.99

Adventure Time Comics

Volume 1
ISBN: 978-1-60886-934-3 | $14.99

Volume 2
ISBN: 978-1-60886-984-8 | $14.99

Volume 3
ISBN: 978-1-68415-041-0 | $14.99

Volume 4
ISBN: 978-1-68415-133-2 | $14.99

Volume 5
ISBN: 978-1-68415-190-5 | $14.99

Volume 6
ISBN: 978-1-68415-258-2 | $14.99

Adventure Time Original Graphic Novels

Volume 1 Playing With Fire
ISBN: 978-1-60886-832-2 | $14.99

Volume 2 Pixel Princesses
ISBN: 978-1-60886-329-7 | $11.99

Volume 3 Seeing Red
ISBN: 978-1-60886-356-3 | $11.99

Volume 4 Bitter Sweets
ISBN: 978-1-60886-430-0 | $12.99

Volume 5 Graybles Schmaybles
ISBN: 978-1-60886-484-3 | $12.99

Volume 6 Masked Mayhem
ISBN: 978-160886-764-6 | $14.99

Volume 7 The Four Castles
ISBN: 978-160886-797-4 | $14.99

Volume 8 President Bubblegum
ISBN: 978-1-60886-846-9 | $14.99

Volume 9 The Brain Robbers
ISBN: 978-1-60886-875-9 | $14.99

Volume 10 The Orient Express
ISBN: 978-1-60886-995-4 | $14.99

Volume 11 Princess & Princess
ISBN: 978-1-68415-025-0 | $14.99

Volume 12 Thunder Road
ISBN: 978-1-68415-179-0 | $14.99

kaboom! A BOOM! Studios Imprint

AVAILABLE AT YOUR LOCAL COMICS SHOP AND BOOKSTORE

WWW.BOOM-STUDIOS.COM

CARTOON NETWORK.

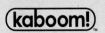

DISCOVER MORE
ADVENTURE TIME

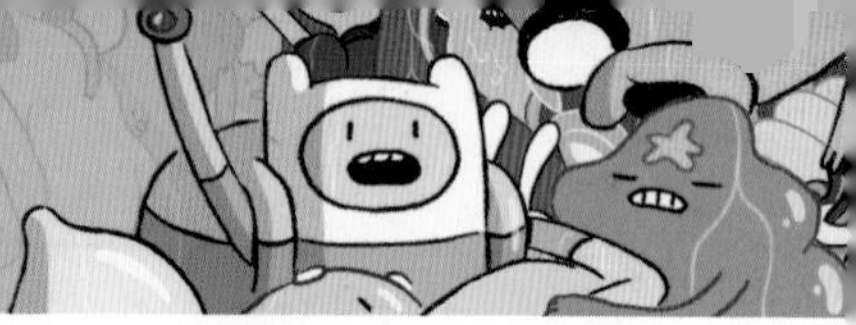

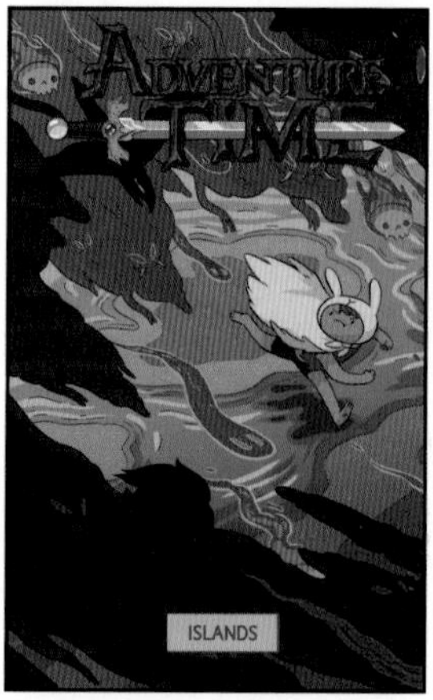

ADVENTURE TIME
ISLANDS

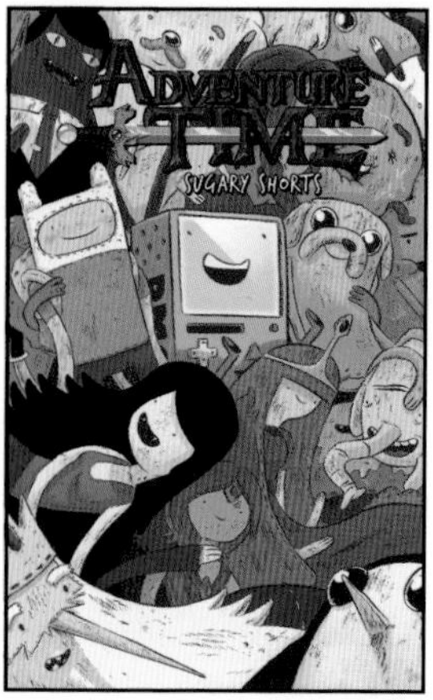

ADVENTURE TIME
SUGARY SHORTS

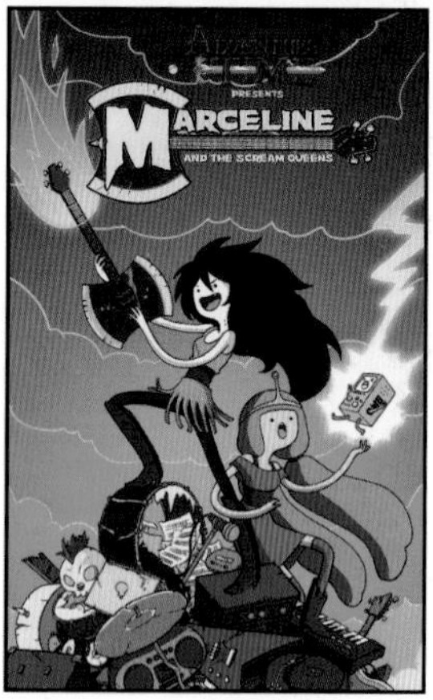

PRESENTS
MARCELINE
AND THE SCREAM QUEENS

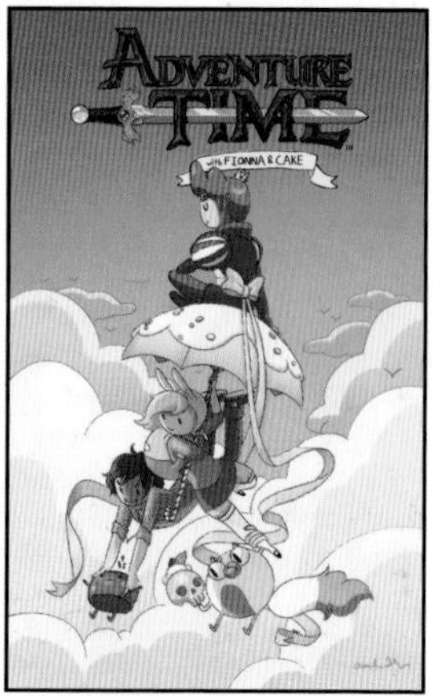

ADVENTURE TIME
with FIONNA & CAKE

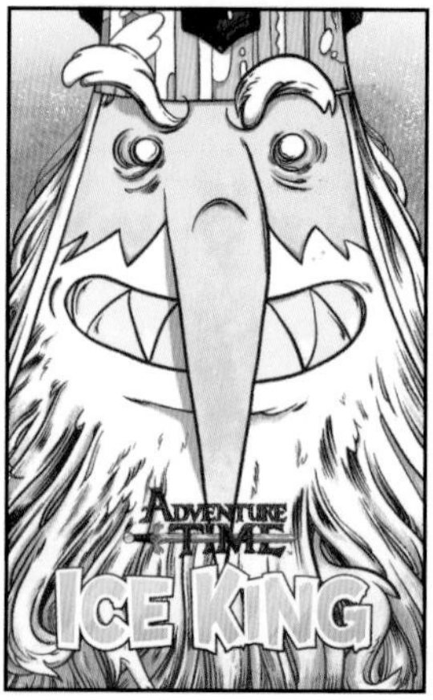

ADVENTURE TIME
ICE KING

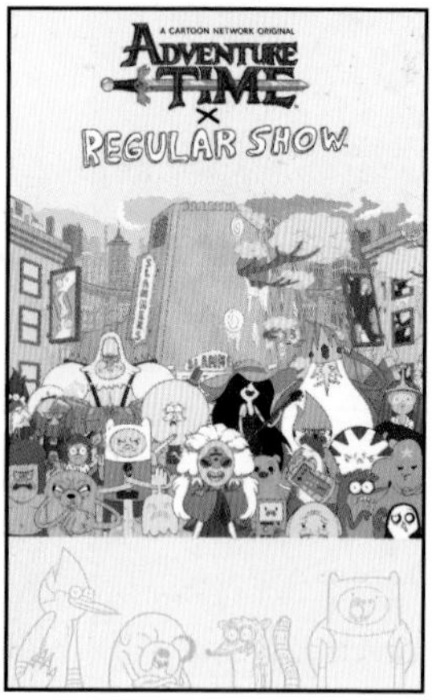

A CARTOON NETWORK ORIGINAL
ADVENTURE TIME
×
REGULAR SHOW

Adventure Time: Islands OGN
ISBN: 978-1-60886-972-5 | $9.99

Adventure Time Sugary Shorts

Volume 1
ISBN: 978-1-60886-361-7 | $19.99

Volume 2
ISBN: 978-1-60886-774-5 | $19.99

Volume 3
ISBN: 978-1-68415-030-4 | $19.99

Volume 4
ISBN: 978-1-68415-122-6 | $19.99

Adventure Time: Marceline & the Scream Queens
ISBN: 978-1-60886-313-6 | $19.99

Adventure Time: Fionna & Cake
ISBN: 978-1-60886-338-9 | $19.99

Adventure Time: Candy Capers
ISBN: 978-1-60886-365-5 | $19.99

Adventure Time: The Flip Side
ISBN: 978-1-60886-456-0 | $19.99

Adventure Time: Banana Guard Academy
ISBN: 978-1-60886-486-7 | $19.99

Adventure Time: Marceline Gone Adrift
ISBN: 978-1-60886-770-7 | $19.99

Adventure Time: Fionna & Cake Card Wars
ISBN: 978-1-60886-799-8 | $19.99

Adventure Time: Ice King
ISBN: 978-1-60886-920-6 | $19.99

Adventure Time/Regular Show
ISBN: 978-1-68415-166-0 | $19.99

kaboom!™
A BOOM! Studios Imprint

AVAILABLE AT YOUR LOCAL COMICS SHOP AND BOOKSTORE
WWW.**BOOM-STUDIOS**.COM

CN CARTOON NETWORK.